□ □ □

"Fluid in its structure and aqueous in its themes, the novel vividly evokes the teeming, sweltering city."
—*The New Yorker*

"Captures the nation's lush history in all its turbulence and resilience . . . flowing gracefully from historical fiction to contemporary realism to science fiction . . . Entrancing . . . Sudbanthad's narrative is not just a tribute to his home, it's an act of resistance against the city's mildew and amnesia. . . . a way of preserving what is otherwise inscribed only on the liquid surface of memory."
—*The Washington Post*

"Remarkable . . . Ambitious and sweeping, yet at once intimately crafted and shot through with fine detail, *Bangkok Wakes to Rain* is a sumptuous accomplishment."
—*Esquire*

"Expertly evokes a sense of place—[Sudbanthad's] descriptions of Thailand are gorgeous; the reader feels transported there. *Bangkok Wakes to Rain* is well worth reading. It's a strong debut from an intelligent, self-assured author."
—*NPR*

"Elegant and restrained . . . A series of glancing vignettes that proceed in roughly linear fashion from the nineteenth century to the near future . . . bear witness to the city's changing landscape. . . . Sudbanthad's serene, almost otherworldly omniscience makes his fictional biography of the city an original and quietly memorable reading experience."
—*The Wall Street Journal*

"[An examination of] hidden, overlooked spaces, where ghosts and spirits and discarded dreams orbit, even as people try to outpace the past . . . [stories] intersect and build on one another, like banana leaves woven to make a floating offering for the water spirits . . . Bangkok is changing too fast, shedding layers of its history like the skins of a snake. Yet the city retains its allure, and the quest to return is like some animal."
—*The New York Times Book Review*

"A sweeping epic with the amphibious city of the title at its scintillating center . . . by turns realistic and mystical, historical and speculative, the book is beautifully diffuse. . . . Sudbanthad's elaborate, time-hopping saga explores class stratifications, intercultural connections and disconnections, and finely textured layers of history, all the while raising fascinating questions about the future."
—*Minneapolis Star-Tribune*

"Sudbanthad spans an entire century in his vast, illuminating portrait of Bangkok, bringing together a cast of characters as they experience love, revolution, and sorrow."
—*Entertainment Weekly*

"This prismatic debut peels back the layers of a Thai manse, whose past residents—among them a disillusioned American missionary and a world-weary jazz musician—still haunt its hallways metaphorically and literally." —*O, The Oprah Magazine*

"[Sudbanthad's] glittering tales of the title city accumulate into a mosaic of jagged puzzle pieces whose chronological leaps make the whole thing come together only more powerfully by the end." —*Vulture*

"*Bangkok Wakes to Rain* is itself a sort of house of ghosts and those haunted by them, in a cycle of vivid life and aching loss . . . The technology Sudbanthad imagines is a marvel, but it's one that might be modeled on what this novel does so beautifully: bringing a place and its people alive through story." —*Tampa Bay Times*

"[W]ith its wide cast and still wider time frames, Pitchaya Sudbanthad's debut rewards close attention . . . . Bangkok unifies his characters' lives and, in a climate of concern for the city's future, amid rising sea levels, so does water, with its fearsome power to transform, disrupt, slaughter, and redeem . . . Sudbanthad's blend of travelogue with social and political history is compelling in his treatment of expatriation . . . the ambitious structure pays off." —*Financial Times*

"Important, ambitious, and accomplished." —Mohsin Hamid, author of *Exit West*

"Gorgeously polyphonic and saturated in the senses, this novel brims with a wistful and gripping energy as it carries us through time and space. Sudbanthad brilliantly sounds the resonant pulse of the city in a wise and far-reaching meditation on home."
—Claire Vaye Watkins, author of *Gold Fame Citrus* and *Battleborn*

"A bold and tender novel with a simple, ingenious conceit—the stories a house can contain, from a city's colonial past to its antediluvian future. Sudbanthad arrives to us already a masterful innovator of the form—a startlingly original debut."
—Alexander Chee, author of *The Queen of the Night*

"Beautifully textured and rich with a sense of place, this is a big, ambitious book. Sudbanthad compellingly captures not only the long arcs of these lives but also the smallest moments, and how those moments linger in memory, how they haunt."
—Karen Thompson Walker, author of *The Age of Miracles* and *The Dreamers*

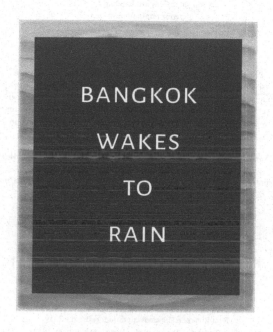

BANGKOK

WAKES

TO

RAIN

Pitchaya Sudbanthad

RIVERHEAD BOOKS □ NEW YORK □

RIVERHEAD BOOKS
An imprint of Penguin Random House LLC
penguinrandomhouse.com

Copyright © 2019 by Pitchaya Sudbanthad

The Library of Congress has catalogued the Riverhead hardcover edition as follows:

Names: Sudbanthad, Pitchaya, author.
Title: Bangkok wakes to rain : a novel / Pitchaya Sudbanthad.
Description: New York : Riverhead Books, 2019.
Identifiers: LCCN 2018042208 (print) | LCCN 2018045835 (ebook) |
ISBN 9780525534785 (ebook) | ISBN 9780525534761 (hardback)
Subjects: | BISAC: FICTION / Cultural Heritage. | FICTION / Literary.
Classification: LCC PS3619.U346 (ebook) | LCC PS3619.U346
B36 2019 (print) | DDC 813/.6—dc23
LC record available at https://lccn.loc.gov/2018042208

First Riverhead hardcover edition: February 2019
First Riverhead trade paperback edition: February 2020
Riverhead trade paperback ISBN: 9780525534778

Printed in the United States of America

BOOK DESIGN BY LUCIA BERNARD

For my family, for all time

CONTENTS

◻ ◻ ◻

I

◻

II

VISITATIONS

Always, she arrives near evening. The last few children in blue-and-white uniforms have finished their after-school work and are plodding along in small gangs or, like her, alone. They don't take notice of her; they have screens in their hands, shoves and teasing to repay, snacks bagged in newsprint to grease up their fingers. In their trail, sparrows tussle over fallen fried crumbs and biscuit sticks trampled to powder by little shoes. A pearl-eyed lottery seller, sensing passersby from footsteps and the clap of flip-flops, calls out over an opened case of clothes-pinned tickets to whoever craves luck.

Her nose picks up the ashen smell always in the air. Somewhere, a garbage heap incinerates underneath a highway overpass; in temples, incense sticks release sweet smoke to the holy and the dead; flames curl blue in the open-air gas grills of shophouse food stalls.

She is a child or a few thousand years old. Would it ever matter? The city will stay this way for her. When she was a uniformed primary schooler herself, walking home along these very streets, she liked to make believe she was a bewildered traveler in a foreign city, drawn forward by alluring strangeness. She couldn't have known then that there would be years ahead when she didn't have to pretend, and years still further ahead when pretending was all she could do.

Fresh, fresh, hot, hot, good for kids, delicious for grown-ups, twenty bahts, twenty bahts. She counts on hearing the soy milk lady's singsongy cry ahead of the others. The thicker the crowd on the sidewalk, the louder the hawkers call out. Stampedes of dusty shoes and shopping bags and stray dogs crisscross near the ground; canopies of sun-shielding umbrellas and twisty headphone cords drift above. The fruit sellers have laid parrot-green pyramids of pomelo on their tables. They holler, "Come, pretty young sister! Come sample this!" and she tells them maybe tomorrow, knowing they'll be at the same spot to greet her the next morning as she hurries to catch the 6:45 at the Skytrain station. Auntie Tofu, Uncle Big Mouth, the Egret: she doesn't know their real names, only the monikers her mother mentioned when boasting of discounts negotiated at the produce scale. The vendors pick up halved mangosteens to show off the white flesh balled inside like an unbloomed flower. It's about the time of the year when these particular fruits become more plentiful, though that wasn't always the case, especially during the calamitous years—lifetimes ago it seems—when orchards drowned and few trucks dared brave watery roads to deliver what little of the crop had been saved. Those days are hardly worth remembering, are they? Everything is now back in its place.

The asphalt before her darkens in the shadow of the building she thinks of as home. The usual guard salutes her from the gatehouse, a walkie-talkie raised to his forehead. When building management first upgraded the security setup to attract higher-paying tenants for the rental floors, she thought the cameras were turning to follow her. She'd find out that the motion was simply an automatic preset and the feeds went to backroom monitors attended by no one. She was young then and didn't realize that there was already scant escape from being watched, camera or no camera.

Eyes are everywhere, pointing down from balconies and windows, through the iron fencing and palm thickets that separate the building's grounds from the unruly street. She can feel eyes on her skin, even now. It won't surprise her to turn around from this walk up the driveway and find the guard peeling her with his stare. Where the building's communal shrine stands, a sun-reddened European family, probably one of the short-term renters, is clicking selfies in front of the week's offerings—oranges and bottled cola—for higher entities and land spirits. The pudgy-faced father turns in her direction, eyes widened, before resuming his pose for another shot.

In the lobby, chilled, purified air welcomes her. How many times has she walked over these granite tiles? Always in a rush, out and in. No letting up the pace. There isn't need for any hurry now. She can take the remainder of her life, if she wants. As she passes, the receptionist behind the front desk barely glances at her, occupied by the telenovela playing on a small tablet that slides out from under her folders when the manager isn't around. There's no customer at the coffee nook, where the receptionist also triples as barista and cashier should someone obey the beckoning paw of the Japanese porcelain cat on the counter.

The coffee venture was part of a flurry of renovations management had embarked upon after she left for abroad. One year, she'd returned to find the lobby's gray walls covered up by prefabricated panels of exposed brick and the waiting area's threadbare sofa replaced by sleeker Scandinavian-by-way-of-Thai-factories chaises and sectionals. Another visit, a spa meant for expats and tourists had opened on one end of the ground floor, and the music from the lobby's overhead speakers had switched from Thai pop hits to rain forest sounds laid over tinkling chimes. Even the elevator bank had gotten a makeover, with footlights installed along the walls and the nicked beige doors refashioned with a few coats of auspicious firecracker red for the Chinese renters.

She stops in front of the call button, her hands clenched. Maybe this will be the time she gives in to the temptation to push it and wait for the arrival bell, a sound she has heard thousands of times. It's nearly seven o'clock. Both her parents should be home from work. Her father's probably watering the plants on the balcony and doing his evening calisthenics routine—arms swinging and legs lifting—in the Premier League T-shirt and shorts he has changed into, and her mother's probably in her favorite chair by the window, arms spreading and folding the day-old newspaper that she always forgets to take for her train commute. Soup is simmering on the stove in the alcove kitchen. It's either the lotus stem curry that her father brings home twice a week from his favorite shop by his office, or the clear tofu soup he likes to make with vegetables left over from other dishes. The TV is on, as it usually is. To break the silence, as her mother says. The evening news anchors—always the genial pairing of a delicately featured woman and a bespectacled man—are at their desk, pitying the fallen and wounded in the day's roundup. At some point, her mother gets up to knock at the windows to tell her father to come inside. Her father pretends to ignore the knock, and her mother knocks again, with louder authority.

The ding of the bell stiffens her back. The elevator has arrived on its own. Its red doors slide open with no one inside, and her own eyes return her gaze from the mirrored wall inside. She dares herself to step through.

She should have known this already: she won't. She'll turn around and walk out the door at the rear of the building and onto the covered walkway leading to the pool. It will already be growing darker out there, no one to look up at the scatter of lit windows. She'll just slip out and leave, as she has always done.

Before she can decide, something interrupts her. She can't say what it is—not a thing she can see, but different from a mere thought, and more than a feeling. It approaches her, cresting forcefully like a wave that has rippled across oceans. It wakes her, as if she were being shaken out of a dream. This is no dream. It's gathering outside of her. It speaks and says without speaking. A dreadful thing's about to happen.

She squints out the lobby's windows. A dry-cleaning delivery van cruises down the drive, the hanger bags having been dropped off. That's all it probably was: a noisy engine startling an anxious woman. She wonders if any of the others also felt it. In the lobby, the receptionist sits undisturbed, her attention still with the telenovela. A tenant stands at the wall of mailboxes, flipping through envelopes. From the speakers, recorded jungle birds squawk out over a synthesized human choir. Her steps clap forward across the marble floor. She pushes the glass doors into the remaining warmth of the slow-boiled day.

It is only so. Many times exiting through these doors, she mumbles the words: *It is only so.* It's a phrase she's said since she was barely more than a child, to steel herself for the unknowable day. A swim teacher first said it to her during a lesson, after a sparrow that had broken its neck against a sky-filled window fell dead into the pool, and she clung to the words as if they were a lifeline thrown to her. *It is only so.* She repeats the phrase three times, out of habit and a need to calm herself, not knowing why she's pacing the circular driveway, looking for what she can't even say.

She suspects the guard is watching her again but doesn't turn around to check. Following the seeming tilt of the land, she lets her feet pull her like hounds toward the garden by the garage entrance, where drivers wait their turn to whirl down the window and tap their entry card. She has long avoided this area for the good chance of running into one of her parents behind the wheel of a car.

The garden is nothing more than a square of yellowing grass and concrete planters. The air here feels thinned out. Her own footsteps, echoing back *one, two, one, two,* feel faded against an intensifying gradient of sensation.

She's suddenly reminded of the few minutes before a concert begins, when musicians run through their warm-ups onstage. She loves hearing those first discordant notes climbing and collapsing in their collective routine as much as the program to come. What are these instruments that now play for her? She hears the flapping of a buzzard's wings, monsoon rain tapping on window glass. Song of harvest sounding across rice fields. Monks' prayers enveloping a hall of mourners. A hand bounding sharply past middle C.

Some uproar above compels her to look up. She sees only the infinity of the bluing cloudless dusk and the darkened rise of the building, but her instincts command her to cross her arms overhead, turn away, and brace.

ARRIVAL

Three weeks after the disappearance of his steamer trunks some-where between the Siamese port and Singapore, Phineas Stevens still held hope for their return. He dearly missed his medical books, drawing supplies, and clothes. The reverend had lent him two sets of shirts and trousers, and each day he washed one in a pan of boiled water and wore the other. It was necessary that this chore be performed daily; here in the Siamese capital, one could sweat oceans in an hour. The heat and the gelatinous air sent his thoughts to leisurely summer swims across Archer's Pond. How he longed for those New England waters—cold, clean, without crocodiles.

At the river port, the Dutch shipping company clerks shook their heads. They assured him that their most diligent men would continue to retrace ship manifests and turn over their warehouses. He suspected them of uproarious laughter as soon as he left.

Outside, he could see that Winston had had better luck at the customs house. At his feet lay a wooden case that looked to hold some mechanical part or another for the crumbling printer, and two small crates—likely pamphlets from the Society to stock their diminishing stacks, which the reverend would claim as proof of interest from the Siamese, ignoring that most had no knowledge of English and that the cooks were using them as kindling.

Winston handed him a yellowed envelope scalloped at a corner by rodent bites.

"For you, Dr. Stevens."

"I'm surprised it has journeyed this far," Phineas said before tucking the envelope into his satchel.

"From your love?"

"My brother."

With the reverend, he spoke freely of his home life at Gransden Hall, but with Winston, who derived uninhibited amusement from the very thought of estate balls and carriage rides through the countryside, he barely mentioned it. Only this morning he'd said, as they set out, "Dr. Stevens, if a sojourn on foot isn't to your liking, you're welcome to ask the reverend if he would hire us sedan chairs, preferably attended by nubiles tickling the air with fronds."

He didn't take Winston's jabbing to heart. Howbeit, he had no choice but to rely on Winston's familiarity with this alien city. The few Westerners he'd encountered were European—Portuguese, English, French, and Dutch—drawn to the country's material riches. The reverend counted no more than one hundred Americans in the capital. The number included some fellow missionaries at Reverend Jones's Baptist mission in the Chinese section and at Dr. Bradley's Congregational mission on the Thonburi side. Then there were the sailors, traders, saloon keepers, and various personages of uncertain character. None made a habit of attending the mission's services.

The sun began to set, the darkened streets readying for thieves. They followed the east bank of the Chao Phraya back to the mission station. The sight of the gates always heartened Phineas. They entered to see again the main edifice, which had been constructed in an indeterminate European style but with much Siamese influence—a high triangular roof for venting heat, and stilts for weeks of flood. Worship took place in the first-floor chapel, an assembly area furnished with rudimentary pews; most days, two of the other lay missionaries, Miss Crawford and Miss Lisle, used it as a classroom for native children. A large tile-roofed veranda that jutted from the room on the south side served as the mission hospital and dispensary where Phineas worked. In addition to the main house, there was enough land for a small orchard of Asiatic fruits that the reverend tended, and a smaller house for the Siamese cooks, who ignored requests for more Occidental meals with winsome smiles. Here good wheat competed in rarity with gold. They tasted bread only in their sleep.

"A fruitful venture, I hope," the reverend said, locking the gate.

"It could have been better."

"In no time, you'll have adjusted your expectations."

It was the reverend who had urged him to accompany Winston on trips outside the mission compound, to "understand the local superstitions for the benefit of our efforts." He had observed how, most days, Phineas sat mute at supper, unable to muster much interest in the others' banter. Miss Crawford and Miss Lisle echoed the reverend's concern, worrying that devotion to work had taken a toll on him. Miss

Lisle made him promise that he would commit to some period of rest. He tried to evade her pleas, but she remained insistent. He acquiesced.

Aside from infrequent call to the homes of local merchants, Phineas had spent the greater part of the weeks since his arrival fulfilling his duties at the mission hospital. He attended to the endless circulation of market peddlers, fishermen, opium addicts, whores, and day laborers, dispensing packets of quinine and acetanilides, purgative oils, and remedies for digestive ailments, conditional on a translated Society pamphlet tied by string to each. There had been a few minor surgical procedures, most to deal with knife-inflicted wounds from skirmishes over wagers on caged cricket fights, and one to address an assault by a mongoose. He cleaved and mended as best he could, given septic conditions and few available instruments.

"We need more medical supplies," he'd said to the reverend, worried about their stock.

"Feel free to send another letter, Dr. Stevens, if you believe yourself more persuasive than I."

The Society historically sent less than what was required. Funds tended to flow more easily to other stations, like the one in Guangzhou, where demonstrable advances of the faith had been made with the local population as well as in the study of regional diseases. Phineas recalled an exhibit at New Haven when he'd been doing his medical training there, of Dr. Parker's studies of tumor pathologies in the Chinese population and the paintings of men and women with bulbous, flowering flesh. These had played no small part in motivating Phineas's own travels to this far-off post.

"Why not? I am after all a white sorcerer of formidable power," he said to the reverend. "Certainly, I can whisper a charm spell into my letter."

Once Phineas had arrived at the clinic to find, before his apothecary cabinet, a spread of square baskets woven from banana leaves. They were filled with offerings of rice, fresh flowers, and sweets. Two clay figures—a man and a woman—had also been left to serve as ghost servants for a chest of enema tubes. It did not delight him that his patients held him in similar esteem as their witch doctors, men who entered into trances to speak the tongue of spirits or who claimed to be able to send ghostly imps to strangle adversaries.

The reverend encouraged the misunderstanding. "A step to faith in the doctor is another to the doctor's God," he said.

Tonight, the reverend tapped Phineas's arm and informed him that tomorrow he'd be accompanying Winston on another outing beyond the compound.

"But what of the mission hospital? Who will tend to the infirm?"

"You'll be far more effective in your duties once you begin to know this country. We can trust Miss Lisle to handle most of the basic cases."

"And what of cases of greater severity?"

"We'll leave those to the witch doctors," the reverend said with a grin, before bidding him good night and walking up to the second-floor sleeping quarters. The reverend occupied the first room next to the stairs. Phineas's was the narrow room between the women's and Winston's. It contained few furnishings beyond a rudimentary desk and a raised platform where he slept on bare wood and a burlap pillow stuffed with coconut husks.

What he loved most about the room were the parrots that gathered in the tree across from its windows. Sunlight poured through the leaves and lit up tiny gold-and-orange flowers along the branches, where the birds perched in pairs. They were colored green and blue, with a necklace of ruffled topaz spots. All day and night they chattered, as if gossiping, and quarreled and sang seemingly joyful songs. Strangely, their noises did not bother him but instead gave him comfort as he lay in his bed, far from the familiar sounds of the wide green valley back home.

Winston wanted nothing more than to shoot these birds—nowhere as meaty as the quail he talked of hunting back in the States, but eating was beside the point. Winston claimed to be able to aim his pistol across the width of a canal and pick off a dragonfly. The reverend would not allow a demonstration of this skill for fear of offending the Siamese, who deplored such killings. They believed that Man was an animal and that, after death, a soul might reenter the realm of the living in the body of a different beast. They would not want to see their fathers shot for some foreigner's pleasure. *They will come for us with sticks and knives*, the reverend had warned.

Phineas woke to the sound of tapping outside. He stood up and stepped through the mosquito net to reach for a scalpel from his desk. A clang, followed by thuds. Someone was out there; he was certain. He unlatched the door and stepped out to the balcony, the scalpel tucked in his fist.

Winston dangled over the wall, having returned from some mysterious nocturnal errand. When he saw Phineas on the balcony, he lifted a lone finger to his lips and winked.

"He is not like us," Miss Crawford had said, after disclosing that were Winston not the only skilled and willing printer available in the capital, he would have long ago lost his place in the house.

"Up late, Dr. Stevens? Too much excitement ticking in that head of yours?" Winston whispered.

"Excitement? For what?"

"Tomorrow's festivities."

This much he'd learned in these few weeks: no occasion for raucous debauchery and superstition went unobserved in this heathen city. His alveoli had blackened from Chinese families burning money to dead relatives; his cochlear spirals had deformed from cannons fired at the Siamese forts to repel celestial leviathans swallowing the moon. The upcoming three-day ceremony, he'd heard, involved a monstrous swing.

In fact, he had seen the swing once, on his way to address a Dutch sea captain's gangrenous arm. The Siamese had raised the red swing beside a busy thoroughfare, where it loomed over no fewer than three gambling houses, an outdoor Chinese opera theater, a Buddhist temple, and a number of gold shops. With unbroken trunks of ancient mountain teak serving as its two main legs, it stood by Winston's estimate as high as fifteen men standing on one another's shoulders.

"You'll see, Doctor," he said now. "I've never before witnessed such daring from mortal creatures, and I have gone eye to eye with Santa Anna's army in Chapultepec."

"I'm certain I won't be disappointed. Sleep well, Winston."

If calamity were to visit me, it would be from this man, Phineas thought. He stepped back into his quarters and latched his door, his heart still pounding. Unable to close his eyes, he lit a lamp at his desk and opened again the envelope from his brother. Inside was a sketch of Gransden Hall that Andrew had drawn for him. What graceful lines, presumably made with soft Borrowdale graphite. There was nothing here for him but crumbly shards of coal, should he wish to return the favor.

He hoped Andrew would soon receive the letter he had sent this afternoon, without the reverend's knowledge, for it also contained a petition to the Society for his immediate transfer to Canton, Rangoon, or wherever else his medical skills could be better applied, with adequate resources and due seriousness of endeavor.

In the same letter he also wrote of his recovery from a mild gastro-intestinal illness, he believed from overripe mangoes devilishly selected by the cooks, and how Miss Lisle had taken charge of his care during that period, cleaning him, performing tasks that should only be asked of one's hired aide or kin. She eliminated marauding mosquitoes from his room and read to him from the few English tracts available to them. *Such magnanimity yields much its intention,* he'd written, and noted how grateful he was to count himself among such kind souls in this alien territory. He continued,

> The Siamese as a race thrive in the aquatic realm. They live as if they have been born sea nymphs that only recently joined the race of man. A traveler arriving at the mouth of the Chao Phraya steams upriver along mangrove beaches until the muddiness yields to long patches of coconut groves, alongside of which one may observe fishing villages where frog-limbed men, with spear or woven trap in hand, serenely perch on poles protruding from the water. Farther on lie endless expanses of wetland grass until the land solidifies into forests of flowering trees, fragrant in the breeze, and banana plants of endless variety. The wilderness gives way to towns where women squat at the shore with their washing and canoes as numerous as autumnal waterfowl in the Hudson's marshes row out, each with its freight of cooped poultry or mounds of fruits ready for the floating markets. And an hour beyond, before one can be lulled to an afternoon slumber, lies the capital, its riverside lined with rickety stilt houses that look incapable of withstanding even the most delicate wake of a modern steamer yet somehow maintain a

mysterious integrity. Their occupants drink, swim, wash away their filth, and fill pots to make soupy meals of their catches, everyone joined in the same confluence of fluids.

It is my conjecture that the waterborne city inspirits our undoing. Its fluvial systems—the natural ones and also the mesh of canals throughout the capital—carry to us miasmata that weaken the body.

Daily, we face our catastrophes, if not by pestilent vapors, then devised by bureaucrats, birthed from faithlessness, self-incurred. I comprehend the Society's preference for men and women of youth, as ample health and vitality are needed to withstand the corrosion of these climes.

I am less concerned for myself than I am for the mission. Since my arrival attendance at service has not increased beyond the dozen or so minority Chinese families converted years prior. Piles of translated tracts and pamphlets lie untouched. Few Siamese pay us heed, unless they are seeking medicine or soliciting us to purchase their goods. The reverend is rightfully proud of what he has managed to achieve at the station under the circumstances, but there are times when I believe him prouder of his bountiful rambutan trees. Miss Crawford and Miss Lisle hold fast to optimism, despite caring for children who prefer craft lessons to the learning of letters and maths. The man Winston, to no surprise, harbors no apparent worries.

Whatever blessings of civilization are accorded to the Siamese will, I fear, bear little fruit. They are a proud, even arrogant people, having yet to come under the domain of a more advanced nation. They seem to regard our own purpose as merely to serve and sustain them in their lifelong pursuit of frivolity. If you ask me, they are full of guile as well, having played off the ambitions of the French and the British, whose territories surround them, so as to profit from the impasse and continue to fly their elephant flag. Without significant headway into the interior of the country—there being no concession for missionary efforts similar to the Treaty of Nanking—I fear the reach of the mission will remain severely limited. Despite the outward friendliness of the Siamese, especially when my medical capacities are needed, the opposition to our presence is profound. That the reverend even managed to secure land for the mission and to procure materials for its construction is a minor miracle.

Another hindrance lies in the people's devotion to demon worship. Few have either the capacity or the desire for literacy, and even the Tripitakas and other texts of their own faith are a mystery to the majority of the people. Seeking solace outside of the passivity encouraged by their religion, the Siamese have embraced the worship of charms and objects, whether a tree or a termite mound.

My dear Andrew, I hope that I have not encumbered you with my distant despair, a world apart from the comforts of our valley, and that instead my musings shall provide you with some thin trickle of amusement. I hereby include a promised watercolor of frolicking parrots to guarantee a lift in your mood. It's very rudimentary, I'm afraid, as I'm forced to get along with the means available. The green comes from soaked pandan leaves, the yellows from turmeric. May their pungent odors fade before your receipt of these words.

Did I tell you in my previous letter what became of the previous occupant of my room? A hooded cobra trespassed the mosquito screen one night, and when the man woke, the snake was roused as well. Not a waking hour passes in that room without my suspicious glance at crevices between the floorboards.

I hold little fear, however, as I consider these present circumstances trials meted by His hand. From my own treatment of patients, I've found that body and spirit are often restored by what most consider tribulation, be it piercing to let foul humors or the administration of black calomel to purge disease and restore balance to the constitution. To be touched by Grace, a soul must not fear enduring harm.

Yet, I must admit, the knowledge of your prayers does provide me with immeasurable comfort. Will you continue to pray for us here, as I pray for you all? Earthly survival, as transient as it will ultimately prove to be, presents a very desirable prospect. By His grace, may I hope to see each morning light?

CADENCE

The way Clyde tells it, the suicidal man was a sergeant, and the band had been trucked to the base to change his mind. "By playing 'My Blue Heaven,'" says Clyde. "His friends thought it worth a try. They told us the song always put the sergeant in a better mood."

It's three o'clock in the morning. The nerves in his knees are shooting lightning. He has just played two sets straight to a room that carries on, chattering and cackling, like he should thank them for letting him play.

He looks for Griang and Marut, but they've slunk away, leaving him at a squeaky vinyl-upholstered booth with these young white officers on their five-day leave from either Utapao or Korat or a few hundred miles east in the big show itself—the country he's more often heard referred to by numbered tactical zones or just "the war" than by its official name of Vietnam. By their accents, he knows these boys are from the South. There are Americans everywhere in Bangkok, he likes to say with a drop of complaint, but he's not unhappy when he catches a familiar drawl through the cigarette smoke, summoning warmer memories of the Carolina shipping town where he was born. Besides, his countrymen pretending to be warrior-gods means good business. The swaggering packs of Americans who clot up the sidewalks on Petchburi Road keep him playing weeknights at the Servicemen's Club and weekends at the Grand Eastern Hotel's lounge.

He should be grateful for what he has going, according to Bobby Blue Eyes. Maybe, but if Bobby comes through, Clyde will be able to look forward to the long-awaited reprieve of a proper show. This time, he'll be the headliner and people will be listening because they've made a point of coming to hear him, not because he happened to be behind the piano that night. He'll play his own songs and none of the standards some Joe Dope might request, waving a twenty-baht bill as if that'd make someone's whole night. *Ring you after tonight's show*, Bobby had said. *Have a drink ready.*

"So this sergeant, what happened with him?" asks a lieutenant with premature gray striping the sides of his head.

Clyde says, "We're driven down this road lined with cinder-block army housing, and I can see ahead exactly where we're stopping, because there's already a small crowd of MPs and GIs around the sergeant's quarters. It's monsoon season, and everything's sunk in mud. They've built us a makeshift stage out of sandbags and pallets, with an upright Baldwin smack in the middle. It's so hellishly humid I can feel the keys stick when I press them, and right away I know the piano's out of tune. They order us to start playing, so we do. Oh, what a disaster. I think about it, and I still want to bury my face in that dirt. When we finish the song, we look around, and they tell us to play it again. Five, six, fifteen, I don't know how many times, and I'm praying that they'll realize what a bad idea this is and also thinking I'll hear a gun pop any moment. Then the door busts open and the man comes out waving his .45 and screaming, 'Stop, you're fucking everything up!' The MPs push him to the ground and that's it." He slaps the table with a hand. "That's how I saved a man's life."

This late, everyone's easy to laugh. He gets Happy to come over from the bar with drinks, four to a hand. There's a toast. He clinks his glass against the others and resumes his pose, propped on his elbows.

If opportunity allows—and he usually finds it—he'll tell his new friends about touring the bases in Europe, sharing the stage with Red, backing up Mabel at packed supper clubs, and, more recently, gripping the railing as a metal bird swerved between mountain cliffs and hoping the piano slotted next to him wouldn't tear from its netting. He likes to dip his voice lower when he talks about the uninvited percussion—mortar rounds being fired into the jungle from hilltop camps. "Then I realize the bang completes my sound," he'll say.

"Clyde, you ever listen to them shows from Hon Tre?" asks one of the officers.

His smile wanes at the mention of rock this, groovy that, and especially the Brazilian stuff the clubs have been asking him to play.

"You like gunk in your ears?" he asks. "Those AFVN know-nothings only play you the riff and hook stuff. And if anyone disagrees, send them to Crazy Legs Clyde. I'll show them what's right."

By now, a man his age has made peace with his stage name. It's all anyone ever remembers. *What the hell*, he once thought. *Oh, what the hell*, he still thinks. Most awful is the obligation of having to still give them the Crazy Legs part, as if everything else about his music hasn't mattered. Worse, that name also means he has to be ever so lively, despite the ruined knees, with his feet flopping and sliding on the stage floor like fresh catch on a dock. Something has to make up for his weakened voice.

"Phone," Happy says from the bar. He slides out of the booth and winks to the lieutenant who has gotten up to let him through. The lieutenant returns it with a courteous nod. *Church boy can't help but keep his good manners*, Clyde thinks.

"So did you get that consulate gig for me or not?" he says into the receiver.

"Working on it," says a voice in piercing, accented English. "But there's something else. A small function. Tomorrow."

"I'm not playing a wedding, Bobby. I've told you that."

"No, Clyde. Not a wedding. Listen, please. It's a private show at a house. The client's a big Crazy Legs fan."

"Bobby, I might as well play on a toy piano at a temple fair."

Morris would have laughed at him for tolerating this indignity. He remembers tugging Morris back by the slide of his horn when a patron kept scraping a fork on the china. Those were splendid times: they played until morning, there at the Roost, and also at Leon's and the Onyx, where, night after night, Clyde listened to music so unearthly he thought he'd heard his bones cry. Even after those joints gave way to the ratholes businessmen ducked in to see girls writhing naked, they kept the jams loud and alive at the few places that hadn't closed, like at Max's basement in the Village, or sometimes up on rooftops in the Bronx, where they kept playing through, undershirts soaked, as the El roared past them in the steamy dark.

"What about that nightly at the Oriental? When are you going to snag that for me?"

"Clyde, that's coming. This is now. This is easy money."

"Hold on. Have to look at my grid," Clyde says, and takes his time to check an imaginary calendar book. "How much bread is this going to get me?"

Bobby Blue Eyes gives him the number, five-figured in bahts, good enough along with what little he has saved for a plane ticket across the ocean.

He has known plenty of cities—starry metropolises with wide, endless boulevards, towns with piazzas empty at dawn, and slums in the shadow of medieval towers—each distinct from the one before, and the countless faces and tastes and smells, each an ocean's width removed from the last. After he woke up from that European dream, Johnny John, who'd flown back from drumming gigs in Asia, suggested he try his luck in Bangkok. He thought he'd swing in for a warm winter. Five years have passed.

Is Morris even still in New York? Not a word has passed between them since he left the States. The most deafening thing he's ever heard is the silence between two people.

"Go ahead, book it," he says to Bobby Blue Eyes.

The pills the bouncer sold him before the show are hitting their notes. In his knees a river is stilled white by winter; in his head a turbid sea laps away the shore. Don't fight it. Roll with the cabin and there's no getting sick, a stewardess once said to him on a plane.

Back at the booth the brandy glasses have been emptied and only one of the boys is there. It's the lieutenant, slumped against the wall on the other side of the booth.

"Where did your friends go?"

"Someplace. They left."

He's visited by the sudden focus that comes to drunks at the height of inebriation. He studies the lieutenant's upwardly curved eyes, made prominent under the barren expanse of forehead; they remind him of the expression on Morris's face, humming a newly hatched tune as they walked down Broadway.

It was Morris who'd fed him the whirly phrases that built up his early songs. Morris, hunched over the desk they shared, whistling and filling music sheets with whatever was abuzz in his head. Morris, who loved even the most wretched parts of him. They'd had a wonderful, tender decade with each other, hadn't they? They'd done all they could so others wouldn't find out, so that, at clubs, they wouldn't walk into abrupt silence where the other musicians sat.

"Did I tell you about when I played in West Berlin with Ambassador Satch?" He pauses to sip his glass.

"Are you okay there, Clyde?"

"As fantastic as ever. Thanks for asking."

His voice feels like it has floated off and he's in a darkened room, listening to someone else say his words. "So this is after I've left New York and am bumming around in Newark. One day I get a call, and it's my old headliner friend saying, 'Clyde, you ever gone east of Queens?' So before I know it, I'm there in England and then Germany, and we're having ourselves a hell of a time, because over there they still love us to death. Then one night, we're at this club in West Berlin, just off the Bleibtreustrasse, and as I'm playing, I feel a chill down my spine, and I notice this fellow standing in the aisle, leaning against a wall, and he's staring at us like he wants to rip our throats out with his teeth. I keep on playing, of course, but whenever I look out there I see this terrible face. Well, the show ends, and the crowd's leaving, and this man's walking up to me. I'm thinking, Louis won't mind if I grab his horn to use in self-defense, but then the man sticks his hand out and barks out something in German, and as I'm shaking his hand, our translator says the man crossed the Wall that night just to come hear us live."

His voice returns to his tongue, like a pigeon to its coop, and becomes his again.

"You want another one?" the lieutenant asks.

"I'm set."

Under the table, Clyde brushes his leg on the lieutenant's. The leg, warm underneath the man's trousers, doesn't move from where his has stopped: the side of the man's calf. A frightened look flashes over the lieutenant's face. How remarkable, Clyde thinks, that a grown man can so quickly become a child again.

□ □ □

A ringing phone wakes him. He looks around and sees that he's alone in his own bed, still wearing last night's pants. The rectangle of morning through his one window shines on the jacket hanging from a chair. It has a nasty tear, the right sleeve hanging on sinewy threads. A dull pain radiates across the left side of his face. When he touches it, looking in the wall mirror, he's glad to find that it's not swollen, just a purple blot he can cover with powder. He remembers now: ambling down an empty soi with the lieutenant, saying the harmless things he usually says to a man he's just met and the lieutenant responding, one-worded. Then out of nowhere, he felt a shove, his collar yanked, and the lieutenant not being so quiet with a pair of right hooks.

"Hello," he says into the phone.

"Making sure someone remembers to show up today."

"Damn it, Bobby. I've been doing this since long before you learned how to chew your food."

He takes a shower in the mildewy bathroom. He takes a bottle of Coke out of the fridge and rubs the cold glass on his face. He patches himself up and dresses. At three o'clock, he walks down the two flights of stairs from his apartment and hails a tuk-tuk in front of the building. As with every afternoon, the roads run thick with private cars and overburdened buses. Beaky scooters and children hawking flower garlands wind through short-lived gaps between crushing fates. It takes half an hour to go just a few kilometers.

"This is it? You sure?" he asks the driver, but the man sputters off without a word.

He stands in the shade of the wrought-iron fence and the column of tall ashoka trees behind it. A servant, wearing a waistcloth like they do in the country, answers the buzzer and lets him in. He follows her down a stone-lined path, past a row of trellises heavy with yellow flowers the shape of gramophone horns, and then along a circular garden pond the color of split pea soup. For a moment, the choir of garden insects falls silent, revealing the sickly sputters of a boat engine. A canal becomes visible through narrow crenels striping the rear concrete wall. They walk along a driveway beside the wall, their footsteps measuring a few tranquil minutes—the sloshing wake, the songbirds overhead—until, finally, he spots a house awash with an air of the ancient in the tree-shaded light. They come to a roofed terrace that reminds him of the porch at his childhood home—his grandma's white-and-green cottage, where he studied how the grown-ups played hymns and where at night, while his family slept, he silently scurried his tiny fingers a nail's width above the keys. This house stands much larger, with two stories of arched windows and decorated eaves and terra-cotta tiles on the roof, much like ones he's seen at villas in northern Italy where he played USO shows.

Inside, the house is cool and dimly lit. His nose picks up the faint scent of aged wood, sweet and dusty, like wisps of tobacco pinched from a tin. "This way. She's waiting," the servant girl tells him in Thai, gesturing down a hallway with her open palm. He steps into a parlor room with sea-blue walls wainscoted in dark teak. A trio of green velvet-backed chairs anchor the room. On the tallest chair sits a Thai woman about his age, wearing an ivory-colored silk blouse and a long brown skirt. The two puppies at her feet spring up to yap at him, and she quiets them with a clap.

"Make yourself comfortable," she says in British-accented English. He brings together his hands, thinking to clasp them and greet her with a traditional Thai wai, but she offers her hand for him to shake. He sits down in the chair facing her and drops his Panama hat on the narrow table beside it.

"A grand house you have here, ma'am," he says.

"It used to be my husband's. He lives in London with his current wife. My son lives in New York, trying to be a starving artist. I'm here."

"All the same, ma'am, it's a wonderful home. All the same."

"Would you like a drink, Mr. Crazy Legs? A water?"

"I'm quite all right, thank you, ma'am. Maybe I'll bother you for that water later."

"And you can stop addressing me as ma'am. Call me Pehn."

"Will do, Khun Pehn. Likewise, please call me Clyde. Clyde Alston."

"I've long admired your work, Mr. Clyde Alston. I must have listened to *Starry Hour* hundreds of times."

"It's been a long time since that album. I'm surprised anyone still knows of it."

"You're being too modest, Mr. Alston. It's a remarkable record. Won't you play from it for me?"

"I've had a few albums since then, Khun Pehn. Sure you wouldn't like to hear my latest stuff?"

"The songs were dear to me during more joyful times in my life. Do you prefer not to play them, Mr. Alston?"

Clyde remembers riding out to Hackensack with Morris to record

Starry Hour at the sound engineer's studio, which was no more than a wood-ceilinged living room with a control area behind glass. The acoustics, though, were better than most concert halls in the city. Afterward, Red and Tony happened to drop in, and they all played on, long after the recording session, everything humming: the air in the room, the blue of the sky outside. Shame they hadn't caught that part on tape too.

"Of course not, Khun Pehn. Just that it's been a while. I might be a little out of practice."

For a long moment they say nothing further. A ceiling fan whirs overhead, and the shrill call of a lone mountain pigeon comes from somewhere outside.

He has never been one for afternoons. He hates how the day hangs so thick and undecided, as if it's staring him down and expecting an answer. Morris would go run errands or play the numbers or both, and then come back some hours later to slap together two of his huge, piled-on sandwiches with cold cuts from the Jewish deli over by Connie's. Winters, they almost never left their apartment on 137th Street unless for a show. They wormed under blankets and drank dirty birds until the next day's light knocked on the window. He'd rest his head on Morris's chest and listen to the growling stomach of the man he loved and think that was the happiest anyone could be. It was on one of those nights that he noticed marks at the bend of Morris's arm. Not long after, he found a kit hidden behind a dresser.

"Not to be rude, Khun Pehn, but Bobby let you know my fee?"

"I don't know who this Bobby is, but yes, here's all of it."

She hands him an envelope, and he puts it in his pants pocket, not bothering to peek. He's curious how Bobby Blue Eyes even found out about this gig.

"So where's this party I'm playing?" he asks, gesturing with his hand in the direction of the garden.

Khun Pehn chuckles, covering her mouth with a wrist.

"Party? This Bobby, did he not tell you?"

She gets up, and he follows her down the hallway under the staircase. The room they enter has bare teak walls and a window that looks out on a vegetable garden. At the far side of the room, Clyde sees a turn-of-the-century piano with elaborate inlaid patterns on the mahogany case and carved moldings on the key bed. Nearby, a man in a white tunic sits cross-legged on a Louis XIV sofa.

"I'm playing for him?"

"Master Rai? He's only the medium. You'll be playing for the spirits," Khun Pehn says, pointing to a wooden pillar by the window.

"In there," Clyde says.

"Yes, mainly. Master Rai counts twenty or so spirits in the pillar. They visit me in my dreams, and I'm tired of it. A woman my age needs her sound sleep."

He looks the pillar up and down. Weathered and knotted, with dark globs of sap bleeding at its base, the pillar reminds him of a giant twig. One magnificent day, he'll cut himself loose from Bobby Blue Eyes.

"What do these spirits want?"

"They're unhappy with me. They think I'm selling the house."

"Are you?"

"Nobody wants me to sell. Nobody lives here but me. I feel as if I'm trapped in one of those boxes they fill up with odd mementos and seal in the ground, so others can dig it out a hundred years later and amuse themselves. Do you know what I'm talking about, Mr. Clyde Alston?"

"Can't think of the exact term at the moment, but yes, I do. What I'm not clear on is my part in this."

"They also told me, through Master Rai, that they haven't heard a musician play for them in ages. My husband's parents brought in ma-hori ensembles. I thought I'd change the tradition a bit."

Clyde lifts the cover and taps out the first bar of a standard. The piano's tuned, depriving him of an honest excuse.

"Khun Pehn, this is giving me the heebie-jeebies. I don't know."

Master Rai, speaking in some dialect, mumbles something that Clyde doesn't catch. After hearing the man out, Khun Pehn says, "He wants you to know the spirits here are very eager for you to perform. And if you'd like, you can invite some of your own."

Standing over the piano, Clyde tells himself that this is no different from any other gig. In a week or two, he'll be gone from Bangkok, and this will be just another of his memories of the place; the mother of future laughs across gin glasses.

"All right, Khun Pehn. Show's on."

"Very well. Shall we?"

□ □ □

Hunched in front of the piano, Clyde sees only the shiny keys and his own softened reflection in the dark lacquer. Khun Pehn and Master Rai are sitting somewhere behind him, but it feels like he's the only one in the room. He wonders when he should start, not used to being deprived of opening applause, no matter how polite and pitiful.

He can't remember when he last played these songs, even on his own. He hopes that his mind only has to pull the familiar levers and his fingers and feet will break into the remembered motions. The keys at the tips of his fingers feel steel-cold. He presses down carefully, as if stepping forward on a lightless street. He slides the chair out of the way.

He begins tapping the floor with a foot, and for a while he rides fast up and down a series of chord changes, quickening the tempo after every few bars. When he reaches a frenzy that verges on his running off with the piano, he freezes and lets his voice pierce through, a grand cry like—as Morris once instructed—the first one outside his ma's belly.

After that outburst, his fingers sing in his place. He opens with the quick-footed bluesy numbers, each about three minutes long, each moody and nervous but not without an underlayer of burgeoning rapture. He then tempers the pace to what might be called a ballad, a reliable crowd melter from when he made the rounds on Fifty-Second Street, a conceit, he admits, to set them up for the bombardment to follow.

Some newspaperman had once said that he played the keys as if they were on a machine shooting out confetti. When he had much of the crowd swaying and nodding their heads at the table, he knew the irrepressible moment had arrived. He'd call them to the floor and out they'd tumble, tugged from their seats by a hand they might only hold for that night. Folks sure went wild, given the permission of a mess.

He shouldn't be surprised by what a song can do. Morris liked him to spread a song wide across the keys and build the chords up high. Each progression begs what's next, and before long, they're exploding further and further and further from where the song got started. Even though he's the one pressing the keys, he has no choice but to hang back and let the music go where it's leading him. He has long known that a song can make a man feel like he's the luckiest being alive or help him smother his loneliness or, if it's in the mood, retrieve to him, with its lengthy reach, times he didn't even know he'd let sink to the murky bottom. This one returns him to the living room with the drab wallpaper and the green sofa rescued from a fire and the dust-encrusted rug where he stood saying to his love, "You think just because you wrote these, I owe you my life?"

It's late in 1967, and they're living not on 137th Street but in a house in Greenville, New Jersey, within earshot of the foghorns that sound from the docks in Elizabeth. They don't play more than a couple of nights a week. A businessman gets bloodied in the Playbill's parking lot, and the white crowd stops coming to Newark.

Morris says to him, "You're running from me."

Clyde says back, "Now why would I say no to playing in Europe with them? You think I'm getting a phone call like that again? You think I should stay here and look at the bugs on this wall and you cranked up on whatever you're on?"

He knows he's breaking a man to pieces. You can't go, I've nothing without you, Morris is going to say, like he does time after time, staggering out of the haze in his blood—no more bothering to hide the habit, no errands, no nothing—to barter for forgiveness with any word still retrievable to that flickering mind. An hour from now, Clyde will be on the early train to the city, and at Idlewild, after splurging on two gimlets in the cocktail lounge, he'll board the flight to Frankfurt, and as the plane makes its rattling escape from the earth he'll stare down at cloudy plumes of dissolving sandbars and dots of seabirds lifting their reedy legs through drowned grass and, like the other passengers, try to forget the end that meets those who fall from dizzying heights.

"Excuse me, Khun Pehn. Might I have that glass of water?"

"Certainly. Is anything the matter?"

"Everything's right and dandy. I need a sip, that's all."

Khun Pehn calls out to the hallway, and not a minute later, a servant girl arrives with a filled glass held high.

"Thank you," he says in Thai, and drains the contents of the glass. It's clean, glorious water subtly scented by a pink-hued tincture that has brought back to his nose the floral wreaths laid around his grandma after she'd found her irrevocable peace. Each gulp helps calm the fran-

34

tic squeezing inside his chest. He's hardly begun to play, but already torrents of sweat have flooded his back and arms.

When he was young, barely a musician, he got booed onstage for the first time. His hands froze, and the noisy disdain grew to fill the room until he couldn't distinguish it from the wall and the piano next to him and all the eyes burning in the dark. He sat there, unable to move, until the club manager dragged him out of the chair.

He's no longer intimidated by a cruel crowd. He doesn't care anymore what other cats say about his playing. But how did he have the gall to imagine that after all this time he might make things right with the man whose life, by word of friends touring through Bangkok, was not claimed by a syringe after all? A man more fearsome to him than any ghost.

"My apologies," he says to the room. He puts the empty glass on a side table and then returns his hands to the keys.

"All right, where was I?"

⊔ ⊔ ⊔

It's another night at the Grand Eastern, and his knees are killing him.

He's wearing his new jacket, cut in cotton the blue of midday. With a stringy tape measure, the tailor had charted wider paths around his body, and now he can button up and still reach for the higher octave keys without feeling the fabric clamp up underarm.

"How's that? Didn't Crazy Legs promise it was going to get wild in here? It did, didn't it?"

He bows to the crowd—this one at least paid enough attention to applaud when they were supposed to—and clambers down the steps, passing the next performer, a Chinese songstress dressed in a red silk qipao. She stands wavering behind the gold-colored curtain, as if it was meant to shield her nakedness, and when she catches his glance, she returns his smile with pursed lips. Already, the crowd's clapping and calling for her before she even walks onstage.

At the bar, Happy taps a finger on the usual bottle.

"Heading someplace else. Just hand over that envelope."

Outside, neon lights remake him in pink and green. It's raining. The puddles, too, brim with light.

He hails a tuk-tuk and tells the driver to turn right when he says so at the intersection of Sukhumvit and a minor soi. They make more turns, past storefronts and stalls shuttered until someone's gladiatorial contender wakes them from its rooftop coop at dawn. This hour, away from the tourist roads and the baited hotels and massage parlors, dark swaths of the city sometimes get so quiet he can hear the whole animal breathe. He tells the driver to stop at a nondescript building with black-filmed windows framed by a strip of Christmas lights.

Stepping inside, he counts maybe two dozen men, some settled into rounded grottoes carved into the wall, others at the bar, lips whispering by ears, arms resting on willing shoulders. Coupled shadows shuffle on the floor to tinny bossa nova. He plops himself on a barstool.

It takes less than five minutes before a young Thai approaches him from across the room. The man has a pale, heart-shaped face, and in the dim light of the club he could be a crane striding past water buffalos in a rice field.

"Louis Armstrong not come here for long time. Sao very sad."

"Well, I'm here. Took the scenic route."

"Louis Armstrong alone tonight? Handsome man doesn't have to be."

"Hey, did I ever tell you about the time I saved a man's life?"

"Sao, good memory. Louis Armstrong tell story many times."

Clyde waves to the bartender and orders overpriced martinis he knows will be badly made. No use not spending the money he now has, minus Bobby Blue Eyes's cut and enough for the suit and next month's rent. He might even use some of it to find a new place, somewhere farther out, with fewer Americans around. A ticket to New York would've cost all that.

"Cheers."

"Chon kaew."

As Sao raises the stemmed glass to meet his, Clyde notices, underneath the tightened shirtwaist, the outline of a switchblade. It's the first time he's seen one on Sao. He's been warned before to be cautious with bedfellows whose passions are for hire, who—so the lore goes—can strangle a man for his wristwatch as easily as they can launch him to the heavens. They all carry some thorn or another, he suspects, and he ought to feel an overboil of fear, hot in his nerves like when the lieutenant stood over him, clench-fisted and panther-eyed in that deserted street.

Instead, he feels relief finding the certain beat of his earthly life knocked a little off its bounce, the few hours to come like cigar smoke curling past the reach of lamplight. So returns a feeling from decades ago, standing outside that big pavilion by the sea and watching the dime-a-dance band twiddle the floor to near explosion. In the middle of a number, the piano man onstage, a brooding angel with his forehead dripping and a vest soaked dark, glanced up from the keys to wink at this boy, and the clear and pounding thrill of the instant ate him live and whole. What has he found since, chasing its quivering echo?

He feels a warm hand fold over his, as if it has been searching a long time for a place to lie down. "Let's get going somewhere," Sao says. "No funny funny. This time Louis Armstrong tell Sao what he wants."

His grandma had looked forward to the eternity that awaited her—the golden-spired cities, the walls of sapphire and amethyst, the springs that would flush out all despair. He's no good for that kind of forever. He wishes Morris had known that, too. Even the most glorious day should carry on only so long.

"Hell if Louis Armstrong knows. He was hoping you'd sing it to him."

BIRTHRIGHT

The connecting flight had been fully booked and he was lucky to have a seat, after much pleading with the Pan Am ticket agent at LAX. He leaned forward to look out the window. Below, the Thames shimmered white, curving across curtains of office towers and stripes of traffic beaded by red taillights. He peered into the glowing rectangular innards of a stadium built long after he had left this city. The green pitch was lit so bright he thought he could hear the cheering crowd. Closer to ground, parking lot lamps painted circles on tiny cars. Billboards topped low-rise office buildings. He couldn't tell what it was that they wanted to tell him. What he wanted to know was whether or not his father was already dead.

From his stepmother's call, he knew that his father had passed out at the pond during a morning swim, luckily in shallow water. His father's swimming buddy, a barrister who had been a colleague, had dragged him to shore and then ran to a telephone booth to call emergency services. Come quickly, Helen said.

It wasn't the first time he thought his father would abandon him. He felt that he'd long been primed for whatever duty it was that a son should perform with solemn ceremoniousness at the end of his father's life.

He boarded the bus. It wouldn't take long to get in from Heathrow. He closed his eyes and fell in and out of sleep, the kind of sleep that comes with short bus rides, momentary drifts into dreams that dimly started and then faded off. He was somewhat aware of a child crying in front of him and cognac exhaled nearby. A man and a woman argued about Gerald Ford in whispers everyone could hear. He woke up when the bus pulled into Victoria Station.

He almost didn't recognize Freddie, waiting for him by a shuttered newsstand. They hadn't seen each other for fifteen years, and at first his half brother looked like any brown-haired bloke waiting for a friend coming in on a late bus from some other English city. Then he recognized the hairline like his own, squared high at the sides, and the same unfortunate ears that winged the fringe of their heads, both their father's gifts.

"Samart," Freddie said with hesitation. "Or would you rather that I call you Sammy?"

"Whichever you'd like. I hope you haven't waited long."

"Not at all, but I did get a few looks from those constables over there. Suspicious man standing alone at a train station. It's the world we live in now."

It seemed fanciful of Freddie to think that anybody could read potential harm into his figure. Here was Paddington Bear, on a mission from the North.

"Am I too late?"

"Actually, he seems to be doing fine. After his CT and echocardiogram, and another night in observation, he insisted on coming back home."

"But that call . . ."

"I'm sorry my mother reached you with such alarm. We can't ever be sure with him, you know."

"I'm sorry I couldn't get here any earlier," Sammy said. Some part of him wanted his father to see him again with eyes still live and aware, yet he could have dealt better with finding his father in the state he'd expected. He felt tempted to turn around and hop on a bus back to the airport.

In the backseat of a cab, as Freddie made polite talk comparing the weather in London and Los Angeles, Sammy could hear his father's bony arms steadily chopping the water, as if keeping time.

"How's business?" asked Freddie.

"It's doing fine, too many assignments or not enough, the usual loony clients, what's new."

"Must be delightful not having to work behind a desk. I think about it, getting up and leaving. 'Fare thee well, billable hours,' I'd yell to the partners, and go do what I don't know. Then I remember I've got Lilith and Alder, and Emily would surely feed me rat poison for the insurance payout."

Freddie envied a false, glorified notion he had of his half brother's life, Sammy thought. He had no idea of the hours Sammy spent calling up ad agencies' finance departments about unpaid invoices, or helping a hired assistant take apart lighting setups and coiling up three duffel bags' worth of cords, or eyeing luggage handlers as they carted away equipment he couldn't afford to insure, much less replace, all for the privilege of beatifying a cereal box or office chair on medium-format film.

"The swimsuit models make it worthwhile," Sammy said. He could sense Freddie's imagination tipping in his favor.

They were being driven on Fulham Road, where he found himself imposing the London he'd known on the London outside the taxi window. Familiar ancients stood under their bowlers and knit caps and waited for the light, and he saw them restored in his mind to who they'd once been—men and women no different from the adults long ago in his own life, their degeneration unthinkable then. They stood alongside impatient young men with their angular trouser legs jutted out like flying buttresses. Who were they? Why were they here? What he least recognized in these streets was the youth. It seemed strange that he was no longer one of them, on streets they should know he'd marked and claimed.

He rolled down the window to take a photo. Nobody acknowledged him. He was another Asiatic tourist snapping future memories of a far-away place.

They arrived at the two-story row house. It was one of those built before the war, kindred with its unremarkable Georgian-style neighbors. Long ago, his father had rented it from a Mrs. Fielding, who had retired to Bath to be closer to her daughters and rarely visited. Eventually his father bought the place. Since Sammy had last been there, the white exterior had been repainted a light slatelike hue, and teal-blue curtains now hung at each window. Someone, probably Freddie, had planted third-rate shrubs out front.

While Freddie paid the fare, he carried his suitcase down the steps to the ground floor and rang the door.

"You're here," said the British woman who'd supplanted his mother. Although deepened grooves now ringed her eyes, and her pale face seemed more cantilevered from her high cheekbones, it was clear that she had once been very beautiful. She drew him close for a hug, and he let her, barely feeling the grip of her arms. She had likely lost some strength in them, but he suspected that she was also being careful with him, the way she might have handled a delicate book at the library where she used to work.

"Hello, Helen."

"Look at you. You haven't aged a day."

He wondered with which age of his she was making the comparison. She could have meant sometime in the 1960s, when he'd come to visit his father before leaving London for good, or how he'd looked in the photos he sent his father from his unannounced wedding in Stockholm, back when he thought he could give marriage a chance with a sweet, healthy-minded woman. Or it could just be something Helen would say to someone she should remember well but couldn't.

"Is he awake?"

"I'm sure he wouldn't mind being woken up to see you."

"No, I can wait until morning."

"We've prepared you a room. It's not terribly big, but there's a comfortable daybed."

"Thank you."

"Freddie, won't you show Samart his room? Freddie?" She walked back to the foyer to check on her son, who'd gone upstairs where he lived with his own family.

Sammy peered down the hall to see a door slightly ajar. He walked over. Inside, his father lay nearly upright, a double layer of pillows behind his back, looking healthy and well preserved, better than what Sammy had imagined of someone who'd just had a stroke. His father

43

still had most of his hair, and his father's skin, the same soft tan of milky coffee as his own, hadn't paled to the blue-veined translucence he'd seen in other elders. Only the small skyline of pharmaceuticals on the nightstand hinted that something was wrong. Sammy snuck out his camera and took a shot. His father, if awake, wouldn't have allowed it.

"I'd say, 'What a sweet sleepy cherub,' if I didn't know better," said Helen, walking back. They both smiled at the man asleep, head down, chin against chest. What more could he do for his father? He thought of the notion he'd had, not to come at all.

"Helen, would you mind if I ring someone later?"

"There's a phone in your room."

"It'll be long distance. I'll pay."

"Don't you worry. You took the trouble to travel on such short notice."

"He is my father."

"Well, I'm happy for him. You're here. It's been some time."

□ □ □

Here he was again, at the place that he and his parents had once called their London house.

For hours into the early morning, he lay looking at the blue and starless dark outside the window. The houses of his father's neighbors seemed unpeopled, the street a thoroughfare for phantoms. As a child, he had looked out in terror at the strange country where his family had been sent, and it was only on a night like this, when the silhouetted scenery had been emptied and he was alone, feeling like a miniaturized figure of a boy in a scale model town, that he had felt comfortable. Tonight, though, the silence and stillness only encouraged his anxiety.

Whether Helen knew it or not, she had put him up in the room where he'd felt most unwelcome in either house: his father's study.

This room might once have served as a small parlor, but by the time he and his parents moved in, permanent shelves had been installed in its walls. Amber light from a lamp outside illuminated rows of books reaching the ceiling. Dread towered over him. He hadn't quite known if these were the same books his father had forbidden him to touch in the old house in Bangkok. He rarely entered this room even when his father was there, glimpsed between hills of books borrowed from the Foreign Ministry library. Some instinct stopped him from announcing himself to the strange figure who now sat in his father's chair and wore reading glasses that seemed like a disguise.

He'd presumed his father to be reading diplomatic treatises or legal screeds befitting a Thammasat-educated rising star of international law, but one day his curiosity won out while his father was away, leading to his discovery that those books on his father's desk had nothing to do with the law. They were instead books that recorded the maneuverings of men and horses on charred muddy hillsides, or the effusive words of Christian saints recounting their myriad remorses, or incomprehensible lines that he would only later come to know as poetry.

Even at his age, he knew that he had more than trespassed beyond his father's warnings not to touch the books or play around the desk. He was glimpsing a kind of nakedness that his father didn't want anyone to see. When his father returned, he didn't ask him about the books. He had waited in the darkened spare bedroom next to the study and watched his father from behind the furniture. When the man emerged from the study, the man would become his father again.

What else had waited for him to come back so it could come to life? Lying on the daybed now, he walked through the house in his mind; he reentered each room—not as they were now but as he'd known them in his youth. With his child's hands, he touched the cherrywood furniture Mrs. Fielding hadn't taken to the country. His fingerprints smudged the long oval dining table. His feet brushed the Persian carpet in the living room, a housewarming gift from his father's friends at the Thai Legation.

He saw his mother in the hallway, practicing her English with the housekeeper, and his father in front of the mirror in the foyer, pinching tight the knot in his tie. Then the people arrived, first as murmurs he couldn't quite hear—his father's colleagues, guests from other countries' posts, some English neighbors they liked. The laughter and singing reached him long after he had been dispatched upstairs to the far exile of his bedroom, Thai and English rising through the floorboard gaps, and sometimes Dutch or French.

He gave in to a succession of recalled moments until he was standing across from his mother in the kitchen, back when the curtains weren't teal blue but ivory. She was wearing a sleeveless crimson gown and frustrated that the liquor for the evening hadn't been delivered.

"Sammy, don't touch anything!"

They had been in London for more than a year. His better friends at school were British—boys with names like Simon and Wendell—and he now went by Sammy, the Anglicized name his mother had picked for him.

The housekeeper had laid out trays of finger foods on the table, formations of toasted mushroom sandwiches and beef Wellington tartlets and cut celery with crabmeat. In a glass dish, a mass quivered.

"What is that, Mother?"

"They call it a trifle. I read about it before we arrived here, in one of the imported magazines."

He had some notion of what a trifle was from mentions in his school reading, but this was the first time he'd seen a specimen. A choppy white foam rose out of it, and underneath the foam, glistening red and purple globules alternated with yellow deposits of custard.

"You can have some later, after the guests. Is your father back yet?"

"No, I don't think so."

"Why isn't he here? I'd have him help put this house in good order. We can't have the farangs think Thais an unkempt people."

Even back then, he'd intuited that his mother's self-regard had been conditionally staked to the success of these evenings. In preparing for them, she had very high expectations for cleanliness, particular placements in mind for their belongings, and little patience for deviation, which was usually either his father's doing or his own.

On this night, by the time his father arrived, an hour later than expected, all was ready.

"My colleagues told me of a library not far from the Legation, and I went to see it. I'll be able to stop there after work."

"I'd have appreciated some help with the preparations. These are your friends and colleagues who are coming."

"Pehn, I never asked for this party."

"You can thank me when they pass up someone else more deserving to give you a promotion."

His father said no more and retreated upstairs to put on a dinner jacket. It might have been the first and only time Sammy felt sympathy at the sight of him, rather than fear of his displeasure.

The guests arrived. After being paraded for the usual cursory greetings and ruffling of his hair by strangers, he was sent up to his room, where, after seeing that the housekeeper had neglected to include the trifle on his exile's plate, he patiently schemed. He pressed an ear against the floor and listened to whatever pierced through—the chortling and silverware scraping and occasional names being called across a table.

When he was sure his parents and the guests had progressed to the back room, he crept downstairs to the kitchen. He found a long spoon in the silverware drawer and held it like an assassin's dagger as he approached the trifle dish. He dug in and excavated the half that was left, in small proper morsels as his mother had taught him.

"How is it?" a voice asked.

He turned to see his father, leaning on his elbow at the doorway, an empty wineglass on the counter next to him.

"Sweet," Sammy said, which was all he could manage without losing his thoughts to his certain punishment.

"Perhaps too sweet, I'd say, like pouring sugar into one's mouth. The British are fond of such peculiar flavors, don't you think?"

Sammy nodded, even though he'd quite liked it. From the front of the house, someone's shrieking laughter went off like a rocket, followed by an eruption of cheers. His father didn't give any indication that he heard any of it.

"Aren't you supposed to be with the guests?" Sammy asked.

"I was there long enough." His father's breath was piney and sour. "Did I ever tell you about when I first heard of this post?"

"Yes."

"The vice minister's secretary came into the clerks' room and said that I was needed, and so I buttoned up and followed him across the courtyard to the upstairs office, and there I listened to the new position assigned me as I looked out the window onto Sanam Chai Road and all the peddlers and wagons whizzing about. The vice minister said, 'Apirak, it's not a leisurely role, but I trust a young man from a family like yours will make our nation proud. The food you'll get over.' And that was it. When I saw your mother at home I said, 'Something happened at work today,' and she said, 'We're going to London. Everyone knows.' She showed me the congratulatory gift baskets that had already arrived from your grandfather's friends. Do you remember that?"

"No."

"Very well. I don't think you were there, now that I think about it."

"I'm not sure."

"What you probably don't know is that your mother cried the entire night. She thought she was never going to see her parents again. I scolded her. I said, 'Pehn, my duty to my country is paramount. What's wrong with you?' and went to sleep. Look at her now, won't you? That's what I want you to learn from us: one must always honor one's duty above one's self-concern. Can you understand me?"

He knew his father wanted him to answer, but he stayed mum. They stared at each other.

"Go back up to your room. What's a boy doing down here this late?" his father said finally, and then he reached for his glass and left Sammy in the kitchen with a white-streaked spoon in hand.

In the morning, he considered what his father had said—it was the most his father had spoken to him since they'd arrived in London—and he understood it as his father demanding some improvement that could be achieved by striving for his father's dutiful example. For a long time, he did try.

◻ ◻ ◻

It was morning in Bangkok when he called. A maid answered and put down the handset. He heard the sharp yelping of the Pomeranians, Kuhn Chang and Khun Paenpradit, and music on the wireless, perhaps a Suntharaporn number. Three minutes must have passed. She picked up when she liked.

"You're there."

"Got in a few hours ago."

"How is he?"

"He's fine, just another scare."

"So he made you fly over for nothing."

"He didn't make me do anything."

"Have you told him about the house?"

"I'm not sure if I should, considering his condition."

"He'll find out eventually."

"Why don't you tell him yourself?"

"Sammy, don't be so foolish. Be a good boy."

"I have to go. It's late here."

After the call, he lay down again, awake in the dark. It was still barely evening in Los Angeles, and the time he'd normally have been sorting contact sheets, or marking notes for the printer, or, likeliest, at his usual watering hole, arguing with Carlo or Henrietta or whoever was keeping bar about some six o'clock news story flickering on the Zenith portable.

His mother wanted his father to know her plans for the old house. His great-great-grandfather, the son of a rice mill laborer, had built it after enriching himself by helping to found a trading company with American and Chinese partners. His father had let her have the deed when they divorced, with the intention that the house would eventually become Sammy's. Now she was fielding inquiries from interested buyers through her society women's circles. Most of their land in the provinces had already been sold for his sake, as money became tighter each year. The proceeds from this sale should be more than sufficient to support her attendance at the galas of her many charities, the kind so dutifully noted in *Sakul Thai* magazine with a photographic record of the sculpted hairdos and shimmery, high-necked dresses in attendance.

He'd met his mother's' friends any number of times on his visits to Bangkok, when they came over to play cards. He'd clasp his hands and do his wai and give an embarrassed laugh and bow to their comments on his handsome looks and prized status as a foreign-educated deg nog. He'd turn down offers of cocktails and use the pack of cigarettes in his hand as a way to escape, even though he didn't smoke much. Out the back door and then around the roofed terrace he went, seeking the afternoon shadow.

It was underneath the banyan tree in Bangkok, with the sound of quarreling sparrows drifting through the canopy, that he fell asleep in London.

□ □ □

By the time he came out for breakfast, his father was already awake. Helen made him eggs, having prepped bowls of yogurt and fruit for herself and his father. Children's footsteps drummed the ceiling above.

"You thought you were going to visit me at my deathbed, didn't you? Are you disappointed?"

"Please don't confuse me with your first wife."

"It's good to see you've retained your bristles."

"Don't mind him," Helen said. "He's very glad you're here. Would you like some more eggs?"

"I'd like some," said his father.

"You know you shouldn't."

"These could be the last eggs I'll ever have."

She divided one and slid half onto his plate.

"So what are we doing today?" his father asked him. "Where are we going?"

"You were let out of hospital two days ago."

"Yes, but I'm not dead yet, am I?"

"The doctors said to be careful about exertion," Helen said. "Can you give that some thought?"

"My son's here. I haven't the slightest worry, and neither should you."

"Tomorrow, dear. Today, you'll rest," Helen said with cheery authority to his father, and then turned to him. "Have you seen what he's done with the photos you sent him? It's like a museum."

"I wouldn't go that far. It's only pictures on a wall."

"Why don't you go show your son?"

His father groaned, if only to protest Helen's insistence, and then motioned him to follow. They made their way to his father's room, where Sammy saw what he hadn't noticed last night. Opposite the bed, where an unremarkable landscape print had hung on last visit, were a cluster of his photos, of a rain forest preserve up in Phrae Province. He'd forgotten he'd sent them and hadn't thought of the trip itself for years.

Now he remembered the telephoto lens he'd fitted on his camera, waiting for the dawn to spread across a green valley veiled by morning mist. When it did, the mountains appeared like islands in a sea of flames. He visited again the screaming white waters of falls too high and hidden to be crowded with sightseers and was reminded of how, descending through a bamboo forest trail later that day, he'd hoped that the photos had somehow captured as well the syncopated howls of monkeys out of sight in the thick growths.

The photos weren't for an assignment. His marriage had faltered and he had left Sweden, telling everyone that he was stopping in Thailand to focus on his art. He had paid for the forest guide and camping gear rental himself. He wanted to trace the path from which his family's earliest fortunes had come: ventures into the teak trade with the northern mueangs. When he was a boy, his father had told him of visiting the same mountains with his own father to see how parceled growths were being felled and floated to sawmills downriver and eventually to feed Bangkok's hunger. Some of the wood in the old house in Bangkok came from those very mountains. In the oldest parts of that house—what had become the Buddha room and the music room—an ancient beam still trickled dark, gummy sap.

"What a glorious view to look on from my bed," his father said now. "Can't believe places like that are still around."

He had not told his father how the view had shifted after the sun rose higher and the morning fog lifted. Through his long lenses, he could see that parts of mountainsides had been stripped bare of trees. To his question about whether the logging was legal, his guide had quickly changed the subject.

"Mother was very upset about that trip. She thought that I was going to either get kidnapped by communists or eaten by a ghost tiger."

"Speaking of my wives, how is your dear mother Pehn?"

"Fine. Radiant, as she might describe herself."

"You visited the old house lately?"

At the mention, he considered bringing up his mother's plans to sell the house. But why upset his father so early in the morning and have to deal with the fallout for the rest of the day?

"It was fine when I saw it last year. The roof was leaking a bit where termites had nested, that's all."

"Have you been following the news over there? What a fine mess. This was not what we had in mind at all. Power was supposed to be for the people, and now those dead students, did you see?"

He nodded, even though he wasn't sure. He didn't have a TV, but he vaguely remembered reading about the protests in a blip of a paragraph in the *Los Angeles Times*, somewhere in the pages he'd thumbed through to check on his Lakers bets. He wasn't surprised that his father still paid attention to events in his former country, but he didn't expect to hear such pained frustration and pity in his father's voice. It seemed that his father expected him to feel the same.

"Yes, those dead students," he said to his father, shaking his head. "A tragic day for Bangkok."

"I still find it strange to hear it called Bangkok," said his father. "It's still Krungthep to me. Are you still able to say the full city name, like when you were a boy?"

"Krungthepmahanakhon...Amon...rattanakosin...Mahinthar... ayutthaya ... ," he said, before stopping. The next parts hung aloft in his mind, just out of reach. He hoped his father would help say them for him.

"It's a shame," his father said. "I think I've forgotten the rest, as well."

□ □ □

In the evening, Freddie's entire family came downstairs for dinner. Emily introduced him to his niece and nephew before herself. The children were about seven or eight years old, and Emily was in her early thirties, a fair bit younger than Freddie, with a friendly, wide-eyed countenance that made her appear perpetually startled. They seemed to Sammy like the families he sometimes dined with in LA. Those occasions always made him feel compelled to be at his most entertaining, as if to convince his hosts that he was worth interrupting their usual domestic routine—an adequate substitute for the TV show they perhaps would have put on had he not come. Tonight, he was at a loss as to whether he should perform as guest or family.

Helen seated his father at the head of the table, and Sammy sat where he intuited he had been assigned, the honored chair next to his father.

"Is it true that when Grandfather lived in Bangkok he lived in a manor with golden pagodas and giants guarding the gates?" asked Alder. "That's what Grandfather says, and we don't know if we should believe him."

"Giants I can't vouch for, but we do often hire seven-headed serpents. Maybe you can see them for yourself someday."

"We've asked Grandfather to take us, but he always says next year," said Lilith.

"Next year," said his father. "Now eat your vegetables."

Helen had made fish—poached turbot with diced bell peppers and a sprig of wilted basil on top.

"I thought I'd give it a hint of Thai," she said, pride hedged by a note of apology.

He had seen right away that, along with the out-of-place bell peppers, it wasn't the right basil, and that the fish, perhaps a bit overcooked, wouldn't have been out of place in an Italian cookbook. A younger version of himself would have outright declared something to that effect. How he used to hate this woman. He'd barely spoken to her when he spent a dutiful week or two here on break from boarding school in Surrey. Her efforts to make him feel welcome had only infuriated him further.

"It's delicious," he said, and took another bite with gusto made apparent.

After dinner, Emily retreated upstairs with the children, and Helen took his father for a bath. Sammy helped Freddie gather and take the soiled dishes to the kitchen, where a dishwasher had recently been installed. For a long moment they stood marveling at it—a white enameled box with shiny chrome buttons now parked between the cramped cupboards.

"Before I had children, they had me do all the washing," said Freddie. "I thought I'd finally outgrown the responsibility, but now they insist that everything be rinsed before it goes in the machine. So why do we even have this expensive thing? I've stopped arguing."

Waiting for each dish with a cloth between splayed hands, Sammy watched how slowly and methodically Freddie rinsed. Perhaps he relished the act, or perhaps he had long ago feared to incur the wrath of their father, should he leave a single speck.

"I'm glad we have another chance to talk among ourselves, brother to brother," Freddie said. "We didn't really carry on with each other when we were younger, did we? You visited so rarely, and then you disappeared with your camera."

Yes, he remembered, the many unfocused pictures of patterned shadows and plays on angularity and easy lifeless subjects. He'd aped Bresson for a phase, then moved on to Man Ray.

"I realize this might appear untoward for me to bring up," Freddie said, "but when it happens, I want you to have reasonable expectations."

"Reasonable expectations?"

"Yes, that's one way to put it."

He noticed that Freddie now spoke in a lowered voice, with dramatic consideration in the half pauses, as if raising some magnificent hidden truth to the surface. This was probably the manner of speaking that he switched to in court, in order to make his arguments sound more convincing. Was Freddie conscious of it? A dog might be unaware that its fangs showed.

"Father knows how expensive it is to raise a family in London," Freddie said. "He wants his grandchildren to have what they need."

"You think I rushed here for his money."

"I'm not exactly saying that."

"You needn't."

"Sammy, if you don't mind my saying so, you weren't ever really here before."

He was glad that Freddie didn't know of his mother's plans, or that, to snuff his protestations about the sale of the house, she'd offered a sizable advance on his inheritance. That sum would dwarf by many magnitudes whatever he stood to inherit from his father. Of course, he could pacify Freddie's concerns by telling him that he had no reason to squabble over their father's money.

"Good night," Sammy said with forceful indignation, and walked away. It felt better to leave Freddie alone with the dumb dishes than to question notions of decency to kin.

◻ ◻ ◻

"Have you told him?" his mother asked over the phone.

"No, I haven't spent much time alone with him," said Sammy.

"Your British accent is partway back. Honestly, I much prefer it to the other ones you've had."

"I'm glad you approve, Mother."

"You only have to find some opening in a conversation. Has he asked about me?"

"No, he hasn't inquired at all about you or Krungthep."

"Well, no matter, you should be happy to hear that my balking has paid off. They've increased their offer."

She waited for his commendation, but he paused as he gathered his arguments and pushed them uphill.

"Here's a thought. What if we don't sell?"

"Why wouldn't we sell? We need three maids just to keep the dust off everything, and with the gardener coming only once a month now, I'm afraid a tiger will creep out of the grass and eat me. And who's going to live here? You?"

"No."

"You can, you know."

"Mother."

"So it's settled. I'm going to keep moving forward with the negotiations, whether you tell him or not. The courtesy is more than he deserves."

After the call ended, he stood up from the daybed and walked to the shelves. His father had thinned his collection, it appeared. He looked for but couldn't find the two volumes of the Arthurian legends bound in faded red linen. They had looked like any of the other old books. It was understandable why his father had thought it unlikely that someone—his son, for example—would reach for them.

He remembered this well: his boyhood fingers feeling the bulge inside the second book. Dozens of letters were lodged in its spine. The ivory-colored sheets were no longer crisp. They had been folded and refolded rather unevenly, as if in haste, and ink had smudged where a thumb had held them for too long. At first, he thought that he might have found a cache of old love letters between his parents, but these were written in English, not Thai. He suspected that he shouldn't be reading them, and so he did, facing the wall in the corner of that study. After so many years, he couldn't be sure of the exact words, but he could retrieve the memory of many memories of them, the words once whispered at his lips later resounding loud as cannon fire in his head.

One letter started:

Last night, I went with Milly and Hannah to a concert at the Conway. Have you much listened to the Ondine

movement in Ravel's Gaspard de la Nuit? The pianist's
cascade of notes caused me to be lulled into a kind of
disembodied trance, and so for the rest of the performance,
I sat in the seat, hands clasped on my lap, but some
otherwise intangible part of me couldn't help but ebb and
flow to you, oh sweet you.

With each instance of remembering, the words in the letters shed
the finality of the past, coming back to him as if they were part of a
past he yet lived.

I've met no one else who's as gentle and capacious in
spirit as you, Apirak, and it's only when I'm with you
that I can so easily feel less alone in the thoughtless,
unfeeling world.

The hair at the back of his neck stood up, he remembered, when
he'd realized that the letters meant for his father hadn't been written
by his mother. This was how he'd first met Helen

What had he done with the letters? He put them back where he found
them and returned the books to their place. He made no mention of the
letters to his mother. If he let them lie buried between some dusty pages
about mythical knights, he might also bury their fate in his life, and the
life of his family. His mother was right. He was a foolish boy.

□ □ □

In the morning, he left the house with his father. Their simple agenda
was to return his father's library books.

With a camera hanging from his neck, Sammy put on his tourist guise and was able to catch the attention of a taxi at the corner. His father, unused to his new frailty, had tried to insist that they take the Tube, but the rain had only just ended, and the many steps down into the station were unlikely to have dried. One misstep, and the opportunity for indignation would be all Freddie's.

"You haven't said a word," his father said in the car.

"Just taking it all in."

"You were last here when?"

"It's been a while."

"You haven't missed much. It's all gotten expensive, and every day's the same—strikes, Edward Heath's bulbous face. I don't turn on the telly anymore."

"You? Watch TV?"

"It's mostly because Helen does."

"Right. Helen, the corrupting influence."

When the traffic wouldn't budge, his father insisted on getting out of the cab, knowing they were close.

They marched up Northumberland, past a newspaper seller shouting, "Standard! Standard!" too loud to the hurried crowd, then wound their way down a narrow alley by Scotland Yard. In front of an overflowing pub, even this early in the day, businessmen from nearby offices stood holding nearly emptied pints at their chests. The smell of burning in the air made Sammy think of Bangkok—of Krungthep.

"Slow down," he said to his father. "You shouldn't be walking so quickly."

His father ignored him. At St. James Square, they passed by bushyhaired ladies in knee-length dresses leaning against the park fence, handbags hung like stilled pendulums at the knees. At the far corner lay the library.

"Hello, Apirak," said a septuagenarian woman at the desk in the issue hall. "Haven't seen you in some time."

"I've books to return. I'm afraid they're long overdue. This is my son," his father said, glancing his way. Sammy took the books out of the satchel he'd been carrying, three linen-bound volumes from a series on European mercantilism.

"Let's have a look around," his father said, and waved him in. His father's cane clacked on the floor as they crossed into a large reading room. Windows that opened on a shady courtyard let in softened sunlight for the silent readers hunched at tables. Wiry brass lamps lit halos on the books in front of them.

"They've been wanting to tear down the wall over there and add more space for periodicals, perhaps higher windows for light," his father said softly. It had always been that way. Being surrounded by old books calmed his father's demeanor, dispelled the usual impatience and severity. The man had been born and raised a Buddhist in a faraway country, but this was his true temple. It had taken the end of his parents' marriage to make Sammy realize that for his father, they weren't merely books but prized transmissions from somewhere "siwilai," as Thais of that generation liked to say of newfangled things from overseas. In London, his father no longer had to be content with reading about a "siwilai" society that he dreamed to reach. Here, he could be born anew within it.

"Is there something you're looking for? Maybe someone can fetch it for you," Sammy said. "We ought to head back soon."

"Just a while longer."

He followed his father to an ancient lift, and they rode it up a floor. There were fewer people in this reading room. They passed a student-aged man asleep in an armchair and a professorial woman who didn't look up. The silence was interrupted only by the buzzing of an electric wall clock.

"My table—unofficially, but they all know it's mine," his father said, pointing to a cranny by a window. "I thought about it as they were loading me on the gurney, worried that someone else would claim it if I was infirm for too long."

"It's a nice spot."

"Who knows if the next time I come here I'll be a sprinkle of ashes. Will you take a photo and send it to me?"

His father sat down at the table, and Sammy lifted the camera to his eye and centered the brackets on his father's face in the viewfinder. He pressed the shutter.

"You met Helen here."

"She was putting away books from a cart. She saw me watching her, and I looked away."

"Obviously it didn't end there, did it?"

His father continued to gaze at the shelves and gave no impression of having heard him.

"We were terrible to each other," his father finally said.

"Who?"

"Your mother and I."

"My memory tells me that you were the one to leave us."

"You can blame me all you like, but I wasn't the only one who transgressed."

His father thought that he hadn't known. A boy knew more than his parents expected him to know: the alien scents they carried home under their coats, the phone calls behind closed doors, the swings in their attention, the overly emotive compensation in their voices when trying to sound honest. They kept their secrets, and he did, too, for them. In the end, he'd sided with his mother because that had long been their arrangement.

Why did his father think to mention any of it now? He couldn't tell whether it was because his father enjoyed petty cruelty, their shared familial trait, or whether his son's opinion now mattered to him.

"Fine," his father said. "I'm finished here. Let's leave."

On the ground floor, the reading room looked emptier than before. The woman who had greeted them at the front desk stood with a few others around a portable radio. His father waved his good-byes. The woman looked up to say, "Be careful out there. There's been a bombing at Parliament."

□ □ □

It was chilly outside, even with the fuller sun, and the air stank of burnt rubber and matches. Sirens blared, unseen, and then dimmed. The old women still stood leaning against the fence. Either they hadn't heard the news or they, like his father, had resolved to remain unruffled.

"We better bash on," his father said, and began walking to the Tube.

Sammy tried to wave down one of the passing taxis, but none were available.

"Do you want to stand here until afternoon?" asked his father. They made their way to Whitehall, but the police had cordoned off the inter-section with blue tape.

"A suspicious something of some sort up there," said a stranger.

"Maybe we should head back to the library," Sammy said to his father.

"Nonsense. There are plenty of routes around this."

A constable waved the crowd away from the intersection but could not tell them where they might be able to cross.

"My father, as you can see, isn't well," Sammy said. "Won't you make this one exception?" The constable continued blowing his whistle.

"Sorry, but did you hear me?"

Sammy's wishes seemed simple: to deposit his father with Helen, to make telephone inquiries regarding a return flight to Los Angeles, and then to remove himself from everyone's ordeals. All these contests of territory, of suffering and vengeance, and the ensuing mistrust and enmity—they weren't his business.

"Samart, you mustn't get so agitated. I've taught you to be stronger than that," said his father, putting a hand on Sammy's back for emphasis.

The touch of his hand there took Sammy to a morning in 1948. He'd been at the old house, a small boy standing over the small circular pond where he had spent many other mornings watching swirls of orange and silver koi send sudden ripples through the reflection of a high-pitched roof with fish-scale tiles and arched windows designed by an Italian architect and shaped by half-Portuguese masons. Leaves from the thick, braided trunks of the banyan tree above skimmed the water in scattered flotillas.

His father, then a towering giant, patted his back. "Will you miss our relatives like they said you would?" he asked.

Sammy shook his head, even though the day before he had clutched his grandmother's wrist, not wanting to let go.

"It's a great opportunity for me. And for you. None of your cousins will have this kind of education and experience abroad. Can't you appreciate that?"

He nodded, but he also must have suspected that later, when he ate and slept and played at the London house, he would feel as if he were only a distant refraction of himself at this house, before which there was nothing.

"Go now. You mustn't let your mother worry," his father said. "You're braver than you appear."

He had tried to believe his father then. He wouldn't now, stranded behind a police line, with a bomb gone off a few streets over and his own luxurious dissatisfaction at how most things had turned out for him.

A white lorry with the Metropolitan Police insignia pulled up at the curb. Sammy thought it might have come from the coroner's office, its arrival having quieted the crowd and suffused the scene with an air of solemnity. The back door swung open to let out two older policemen in regular uniform, and then a rough human shape, its limbs padded thickly in drab-colored material. Only the hands were of normal proportion, almost naked but for thin gray gloves. The figure wore a helmet that looked like a motorcyclist's except for the Plexiglas plate screwed over the face—a man's, it appeared, though Sammy could barely make it out through the thick shield and the mist that pulsed when the face breathed. The figure stood heavily on the pavement as the others inspected the suit.

Sammy raised his camera and began taking photos.

"Samart, you're still cross about that bit at the library," his father said.

"I'm not."

"Never be afraid to announce one's mind. You need to learn this."

There he was again, the dispenser of paternal wisdom. It felt to him that his father was offering both a suggestion for his son's character and an explanation for his earlier insult to his ex-wife. No need to say anything in response, Sammy told himself.

"She's selling the old house," he said to his father. "It's going to become a condominium."

His father's eyes widened for a fraction of a second, but all he said was, "I imagine it'll fetch a fair price."

"More than fair."

"Will you see any of it?"

"A good sum to tide me over."

"Then it's for the best."

His father's calm reception caught him off guard. It would have been satisfying to see a sudden swell of disbelief or disappointment—or both—break across that face.

"I told her that we didn't have to sell."

"Shush," said his father. "It's done. Nothing more to say."

One privilege Sammy enjoyed about his line of work was that it allowed him to disappear, bodiless, into the rectangular world within his camera. As the man in the bomb suit walked away from the lorry, Sammy raised his camera again and pressed the shutter without bothering to adjust the depth of vision. A police wagon pulled in and blocked his view, and he moved closer to get another shot from between shoulders and parked cars.

"Stay here," he shouted to his father, without taking his eyes off the viewfinder. As the man walked farther ahead, Sammy followed.

He noticed how easily the man swung his limbs, even with the thick padding. He lurched forward, under the airy winter clouds and the Edwardian-era shopfronts with the touristy merchandise in their windows, bringing the fear of obliteration into focus on this otherwise mundane weekday and ordinary street. Sammy wondered how the man might gauge the probable course of electrical current wired from a car battery or what preparations he had made to deal with it, or how much confidence he had in the steadiness of his hands. He pressed the shutter again and again, trying to capture the vision of a courageous knight, persistent in the protection of life and property from devastation.

His father. Sammy looked back to see an old man leaning forward on his cane. His father wasn't looking at or for him. His gaze seemed fixed on someplace invisible to everyone else. It was the same expression his father had while reading—the concentrated attention that had always made Sammy want to call out to him, to return him to the world they'd shared. But each time he'd been afraid to go through with it, not for fear of reprimand but for fear of fraying whatever fibril still attached his father to them—his mother and him. It turned out that his father had been elsewhere all along.

Sammy turned back, but the man in the suit had rounded the corner and was out of sight. When he turned again, so was his father.

OUTPOUR

There were a few thousand people crowded in the streets at first, and each day their number grew by thousands more. This many people, some swore they could feel the roads sag beneath their shoes. They moved together like a giant animal, each tiny human a cell of the beast. Strangers became dearest friends, ready to die for one another. Nemeses from rival schools passed around cellophane bags of milky iced tea and, later, bottles of cane rum.

It was supposed to rain, they in the animal had heard. When it didn't, they saw it as an auspicious sign that the heavenly deities were with them, and when it did rain the next day, they took it as a test of their heart and commitment. They sat and squatted in makeshift newspaper ponchos and under umbrellas, listening to the impassioned speeches of their friends and fellow citizens.

The animal obliterated silence with its chants and roars. It demanded a constitution. The arrested student leaders must be released at once.

These disturbances to the nation's peace and prosperity, as the officials would refer to the animal, started as murmurs at university lunch tables that within a few months grew to megaphoned outdoor speeches. The military government, led by the field marshal who had overthrown the previous government, had promised that power would soon be restored to the people, but in the two years that had since passed, the prospect of a civil democracy had faded and discontentment had grown. Every cup of rice cost more than the last. Workers had to keep walking out of factories to have a chance at fair wages. The influence of the Americans and the Japanese was ruining everything.

Anger spread all over Krungthep through mimeographed flyers handed out to passersby, and by impassioned voices on unsanctioned radio broadcasts and street corners, where crowds—not just university students but also bus drivers and street peddlers—stood to listen until they, too, became part of the beast.

When the animal grew even larger, the masses inside it swelling into tens of thousands, it spread up and down the length of the capital's grandest avenues. When it needed to sleep, cardboard and scraps served as mats. When it needed to eat and drink, money was pooled to haul in pickup truckloads of water canisters and sacks of rice. Meals were cooked in open-air kitchens, supplemented with whatever the street hawkers were selling.

At a multigroup committee meeting, one of the demonstration organizers brought up reports that the toilet situation was getting dire. If they didn't want to lose the support of surrounding residents and merchants, a solution needed to be found.

They looked at one another, hoping someone would know what to do. Who had any idea how to build toilets?

A hand went up, a young man. They asked him who he was and what he had in mind. The young man spoke in a low voice, and the crowd yelled at him to speak louder.

He was—he said, at slightly higher volume—a second-year engineering student, part of the agricultural university's faction. Back home in Prachuap, he had helped his father set up toilets on fishing boats, and he was also the boy who had to clean them. If he had more time, he could likely design a better setup, but the most expedient solution that came to his mind would require only some hacksaws and metal pipe, or if that wasn't available, thick hollow bamboo would do. And buckets. Many, many buckets.

Get this patriot what he needs, the committee commanded their underlings. The students around him patted his back and exhorted him not to fail them. He wouldn't, he promised. The animal would continue to grow. The fates of their generation and generations to come would hinge on its decisive victory, and he would tend to his part.

Over the next day, he built a row of makeshift toilets that emptied into an already filthy canal. Open-air for the men, and for the women a separate row shielded by donated curtains. The committee asked him to supervise the cleaning shifts, and he agreed to the thankless assignment. Volunteers would often disappear when their turn came. The ones left were able to convince a nearby mechanic shop to let them borrow a long hose. When the inevitable clogging problems occurred, he was the one to wrap his nose under perfumed cloth and open the affected joints.

It was worth it, the engineering student said to himself. The animal he was part of was about to save the country. On the radio, the police proclaimed that no force would be used against the animal. The animal would be victorious if it didn't back away. It would grow larger and stronger. It would spread through the streets of Krungthep, and with every step that it lurched forward, all the world would hear it coming.

□ □ □

Marching with the crowd toward the rallying point at Democracy Monument, the engineering student registered the sublimity of the scenery and circumstances around him. Just over a year back, straight out of secondary school, he couldn't have foreseen himself as one of the nameless many—now more than three hundred thousand, one newspaper estimated—chanting at the top of his lungs, raising his fists to join the others.

It was October 1973. Any other year, the students would have been worrying about examinations and, if they'd scored well enough to genuflect for their diploma, about whatever was to be the rest of their lives. For the engineering student, October should have meant looking forward to the start of the term break; he had planned to board a train at Hua Lamphong and ride southward to his home village, staring out the window at the passing scenery of salt farms and crop fields crisscrossed by hastily dug red-dirt roads and the distant peaks of the mountain ranges that bordered Burma. It was the reverse of the view outside his train window when he'd left his hometown for Krungthep, having promised his parents that he would bring back pride and honor for his family.

Before his arrival at the university, he'd had no idea there was such a thing as protests. In his home province of Prachuap, if anyone had a grievance with the governance, they might approach the village head-man, who might, depending on the breadth of the complaints or whether he had won or lost at high-low the previous night, gather other elders to his house. Generous quantities of home-distilled rum would be passed around, and by the next morning few would remember their grief or the promises made to them.

His family back home knew little about his involvement with the protest groups. In letters to his mother, he mentioned only the things he wished their village had—uninterrupted electricity and multistory department stores selling all kinds of merchandise, even though he couldn't afford most of it. And the things he wished Krungthep could have of Prachuap—the cool, breathable air wafting from the sea and the long bands of stars whitening the night sky. He told his mother he was eating well and never skipped meals. He talked of his new friends and all the good, supportive professors he'd come to know.

The truth was that he didn't have very many friends even in his own department, preferring to spend the hours outside of class listening to his records while finishing up his problem sets. He was polite to a fault, his manners betraying a palpable shyness that arose from not wanting to inconvenience others, from not being from the capital and not being conditioned to speak in proper, unaccented Krungthep dialect or to dress other than in the requisite university dress of white shirts and dark pants. He found comfort in the empty back rows of lecture halls and on the outdoor benches that were too sunny for the capital-born. There and in his room he could concentrate on his studies, at the least, and advance himself.

After he finished his problem sets, he liked to lie down in the dark and put a new record on the player. The records weren't even his. He had been asked to safekeep the collection and the turntable that came with it while a fellow dorm resident took a term off to sort out family matters. That neighbor never came back. At first, the engineering student didn't know what to think of the music. There was enough of it to fill two whole rows on his shelf, mostly of American jazz musicians. He had never listened to anything but loog-toong his whole life, with its folksy, upbeat declarations of love and hardship and the strangely comforting shrillness of the singers' voices, but this trove of jazz records had cost him nothing, and so he listened to each of them, to erase the silence in his room. The bass line made his fingers move as if he were bouncing an invisible ball. The squeals and fusillades coming out of the speakers sounded like nothing he'd heard before. He soon grew to prefer the air in his room ungently massaged by horns and pianos before he breathed it. He lay on his sleeping mat and felt his matter vibrate and dissolve. It occurred to him that he was not only communing with the songs he was listening to but also that he was making out what might be called songs that had all along been sounding from somewhere inside himself.

One night, as he was listening to a Coleman Hawkins LP, the lights went out in his room. A fuse had likely blown, as often happened in a run-down dormitory seemingly sewn into place by the jumbled wires creeping along ceilings. The darkness forced him outside to sit under a streetlight with a textbook for the next day's fluid mechanics class. Another young man was already there, crouched on the ground with markers and a rusty art knife. The young man asked the engineering student if he was the one who listened to jazz all the time. The engineering student apologized if his music had been too loud. The young man said not to worry, it helped cover up the all too frequent masturbatorial groans from a nearby room. The young man showed him the layout he had been working on. It was a flyer for an upcoming student group meeting. There would be food and refreshments, the young man said. Come.

So the circumstances that had sparked his involvement with the politics of his peers could be described as accidental, or fateful, or entirely typical for a university student of that era. For the engineering student, curiosity and hunger both proved to be compelling motivations. He went to the meeting, then became a regular attendee. The noodles served were tasty and free, and he was absorbing new thinking about why things weren't working in his country. He volunteered to help with routine organizational work, readying venues for future meetings and coordinating with the art students to make sure that sufficient quantities of posters and pamphlets were printed. As often was the case with student groups, turnover was high, interest and participation varying with class schedules and whim, and one could rise in rank simply by showing up. By early 1973, the engineering student had been entrusted to help plan matters of transport and logistics for campus gatherings. At meetings, he wore an armband that gave him authority he found discomfiting. The other students no longer called him by his name, Siripohng, or worse, Ai Pohng, the way someone might yell at their dog. They addressed him as Bigger Brother Pohng, which caused him to bow slightly each time.

The day of the protests, they shouted, *Run, Bigger Brother, run!* Gunfire had erupted as they marched toward Phan Fah Bridge. He ducked and crawled behind a telephone booth, glass shattering above him. From the shortcuts he took getting to class, he knew his way around the side sois and alleys that veined the old city. He ducked again and ran low toward Bang Lamphu. He heard explosions in one direction and then another. Somewhere close, men and women screamed, but he couldn't understand their words. The air thickened with an unfamiliar chemical smell. His stinging eyes let out torrents. He ran headfirst into a tree and fell over, bloodying an arm. He was lucky that an old woman shuttering her fabric shop took a look at him and pulled him inside. He felt his way on the tiled floor and followed the slaps of her bare feet upstairs. She washed his face with tofu milk from a steel bathroom bowl and covered his eyes with a wet rag. He spent the night in the woman's spare room, wearing her late husband's pajamas and listening to the gunfire and the engine noise of personnel carriers that rumbled through the streets.

When he heard the radio announce that the field marshal had been removed from office and expelled from the country, he wept with happiness.

He would later find out what had befallen his friends—he could certainly call them that now. Most hadn't been hurt, but more than a few had been torn through by M16 bullets. The fate of others was unknown, but their demise was assumed after they began appearing in the dreams of fellow students, asking for a cigarette or a Coke. Siripohng would also learn that, for his appearance in the lower ranks of the protest's organizational charts, he had been suspended from the university. He considered it a better fate than that of the more prominent student leaders, who had been forced to flee to the mountains to escape serious charges and the possibility of sudden, involuntary disappearance. His professors assured him that when the pressure died down, he stood a very good chance of being able to continue his studies.

He stayed in Krungthep instead of returning to Prachuap. He told his mother that he was taking time off to make money from an apprenticeship at an engineering firm, to help further his job prospects after graduation. He worked in a print shop, making illegal copies of textbooks for university students, and did weekend shifts as a hotel porter. Each night, after he returned to his rented apartment, he listened to the jazz records, which he now considered his. It wasn't a bad life, he told a coworker at the print shop. The steadiness of his days gave him comfort, and he could have stayed on that course for a good long while, waiting for the all-clear to renew his studies. Then he met her.

He had been keeping up every now and then with his student group friends. If he wasn't working, he showed up at meetings, now held off campus at locations known only to those who'd been vetted. He was glad to be back among his fellow students, although there were many new faces he didn't recognize, and he had to overcome his shyness at each new introduction. Many of the students still called him Bigger Brother, his prestige only having grown for his reprimand by the authorities, although he secretly felt he had not earned the titular respect because he had been safe inside while others stormed police headquarters or carried wounded colleagues out of danger. Yet when he tried to downplay his role, they commended him even more. *What humility. We should all look to his example.*

He met Nee at one of the meetings. He noticed her immediately, because she had come in from the monsoon rain, and unlike other arriving students, she didn't seem too excited or unhappy about being drenched. She removed the sheet of newspaper she had wrapped in a protective cone around her head and sat down in a chair in front of him, her white blouse a shade darker where it hung wet from her shoulders. Her hair was cut in a bob just above her neck, and she had long, oarlike hands. When she flipped her notebook, which had the insignia of a more famous university than his, he marveled at her immaculate handwriting.

He ended up working with her on a subcommittee to restock supplies, and he tried his best, at the biweekly meetings, not to prolong his glances in her direction. In the end, he didn't have to gather his courage to pursue her, this unimagined, noncolor printed woman; it was she who suggested that he take her out.

He took her to an air-conditioned restaurant famous for its grilled chicken and sticky rice, one of his staples. The next time, they went together to see a foreign movie at Chalermthai Theater. It was an American cowboy comedy that made her laugh and laugh, and he tried his best to keep up with her laughter even when he didn't quite understand the jokes. The strange world that she loved to watch befuddled him. People went around indoors with shoes on, on floors lined with furry cloths. They had times in their year when their streets turned into ice cups but without the Hale's Blue Boy syrup. She admonished him for not realizing there was such a thing as snow.

She was only a second-year in nursing, but because she was a Krungthep woman he developed a fear that his country boy origins would doom him. He was well aware that he didn't have an impressive job and wasn't even an official student anymore and that he lacked the knowingness he often saw in his student friends, who competed over which social theorists to read or which foreign cigarettes to buy. And because he feared he would lose her to someone from a higher social, economic, or interestingness stratum, he grew jealous of her male friends. They often fought, and then they made love with the kind of reconciliatory passion abundant in youth, the first time unplanned in his room and the second time in a hotel room he'd reserved under a different name, out of fear—irrational, he admitted to himself—that someone he knew would see his actual name on the guest ledger and report back to his mother in his home village.

After almost a year and a half had passed, Nee decided he was fit for a meal at her mother's. She'd insisted that she wasn't from a wealthy family, but he worried that she was trying to be modest. To his relief, it turned out that her mother owned and ran an ordinary sundries shop in a suburban Krungthep neighborhood. The store sold newspapers and magazines out front and snacks, lozenges, and soft drinks inside. On the first floor, behind the shop, was a combined kitchen and dining room, and upstairs were the bedrooms and the rest of the living areas. In a corner of the dining room, he stood in front of a glass cabinet filled with swimming trophies and medals from Nee's secondary-school meets. Sit, he was told, and he did, before a small spread of stir-fried watercress and a sour catfish curry and a fluffy golden omelet that hid a mound of sweetened ground pork.

After the dinner, he told her mother that she should have opened a restaurant, which her mother took as flattery but he had said with the utmost earnestness. He found out that his girlfriend—after the meal, he felt more assured calling her that—had a sister living in Japan, where she had opened a Thai restaurant. His girlfriend's father, who had died of a heart attack five years before, had been a teacher and handsome, the very portrait of moral fortitude, judging from the black-and-white face staring down at him from a wall. Still, he was glad Nee more closely resembled her mother, who had retained an unassuming, approachable kind of beauty that reminded him of actresses from older Thai movies. He would learn afterward that her mother had instructed her to bring him for more dinners. It made him glad, for reasons beyond the food. He loved the sense of family the dinner granted him. He missed his own family, and this was as close as he'd felt to coming home, without having to lie or feel ashamed about his failures.

Each week, he looked forward to their routine: Friday dinner with her mother, catching a new movie, helping out with the student group's activities. Sometimes, when tips at his hotel job allowed, they even splurged on steak or macaroni at a Western restaurant. They fought less often. He felt sure that he loved her, but he also wondered whether what he felt was really love or some kind of nameless, pleasurable emotion that had simply formed out of relief from years of not having. Matters of love had grown more complicated than he'd ever imagined. His parents had gone about it the way people had done for generations:

after the astrological questions had been satisfied, a parade of dancers and merrymakers had appeared at his maternal grandparents' house and his grandfather's permission was requested. When it was received, his father and mother were engaged. If a ceremonial parade like that were to appear on a Krungthep street, they'd get run off by a haphazardly driven bus.

The thought of marrying Nee crossed his mind more than once. He had been unable to believe that she had happened to him, in this life. Before her, he had thought that he would have to return to Prachuap and find a bride among the fishermen's daughters with whom he might have gone to secondary school and who probably only remembered him as the smart but unbearably quiet boy who had won a provincial scholarship to a university in the capital. He planned on returning to the university; he'd heard that others had had success in their petitions for readmission. It wasn't that he missed studying engineering. He no longer wanted to feel like he was wasting away in menial jobs that made little use of his mind. He needed again to be able to speak to his parents without shame. He wanted Nee to feel proud to be with a respectable someone.

He hoped that, with time, enough courage would gather inside him that he could bring up the question of their future together. If not, he would swig one of those energy potions truck drivers drank to stay awake, and he would down a shot of the strongest, dirtiest rum, and he would tell her that they needed to talk, and he would be ready for whatever she might say.

He was thinking of bringing up the subject as they lay next to each other in his rented room the night they heard the news on the radio. The field marshal had flown back from his exile in Singapore. It was October 1976.

When Siripohng turned to face Nee, he sensed that it was not her love for him that had blanked her eyes but shock that was quickly turning into rage. He knew their student friends wouldn't allow for this: the man whom they held responsible for the death and suffering of so many of their classmates, setting foot again in this country—in the guise of a monk, no less. He told her he was afraid of what could happen in Krungthep now, and she rebuked him for having any fear at all. When she got dressed and left, he couldn't tell if she was more angry at the news or at him.

He didn't tell her that he feared nothing for himself. Ever since the protests three years ago, he had been waking from nightmares. In those dreams, the streets of the city had emptied, save for the lone passing figure of a night watchman, who did not acknowledge him and whose cymbal claps would fade to reveal the sound of approaching footsteps. He knew to launch into a sprint, as he had done through alleys that October day, only this time there wasn't an old woman to pull him inside to safety. As he looked over his shoulder to see the men behind him, their faces obscured by shadow, he worried for the woman he loved. They would also come for her, he was sure.

"Run, Nee!" he would scream to her, always waking himself. "Run!"

□ □ □

Nee knew she had to leave before six in the morning, the hour her mother rose to water the myrtle in front of the shop and bring in the bundle of wholesale newspapers, still delivered in her late husband's name. During the last protests, when Nee was just a first-year, her mother had been able to evoke the memory of her father with effect. Your father would have wanted to see his daughter graduate, intact and alive, she'd said. Nee had stayed away from the batons and bullets that time.

The antigovernment rallies since the field marshal's return had intensified, and a few days before, two people putting up protest posters were beaten to death, the police unable, they said, to determine the parties responsible.

Nee guessed that her mother had prayed to higher deities and land spirits that her father's name wouldn't lose its power. It hadn't, but she wasn't going to stay home anymore. A dead father could only hold back so much, and a living mother for only so long. Her mother must have suspected so. She'd known that Nee had been staying late after classes to go to the demonstrations, but now that more blood had been shed and more protests were erupting in provinces north and south, she told Nee how familiar it all looked: the gabbers in suits on the TV and the gun-wielding men iterating the usual about national stability and the enraged young people vowing not to let their friends die in vain. Her mother again invoked her father's name and implored her to stay home. Nee assured her mother that she would, knowing that she had lied.

When Nee tried to leave her bedroom the next morning, she found the door locked from the outside.

Her mother should have known better than to underestimate her resolve. Nee stood on a desk and climbed through the transom as quietly as she could, imitating the little yellow lizards that silently darted across her bedroom walls and ceiling at night. On reaching the floor, she was careful not to step where the boards creaked, and then she tiptoed down the stairs.

She commanded herself not to look in the direction of her father's photo, but she needn't have looked there to see her father's face. He used to get up about now, waking earlier than her mother did to help ready the shop before heading out to teach at a secondary school. She often woke a little after her father, and she'd go down to help him set up the newsstand. She restocked packs of cigarettes in the glass case and cough drops in their tall tins. She mopped the floors and threw away dead roaches. How she resented Nok, who never bothered to do the same and yet never seemed to suffer any loss of love from their father. She figured that her father had applied to his daughters a position of neutrality similar to the one he maintained in the classroom, doing his best to avoid favoring any child over the other. She didn't blame him; she blamed her sister, now absconded overseas.

Nee had spoken to Nok a few nights before. Nok worried, like their mother, but Nok wasn't as persistent. It took very little to change the subject with her. This time it was the hor mok their mother had cooked the weekend before.

"She made it with knife fish from Brother Whiskers and banana leaves from Grandmother's trees," Nee said.

"Oh, I would lick the phone if I could taste it that way."

She loved hearing Nok gasping and moaning with jealousy five thousand kilometers away.

After promises to ship some Thai magazines, Nee said her good-byes and hung up. Now it occurred to her that the phone call with her sister might have been their last. The same with this walk through the unlit store in the near morning. She should appreciate it: the ordinary and mundane that was hers, like her knowledge of where to step forward in the dark to avoid the shelves and the stacks of rice sacks, and how much she loved to hear the muffled call to prayer being sung from the nearby mosque at this hour—the things that wouldn't matter to anyone else if her mother's fears were to come true.

It was very early, but customers would soon be on their way—the housekeepers for the rich stopping in for detergent and cooking oil, the pedal cabdrivers for their morning bottle of Red Bull. The day bloomed with gossip and laughter among neighbors and customers. They complained about the weather, they asked after daughters and sons, they traded last night's leftovers saved in rubber-banded bags.

As Nee slid open the shutters, she reached out to put her palm on the wall. Along with her family, she would most miss this place, should some ghost of herself persist in another realm.

Siripohng was waiting outside, in a white shirt and dark pants, student attire. "What's wrong?" he asked her.

"Nothing. Speak more quietly. My mother has very good hearing," she said, wiping the corners of her eyes by pretending to smooth her hair.

"We don't have to go today," Siripohng said. "I think things might get even worse than last time."

"I'm a nursing student. I need to be there, especially if people start to get hurt. You can stay here with my mother if you want."

When her mother realized that she was missing, she would hurry to the store's altar and light incense sticks with her husband's old lighter, before clasping her hands at her forehead to make pleas to the deities. *Listen, and help us, your humble calves*, her mother would mutter, her eyes closed.

Nee looked at Siripohng. He hadn't said anything after she'd hissed at him. Her friends had told her that she was the cruel one in the relationship. After the fights and the horrible things they'd say to each other, she could count on him to circle back, repentant and yielding. She didn't know if this was how love should be, but it was what they had, and she had had her heart torn up before by men unlike Siripohng, whom she could read with nothing more than a glance at his face. He looked nervous this morning, and she was mad at him for giving her own cowardice the excuse to scratch at her.

She padlocked the shutters closed and said to him, "Hey, stop being so scared. Let's go."

□ □ □

They walked for hours that morning. To avoid paramilitary groups rumored to be harassing students, they had thought it safer to take a route through back alleys, wearing staffers' jackets from the hotel where Siripohng worked over their student clothes and wandering through innards of the old city that she'd never known were there. Siripohng had claimed to know where he was going in the endless maze of shopfronts and homes, and when she realized that they were lost, she wasn't angry. Here they were shielded from the horns and engine rumbles of the main roads, and as they walked farther into the alleys, the air around them seemed to change. The sun no longer scorched them; trees and overhanging roofs shaded their path. It might have been evening, in this dimmed quietude. The shops inside the teak houses they passed seemed open for business but unlit. A girl in a pah toong dress, her features obscured by the hang of her long hair, leaned against a table, mending a bamboo birdcage. Pale-skinned women stood behind salon chairs, trimming the hair of ancient customers who sat blank-faced in front of mirrors. Shirtless, pigtailed children ran loops in the streets and disappeared into the shadows of deeper alleys.

Nee and Siripohng didn't speak to anyone, not wanting questions to be asked, and no one spoke to them. They walked and walked, until the alleyways, the shops, and the faces they walked past all began to feel familiar. At times, they wondered if they might be walking in circles, yet some part of them wished that they could keep wandering through the alleys, never get to where they had set out for. They would diverge to a separate place, removed from the society and people they'd cared for or even loved, so they could finally feel unburdened by the weight of the future they'd dreamed to be theirs. After a turn that they recognized to be informed more by chance than by certitude, they emerged into a produce market and were again welcomed by the searing noise of the city.

It was almost noon when they reached the campus and entered the quad through a little-used entrance. Their feet ached and they were thirsty, but their discomforts couldn't outmatch their elation at joining the thousands of students already there. At the football field, they met up with friends who unrolled a spare rattan rug for them, and for the rest of that afternoon Siripohng held an umbrella over Nee as he sat watching satirical plays performed on the stage and she lay napping beside him.

When evening came, they ate chicken-fat rice from newsprint bundles unwrapped across their laps. They laughed at the comedic performances and sang more songs and clapped for the speakers who got up to rile the crowd. They talked idly with friends about telenovela episodes and books, as the half-moon arced above them, and then they went to sleep on the dew-touched rug to regain their strength.

□ □ □

It sounded like thunder, but there was no storm. Early that morning, two bombs landed on the football field and shrapnel tore through the crowd. Many were still asleep. The ones woken by the noise screamed for their friends to wake up, and some never would.

Sulfurous smoke poured from the university fences. From the loudspeakers, a desperate young man's voice cried out, "Please stop shooting! Please stop shooting! We're only students!," over and over, but the gunfire went on.

Siripohng lay spilling out on the ground. Nee dragged him behind a concrete wall and tore off his shirt, revealing two torrential holes under his ribs. She didn't know if he could hear her, but she told him that his wounds weren't bad and she was going to get him to the student medics. He only needed to stay calm, she told him, but he kept trying to say something as blood gurgled from his mouth. Run, he was saying. She refused, but he insisted, gasping. To stop the bleeding, she bunched his shirt over his wound and pushed, but he continued to pour out. His shirt was red, as were her hands and the ground around them. He asked why the sound system was getting so loud. She didn't understand what he meant, hearing only terrified shouts and more gunfire, closer. Then his eyes rolled back and he stopped speaking. His body began to shudder. His legs kicked.

Nee knew that he was drowning, and she couldn't bear to stay. She ran, taking off with a small crowd fleeing down narrow walkways between buildings. They ran past the all-seeing face of the university's clocktower, and when they made it to the river, they splashed in like children.

Gunboats approached. Nee expected someone to shout out and demand surrender. Instead, muzzles flashed white. Underwater, she could still hear them. She was lucky to be a good swimmer. From her high school meets, she knew how to hold her breath for precious minutes. She broke the surface farther out and hid behind a drifting patch of water hyacinths. Green snakes were said to make homes of them. She had no fear of snakes that day.

Daylight arrived. On the shore, men moved in efficient swarms. Nee watched them drag students by the hair. Up by rope they went, dead or alive, and dangled beneath the dotted shade of bodhi trees. Cans of gasoline appeared. Near the river landing, heaps made jagged with legs and hands blackened, their matter joining the tea-colored smoke rising elsewhere on campus. She couldn't be sure if it was because her ears were full of water, but by afternoon all sounds had disappeared. It was the quietest she had ever heard the campus, not one sparrow noisy over classroom roofs. She felt like she was somewhere else, watching a terrible silent movie.

Cold and tired, she hung on to the hyacinths for hours. Waiters at a restaurant down the river snagged her in with the same long-handled bamboo stick they used to push floating trash from patrons' view.

II

FALLING

For most of the year, the swing served no significant function other to provide a tall perch for sparrows and vultures, but at the start of the lunar year, it became the site of great Brahmin festivities in the Siamese capital. Phineas had promised the reverend that he'd go forth and observe the local customs, and so it came to be that, on the appointed afternoon, he went to meet Winston at the gate. Winston was dressed in his usual squalid shirt and vest, but with a cloth wrapped around his hips, the way many natives dressed.

"Doctor, you have to try it for yourself," he said, pointing to other cloths he had hung to dry outside. "The breeze fans right through."

Phineas demurred, and so they left the gate, and before long they were proceeding down gravel roads he had not taken before. "It's a swifty shortcut," Winston said, with a smirk. His duties as the mission's printer necessitated visits to ink shops and paper traders all over the city, but Phineas seldom ventured on foot this far from the compound, and when he did, he mostly took the wider, less crowded avenues, with patrolling constables and at least some hope of spotting a threatening gesture before harm arrived.

The capital, the reverend had told him, had been built with heavy inspiration from Ayutthaya, which lay a day's journey north at the junction of three rivers. The old capital, much like the current one, manifested as an intricate latticework of long bustling thoroughfares lined by grand temples and pagodas. Little of them would survive destruction by Burmese invaders, but the building plans and spatial alignments served as a model for its eventual successor.

Phineas wondered if any of the lunacy before them had also been inherited. The farther they traveled toward the city's center, the greater the variety and concentration of people and sights. They walked alongside long-robed Chinamen and orderly columns of monks and caged fowl on pushcarts, past vegetable piles and fresh manure not inches apart, past singing girls cracking coconuts with bludgeons, past babies dozing in their hammocks and leashed monkeys and lesion-scarred beggars. At corners, laborers squatted in front of eating houses, digging into bowls with their hands. Sari-wrapped Hindu women beckoned them to step into their crammed fabric shops. Roadside elephants crushing sugarcane stalks in their jaws watched them with indifferent eyes, as did red-mouthed elderly Siamese chewing betel nuts under their stilt-propped shacks. They crossed over canals where canoe-borne vendors sang out their wares and held high assorted fruits and skinned carcasses for inspection.

At a bridge, children spreading their eyelids with their fingers to mock them were soon joined by older youth carrying bamboo sticks and reeking of rice spirits even from afar. Phineas paused to gauge their friendliness. Winston chuckled and advised that they keep walking.

"You think this little walk is fraught with peril? Let me tell you of my days outside of Madurai, printing scriptures in Tamil. We were surrounded by tigers, with only crabapples to fling for our defense. One would have eaten me if it weren't for a good throw from this very hand right here."

"Winston, unlike you, I do not look forward to physical squabbles as part of my daily nourishment."

"Well, why don't you then?"

Phineas ignored him and continued forward. He could see by then the red curve of the swing arching over the trees. High on one of its legs, he observed burn marks where lightning must have struck it some time ago, but that damage apparently hadn't halted the custom. He could hear the roar of the crowd, wild and hungry, as if a battle was about to commence. He and Winston hastened to the viewing area, wedging themselves into the gathered masses.

For the want of silver, men risked flesh and bone to clench their teeth on silken satchels. Phineas saw them carried by the swing through the blue of the sky, as high from the ground as the tallest church steeples in a New England valley.

During upswings, the satchel biter at the front of the plank lunged forward, his body extended beyond the plank, his mouth agape, sharklike. His adjacent companions, one on each side, attempted to steer the plank by shifting their weight, while a fourth man, in the back, squatted down to lend greater velocity to their ascension, to the cheers of the immense crowd.

The swing creaked steadily as the plank swung in the air. The biter tilted his head and, with a swiping bite, snapped off one of the three satchels suspended from the hanger. A storm of voices rose and swirled around him and Winston, and soon they joined those voices with their own.

They lingered for what felt like hours. After that team had grabbed all the satchels—the highest weighing three taels—another foursome readied. Simian boys with dangly arms scrambled up the swing to hang new prizes.

Winston told him to remain where he was and, minutes later, returned with grilled ears of corn from a woman roasting them beside the street. Some of the Siamese pointed and stared, as if amazed to see that they ate the same food. Again the swing took flight, and again the crowd roared.

In the heights that Phineas saw them reach, it felt as if he, too, were reaching the summit of human daring. In his mind, he resurrected his own feats—running across the old field at the college, where on trampled grass his peers cheered him on to set a record in the upperclassmen race—and also those of others: the men who'd found more than they'd before known of themselves at the Colosseum in Rome, on the Aztecs' game courts, in the gambling halls of New Orleans. And the crowds, the same here as any other. How they all yearned to see acts that defied common expectation, that could push a man across the membrane that separated ordinary life from the imagination of better. The whole of human history depended on this desire.

He soon saw the horror that could come of this desire as well.

On the downswing, a biter lost his grip. The crowd, sensing that something was wrong before he fell, burst with shouts and then exploded into a louder collective cry. The man tumbled sideward as the plank swung fast to the ground. It threw him a distance of at least ten yards. He missed one of the swing's legs by an arm's length, dervishing in a cloud of red clay dust before coming to rest in the road. At once, Phineas began to make his way toward the man, pushing forward while exclaiming, "Mawh! Mawh!," hoping his intonation sufficient to declare his status as a physician and not a pot for boiling.

Some of the ceremonial guards had already gathered around the man. From his apprentice days, Phineas knew how much harm could be inflicted by aid from the well intentioned but unlearned. He shuddered as they carried the man by his arms and legs in the direction of an open pavilion. By then, a new team had already been ushered to the swing. The ceremonies must continue.

"Mawh! Mawh!" he yelled again, his palms raised high, so as to signal to the guards to desist from whatever they were doing to the man. He felt justified in his worries as soon as he reached the group. The biter was in a worrisome state. Phineas could see at once that the man had broken his fall with the left side of his body. The abrupt bend in the man's shoulder made clear a broken clavicle. The man's face had been deformed by the impact. A convexity on the left side of the lower jaw told him where bone structure had compacted. A long gash in the arm burbled crimson. Phineas tore off the strap that had fastened his headdress and used it to constrict blood flow in the brachial artery. The outpour slowed to a trickle.

When Winston arrived at the pavilion, Phineas yelled at him to find a cart so that they could wheel the man to the mission hospital. The surgical tools there might offer the man some hope of continuing his days.

"Kwian! Ow kwian mah!" Phineas yelled to the ring of onlookers that had formed around the pavilion. None responded. The guards remained where they stood, seeming more bewildered by the presence of two Occidentals than by the man's injuries. Above them, red-clad women leaning from veiled windows watched indifferently.

A boy no older than five threw himself on the man. The boy's head was shaven, aside from the customary tail at the back of his head. At first, Phineas believed he was crying, but he soon saw that the boy bore no tears in his eyes. The child scowled at him, in a rage, as if he were the one to blame for the man's wounds.

"Is this your father?" Phineas asked, with his best pronunciation in the native language.

"Yes," the boy answered.

"What is his name? What is yours?"

He learned that the man's name was Bunsahk. The boy was Bunmahk. Phineas felt sorrow for the boy. He would save the man to fulfill his physician's oath, but he would call on Him to guide his hand for the boy's sake.

"Bunmahk, I'll do everything I can for him," he said to the boy's unchanging expression, acknowledging the responsibility it demanded. "Where's the cart?" he called out.

No cart came. Instead, the onlookers parted to let through an older man dressed in a manner not unlike a Buddhist monk. Instead of a saffron robe, however, he wore over one shoulder a sash made of tiger hide. He was not shaved bald like the monks but had half a head of hair that hung ribbonlike down his neck to meet an arrow-shaped beard and an orbit of wooden rosaries. He carried a walking stick made of driftwood, at the top of which hung a lacquered gourd with carved eyes. A dozen men armed with scars accompanied him. The old man stabbed the ground with his walking stick and commenced to shout at Phineas, while pointing at the man Bunsahk. Phineas asked Winston what the man was saying.

"He says the injured fellow here must have offended the snake god in some way. He says that the lone hope for the man is the immediate undertaking of an apology ritual."

"This man is dying," Phineas said to Winston, his eyes still on the old man.

"They want the man to be taken at once to the ceremonial house." Phineas did not know how to respond to this madness. He asked Winston to make it clear that he was a trained physician, and what this man needed was for his wounds to be sutured and cauterized as soon as possible.

"What the witch doctor thinks is that you're obstructing him from doing what he must do for this man. And so does this crowd."

Bystanders now stood shouting at them. The men around the witch doctor began to advance on them, as if they were townspeople back in the States cornering a pair of boars.

He saw his father and mother answering the door to hear of his demise from a Society member. He saw his brother reading in the papers: "Missionaries Murdered and Mutilated by Siamese Mob." He thought of the reverend and the schoolteachers, and the troubles that would visit them, were he and Winston to pass from this earth in this manner. Worst, he felt his limbs soften, numbed, as the men moved closer. The strangest memories arrived in those seconds: the smell of his mother's roast; a view of the Hudson in autumn; poor Annabeth, so young.

He feared. There was no other adequate word.

Even if he were to succeed in bringing this man Bunsahk to the mission hospital, he would likely have brought back a dead man. The wine- and ash-colored bruises on the man's torso suggested hemorrhaging within. He expected to see, at any moment, the man's soul rise out and drift up toward the tall swing in search of the satchel that had eluded his bite.

His musings were interrupted by a nudge from Winston, who, lifting his vest slightly, revealed the curved wooden butt of a sidearm.

"I can fire one skyward and scare them off. If that doesn't work, there's five more in the chamber," Winston said.

"No, there's no need. We've done all that we can here."

"Hold on, and listen. You just worry about getting him to a cart. They won't make it past me."

"Let them have the man."

"What? Are we going to let him die so pitiably?" asked Winston with such passionate fury that Phineas half expected him to draw the gun and shoot the man dead.

Phineas said nothing but lowered his hands to his hips. Winston dropped his hands from his vest. The men reached Bunsahk and lifted him onto their shoulders. They walked off, the witch doctor leading them.

Phineas heard the boy shout after his father. He did not dare look in the boy's direction.

After they returned to the mission, they made no mention of this incident to others. When the reverend asked if he had enjoyed observing the festivities, Phineas told him that he had and thanked the reverend for suggesting he attend. They ate well that night. The cooks had, for once, made a fine meal of stewed chicken in the Dutch style, under Miss Lisle's guidance.

Later, by the light of the full moon, he again crossed paths with Winston on the second-floor deck. Winston was leaning on the railing, his expression that of a man in a waking dream. When he did not show his usual smile, Phineas asked if he wanted to speak further about the day's matter.

"It's fine, Doctor. There's no need," Winston said, before retiring to his room.

Unable to sleep that night, Phineas wrote to his brother about the day, asking Andrew if he wouldn't have chosen the same course. He described the incident in fine detail, desiring to provide Andrew with all the necessary facts to arrive at the same decision that he had made and portrayed the witch doctor in a manner that would help Andrew understand the frustration and fear that had overtaken him, surrounded by a crowd of angry heathens.

Will you see that I acted within the bounds of good reason? he asked in conclusion.

Then he added:

> If you should find yourself in the city on business in the
> next month, please make inquiries with the Society about
> my transfer request posted on the fifth of November. It
> gives me great concern that my pleas have not been
> answered and that I'm left here, with troubled mind and
> spirit, to wonder if my ordeal shall last in perpetuity.

UPRISING

They always figured a way. The old gap had already been boarded up, but it was only a matter of finding another. The past few hours had yielded far too little, and their hunger grew as morning diminished the cover of night. Hushed barks kept the pack on the move. The short-haired one nuzzled and pawed the bottom edges of the wall, tracing eights with its long bushy tail. The mangiest of them trailed a few steps behind, followed by the cripple, who was the oldest of the pack and the only one who remembered a time when the city gave up steady riches. Before the arrival of impenetrable bins, piles left at the sides of roads kept them from starving. There were more of them then—allies, enemies, momentary lovers. The only ones left were those gifted with the swiftest legs and a nose still sharp enough to detect faint promises in the fumes.

A wood plank bent loose with a push of a muzzle. They entered one by one, scraping their fur against the edges of the widened opening. Inside, the scent of dry, pulverized earth overwhelmed them. They pointed their noses upward and sniffed harder. Days ago, they came across unspoiled stringy foods a two-legger had thrown out, and before that, an unsecured trash basket brimmed with salvation. They crossed quietly over small gravel fields, stopping here and there to smell milky puddles. They took care not to disturb the big metallic animals that they knew would soon wake to life as men climbed the dark skeleton above them and showered the ground with fiery stars. With each return of daylight, the skeleton rose taller. The sun shone behind it, peeking through.

Mounds of sand, damp from the night's dew, swallowed their legs. The crippled one fell behind, letting out an unanswered yelp. The other two looked back, as if they had meant to wait, and then disappeared around the corner. The crippled one quickened its hop. Up ahead, where the skeleton rose from the ground, it came upon a smaller structure it recognized. The old dog remembered the welcoming light that spilled from the rectangular openings. From one of them, an older woman stepped out from a gate to leave a metal bowl filled with all that it could want. Inside, two furry faces watched unhappily as the stranger ate food that could have been theirs. That was a lifetime ago.

◻ ◻ ◻

Incense smoke couldn't hide smells steaming from the chicken Juk had left out for the ghosts. Waving a neon green construction vest with both hands, he shooed off the dogs just before they could get close to the food. He watched them retreat to the sand mounds and then edge back to where they thought safe and he thought disrespectful. He picked up a rusty bolt from the ground and threw it at them. Off they scrambled for a few meters before returning with another dog, a limping mutt he recognized from having seen it clipped by a truck the month before.

When he was younger, Juk might have admired their brazenness, but now it annoyed him that these dogs weren't intimidated by him. If they could know how fearsome he had once been, with shoulders like an ox plow and arms that could lift two burlap sacks of rice over his back. When he was no older than fifteen, he had tried to swim across the Chao Phraya River—the pagodas of the temple on the other side merely shiny needles—giving up only after he woke gushing water from a bottomless dream, his mother in the gathered crowd, delirious from believing her oldest son dead. Then his bones had turned to cork from twenty thankless years of helping move the steel beams and cement bags that lifted Krungthep upward. His muscles pulsed with pain when he tried to sleep. And now these dogs, along with everyone else, conspired to take away what dignity he had left.

"Ai Gai, do you think this is funny?" he asked his nephew, who had done nothing to help but had the nerve to chuckle. "Now you'll stand in front of the food until the ghosts are done eating."

"Loong Juk, how am I supposed to know when they're done?" Gai asked.

Juk checked the time on his watch. He guessed that twenty minutes should be enough for the ghosts to finish eating. Any less, and he feared they would give him nothing or, worse, come demanding much more that night.

"You think you're so clever? I'll tell you when."

Juk could tell that Gai was barely awake. Not long before dawn, he'd heard the boy lie down on his mattress pad. He had thought of confronting the boy about having snuck out, but he didn't want to be the bad uncle who replaced the cruel father. They would have fought, and it would break his heart to see the boy standing there, expecting blows to land. It was good enough that the boy returned from wherever he had gone and, at the least, that he knew better than to steal from his uncle's cash tin.

"Loong Juk, will this be the week that the ghosts reward you? Don't forget to share your lottery jackpot with us!" shouted the ironworkers heading up the ramp. They were about the same age as Gai but entirely different beasts. As his nephew washed off buckets on the ground level, they quick-stepped across narrow beams, guiding steel sections the length of train cars into place, the city a whole sky below.

"You cursed lizards! I will laugh when the ghosts come to wring your necks!"

The workers grabbed their throats as if strangled. They shouted, "Help us, Loong Juk! Help us!"

"Gai, are these the hell creatures you're hanging with? Your mother would be so proud."

"No, Uncle. I've never even spoken to them."

Gai's voice was louder than expected, and Juk turned to find his nephew beside him.

"Damn, Gai, why are you standing here?!"

Juk looked toward the ancient house, where under the crosshatched shade of the netting and scaffolding protecting it from the construction above, he had left the offerings on an entrance step. He saw two dogs locked together in a furious dance, each with jaws clenched on a leg of the chicken. Another, the limping one, had its face buried in the bowl of boiled eggs and rice. It was the only one to glance up and look at Juk eye to eye.

"Ai Gai!" he yelled. His nephew ran to the house as the dogs scampered away. Only aftermath lingered. From an upturned bowl, white beads of rice mingled with sand. A bottle of Thai whiskey lay on its side, the ground anointed.

Juk dropped to his knees in front of the house. How long had it been here? A hundred years? A thousand? Even under the netting, he could make out a roof covered with aged scallop-shaped tiles and, underneath, patterned masonry work of a type long made extinct by cement blocks. Through gaps between shuttered windows he thought he could see the faint contours of rooms with ornate, paneled walls—once grand for whoever lived here and now a luxurious home only for geckos and ghosts.

He raised his clasped palms and pleaded loudly so that his voice would carry through all the layers of this realm and all heaven and hell, "Please, don't come for us! Little us meant no disrespect!"

And then to Gai: "We're fucked now, you hear?! Fucked!"

◻ ◻ ◻

From below, Tohn heard what sounded like screaming, but unable to make out the words, he let himself believe that the workers were just horsing around again. If something serious did happen, he'd find out well before his walkie-talkie lit up. Sound traveled easily up the floors. A man could carry on whole conversations with a friend ten stories above. He often listened for his name. In front of him, the workers smiled and bowed and returned questions with docile replies, but Tohn thought himself smarter than to believe them.

"Smell that. The freshest air in Krungthep," he told Prateep, the construction manager.

Tohn thought he could smell the moist, dirtlike scent of rain, the same smell he remembered from hunting in the mountains with his father during storms, when they could creep closer before the wild birds flushed. There, leaves shook as falling raindrops answered the cries of tree frogs. Here, walls of water poured on the city and reduced its streets to streams of floating garbage.

Had Khun Prateep even heard him? He stood rubbing his fingers on the rivets of a steel beam. Sometimes Tohn thought he could smell saltiness from the sea, less than an hour's drive away. A few years ago, at a different construction site, he was sure he smelled a trace of gunpowder after coup plotters attacked an army building.

"Will the the eleventh floor be done by the the fifteenth of next month?" asked Prateep.

"Most likely," said Tohn. "But, Khun Prateep, delays can't be predicted."

"That's unacceptable," said Prateep.

Tohn hated the commanding way Prateep said it. It reminded him of the way rice buyers talked to his father after harvest was over. Prateep had joined the firm a decade after he had, but it was Prateep whom the company selected to send abroad to apprentice at a partner firm in Berlin.

"Do you have reason to be skeptical?" Prateep asked.

Unable to muster an immediate response, Tohn smiled to hide his anxiety and looked down, as if the correct answer had dropped on the unfinished floor. "You know, it took longer to lay the foundation and posts to avoid damage to the old house. And now we're routing materials in a way that's less than optimal. The extra minutes each day with each truck and worker add up."

"I thought we discussed this," Prateep said.

Tohn said nothing. They were standing near enough to the side of the building that he could see the majority of the site. The roof of the old house was missing shingles at one corner, where earthy debris had let saplings take root. He was the one who'd supervised the cutting of the trees that had been here. Three men holding hands couldn't wrap their arms around some of them. They were the largest, possibly the oldest, trees he'd seen in Krungthep. Under their enormous twisted roots, he imagined a society of snakes coiled coolly in earthy burrows.

At the east side of the house, a circular outline of the old garden could still be seen. After digging out its paved stone slabs, workers piled them not far from the ramp. From this high, they looked like small hills of giants' teeth.

Prateep sighed. "I know it's an odd requirement, and I've talked to the boss about the additional complications, but the plans won't change, especially with the partners now thinking that they'll be able to use the Sino-Colonial architecture of the house to attract foreign tenants."

The project had had its plague of delays. There were hearings with academics and preservationists, only a handful, but the bad publicity forced them to keep intact much of the original house as part of the lobby, as a concession. Then financing from a Japanese bank fell through, and for many years the site sat soot dusted, fenced by corrugated tin sheets colonized by parliamentary campaign and energy drink posters. It then took another five years for construction to make any real progress.

"You have to believe me, Tohn. I've tried my best with the project timeline. Do you think me an unreasonable man?"

Tohn shook his head. He thought of his son, a second-year at a local primary school, and the pride his son showed pointing up to the metal dragons perched at the side of rising towers and saying those were his father's buildings.

"Of course not, Khun Prateep. You know best."

□ □ □

Don't worry. Bamboo's just as strong as steel. That's what they said to a new kid stepping onto scaffolding for the first time. This high up, the chances of a rod snapping was the least of anyone's worries. Sudden wind was more fearsome. So were slick spots purple sheened with machine grease or, worse, someone's burlap sack heavy with screws, knocked over from many stories up. Posters the managers put up before a site visit by foreign investors showed figures wearing steel-capped boots and harnesses and bright orange hardhats and warned of drinking on the job. It was a wonder how anyone could survive for long in those restrictive conditions, without their bare toes divining their next step or a quick swig to soothe a yearning heart. Greater dangers waited for them in some stray thought of parents back in the village, or of the ivory-skinned girl on the cosmetics billboard across from the site, or of rage smoldering in the gut after harsh words had flown across a ring of dice rollers. All they really needed was a rag they could wrap around their face, so the brute light twenty stories up wouldn't scorch off their skin and cement powder wouldn't turn their lungs to stone.

"Faster! A constipated ox would have already made it up here," Lek yelled to Gai.

With one hand the boy found his grip; with the other he held on to a bucket. It was the boy's second week on the high floors. With the new deadlines, the workers did double shifts, and anyone older than ten was brought up from the shacks to climb over steel rods and smooth them with wire brushes, or, like the boy here, to deliver cement sloshing inside plastic buckets.

"I'm going fast," Gai said. "How the hell can anyone can go any faster?"

"All you little ingrates just want to go back down and eat and sleep, none of you worth the rice you're fed. At least you didn't spill this one."

Lek took the bucket from the boy and poured the gray slush over laid rods.

"When I was your age, I could haul up two buckets at a time. What's with you? You don't want your day off?"

They had worked for six weeks without a break, with the promise of one to be given if enough floors had risen. Songkran was a few months away, and they couldn't bear the thought of having to stay behind in Krungthep that holiday week. The managers knew that about them when the extra shifts were announced. What prouder accomplishment could there be than to still be on the payroll and also able to return to one's home province as the new year's bearer of a ring for one's mother or a Walkman for siblings?

Gai grabbed the emptied bucket and clambered down the nailed lattice of bamboo. He lowered his bare feet rung by rung, feeling for the ridges on the next rod, until he felt a steel beam firm underfoot. He balanced himself and stepped heel over toe until he could hop on to the hardened concrete on the floor below.

"Ah Lek giving you shit again?" asked Waen, who lived in the same row of shacks as him and Loong Juk. Gluey and Baby Boy didn't hold back their laughter.

"No, Ah Lek's just pouring the slab," Gai said.

"Don't lie to me. Do you think I'm blind and can't see that look on your face?"

The others were only a few years older than Gai but acted as if they were a decade apart. Gai trailed behind them and the other young workers when they went at night to the new multistoried department store, to feel the air-conditioning whisper on their skin and to stand in front of a color TV and watch things blow up in dubbed farang movies.

"You tired? Sleepy? You wish you had some of the good stuff, don't you?"

"Gluey, he's too young for that."

"Your sister's too young, and nothing's stopping her from sucking my cock."

"Shut the hell up! I'll swallow some good stuff and fuck seven generations of your ancestors."

Gai knew what the good stuff was supposed to do for the workers. An older kid had said it made him feel like Ultraman, fifty feet tall and able to shoot gamma rays from his arms. Eyes pried awake and muscles surged with elephantine power. All day they could work, stopping only to pee and shit. The designated dispenser, Loong Bood, was allowed to roam freely, floor to floor, hawking cigarettes, hard candies, lottery tickets from a basket. When prompted, he would lift a tin of cough drops to retrieve a small plastic bag with colored pills, often blue, sometimes orange or white. Knowing Loong Juk would come after him with a cleaver, Loong Bood never sold any to Gai.

"Get me some," Gai said.

Waen shook his head. Gluey and Baby Boy howled laughing.

"Little Gai wants to be a big man. Does the big man have the money?"

"I'll pay you later, I promise."

"You show up with some cash, then we can talk. And isn't that Ah Lek yelling for you?"

Gai heard it, as well: his name shouted from above. He grabbed a filled bucket and ran back to the scaffolds. As he climbed one-handed up the bamboo rods, managing to keep the bucket from slipping out of his other hand, he wondered how soundly Loong Juk would sleep that night.

◻ ◻ ◻

All the sparrows. Hundreds of their tiny bodies made undulating ribbons in the sky above the cluttered spread of roofs and TV antennas, flecking the vacancy between newly risen buildings with the brown of their feathers and the gray of their shadows. The weary among them alighted at the edge of balconies and, before they swooped again toward flight, took care to leave mementos of their visit.

Finished, the latest building stood twenty-seven stories tall. People in the neighborhood called it the corncob, with its sticklike shape ringed by half-moon balconies that jutted out, floor after floor. It had been painted white, but with the traffic always languishing just below, the industrious fires of the city's coal cookers, and the rains depositing what factories had breathed out, streaks of soot and grime ran soon where rainwater had poured off. Just over a year into its life, like the other buildings that had risen alongside it, this tower was well on its way to looking as if it had been there since the time this city was not a city but a mosquito-breeding marsh, when merchant galleon captains paid the flooded grassland no mind as they floated upriver to reach Ayutthaya, hundreds of years before Burmese soldiers laid torches to it.

What survived even in memory of that glorious former capital, beyond the facts and dates schoolchildren were made to memorize from the history books? Most modern citizens of Krungthep had difficulty recalling events more than months past.

And yet this building was already rumored to be cursed. The empty old colonial-style mansion at the base was said by locals to have been owned by a wealthy family whose members mysteriously disappeared, one by one, until none were left. There had been numerous construction mishaps, with one worker losing an arm and others their minds.

Then a young worker had fallen to his death, and TV vans and reporters had shown up in front of the construction site for a week to cover
the incident. All of decent Krungthep was appalled. "Safety standards
have to come first," a member of parliament said to cameras. "What
happened to this boy mustn't occur again."

By the next week, few in Krungthep thought of the boy. The city's
eyes had shifted to fresher news of deaths and mayhem that reminded
them again of the mysteries of karma.

Construction resumed after adequate sums changed hands between
the right parties. The building rose to completion and so did the enormous billboard outside, enticing passing motorists with a list of features and amenities and, in disproportionally large font, the office
number to call to rent or buy.

At one of the balconies of this building, a woman slid open a screen
door and stepped out. She puffed mist from a squeeze bottle at trickles
hardened by weeks of relentless sunlight and began to scrub with a
bristle brush. Potential renters were due to look at the unit in the
afternoon.

□ □ □

"All clean, Nee?" Duang asked the office girl returning from the unit.

"Gleaming."

Duang nodded her approval. A year ago, she had had her hesitations
about hiring a graduate from a reputable university for the job. She
didn't want anyone who might think herself above the necessary labors
when the housekeeping crew was overwhelmed or the maintenance
staff had all gone out on another drunken lunch, or anyone who'd leave
as soon as she could find another job. What made this girl stand out
from the hospitality industry applicants was her degree in nursing, a

profession that Duang knew to require the ability to endure many lifetimes of thanklessness.

"Your CV here says that you worked for a while as a nurse. Are you sure you shouldn't be applying for a job at a hospital?" she'd asked.

"I only finished the degree because I didn't want to disappoint my mother," said Nee. "Then she became sick, and I ran her sundries business at our shophouse so I could take care of her. It took some years after she died for me to realize I'm not meant to take her place. I need to do something else."

Duang's own mother had been a nurse. She'd come home exhausted every night and fall asleep on the sleeping mat in her work clothes. When, as a girl, Duang slid over to sleep beside her, she could smell her mother's work—the lingering chemical scent of sterilizers and medications, the trace stenches from air around the old and ailing.

"Let me tell you. I've met with ten other people who can all do the job. I could pick someone younger or with experience in this field. Why do you think I should choose you?" Duang had persisted. She'd expected the girl to talk about having bountiful energy and highly developed problem-solving skills. Instead, Nee went to the window and pointed to the pool.

"I can teach swimming," she said. "Wouldn't swim classes be an attractive feature for prospective tenants with families?"

Duang hadn't considered such an idea. That bright blue rectangle of water was only meant to look clean and hypothetically enticing for potential buyers and rental tenants.

Maybe it was the memory of her mother that had compelled Duang to hire Nee over the others, or maybe it was the sense of something kindred in the girl's desperation, despite business-minded logic telling her to go with someone else. She'd had no reason to regret her choice. Devotion and diligence seemed like words deployed as a matter of course in talking about employees, but with Nee, they were real. She'd watched Nee pick up phones on the first ring and then, call after call, hurry to the service elevator to take care of whatever issue had been communicated. Windows had turned to waterfalls during heavy rain. Red ants had taken over a potted shrub on the courtyard walkway. Garrulous bats were mating over someone's door, wire-chewing rodents discovered after they'd brought on their own immolation. Showers streamed the red of clay roads, stray dogs slipped into the lobby, and a farang tenant, wearing only a sheet of the morning's paper around his waist, once knocked on the glass door of their office to say he was locked out.

"Anything new with 12A?" she asked Nee, who was putting away the cleaning supplies.

"Syphilis. A housekeeper saw the medication bottles in a trash bag."

"Ha! I knew it. Suits that gigolo. And what about 20E—Mrs. O?"

"Still depressed about her cat. Still wearing black."

"And what's going on with 25C's kitchen faucets?"

"No water, still. Just this noise. Like this."

Her teeth clenched, the girl made a hissing sound.

"Take care of that today. You know who owns that unit."

"I'll find a way to tell Kuhn Pehn. The plumbers told me they would fix it last Friday."

"They're the worst. I'd fire them if they weren't cousins of the new director at the mother company. Remember my name for him? Khun Camel Face?"

They let out the laugh of sisters and school friends. Duang would never admit it, but she wanted the girl to like her. Sometimes she felt guilty for having Nee do more work than listed in the original job posting. After all, a decade ago, she had been an office girl herself.

Nee had no idea of her luck, not having a man for a boss. Duang couldn't shake off the memory of one old boss, and how he'd bend down to ask how her day had been, his shoulder pressed against hers, his breath stinking of tobacco and the grilled pork fermenting between his teeth. There were mornings when she wept on the bus to work and had to steel herself on the way, stopping to face a wall and flipping open her pocket mirror to reconstruct the face that had washed off.

"Khun Duang, your two o'clock's at the reception desk," said Nee, hanging up the office phone they shared.

Duang undid the clasp on her purse and took out the mirror, its red plastic shell faded a shade and scratched to dullness by loose coins. A face made of memories returned her gaze. She no longer had the firm, lush skin of the office girl that she had been, with no real need for foundation, as tan as she was. What Duang now had was her title as building manager, and a sickly teenage boy who'd inherited her husband's most self-defeating genes, and a secondhand Toyota nicked by motor scooter handlebars. On weekends, she crossed the river to Nonthaburi to visit her mother-in-law, and on holy days, she made alms at the temple, so that her next life would be fuller and richer, with maybe a husband possessing soap-opera-star looks and at least an engineer's dependable mind. If she hit her leasing goals this week, she promised to buy a week's lunch for the monks, to make up for any wrongs committed.

"Nee, how do I look?"

"As gorgeous as always."

□ □ □

Mohd and Mehta stood in the building's lobby and stared at the ceiling. Sometime long ago, workers had pressed tin tiles on die shipped from Italy, and up there the patterned flower petals and curled vines remained, an overhead gesture toward an orderly Renaissance garden, warped at the edges by the tropical heat.

"So gorgeous, isn't it? This was all part of a trading family's mansion built in the 1910s," said the woman from the building management office. "I don't know if you believe in feng shui and all that, but this land, let me tell you, has brought much luck to everyone who has lived on it. Only good, prosperous people have the karmic merits to live here."

"Khun Duang, there's a chance I might qualify, but I'm not sure about my wife."

Mehta nudged Mohd to show that he was joking, and she responded the way she always did, with a shove on his elbow, enough to make him stumble a step.

They had spent a honeymoon week in Florence, where they tried to appreciate the authentic pasta dishes, but by the third day they succumbed to adding a few drops of fish sauce and sprinkling crushed Thai peppers they'd been warned to bring along. The ceiling reminded Mohd of the Florentine architecture that she so loved—the geometric domes and intricate facades of a stony city lit by its own pale glow. It felt strange that she would have any reservation about walking through this lobby and its heavenly ceiling and rarefied wood walls, but then she realized that what unnerved her most was the thought of living in a place who knew how many stories up, like seabirds nesting on the face of a cliff.

"Which floor is the unit on again?" she asked.

"This one's on"—the woman checked the printout—"floor twenty-five. Now that's a nice auspicious number, let me tell you. Follow me."

They rode the elevator, which the woman pointed out as being very speedy, never any long wait to hear that arrival bell. The unit was on the south wing of the tower, at the far end of a hallway, nice and quiet, and well lit throughout. Inside were two bedrooms, each at opposite ends of the hall, for maximum privacy, and a high-grade kitchen with Japanese appliances, an oven optional, as not many Thais wanted them but the expats expected one, and, true, only one bathroom, but more than sizable and well equipped with hotel-quality fixtures in fine porcelain and polished brass.

"The best part is this view," said the woman, her hand sailing across the living room windows. Out there, the city crawled and rose and stretched and liquefied into the horizon. They could see the creamy body of a river in the far distance. A wind blew through a slit of open window and whistled its uneven song.

"To be honest," Mohd said, "I hadn't ever thought I'd live this high up. What if there's a fire?"

It was Mehta who thought they should look at moving into one of these newfangled condo buildings. They had visited housing developments, those they could afford an hour or more outside Krungthep proper, even with willing traffic, and laid in rectangular plots, each house a few arm's lengths' away from identical neighbors. His mother wanted them to continue living with her, but Mohd had tired of the power struggle, every conversation a careful play of diplomacy, every silence an occasion for sharpening blades in their minds.

"I understand your concerns," said the woman. "That's why we've installed sprinklers and a top-of-the-line alarm system, just like ones they have in Tokyo and New York. Only the best, let me tell you."

"This is Krungthep," said Mohd. "Will they work? Will the firemen make it in time at rush hour?"

Her husband glared at her. It was so like Mehta to be mad on behalf of a stranger, especially one with makeup caked on her face. Didn't he notice? Could he even tell?

"Mohd, just look out there," he said, walking to the window. "Khun Duang, you really have this view doing all the work for you."

"Khun Mohd, I have to ask," said the woman. "Do you have any children?"

"Not yet. We will."

She hadn't yet told Mehta. This certainly wasn't the right time for that kind of announcement. Still, her hand reached up to touch her waist.

"Let me tell you, when you do, you'll love the kids' activities scheduled in the common garden, with the playground soon to be finished. Also, our new office girl is going to start teaching children's swim classes on weekends."

"Forget about kids," Mehta said. "With a pool like that, I'd go for a dip every day."

He giggled with the saleswoman, who made it seem like he had said the funniest thing she'd ever heard in her life. Harmless, he'd say later.

"This building," said Mohd. "It's where the young worker fell off, isn't it? It's the one people are afraid would be haunted, so the prices came down, which is the reason we're here."

She remembered a reporter donning an orange hardhat in front of a construction site. She had been watching the late-edition news, alone in her bedroom and Mehta away at some work meeting. Just a few more hours, he'd said on the phone. All the bosses are here.

"Mohd, so many new buildings have gone up recently. Why would you think it's this one?"

"I don't know. It's just a thought that came to me."

"I have to apologize, Khun Duang. My wife can be so superstitious for such a well-educated, professional businesslady."

"Actually," the woman said, "the prices are down because the owner of this unit is someone who owns several units here, and she is superstitious about having an even number of units rented."

Mohd turned away from the two of them to restrain herself from slapping Mehta. No, she wouldn't explode on her husband, whom, she knew by now, and should have always known, to be a man who felt he had to be adored by everyone, especially those taking advantage of him. She walked to the window to leave him and the woman to their enthused admiration for the bright wood floors and the built-in AC or whatever.

From somewhere outside, a sound clapped against the window. The glass hummed. Not far off, a white helicopter sliced across the sky with blurred rotor blades before diminishing into an insectile speck as it wove behind mirror-skinned towers. There was something in the choppy noise that helped calm her: the assured steadiness powering the uplift of the machine. It occurred to her that the pulsing of her own heartbeat, sending life to her womb—more forceful than she'd ever felt it—had the same rhythmic shudder.

She felt a tap on her arm. It wasn't Mehta but the woman, whose eyes had softened as if ropes behind them had been cut.

"Don't worry, Khun Mohd. Let me tell you, no one has died here, and there are no ghosts."

"Yes, I'm probably mistaken."

Of course this was the building. The view was the same as from the news segment when reporters went up with police officials to inspect the scene. What haunted her most was the blank expression of one of the boys, seen in a cropped and magnified family photo, the nickname captioned in white letters: Gai. Before seeing that dead boy, she had considered giving the same name to her child, were she to have a son.

By the time they left the building, it was nearly dark, and they had signed themselves to a down payment amounting to the entirety of their savings. Mohd asked the woman if they could see the unit again on their own, and they were given a key they could slide under the office door afterward. Up again they went, to survey the fractional share of the city they would claim as theirs. They flushed the toilet and flicked the kitchen lights off and on to make sure the place was all there, as if it might have fallen apart the moment they'd agreed to lease it. Let Mehta have his roosting place, she thought, tracing a finger on the bathroom grout. Here, she would make sure he gave their child the vigil of his love.

Down they returned to walk on paved ground releasing back the warmth of the afternoon's sun. She heard again the street song of taxi horns and motorcycle sputters and hawkers calling out their goods. She would not miss it at all.

MONSTERS

I t was morning, and the breeze blowing from the direction of Osanbashi Pier still smelled faintly of the bay. Nok and her husband were clearing the airborne sting of chopped chilies through the restaurant's front door when a familiar white van pulled up at the curb—the ingredients supplier, but two days earlier than scheduled. Instead of the usual Japanese man who sweated like he'd stepped out of a hot spring, Khun Ubol walked in with the pushcart. He'd come himself, he explained, because he had decided to pack it up and return to Krungthep.

"Don't worry, Khun Nok, Khun Maru," he said. "You'll soon see this cart, as full as it is today."

Nok knew too well the easy assurances of her countrymen. Maru, born here in Yokohama and accustomed to fulfilled obligations, didn't understand her doubts, not until he talked to Khun Ubol's successors. From them they learned that their deliveries would cease while very specific import licenses were being transferred. This meant the licenses would enter the backlog at the customs office, a month could pass before shipments resumed, and none of the other importers in Chinatown would deal with orders as small as their restaurant's.

This was 1983. Thai food wasn't very well known then. They'd be lucky if the Chinese grocers stocked enough Thai fish sauce to last a week. Khun Ubol was the supplier for those places, too.

"First, we'll run out of galangal," Nok said to Maru after Khun Ubol left. "This is the end of tom kha gai."

"This isn't the end of anything. We're going to find another supplier. Close your eyes for a minute and breathe."

The door chime rang. Nok pushed Maru back into the dining area, so he could greet the arriving customer. It was Khun Chahtchai, one of the regulars. He was a Thai man in his sixties who came to the restaurant every week for an early lunch right when they opened and left well before other customers arrived. As usual, Khun Chahtchai seated himself at the table next to the corner window. As usual, Maru greeted him in rudimentary Thai but with a customary Japanese half bow.

Before Khun Chahtchai could get a good look at her, Nok went into the kitchen and brushed away tears. Unlike with Maru, she couldn't make problems go away by closing her eyes and believing the best would happen. Instead, her worst fears tended to become more and more vivid. She saw their menu at Erawan—basically a photocopied page inside a plastic sleeve—with half the dishes crossed out, the remaining clinging on like animals on an endangered species list, begging for survival.

◻ ◻ ◻

"Nok, I can look into how much shipping container space might cost you," said Nee. It was midevening for Nee, the time for their usual telephone rendezvous. Nee had been running the sundries shop, now that their mother could only float in and out of medicated sleep on her wicker chair, and Nok knew her sister was trying not to sound tired.

"But, Nee, I'm not Khun Ubol. I would still need licenses. Everything's going to get stuck at the port and spoil."

"Can you grow some of what you need?"

"Like the chili plants barely sprouting on my windowsill?"

"How much of anything do you still have?"

"Nee, I think I'm going to have to close down Erawan."

"Nonsense. You're going to get your hands on whatever you need."

Her sister's words always calmed Nok. Nok had been a sixth-year and Nee only a third-year when they swam at secondary school meets, but Nee wasn't afraid to go up to older teammates and show ways to push off and angle stroke. For Nok, the purpose of her own swimming was to impress their father, most of all. Nee swam because she thought they had a chance against the schools with their own pools. She trained them better than their coach.

"An airlift is what's going to happen," Nee said. "How many students do you know?"

They gambled that Thai students at nearby universities couldn't bear to see the restaurant close. Returning to Japan from their summer break, the students would act as couriers. Nok would make the pleading phone calls, and in Bangkok, Nee would deliver ingredients to the students, even help pack to make sure suitcases filled up. Nok never fully believed the plan would work, but what choice did she have?

◻ ◻ ◻

The morning the first suitcase was due, Nok developed a sudden routine of grabbing the broom and stepping outside the restaurant. She brushed it over bare spots on the sidewalk she had swept an hour earlier, her eyes on the intersection closest to the subway station. It was a familiar view. Store signs jutted from the side of low-rise buildings. Office workers walked unhurried beneath wide-leafed trees spaced apart at exact intervals. Sidewalk tiles gleamed white, like teeth. She had told Nee that this part of Yokohama had the cleanest streets on earth. Just walking on them cleared minds and absolved sins.

Standing there outside the restaurant, Nok felt her heart leap at the sight of anyone who remotely looked Thai. She felt sure that the airport customs must have seized everything. When she spotted a figure rounding the corner, wheeling luggage, she dropped her broom.

"Sawasdee ka!" she yelled out, and waved with an outstretched arm.

"Sawasdee ka!" the young woman called back. They both clasped hands to their noses and bowed their heads.

"Come in," Nok told the woman. "I thought you might come sooner, but never mind, you're here."

Maru opened the door. Nok rolled the American Tourister suitcase to a corner, laid it flat, and opened it. In the still-empty restaurant, she felt free to laugh and clap at the jars of fermented fish. With careful hands, she helped Maru lift out bricks of tamarind pulp as if they were newborns. She had been so eager to do away with weeks of improvising what they could—yatsufusa pepper powder for Thai roasted chili powder, dried fish flakes standing in for cured Thai prawns. They'd even had to reduce the palm sugar in her mother's recipes by half, and then by half again.

Nok thanked the woman while Maru carried their bounty to the pantry. If careful, they could make it last a week and a half.

"Do you know anybody else flying back?" Nok quickly asked.

Through summer's end, more suitcases arrived at the restaurant, with Nee's help. Nok no longer felt ashamed serving food below her expectations. Still, with what they paid the students for each bag, costs at the restaurant doubled. Many nights, Nok couldn't sleep. While Maru snored, she lay there and tortured herself thinking about how she'd ever gotten into this situation.

□ □ □

She had met Maru some years before, in 1972, when she was hired as a grad student trainee at the Tokyo architecture firm where Maru was a senior draftsman. They married before her visa expired.

Few companies would hire her, a non-Japanese and a woman, after her program ended. Maru, never quite suited for desk work, also wanted a way out of architecture. So they moved to Yokohama and with the small sum left to him by his father opened Erawan, the only Thai restaurant in the area, as far as they knew.

That year, before Thailand's tourism boom, most Japanese had yet to dust their feet with the beach sands of Koh Phangan or walk across fairways carved into valleys where their forefathers had succumbed to malaria and Allied bombing raids. Passersby, if they stopped at all, peered into the windows with shaded eyes before stepping back. The restaurant survived on the few who didn't, and the shifting mass of Thais—students, immigrant workers, and women whose occupation they left unasked.

Late afternoons, Nok's favorite time of the day, students came by after classes. She lingered in the dining room and listened to them douse each other with Thai curse words and exchange nam-nao soap operas on static-scarred VHS tapes.

Maru watched the shows with her. If he didn't understand what was being said, he could guess it by the actors' disregard for subtlety. The students loved it when Maru updated them on a storyline. They asked with wide smiles, "Big Brother Maru, did you like what happened in the *House of Golden Sand* finale?"

There were months when they scraped by, their profit margins as fine and thin as their slivered shallots, but Nok resisted the thought of giving up the restaurant. Where else could her people go to taste this food? What would she do without them here?

□ □ □

"Khun Nok, did prices on the menu jump again?" Khun Chahtchai said one morning. "And the hor mok tastes different to me. It has a strange saltiness, a sharper kind, and it's less fragrant than usual."

Nok had said the same thing to Maru the night before. Student travel delays that week meant that they were down to the last jar of kapi. They'd resorted to diluting it with pulverized fishmeal and heaps of salt.

"We've had a problem with getting ingredients and had to adjust. I'm sorry if it's a complete failure. Consider this one on us."

"No, it's actually delicious in a new way. But you'll have what you need soon?"

"Yes, our new supplier should get their act together by the end of the month."

"Well, let me know if I can help in any way. I have associates who can probably get you anything you want."

"Thank you, but we wouldn't want to trouble you."

"It would be no bother. We have to help each other, Khun Nok, especially here."

Nok knew what he meant by *here*. She nodded as she clasped her hands to thank him for the thought and then returned to the kitchen to check on a pot of seafood stock for tom yum goong.

Maru cleared the table after Khun Chahtchai had left. He held up the blue fan of thousand-yen bills left as tip.

"What did you say to him?"

She shrugged. Maru, always prideful, would have chided her for revealing their situation to an outsider. She put the money in her pocket and told him the grease bins needed to be emptied.

◻ ◻ ◻

When asked why she had chosen the name Erawan for the restaurant, Nok talked of how traders brought the elephant god to Thailand from India by way of the Khmer empire. Erawan stood as large as a mountain and had thirty-three heads, each with seven tusks. The god Indra rode him into wars against demons, but in peaceful times, Erawan nourished the world by drawing water to the sky and returning it as rain. The story delighted customers, but the real reason Nok chose Erawan was that she had been to a Thai restaurant with the same name while visiting cousins in Los Angeles. She learned about the myth only after Maru found it in a Japanese guidebook. Eh-rah-wun, he said, the same way the local customers did.

She used to interrogate Maru about why he married her instead of a Japanese woman. Maru shook his head and mentioned love in a blur of words, maybe thinking it was what she wanted to hear. He didn't realize that she was asking him to accept blame: for his family's treating her only with closemouthed politeness, for confused department store clerks' apologetic bowing and slowed words, her fluent Japanese secondary to the fact of her darker skin—the color of delicious pad see-ew noodles, as Maru had put it.

Those early years in Japan, Nok called Bangkok every night. She asked Nee about their mother's diabetes and visits to the doctor. At some point, Nok would notice her own voice faltering, a signal that tears were brimming at the corners of her eyes, her lips tucked in, the way she had often seen them in the mirror in the middle of a cry.

"Mother is so lucky to have you. I'm here, useless," Nok said.

"Are you in one of your moods again?"

Nee reminded her of the reasons. Maru. Perfectly surfaced asphalt roads and supermarkets selling foods unvisited by orchestral flies. When Nok and Maru had children, they would never have to wade through a flooded city to get to school or stop their cars to let armored trucks pass on their way to an appointed coup. Their children would be Japanese and Thai and have a clean, ample chance to be the better versions of both.

Nee didn't know Nok's other reason: she didn't want the burden of choosing to stay in Bangkok. Nok would have had to answer to her duties as eldest child and devoted herself to the care of her elderly parents. Her acceptance into the graduate program in Tokyo gave her an out. After her father passed away, and with Nee inclined to take charge, Nok felt she had leeway to shrug off her karmic balance sheet. She loosened the grip that had held her and flew off to a new, separate life. Nee would take her place.

Nok now knew that while Japan let in foreigners, it was only by so much. After years spent circling an invisible fortress, thinking that if she searched hard enough, she would uncover a way inside, she had realized that her place would always be across the moat. She didn't know if she'd ever have children here.

□ □ □

Deeper into the semester, fewer students made the trip from Bangkok. The importer's documents should have gone through, letting them buy all the dried chilies and canned quail eggs they needed. But there were new delays.

"What do you mean it will be another month?" Maru yelled into the phone.

Nok looked in the pantry and regretted having thought it safe to use up the good fish sauce. She mixed what was left with the most pungent shottsuru she could find. If all else failed, she knew Nee would rather have her sink all her pots in the bay than further desecrate their mother's recipes. Thankfully, no one who'd tasted her mother's dishes was there to taste what she was making.

"Your sour curry. Did you change the recipe?" asked Khun Chahtchai after a sip.

Nok clasped hands at her chin and asked for forgiveness.

"We had to use Japanese fish sauce. It's all we have right now."

"Actually, it's the sourness that's different."

"We're also low on tamarind paste. I'm so sorry for such an abomination."

"Still having trouble with the importer?"

"It'll be yet another month, they said, but we don't know for sure."

"All right, this is getting serious. Do you want me to help?"

Nok checked to see that Maru was safely back in the kitchen. She nodded.

Khun Chahtchai got up from the table and knocked on the window. A middle-aged man in a gray suit appeared from a parked sedan. His pale face, wide and pockmarked, floated in like the moon.

"Khun Nok, this is Gahn. You can tell him what you need."

"If it's not too much trouble," Nok said, and made a list on a notepad.

Gahn read it and chuckled.

"This? Trouble?"

Nok was hopeful, but she was also used to men from her country talking big and not doing much. That night, she scanned the papers, circling housekeeping or office cleaning jobs for herself and draftsman positions for Maru. She imagined what she would tell Nee: that the restaurant was doing well enough, but they had decided to close it because they missed architecture too much.

One morning not a week later, Gahn knocked on the restaurant window. Maru went with him to the van parked outside. It took those two men five trips to carry in the boxes. There were so many, they had to stack some in the bathroom.

"How much do we owe Khun Chahtchai?" Nok asked Gahn.

"Him, nothing. But how about a glass of olieng for me?"

□   □   □

Khun Chahtchai's supply chain lasted as long as it took for the import licenses to clear. Subsequent shipments arrived via a deliveryman wearing a sweaty hachimaki around his forehead as he pushed a handcart from the supplier's truck to the door.

To atone for her subterfuge, Nok came up with new specials—curried banana flowers, lime-drenched seafood salads with fresh fish roe. She started making for Japanese guests desserts that had been offered only on a secret menu to Thai students, meant to ward off homesickness. She perfumed coconut milk with pandan leaves. Customers' eyes widened when they held the bowl to their nose and smelled sun-warmed fields.

"We're in your debt," she said to Khun Chahtchai. He waved his hands in front of him before she could say more.

"Khun Nok, you and I are not strangers. This is what we people do. And your dishes are treasures that must be protected."

"I'm only cooking my mother's recipes. She'd be mad at me for ruining them."

"She'd be proud to know her daughter is more than worthy."

Nok tried to dismiss Khun Chahtchai's commendations as flattery, but it felt better to see them as earned praise from an elder. She looked forward to his visits even more than those of the students. When he came for his early lunch every week, she made sure to be extra mindful in the kitchen to deserve his compliments.

Khun Chahtchai told her that he had chosen to retire in Japan because his most fruitful business investments had been made here. He had grown up in the Ayutthaya countryside, not far from where her father had, it turned out, and had worked his hardest to defy his birth-given destinies: a lifetime bent over, calves muddied, hands clutching stalks of rice, or, at best, trapped in decade-long waits for minor promotions as a guardian of civil office forms. She wanted to know more about his life but didn't feel it appropriate to pry further. Sometimes, his eyes drew closed as he chewed, and she left him to that ceremonial state—serene and monklike, her food necessary.

That same year, with the restaurant saved, she and Maru moved to a larger flat in the Aoba Ward, not far down the Blue Line. The first day there, they celebrated in their new living room by walking side by side, arms and bodies stretched as far as they could, until they sailed into the opposite wall. She took photos, so that Nee would see her and Maru standing on the sliver of a balcony, similar beige-colored buildings behind them. On the street, schoolchildren shuffled homeward in orderly clusters under the curved sag of telephone lines that carried voices across the sea.

◻ ◻ ◻

At first, Nok thought the students were horsing around. Maru was taking orders at a table and she was deveining shrimp at the counter when one of them got up and walked over to Khun Chahtchai, who had arrived later than usual for his lunch and was still finishing off a bowl of noodles. The student stood over the older man and asked for his name. Khun Chahtchai didn't tell him and instead asked the student to go back to his own table.

"It's almost October," the student said, and then leaned over Khun Chahtchai's bowl and curdled a ball of spit into it. Gahn, after seeing what had happened through the window, rushed in, fists clenched. The student's friends started yelling about who was tougher. Everyone except the lone table of horrified Japanese customers rose to their feet.

"You water buffalo, sit back down right now," yelled Gahn.

"You think we're afraid of you? You think you can sit here and scarf down your food?"

Maru stepped in and begged for calm, exerting his authority with deep bows in every direction.

"We don't want any trouble! Please!"

Khun Chahtchai got up and leafed through his wallet.

"Khun Nok, Khun Maru. I apologize for the disturbance. The kuay tiew was very delicious."

After Khun Chahtchai and Gahn left, the students returned to their seats. Nok stood fuming.

"What happened? Do you guys think this is a Muay Thai ring?"

"Sorry, Sister Nok," a student said. "We didn't meant any disrespect, but it's him, we're sure of it. It's the colonel."

◻ ◻ ◻

The colonel. She had nearly thought he was a myth.

When it happened in 1973, she was already in Tokyo. When it happened again, three Octobers later, she and Maru and had just opened Erawan, and Nee was studying nursing at Thamassat. Nok knew Nee would be at protests against the field marshal's return from exile. Nee had told her over the phone how she had fallen for one of the leaders of the campus activist groups and that she would be joining him at the university rallies. Nok told herself that she couldn't have stopped her sister. Nee took after their mother, who, pretending to sell fruits on the street, had monitored Japanese troops for the Thai resistance. After the war, Thais would no longer need foreigners to hold guns to their country. Prime ministers and parliaments lasted as long as afternoon rains.

At that time, the Yokohama National students at her restaurant had begun to follow a new soap opera, with many villains, no VHS tapes needed. There were rumors of paramilitaries and armed scouts trucked in from the border. Talk of CIA involvement steamed over plates of basil chicken.

Nok couldn't say where she was or what she was doing when the 1976 crackdown happened. She was probably, as usual, letting days lap against her life. She got up early in the morning to prepare broths and curry pastes. She helped Maru haul trash bags to the curb and sweep the sidewalk. At the old flat, they made love, their bodies framed by the padded mattress that they would fold away in the morning. She showered before bed, and then sometime too soon after, the alarm clock would wake her to open the restaurant again. How could she be expected to do anything else?

□ □ □

Later that week, the students who had confronted Khun Chahtchai returned with proof that he was who they'd said he was. They showed Nok a Xeroxed newspaper photo of a uniformed man with an eye shut and an elbow steadied on a campus wall. The arm ended in a pistol. The gray-haired man firing it looked like the one she had known to compliment her on her broth.

He was Khun Chahtchai. He was the colonel, the man responsible for training and organizing the paramilitaries who'd joined that morning attack on the football field, seven years ago. He'd been exiled after the coups and countercoups that followed. He was said to have left the country with a good deal of offshore money, origins unknown.

Nee was alive, though, wasn't she? Was there any reason to be personally upset at Khun Chahtchai now? Yet Nok also knew that Nee had escaped a horrific fate only by luck, or destiny, or karmic currents like the one that eventually brought the colonel to savor meals in Japan at a restaurant owned by her sister, of all people, of all places.

Khun Chahtchai didn't come back. Instead, in the following months, Gahn returned every other week, late in the morning, before other customers arrived, with a stack of steel bento boxes. Maru took them to the kitchen and lined them up at the prep table for Nok to fill, the orders written in marker on the lids. Most of the time, she didn't even see

Gahn. He waited outside, sipping his customary olieng, until Maru came out to the car with an armful of meals. When Nok went out to the car to talk to him, he bowed to her with clasped hands and complimented her on the last batch of dishes. She made no inquiries about his boss.

"Aroy-mahk," he would say, and pat his belly, before walking back to the driver's side with the assured gait of a former soldier.

One day Gahn showed up late, close to noon. A student, the very woman who had first delivered suitcases to the restaurant that summer of need, stepped out to yell after him, "Go serve your murderous master, you tailless animal!"

Then she looked at Nok with accusing eyes.

□ □ □

When she was young, her mother had taught her to never forget generosity. If you did, in the afterlife, you were destined to become an abominable creature her mother claimed to have seen in her youth. It stood as tall as palm trees. Out of a mouth as small as a needle's eye, it whistled its eternal torment. When she grew older, the threat no longer worked.

"He's not Pol Pot or Idi Amin, but do you think cooking for him is on the same side of disturbing?" asked Maru.

"Please go to sleep."

"I mean, you're okay with it?"

"He was good to us, remember."

"I know, I know. It still feels strange, though. At least, to me."

Maru didn't know that Nok had felt unwelcome in her own restaurant, even when no one else was around. She regretted not having let it close that summer, although that would have killed them financially.

On subway rides, she flipped through Japanese women's magazines picked up at the station kiosk, as if there, between the how-to pictorials of women joyfully baking danishes and making seaweed soup, she would find a solution for this exact predicament.

Nee called very late one night.

"What's the matter? Is everything all right?" Nok asked.

"Did you think because you're over there I wouldn't find out?"

Nok could have admitted it. She had counted on Sagami Bay and, beyond that, the long fractured curve of the archipelago and its flowering of islets, and then the sea, vast and all-dissolving, to protect her.

"Is it true?" asked Nee. "And with Mother's recipes?"

□   □   □

What happens when a woman does something unforgivable? That woman might set out to repair her wrongs.

Nok told Gahn that she wouldn't be making food for his boss anymore. He laid crisp bills on his empty glass for that last order and drove off. To whomever of the students would listen, Nok offered her deepest apologies. She hadn't known who the colonel was. She was only a cook, and she'd understand if they refused her food. Most eventually came back.

With Nee, she didn't know what to do. Nok called and began speaking as soon as Nee picked up the phone. Whether Nee listened or not, she couldn't tell. Nok spoke into a long, hollow silence, the loudest sound she'd ever heard, and after a while, the dial tone came on. She took it for granted that, in Thai, to say sorry was to ask for punishment that wouldn't ordinarily be meted out.

The next day Nok called, and Nee didn't answer. The next week Nok also called, and again Nee didn't answer. Things were busy at the restaurant, and so Nok resolved to wait for a month and let Nee calm down before calling again. She came up with new specials for the Thai students' version of the menu. She rearranged the kitchen equipment and tools, to the annoyance of Maru, who couldn't find what he needed anymore.

When it was time, she picked up the receiver and dialed. As if she were there in Krungthep, she could hear the phones ringing in their house, first in the back room where they used to eat meals at a circular table overlooked by a framed photo of their father, and also upstairs in the hallway between their bedroom and their mother's, the phone and a notepad the lone occupants of a small side table. Nee didn't pick up.

During their grade school breaks, she and Nee used to stay at their grandmother's house. The water out in the provinces was cleaner than in Krungthep, and they spent many afternoons swimming in the nearby canal. It was there that they visited the nagas. They would duck underwater for as long as they could and come up to talk about the wonders they'd seen in the serpentine world below their kicking feet. They told each other of the giant snakes who came to greet them at a great city built of gold and jewels, and how the nagas would let their guests ride on their outspread hoods. Nee could stay under for longer than Nok could and always had more to say. Nee asked Nok if she had met the Cobra Prince with the chariot pulled behind a giant school of catfish or if Nok had visited the cave where eels played music by plucking their stretched bodies. Nok affirmed that of course she'd seen these things, days ago, but wanted her sister to see them for herself. Then Nok lifted herself onto the steps, saying that she was sick of swimming.

One time, Nee came up from a dive to find Nok teary-faced. Nok had been treading water and watching the cranes land in the nearby fields, afraid to move. Her sister had been gone for so long. She had called out

Nee's name and nothing answered her but the stray dogs across the bank. The next minute went by, and then another. She really thought she was never going to see Nee again. "That's nonsense. I'll always come right back," Nee promised her.

Did Nee really mean it? Nok held the phone closer to her ear. She heard it ring for the fifteenth time, and then a voice cut her off in Japanese to say that the call couldn't be completed.

She hung up the phone and turned off the lights. She lay down next to Maru, who was already asleep, and listened to herself breathe in the immense dark—awake and alone.

FLIGHT

U p they woke from their blue-lit sleep to find their houses in shards. Stunned by the brightness, they cried out of pain they would come to know as hunger. Crying was all they could do, and it seemed that nobody would answer their pleas, until large shadows landed over them to drop gifts into their waiting mouths. They tasted what they would all their lives go on to seek. Wet bits slid down their throats and satisfied their bellies. Their knowledge of this mysterious place came through whatever they tasted: the slick limbs of frogs, still-writhing bugs, the head of a minnow.

The large shadows hunted in the wide watery fields beyond the colony. Throughout the searing day, they followed the wake of creatures larger than themselves. They waited patiently near gray, horned behemoths at rest in the water, and sometimes even stood on the expansive territory of those behemoths' bodies to pick off small snacks for themselves. The real bounty came when the behemoths roamed. Wherever the behemoths stepped, smaller creatures scattered out of the way. It took only a quick lunge with a ready beak to capture those small creatures. For the winged hunters, their prey's final dance in their grasp satisfied the overwhelming commands they felt they had to answer. These commands were simple: seek enough creatures to feed the young and themselves, and protect the young from harm.

The sole tasks of the young were to eat and plead. When they felt the approach of their parents, they made sure to cry even louder. They opened their mouths and waited to feast. When they grew strong enough, they learned to knock over their brothers and sisters when their parents returned, and in turn they felt the slaps of their siblings' wings.

There were many more younglings in the colony's other nests. They all watched for their parents, and they also watched for the villains they knew they had to fear. Watching a snake winding up a branch, they cried louder than when they were hungry. They shook with horror when they looked up to see larger birds with humongous wings circling the colony. They quieted when their parents managed to chase away the villain or when some other youngling had been taken to appease the villain's hunger.

Then they quickly returned to their tasks. High above the ground, they ate to grow larger than the others. They ate to become larger than they were, so their wings could take them through the air. The unlucky ones fell off the tree and lay crying until they no longer cried, or never made it back from those early attempts to explore farther from the colony. Along the high grass, they stalked crickets while being stalked themselves. They didn't see the pair of eyes floating closer and closer. The unlucky paid dearly.

The rest grew strong enough to join their parents and uncles and aunties in the fields. They waded for their own food, stepping across the shallows silently. Their chests filled, enlarged. Their hearts ballooned with the reach of their white wings.

They now easily took flight on their own, gliding across the green, watery fields. They flew where they thought they could hunt, and an expedition could take them out of sight of the colony. They knew, though, to turn when they neared the hazy, greenless lands. There were no gray behemoths there, only strange, rocky outcrops and small mountains and fast-roving animals that smeared them bloody against hard strips of flat land. This was the territory of the wingless giants. The winged knew to keep away from them. The giants usually didn't pay attention to the winged—only a small group came to walk the fields for days, their backs bent over—but sometimes the giants revealed stringy shapes that flung fast, piercing rocks skyward. The unlucky dropped out of the air and paid dearly.

The lucky stayed in these fields for as long as they needed. When the air thickened, the hard rain would come. Many in the colony lifted and flew north, where they wouldn't be battered and awash in the trees. Some stuck around and took their chances. They watched the giants pluck from the fields. They followed the gray behemoths and ate their fill of smaller creatures.

□ □ □

The winged who went north returned after the rains had lessened. They didn't always come back but usually they did, finding comfort in the familiar squares of watery fields.

Those who had been younglings were now old enough to have younglings of their own. The males danced with their heads and necks

and showed off their feathers. They clapped their beaks together amo-
rously to those they were wooing. They pretended to shoo off any who
seemed interested, but it was only a ruse, so that they could pretend to
be stronger and more attractive than they actually were. Slowly, half
convinced by the other's bluff, they approached and gently picked at
each other's feathers with their beaks. When they finally reached
agreement on their relationship status, they built their homes.

They looked for trees like the ones they'd cried from as younglings.
If they found an old nest that suited them, they made repairs, and if
they found none to their liking, they went into a frenzy of construction. Out across the fields they flew to steal back twigs and strips of
hardy grass, and with those pieces they wove the beginnings of their
domestic future.

They knew the routine. Once their young arrived, encased in delicate orbs, they stood guard and launched themselves furiously at any
encroaching danger—the usual snakes and squirrels and larger birds,
but now also new furry animals with pitiless eyes and pointed ears that
roamed from the hardlands.

When sunlight felt like fire, they spread their wings to give shade.
When it rained, they covered their precious orbs with their bodies, to
keep their future warm.

After their young hatched, they took turns gliding out to find food
and returning with beakfuls to satisfy the ceaseless, noisy hunger. As
they flew, they noticed that the air under their wings felt different
from the year before. The winds were heavier and hotter. Their breath
vaguely smelled of stone.

They flew farther than their parents did to find enough to feed
their young. They speared fewer frogs, and the schools of minnows
weren't as thick. They flew home, tired, with less in their beaks, and
then rushed off to find more. There were fewer gray behemoths that

they could follow—the ones that were around were old and barely moved.

They kept to their routine. The young—those who lived—grew larger, as they themselves had once grown, and attempted flight, as they had. Those who succeeded left the fields for the north with them when the air began to steam thick in their beaks.

Later, when the wingless giants again began to group in the fields, they weren't as numerous as in previous times. Yet the hardlands seemed closer than it had been before.

□ □ □

Time after time, the colony left and returned. They found new mates or resorted to old ones. They discovered nests they could repair, or they built a new home for their future young. They hunted. They ate. They mated. They watched over their precious young. They hunted. They fed gaping mouths. They saw the young grow; they saw the young die.

Some didn't come back to where they'd grown. They stayed at the fields where they'd found refuge, or they chose to fly elsewhere.

Those who did return recognized the colony where it stood—the same tree with widespread branches, the same cluster of spiky grass that surrounded it. The tree, though, stood in a field smaller than it had been in the times before. Old nests, no longer repaired, had fallen from the trees. The leaves didn't look as green.

They found only a few gray behemoths and couple of wingless giants wandering the fields. The frogs tasted different, and so did the minnows. The hardlands seemed closer than it had been before.

Then they fled again when the air thickened, and the fields began to steam.

Many didn't return in the season that followed. Those who did joined with those who'd stayed. They went about their business, following the same commands as their ancestors. Where they could find trees, they built nests out of twigs and dried grass and mysterious shapes that let light through. They mated and fed their young. Their young grew. Their young died.

They hunted in new waterways that flowed alongside hot, flat strips of land carrying fast-moving, large-eyed creatures. Many no longer remembered the taste of grasshoppers, once so plentiful. They dissolved away their fondness for field mice. Instead, they hunted fatter, flight-ready versions of the water bugs they'd known. They lunged at mice-like creatures with far longer tails—at least, those that had not yet grown as large as they were and could strike back with sharp teeth. If their hunt yielded little, they soared through the sky and landed at fresh rotten mounds and tore away at bouncy white rectangles the giants had left behind, to get at the nourishing bits that remained inside.

Fresh rocky outcroppings rose where there once had been wet fields. Sometimes, mountains spired higher than they could fly.

IMPASSE

Nee had never seen this part of Krungthep so empty. Only sparrows dared to make noise.

Even this far out from the happenings in the old city, few private cars braved the roads. Most of the shops along Petchburi had closed, their metal shutters pulled across or down. Outside the few that had stayed open, shopkeepers sat idle, watching for trouble and probably wondering whether their decision had been wise. The streets otherwise looked the way they did any day, save for the military jeeps guarding major intersections.

All week, the radio stations had been broadcasting either a dead monotone or speeches that might as well not have been made, for the emptiness of their words. Don't join the rallies. Trust the council in charge. Nee wasn't surprised when she heard that the men with guns who had taken power last year were now backing away from their promises. For the good of the country, the general's tenure as PM wouldn't be temporary, they said. Hundreds of thousands responded by flooding the streets and holding rallies in Sanam Luang, despite warnings for law-abiding citizens to stay home. Nee was one of those who didn't comply, although she wasn't headed to the protests. She was going to get to the hospital, because she had promised that she would.

All she had taken with her was a small purse and an umbrella to shield herself from the sun. No buses were running, and any taxi would have asked for more than she could pay. A blister threatened to ripen on one heel; even her good walking sandals had betrayed her. If anyone thought it fine to shoot a middle-aged woman walking in discomfort, let them. It wasn't her first time staring down rifles.

Still, she shuddered when some shophouse resident slammed window bars shut. A darting stray dog startled her. She felt her arms and legs move in spastic jerks, every muscle electrified. She breathed in quick, shallow gulps, as if the city was fast running out of air.

The hardest to calm was her mind. Her ears hadn't registered gunfire, but she thought she could hear guns reporting from every direction. The howls and the hurried steps of hundreds sounded out from an invisible place that could only pierce through when the blaring and rumbling of the city fell this silent. She tried her best to ignore a faint voice calling out her name.

She was better steeled by the time she heard the thunderous roar of motorcycle engines behind her. A dozen or more scooters and sport bikes raced past, honking their horns and waving flags, followed by another dozen right behind them. One rider came to a stop at the curb and with an apologetic bow said, "Excuse me, auntie," before leaping from his motorbike to spray paint STOP THE BARBARISM, YOU DE-SPICABLE WATER LIZARDS on a wall and then sprint back to rejoin his group.

Although she couldn't see the man's face through the helmet, she could tell from the energetic, unconsidered movements of his body that he was young, probably in upper secondary school or the first years of university. She thought she'd glimpsed in him a secreted gentleness that she had known and never found again, and as the faceless, nameless man sped away, she couldn't help but ask the deities of the land and heavens to keep him safe.

Refreshed terrors from sixteen years ago threatened to flood her mind. Feeling weak at the knees, she staggered for another block before leaning on a telephone booth to regain her breath. Through her blouse, she clutched the monk's amulet her late mother had given her, and although she couldn't say she wholly believed it to endow her with a protective halo, she found comfort feeling its triangular shape. She wouldn't turn back, Nee told herself. She'd fled one too many times.

A low tremor pushed aside the quieted air. The sidewalk trembled under her heels. A giant green beast lumbered at the intersection and then rolled forward. Through its skin of armor, she could see young men's faces in the shadowy hold of its belly. The muzzle end of rifles swayed in front of them. She wanted to call out and tell those faces to please turn back, they need not stain their better karma, but she kept her mouth shut and kept walking. Nobody shot her.

An hour later, she arrived at the hospital. The pharmacist thankfully on duty at the counter read the physician's notes inside Khun Pehn's file and, mistaking Nee for a daughter, said, "Your mother's canceled her last three appointments. The doctor needs to know whether the medication has been effective. Can you please remind her to come in?"

◻ ◻ ◻

"Hold on. Coming," Pehn hollered to the door, as she turned toward the chairback to push herself up. She would have added that rude little buzzer to the list of things to address with management were it not that she sometimes did remove the hearing aid, and a knock wouldn't register any louder than a sparrow's sneeze.

Standing, she became desperately aware of the messiness of the place. The maids wouldn't arrive for another few days. She thought she could feel tiny, pebbly specks under her bare feet. Especially around the TV and the stereo speakers, enough dust would soon settle for her to be able to carve a stark line with a pinkie. Not that she should worry about making an impression with Nee, but one ought to have standards, no matter the visitor. *A woman your age will benefit from a smaller place with more manageable upkeep,* they'd said. But with the house, if a room hadn't been to her liking she could quickly find refuge in some other, while the offending room was put in order by her live-in maids. Now she had to wait for a crew of three migrant workers and their supervisor to arrive twice a week, as scheduled by the company Nee had helped her hire. Without many of her old things around the house, there was only more bare surface for more dust to colonize.

There was one thing to be thankful for: no great pain shot up her legs as she shuffled across the room. What would she have done without the glucosamine pills her bridge partners had told her about and that she had gotten her son to ship to her from the States? So what if her son had read somewhere that the medical evidence was suspect and initially refused to, in his words, waste her money and his time on pharmaceutical sorcery? It made no difference what the scientists said. How an old woman felt about her physical misery probably never figured into their graphs and charts. All she knew was that her knees felt like they'd been filled with river stones, and moving a few leg muscles, walking across the condo, felt as if she'd resumed some ancient forward trajectory long petrified.

She should be thankful that she still had her wits. For her sharpness at the card tables, someone had anointed her the Invincible Sword, after the popular Hong Kong martial arts series, and the name had stuck for more than a decade now. She made them sweat, for sure. Take out the handkerchief and dab your forehead, ladies. Oh, the look on Gaew or Ploy, when they realized they had to throw away their most valuable cards after a squeeze play she'd run. It was all in good fun, them emptying one another's purses and donating winnings to charities, or so it was claimed. The last time she went was a month ago. Their numbers had noticeably thinned in recent years, and every reconvening brought her both joy and melancholy. They'd likely soon be seeing one another again at yet another temple, dressed in black and lined up to toss fragrant woods into the pyre. She'd added two new funeral books to her unfortunate collection just this year, and they were only partway through 1992.

"Almost there," she said, nearer to the door. What a pity, what a shame, she muttered in her head, addressing the universe.

□ □ □

For Nee, stepping into Khun Pehn's condo always felt like walking into an architectural magazine spread, with the white-and-gray marble floor tiles blindingly bright under the light-colored furnishings, the pillowy chalk-hued sectional sofa and the glass-top coffee table made from ebony, and the pale cowhide spread out in a small mound, as if a gigantic animal had collapsed and sunk into the floor. There were few things on the shelves and fewer on the credenza. The one piece of furniture that somehow breached this sensibility was found in one corner of the living room: a somewhat faded and tattered green velvet chair that seemed to have been left behind from another century. It was where Nee knew Khun Pehn liked to listen to the the traffic and news radio and, judging from the half-full teacup on a side table, also where she had gotten up to answer the door.

Nee clasped her hands into a wai and bowed, the bag dangling against her chest.

"They wanted you to come in, ma'am."

Khun Pehn didn't acknowledge the secondhand request. "I hope it wasn't too bad out there, my dear," she said.

"The city was just a little quieter, that's all."

Khun Pehn was wearing a short-sleeved house dress with tan floral prints that would have looked dowdy on any other tenant her age. She reached into her dress pocket and retrieved a wedge of folded red bills.

"Here's something for your trouble."

"Please, no, Khun Pehn. I was passing through that part of the city anyway."

"Well, I can't have you leave empty-handed or empty-stomached. You'll stay for some sweets and tea, won't you? Mrs. Reinhardt made a marvelous meringue cake."

"I really should get back to the office, ma'am. I bet I have a hundred tenant messages waiting for me."

"Those messages can wait. Rather than get into fisticuffs with an old lady, I suggest you reconsider."

Nee knew better than to say no again. This was the one unit in the building where she was guaranteed to arrive at least two or three times every week, be it because of slow drains or audacious ants or the occasional promise of a tasty gift brought back from a trip to the provinces. There was the time Nee declined a second tray of coconut custard brought from Hua Hin by one of Khun Pehn's bushy-haired card shark friends, and Khun Pehn went to the door and locked it, telling Nee that she was not to leave until she agreed to the offer.

"One slice, ma'am," Nee said now, an index finger raised.

"Wise choice. Wait here."

As her eyes followed Khun Pehn down the long corridor to the kitchen, past bedrooms once reserved for beloved pets, now empty because Khun Pehn feared new animals would outlive her and have nobody to care for them, Nee thought of her one-room flat, a fraction of the space of this condo. Her windows certainly didn't give onto a city seemingly constructed in miniature. The neighbors had decided to open a dry-cleaning business, and racks of plastic-shrouded customers' clothes now crowded half the street in front of her building. There were noises of all kinds: megaphone announcements from vegetable-hawking trucks, other neighbors yelling for their dogs to come back in, engine sputter from the scooters making delivery rounds. The pristine noiselessness in Khun Pehn's apartment always overwhelmed her.

A sharp squeal cut through the calm. Nee's immediate thought was that Khun Pehn had gotten herself a bird, maybe one of those colorful Amazonian specimens she'd seen on TV, but the sound had come from a small black box with knobs and dials.

"All morning, this voice," said Khun Pehn, returning with a plated cake in hand. "It very much sums up what's happening right now, don't you think?"

◻ ◻ ◻

Pehn had first learned that there might be something truly wrong the night before when Urai called and told her to stay put in her building the next day. Pehn didn't think too much of her friend's warning.

Everyone had heard a rumor from someone who had an uncle or brother who was an officer of some sort. Troops were being trucked in from the provinces. There was going to be a crackdown on the protests, some were saying. There was a new coup in the works to upturn last year's coup, said others. What did it matter? She'd survived more than a handful of national upheavals, and she guessed that, once again, nobody knew anything. It was late, and she had a doctor's appointment the next day that she was going to cancel.

Then she woke to the sound of children playing in the hallway outside. Even if schools hadn't announced delays for the opening of the term, parents weren't going to send their kids out there. But what could be done for an old lady who'd waited too long to refill her prescriptions at the hospital? It wasn't as if she could go to the pharmacy a few sois over for the kinds of medicine she needed.

Thank the deities for Nee. The least that could be offered to her was this slice of cake and a fresh cup of tea, and perhaps later that small billfold would find its way into Nee's unwatched purse. Nee would later return it, as she had always done. This back-and-forth had become a ritual of sorts. At this age, a love for repetitive, childlike games returned anew.

"What do you think?" Pehn asked.

"It's very delicious, ma'am. Mrs. Reinhardt should open a bakery."

Pehn thought of Mrs. Reinhardt in the hallway late that morning. Pehn had invited her in, but Mrs. Reinhardt needed to watch her grandchild, who was among the children happily kicking a toy ball up and down the length of the floor.

"Would you like cake?" Mrs. Reinhardt had asked her.

"You know I won't say no to a piece," Pehn replied.

"No, I mean a whole one, Madame Pehn. I can't stop baking when I'm nervous, and I've already made three cakes since I got up."

Pehn noticed the anxious terror peeking from behind the woman's friendly eyes. The farangs scared so easily, Pehn thought, for people who could book themselves a flight tomorrow and leave this all behind. What an exciting episode they'd have to tell their friends, of their near peril in the turbulent East.

Was Sammy like these farangs who flitted about wherever they liked? She used to think her son would tire of all the moving and hopping country to country, and finally come home or at least find a nice place to stay put, but she could still count on every few years receiving in the mail photos he'd taken in a new city, the most perfect place for him, he'd say yet again. Whatever was in his head? For so long, she had thought he stayed away from Krungthep out of anger and resentment toward her and Apirak, inevitable considering the mess they'd made of his youth. She thought she'd given him everything he needed to overcome whatever damage they had inflicted, but he still didn't have the wherewithal to do better for himself. Instead, he appeared to derive pleasure from fouling up, and it was this sick lust for self-punishment, she had long been certain, that most moved her son. She had thought to offer to pay someone for lifelong sessions of whipping and yelling, if suffering was all he really wanted.

How mistaken she had been. Theirs was no exceptional story, she realized, only the one of so many mothers and sons, where love and affection alternated with distrust and wariness. *Why did you abandon me?* he seemed to cry, still reaching for her. *Why have you abandoned me?* she'd respond in her way, grasping for him. Such a lamentable cycle that had cost them both dearly, especially him, her poor boy. She wondered every day if she had done everything she could to extract him from it.

"Have you noticed, Nee, that the photo on that wall is different? My son, Sammy, recently sent it to me, and so into the frame it went, replacing the one he last sent. I don't know why he only sends me the photos that will trouble me. The prettier, much more pleasant ones he takes for advertisement clients he never shows."

Her gaze shifted Nee's to the photo on the wall.

"I haven't told you very much about him, have I? Well, the next time he's here, I'll make sure that you two meet."

□   □   □

Nee did notice that the photo on the wall had been changed. The previous one had been of a brick building in New York. She recognized that city right away, as if it were a scene from a movie she had seen in her youth. A few of its windowpanes had either broken or fallen off, and the pavement outside was strewn with loose pieces of masonry rubble. In the entrance doorway, up one short flight of the front stairs, a blond-wigged woman who looked to be in her seventies or eighties stood half emerged, draped in a tattered fur coat. Nee couldn't tell if the woman had meant to express displeasure or surprise on finding herself captured and fixed on film by a stranger ambushing outside the door, or if her scowl had been no more than circumstantial permanence. Nee tried to imagine herself in this strange woman's head. On a different day, or likely, a different decade, the woman might've felt flattered that someone, out of the blue, would want to photograph her. If only the camera could find her when she wasn't a wrinkly-faced thing hesitant to step out into the street, but what could an old woman do but yell at the young man to scram and slam her door shut, all too late?

The newer photograph that replaced the photo of the old woman had also been taken in front of a building. This one was of a single-story shopping center somewhere with palm trees in the distance, where the sun shone brightly enough to reach inside smashed windows to reveal a mess of scattered, unpaired shoes and crumpled cardboard boxes on the ground. There were sooty streaks coming from a storefront next door but the photographer had cut off the view, so that he could bring into frame a policeman in a tan uniform, who stood with a rifle rested on his shoulder, guarding the aftermath. She guessed that this must be in an American city. She'd seen buildings like this in Hollywood movies, but not in this kind of shape. What kind of grievous thing had happened for Americans to attack a shoe store? Why must there be so many men with guns, everywhere?

Nee hadn't kept up with international news. Enough troubles were already making everyone dangerously nervous in Krungthep, and she had avoided looking at the papers, resolving to busy herself with the building. She found repair people for the lobby's HVAC units and made sure the landscapers did a thorough job with the hedges. She scooped up broken-neck sparrows from the grounds, before any tenant noticed. The times that she did glance at the headlines or when a coworker brought up the latest, her undying rage returned and she'd have to step out, either for a long calming walk or a swim in the pool, to keep herself from catching fire from the inside out.

Nok would love for that to happen, wouldn't she? If Nee went berserk or had a breakdown somewhere public, it would only confirm Nok's accusation that she was crazy and unreasonable.

It was unlikely, though, that Nok would ever find out. They hadn't talked in almost ten years, not since Nee had found out about the colonel. At their mother's funeral, they barely glanced at each other. Nee chose to sit at one end of the temple hall and never walked by Nok, who stayed at the other end and flew back to Japan right after the cremation. It was probably for the best. They avoided a scene when there were so many relatives around. Their mother sometimes appeared in a dream to lament what she called their senseless, lingering feud, and

Nee would tell her to stop meddling in the business of the living. Then she'd wake herself up.

Every new year, the phone rang very late at night, and Nee never bothered to get up. It could be one of her friends calling with well wishes, or it could be Nok. It didn't matter either way, she'd tell herself. She'd let the phone ring and ring and ring, until silence was hers again.

□ □ □

Another squeal crackled from the black box on the end table, followed by a high-pitched voice rapid-firing curse words pertaining to the mother of anyone listening. Static hissed for a moment, before a gruff voice returned equally rich insults, with the threat of bullets.

"I bought the CB set a year ago, after the last round of unrest," Pehn said to Nee. "As you know, the TV and radio news aren't going to tell you much of anything. This has a receiver that can pick up most of the police and military channels."

"And what have they been saying, ma'am?"

"You have it backward, my dear. I've found that one can learn so much more from what hasn't been said. For example, I probably don't need to say anything now because you'd already know what I heard."

Worry washed across Nee's face. Pehn feared she had upset the young woman.

"I'm probably wrong," Pehn thought to say. "What does an old woman like me know about what they're really saying?"

"No, ma'am. You're not wrong. It's going to get worse. I've seen it before."

For a while, not a word passed between them. Nee remained where she was at the sofa, looking out the window.

Pehn didn't think it was the scenic skyline that had captured her attention. The young woman was elsewhere, even as she sat here. Nee had said little about herself, and it was only from other staffers that Pehn had learned that Nee had graduated from a famous university in the mid-1970s, which meant there was a good chance she might have taken part in the student protests then. The horrific photos of bodies burned and blackened, bashed and pummeled until their faces seemed like overripe fruits. The young lives extinguished in the grand thoroughfares where they'd gathered.

She remembered great tension and fear all around the country and especially in Krungthep. She wouldn't deny that she'd felt it, too, as one of the many terrified that these students and their fiery passions would upturn everything for the worse and maybe even destroy the society she'd cherished.

It was bound to end in this violent way, she thought then, and in the years after, those killings became a thing that happened further and further from her. After all, her hands weren't involved in hurting anyone. She wouldn't carry any guilt for only having happened to live in a certain city in a particular terrible time. She even felt some vindication when news arrived of the mass killings in Cambodia, only a few hundred kilometers east. Those communists wanted the same fate for her country, she was told.

But was it really vindication when she couldn't shake away the suspicion that those young people had paid too high a price? Need those kids have been sacrificed the way they were, to a game of musical chairs at the Government House? She remembered feeling so afraid of whatever might disturb her beloved Krungthep that she could feel it justifiable that someone's grown child was hanged from a tree as a cheery mob beat his lifeless body with a chair. She had let herself forget that they were sons and daughters. They were young people who cared about their future. Many would have become mothers and fathers themselves.

She wasn't a woman prone to anger and frustration, but one grew old and couldn't help but remember—it was all one did—and many times these past few months, seeing the country again falling into chaos, she couldn't help but think of those students from years ago.

They'd died, and the game of musical chairs kept going anyway. Ramwong dancers old and new—with faces powdered, arms outstretched, and hands curled back—went round and round to never-ending cymbal-clanging songs. When she looked out the window at the spread of this city and the grand dance still in motion, she wondered if she wasn't going mad with shame.

"Would you like to try it?" she said to Nee.

"Pardon me, Khun Pehn?"

"I'm talking about the CB. The squealing voice you heard earlier."

"The voice, ma'am?"

"Yes, they've been calling it Sharpy. All you have to do is to heighten your pitch, maybe with a little raspiness, so that you sound something like a jungle gibbon. That's what I was going after, and then the other CB people were quick to catch on."

"I'm speechless, ma'am."

"No, you are not. Go ahead, push this button with your thumb. There are so many others out there doing the same, we won't be found out. Say anything you want. Like this."

◻ ◻ ◻

Squeeeeeeeeeeeeeaaaaaaaal! Hello, my pretties! What's with the commotion all round the city! Are you celebrating your mama's new lover?

Squeeeeeeeeeeeeeaaaaaaaal! Squeeeeeeeeeeeeeaaaaaaaal! Sharpy had no idea they could dress up water buffalos and make them like look so convincingly like men! It's so hard to tell who's who and what's what!

Squeeeeeeeeeeeeeaaaaaaaal! Sharpy would like to know which witch doctor they've hired to help fill up the Capitol! What choice pickings from all the graveyards! It's a pageant of hell creatures reborn as head-nodding politicians!

Squeeeeeeeeeeeeeaaaaaaaal! Sharpy wants some lucky numbers for the lottery! Maybe Sharpy will pray to the water cannons and make rubbings on the armored trucks! Surely they're there for our good fortune!

Squeeeeeeeeeeeeeaaaaaaaal! It's Sharpy again! Miss me?

"Shut up, Sharpy," barked a voice over the radio. "We will hunt you down! Whatever it takes! We will drag you out to the streets and slap you bloody in the mouth!"

Squeeeeeeeeeeeeeaaaaaaaal! You water lizards!

"You will regret being born, Sharpy! You will regret this day!"

Squeeeeeeeeeeeeeaaaaaaaal! Roger that! Sharpy will talk to you later, my dearest water lizards!

□　□　□

Nee put down the handset and joined Khun Pehn in giggling on the sofa.

"It feels better, doesn't it, Nee?"

"Yes, I think so, ma'am."

"I never would have guessed you to be so expert with expletives. I must be more careful to avoid your wrath."

"I grew up near a market, Khun Pehn. What the hawkers could do with insults rivaled the poetry of Sunthorn Phu."

"And I thought my early schooling at Krungthep's finest institutions served me well. My classmates and I adored cursing each other, mainly because our parents would be so furious if they ever heard us speak so improperly."

They shared another round of giggles. Khun Pehn's laughter reminded Nee of her own mother's, and she wondered if somehow all the women of that generation had been taught to laugh the same way. Had she inherited it too?

Squeeeeeeeeeeeeeaaaaaaaal! Squeeeeeeeeeeeeeaaaaaaaal!

The eruption of taunts from the CB radio returned Nee to the condo tower, where Khun Pehn's eyes had widened. The old woman's pale lips trembled soundlessly.

"What is it, ma'am? What's wrong?"

"There."

Khun Pehn pointed to the window. It was dark out, but enough blue had lingered in the sky for Nee to make out smoke pluming in the distance.

◻ ◻ ◻

They stood watching at the window, even after it had become too dark to see. More squeals, more taunts from the radio, with little apparent effect on the mayhem. More men spoke on the television, more commands for calm, for good citizens to stay off the streets. More plumes appeared before the darkened night veiled them, and then the skyline again looked the same as any other night: a nighttime sea crowded with fishermen's lights. Behind window glass, they couldn't smell smoke. They couldn't hear sirens or shots. The city lived and died another world below.

Nee fell asleep on the sofa, and when she woke again, she found Khun Pehn still there on the green chair, awake.

"Nee, please stay the night. It's too dangerous to try to make it home."

"I don't want to trouble you, Khun Pehn."

"You'll find a bed as good as any in my spare room. It's where my son's supposed to sleep when he visits."

They waddled together down the hallway and turned on the lights in the bedroom.

"You know where the bathroom is. Towels are in that drawer. If you need anything, knock on my door," said Khun Pehn.

"Thank you, ma'am. I'm sure I won't disturb you."

Now she was alone in this room with more photographs by the son. Aside from ones taken at what looked to be a Thai mountain, the majority of them were of strange people in cities she didn't recognize, of shadows and silhouettes beautifully cast on languid afternoons alien to her. In one, Nee could see the shape of the son faintly reflected in the rearview mirror of a taxicab, the ancient bearded driver looking back, midshout. A beautiful woman sat smoking on a rooftop with a Persian cat perched on her shoulders. Children spraying graffiti on a wall. Confetti covering an entire police car. A black-and-white forest of legs on a rainy sidewalk.

Would she wake up inside one of these photos tonight, like she often did after watching foreign movies? She had watched many, back when going to a packed movie theater didn't make her feel feverish with terror. Instead of helping her escape somewhere else, movies trying to scare her or make her laugh only reminded Nee that her life no longer felt real.

By all appearances, it seemed to Nee that she was the only one who had had trouble rejoining the garden of fantastical delights that was Krungthep. Her friends feasted at new restaurants serving sukiyaki and burgers, and followed popular TV serials, and could tell her who sang what on the radio. It didn't take them as long as it did her to look for work. They still worked as nurses. Most eventually found someone to bring home to their parents. Fewer wedding invitations now arrived to her in the mail, replaced by cards announcing kids' birthdays or piano recitals. Every reunion or chance meeting became a traveling exhibit of wallet-sized photos of children, and when conversation drifted beyond their school accomplishments and future careers, she saw the panic in her friends' eyes before their quick turn to familiar shores.

At one of their get-togethers, she complained about never getting enough sleep. "I keep thinking that I'd never wake up because bombs would start falling," she said. It was a quiet admission meant for a friend she felt she could be honest with, but someone else behind her had overheard.

"That used to happen to me, too," said the voice that interrupted them. "I would be up until I heard roosters crowing at sunrise, not a wink of peace. Then you know what I did? I gave in and let myself go back to that night, and I'm curled up on the football field at the university again, and I can feel all my friends around me in the dark. That's where I close my eyes. That's where I fall asleep."

The voice belonged to an acquaintance from another class year, an ontology nurse and mother of two who had also been on campus that October day. The woman grinned and nodded, as if to apologize, and then turned back to her own table.

But wait, she wanted to say to the woman. *What if someone's waiting for me at the football field? What do I say to him?*

□ □ □

Those pills don't go down easily, thought Pehn on the way to her bedroom. What a folly, having to swallow so many, three times a day. Perhaps she wasn't taking them with enough water, but this late, she didn't want to take in too much for fear of being wakened for so many bathroom trips. She remembered comparing pills with her friends, opening the lids of their partitioned boxes to reveal the pharmacological rainbow within, boasting of how many they took. All dead now, she supposed. She'd outlasted most. Better to be the Invincible Sword, all right.

Earlier in the day, though, she had surprised herself with a moment of envy for her old bridge pal, Gaew, relegated to a corner in her son's living room, there to be respectfully handled from bed to chair and back in the course of a day, always the sweetest gummy smile on a face questionably aware of the whys and whats of her routine, or anything, really. Lucky Gaew, not having any cognizance of current events, just happily in and out of the world, one hour reanimated by CDs of old dancehall songs the home care nurse played for her, and then the next back to blankness when the songs ended. Maybe that was as good as could be expected of anyone's last years.

In the bathroom, she plugged the tub drain and turned on the cold water, so that she'd at least have some clean water on hand. The power could go out, and she didn't trust the generators to last for however long this was going to go on. She sat at the edge of the tub as the water gushed. If she closed her eyes, it could sound like a waterfall. There was that country jaunt, a while ago, before Sammy was born. Which waterfall in what province, she couldn't remember. Blankets had been laid, and spiced punch was being ladled into tiny glasses with handles, and someone had hooked up a portable turntable to the car, and the most jubilant piano music soon poured out to jiggle legs and feet that had drifted so peacefully in the current. Apirak pulled her hand so they could get up and join the others wriggling away, and for a while she danced with him, but then she loosened his hands away to swing her limbs and bob her head on her own, her eyes half shut in private ecstasy. What a fine afternoon that was. She'd thought there would be many more like it. She would later ask the name of the record. *Starry Hour*, Clyde Alston, someone said.

It was because of this recollection that she'd taken so long to greet Nee at the door, needing to stop in front of the mirror so as to check whether or not her eyes had noticeably reddened. Tears came too easily, provoked by something or another otherwise dismissible thing, like the few scratchy notes from a song she'd caught playing in her mind. Call her selfish for letting a personal remembrance draw the first drops out of her eyes while her country burst into flames. What tremendously upset her today was what she couldn't remember anymore: Apirak's face, which she never saw again after her return to Krungthep, and which, for many years, she would have paid a good deal to forget. But would she really have? For years she relished, as she now realized her son also likely did, the familiar leisure of self-pity. Forgetting would have starved her of it. Forgetting was the thing one was supposed to do after calamity—not realizing the danger of confusion when someday the living would come to feel like ghosts, and the long departed came back to life when they liked anyway.

Outside, a bang sounded loud enough to rattle the windows. Pehn didn't look up from the hand she'd dipped into the water, to feel it swirling cold between her fingers. She only now realized, having half filled the tub with provisional water, that she had forgotten to take her bedtime bath, a habit from her time in London. A few years back she wouldn't have hesitated to pull the stopper, so she could refill the tub with warmer water. She wouldn't do that now. Before reaching her this water had flown and fallen, swirled through veins of enlivened animals, washed away mountains, and drowned the unlucky. Who was she to waste all this good water for an expiring woman's comforts? A thing inside her chest had stayed her hand from reaching for the stopper, and that thing was instead compelling her to cup a small ocean and raise it to her lips and drink.

HEIRLOOM

Sammy could count this as one of his annual trips to Bangkok to visit his mother, but on this trip, he wouldn't see her. It was his first time in the city after she had passed away, back on his own to sort out what his mother had left him, which was everything.

He had made many trips in the last year. Her death from lung cancer wasn't sudden. She had known for some time, since the visit to see her doctor for a cough that wouldn't go away. He rode straight from the airport to the hospital where his mother had had surgery, and slept in a cot by her bed. All other trips, he refused the spare bedroom that his mother had set aside for his visits and stayed at hotels. He gave her the unsatisfactory excuse of needing a separate place to focus on his work and call clients, but the truer reason was that he felt useless and sad watching the home health aides help her bathe and use the restroom and eat puréed foods a half spoonful at a time. He slept in at the hotel during the day and visited his dear mother in the evening, staying long enough that he could usually make an excuse of having to get back to the hotel for a conference call with Los Angeles. A part of him denied how little time his mother had left. He wanted to suspect that she might be playing up her illness so that her son would take pity on his poor mother—exactly as she'd described herself more than a few times.

When her end did come, with all kinds of tubing and apparatuses strapped to that pale, withered body, as if the machines had been the hungry culprit feeding off her, he couldn't believe that it had actually happened, even as he stood greeting her friends and his relatives who were more strangers than family at the temple pavilion, even as he threw fragrant woods into the fire licking her coffin. She was gone, scorched to gritty powder and then scattered at the mouth of the Chao Phraya, where they used to walk along shaky boardwalks and search the beach for mudfish.

It took him a week of endless sleep at the hotel before he could bring himself to visit the condo unit where she had lived. As rain dripped ceiling to floor in the exposed hallway, a woman stood outside the door waiting for him. An hour had passed since their appointment.

"I'm sorry, Khun Sunee. The street floods, the traffic," he said, a lie.

"It's okay. I came up late because I didn't expect you to be on time. Your mother often talked about you. Please, feel free to call me Nee."

"Don't believe everything my mother said."

Sammy didn't tell Nee that his mother had talked about her—the hardworking, attentive young woman who helped out with calling repairmen and sometimes even doing the job herself. It was a ploy his mother had tried before with society girls, daughters of friends, and bridge table acquaintances, and long given up. He should meet so-and-so the next time he was in Bangkok.

This one was not as he had imagined her. She looked to be in her midthirties, about fifteen or so years behind him, and rather tall, with long straight hair parted to the right and rounded eyes like portholes on a ship.

The thing that most surprised him, having met other women by way of his mother, was Khun Nee's skin, a few shades darker than his own. The fact tickled his suspicion. He wondered what his mother had in mind with this reversal, a gambit he was sure.

Dear Mother Pehn had tried many of them from thousands of kilometers away, dangling obvious bribes or casting herself as helpless to nurture his guilt, but he had refused to comply. Part of it had to do with his own ironclad stubbornness, and part of it grew from long-standing resentment—the reason they hadn't talked for a few years at one point in his forties. This condo unit and the others she rented out were part of the package deal she'd made with the developer for the estate that had been in his family for more than three generations.

Now only the Sino-Colonial facades of the old house remained at the base of the condominium building. The front opened into a marble-floored lobby, and the side wing, where his childhood bedroom had been, now served as entrance to a day spa offering massages in some vaguely Nordic tradition. Along the roofed terrace, strange vinyl-padded furniture lay scattered about in disuse, a sad shadow of the woven rattan chairs where he'd sat with his grandparents, reading or playing chess under the slow whirl of a wooden fan. In the garden, most of the majestic trees had been felled, and worst, the koi pond where he had spent so many afternoon hours gazing at swirls of rippling fins now lay under a driveway to the parking decks.

Sammy had acquiesced to his mother about the sale and then regretted his acquiescence, and out of that regret came a long period of bitterness and blame that he thought was just punishment for them both.

He didn't know what his mother had told Nee about him. He could only stand by his own story: that he had refused to come back to Bangkok after boarding school in Surrey, where his mother had sent him after his family's dissolution. At university, he baited her with plans of education and advancement, first in international law, then in architecture, and, finally, photography. He bought expensive medium-format cameras to justify himself. He spent a decade wielding them in London, another in Hong Kong, a few years in Stockholm as a married man, and then in Los Angeles, alone.

Now his mother was gone, and it was a son's duty to honor the remnants of her. With Nee, he wound through the rooms. Some of the things his mother left behind he would have recognized anywhere: the gold-capped fountain pen dented with the teethmarks of his first dog or the rattly wooden abacus his mother had used to figure out the bills. She had kept them all in perfect order and at their assigned places, leaning in doorways to tell the maid exactly what to put back where.

Unnerved, he uncapped his 35 mm rangefinder and began snapping pictures of the place.

"She spoke very proudly about your photos," Nee said, recalling him to this world.

"Of course she'd tell you that. I wouldn't hear any of it, though."

They paused at a window. Twenty-seven stories down, children splashed back and forth along the edges of a pool. Their laughs and screams barely pierced through the great babble of the city.

"For extra money, I teach weekend swim classes down there," Nee said.

"I've thought about adult swimming lessons, but there's a chance I'd already float on my own," he said, patting the spillover flesh at his waist.

When she didn't laugh, he took it as a reminder that he was supposed to be in mourning. She didn't understand that he had not bothered with the business of somberness and tears because he wanted to prove to his dead mother that he was no longer a child. Yet when they opened his mother's bedroom closet and he saw clothes hanging from metal hangers, no thinner than her body in the last year, he snapped a photo and then wept.

In the States, this would be the moment when he'd expect to receive some variation of a consoling embrace. Nee stood there, looking down at her feet, and let him cry. Then with one hand, she patted him for a fraction of a second on his shoulder.

"If you don't want to keep them, I can give them away," Nee said, looking at the clothes.

"Please. Thank you," he said, trying to dry his face with bare fingers.

"Let me know how else I can help. I'm in the management office nearly every day."

□ □ □

He was touched. He thought of Nee as soon as he left the condo building, wondering what kind of excuses he could make to see her again, and he thought of her again that night, wading in the hotel pool by himself and gazing at his emptied plastic martini glass.

After a few days, he dropped by the office and asked Nee if she would join him for drinks at a hotel bar by the river, half certain she would say no.

That evening—their first rendezvous outside the condo—they sat at a slim windowside table and watched the dim lights of ships float seaward. He hadn't heard a ship's horn blast for decades, and he told her that it sounded unreal, like a sound effect in a movie. He talked about old radio serials lost to those born after the '50s; he was probably part of the last generation to remember sleepless nights, as a child, counting the hourly gongs of night watchmen. She talked about listening to the radio with her father and hearing songs on vinyl records for the first time when she was a university student, but now she only overheard other people's music. He learned that it had been a little over ten years since her own mother had passed away, and since she didn't mention any brother or sister, he assumed she was an only child as well. He told her that things might have been easier between him and his mother, had he siblings to share the tension. It felt strangely good not to feel that tension anymore.

The admission felt easy. She was pretty much a stranger, but he noticed that, with her, he wasn't afraid to open up parts of himself he had long kept sealed. He wasn't afraid to tell her that he hadn't had a paying assignment in more than a few years and no longer cared, or that, in the old house where the tower now stood, he once saw at the foot of the bed his grandfather's ghost, narrow-faced and blued, like in old tintypes.

He was curious why Nee hadn't married, the usual course for Bangkok women of her age.

"I should ask you the same question," she said.

"I was married, abroad, but I've forgotten so much of it that it feels like I never married."

"The not-remembering doesn't really work, does it?"

"No, not really," he said, without pressing further.

After that night, he didn't know when he should expect to see Nee again. He called up his travel agency and asked about return flights but, because he was thinking of her, he did not book one.

In matters of romance, all his life he had been able to play up indifference and aloofness to his advantage, as his friends often advised him. When he called the management office, he hung up on hearing an assistant pick up and then called again a few minutes later to leave a message. When Nee did call him back days later, apologizing for not spotting her assistant's message slips sooner, he heard, to his chagrin, joyous music in the voice that escaped his mouth.

He asked her what she was doing the next weekend, and she mentioned that she often went on long walks on her days off. Everybody in Krungthep who had the means hopped on air-conditioned buses or drove their cars. Her friends all thought she was crazy for going around on her feet for any purpose of leisure.

"When did you start taking these walks?" he asked.

"Not long after I graduated, I remembered that I used to love going to see the movies. My mother pressed me to go, to get me out of the house. She gave me money, and I went to see a movie by myself. It was some Hollywood action adventure or another, I don't even remember. I was paying more attention to the crowd. I watched everybody else gasp at the stunts and laugh at the romantic banter, and I decided that I couldn't bear it anymore. If I stayed, I would become them, and I hated the idea, even though they were probably all fine people out to have a good time. I got up and walked out of the theater. It was a bright afternoon, almost harsh, but I walked many kilometers home. There was something in that walk and my steady step through the city—foot out, foot out, foot out, foot out, foot out, foot out, foot out, foot out—that made me feel less nervous. This was before I was hired at this building and had access to a swimming pool, but I still walk when I can. If I'm not swimming, I walk. If I'm not walking, I long to swim. I love diving into that blue water and dissolving. Does this make any sense?"

"My father swam," he said, offering no more. "I don't swim, really, but I'm pretty good at walking. Can I join you on one of these walks?"

"I don't think you'd enjoy it."

"No, I'd love nothing more. There are many Bangkok neighborhoods that I never saw when visiting my mother. Please, show me."

So they wandered together. Those first few weekends, they wound their way around Klong Toey alley markets crowded with stands that sold underwear and sun-dried sea creatures on the same table. They trekked through sois on the Thonburi side of the river, following its gentle turn southward, the murky water mostly invisible behind buildings and homes, until they saw it again through temple grounds. They wormed through dusty new suburbs edging the city outward and up highway tributaries choked with overloaded, market-bound trucks and their spindly sugarcane stalks and deathly silent animals, and when they tired, they hailed a two-rowed passenger truck to return to the city proper. These afternoons walks were always sun seared, and the traffic fumes overwhelmed even a longtime Angeleno's smog-encrusted lungs, but Sammy couldn't get enough of seeing the city with her.

But she said no to his question of a walk in the old city. "You should go without me," she said over the phone.

"It would be a far more enjoyable walk if you'd come," he said.

"No, I'd rather not. I went to university around there. I've seen more than I needed to see."

So he went on his own, camera in hand, camouflaged amid the ant-like columns of tourists threading past the famous temples and palaces. His father once pointed out to him, as they rode a trolley car to the Khao Din zoo, that many of these places had been situated to mirror where their predecessors had been in the old capital of Ayutthaya, before it was sacked by the Burmese. He did now as he had done then, as many of the gawking farangs were also doing: he raised his camera and took photos.

At a corner shop by the great red swing, he stopped for a bag of icy olieng and thought of Nee as he stood sipping through a straw. It was clear to him that he was upset, almost angry, that she hadn't come with him. Part of the point of this solo walk was to show Nee that he didn't need her to explore the city of his birth. He figured that she must not have wanted to feel she had to act as tour guide here, like the many leading their throngs with a brightly colored flag held high. He wished that she could see how he'd hardly needed to unfold his map. He had visited many of these places when he was a boy, and he was surprised at how much of them he hadn't forgotten. He knew all about Bangkok too.

He would tell her so a few nights after, while showing her photos he'd taken on that walk. He was no longer staying at the hotel. It was his first night at the condo that was now his, and he'd invited her to come up and have dinner with him. On the other side of the long dining table, he'd laid out stacks of black-and-white photos, two to a column, the way he arranged his portfolio books when showing a new client.

"You have a good eye," she said, touching a photo of a woman, her back to the camera as she wove a wisp of bamboo into a birdcage. Light poured through the tree leaves above to dapple the woman's otherwise overshadowed back.

"I'd hope so," he said. "I've probably been taking photos since I was eight. My grandfather gave me one of those Kodaks you held at the chest to look through. Like this." He pretended to look down at a boxy shape he made with his hands.

"Hey, you took this one of me," she said, pointing at a photo he had been careful to include in one of the middle stacks. It was taken during their stop at a temple somewhere by the river. They had asked the monks to perform a merit ceremony, and the photo showed her half kneeling under the shade of a tree, pouring out ceremonial water from a silver bottle to let good karma flow onto his recently departed mother, onto their dead ancestors, onto souls they'd wronged in lives past and present, onto the guardian spirits of the places they lived, and, with whatever was left, onto all the realm's pitiful wandering ghosts.

"I couldn't help it. I hope you don't mind."

"It's okay. I don't."

"I'd love to take more photos of you," he said. "Can I?"

"Yes, I guess."

He took her response as the signal he needed to reach for the camera he'd put in position on a table nearby.

"Now?" she asked. He only nodded and raised the viewfinder to his eye and, on seeing Nee gazing down with a suppressed grin, pressed the shutter. She looked up at him, and when he saw that she wasn't mad, he pressed the shutter again.

"Come with me. Let's go where the natural light is more diffused."

She didn't refuse. She followed him to the living room, where he pulled closed the gossamer curtain. He motioned her to turn this way and that to help her pose, and then he guided her by a tap or a brush of his fingertips.

"You're a natural," he said. It was a reliable line, one he'd said so many times that he only had a dim awareness of saying the words.

He went through a whole roll of film before he leaned in for a kiss that turned into hungry devouring.

They walked together to the spare bedroom that his mother had set aside for her son, instead of the master bedroom where his mother once slept. They took off their clothes and wrapped themselves around each other.

Always, he treasured the newness of another's naked body, each a country with its own strange language of flesh and bone. With Nee, he detected a growing vacancy between them as their bodies entwined. She seemed to have retreated into a separate room within herself. When he tried to follow, by look or touch, she responded, but her every passionate look and gesture served only to distract him from the secret material that sealed the place where she had dived through. He pretended not to notice.

Anyone else might find it maddening to be with someone who could seemingly vanish during such intimacy, but he found familiarity. She was revealing who she was, and so was he, in turn receding into his own separate place as he moved and collided with her, savoring the pleasure of their bodies from a distance far above the performance. Where did she go? Who was she thinking of? He wouldn't ask her, not wanting to answer the questions himself.

□ □ □

For a good while, more than two decades before, he'd thought himself happy. He had met a woman, a stewardess, at a Swedish expat's midsummer's party in New York and within a year they were married and living in her home city of Stockholm.

Weekends, they drove out to her parents' island villa on Blidö and he chopped firewood, every once in a while stopping to wipe his brows and gaze out to the serenity of the bay. He learned when to switch from hard to soft k's with the new words he was picking up, and how to make gravlax out of a whole fish in their flat's cramped kitchen, and what sweets to bring to fika with the new friends he was making through Anja. He leisurely dissolved, bit by bit, into that life.

Who did he remember when he thought of his former wife? The most he could now recollect of Anja was the memory of remembering her. She returned to him not as one whole person but as an apparition in parts: a collection of stills that appeared to him for no longer than the flash of a strobe light. For a moment, he could breathe in long dissipated whiffs of rose and jasmine in her perfume and hear the sigh she let out as she turned over to get up in the morning to catch a flight. She had wanted to quit her job and find a new one without as much traveling involved, maybe go back to university and work toward an advanced degree.

The thought of her body still excited him. In his mind, he liked to pose her as she had appeared in bed on a sunless day. He could feel her shoulders again, and her reedy runner's arms, and the give of her breasts cupped in his hands. He liked the way other men looked her over and how they winced at him.

There were, of course, other memories. Their last year together echoed with shouts and cries. Shattered pieces of their belongings scattered where they'd hit the floor.

He didn't like to reanimate those times. He most cared for the parts of his life that made him happiest to think of old happiness.

□ □ □

Nee called him out on another trait of his: he avoided confrontation. She said this after they had waited half an hour for a restaurant table and then lost it to a family who sidestepped him and sat down. They were at one of those places where the food was so revered the staff didn't care if customers stared each other down and fought over chairs. He had volunteered to guard one table that looked to clear out, telling her and her friends to feel free to go use the washroom or grab a smoke.

"They had kids," he said.

"They could have come with a whole orphanage, but still," said Nee. He could see why his mother had picked her.

They were there with half a dozen of her old classmates, and he had failed them. It had been about three months since he'd begun seeing Nee, and he'd earned an invitation to join them on an outing. He had long been curious about the lives of Thais to whom he wasn't related, and he knew Nee admired her friends, whom she thought had done so much better than she in their professional lives, grateful that they stayed in touch and never treated her differently. She kept careful guard of them, and only when he'd proved himself to be worth their bother was he allowed to circle closer. Theirs was the kind of friendship forged only in the fine weave of Bangkok schools and universities. As infinite as the city appeared, its people moved in the same clusters from birth to death.

To their credit, her friends didn't make a big deal about the table. After they were finally seated, they clinked foamy glasses of Singha and Kloster with his and kept him in conversations they could have carried on without pausing to ask for his thoughts.

"Nee tells me you're a photographer," one of her friends said. "You must have a great eye."

"It's the light and equipment, really. I simply press the shutter."

"You took some great photos of Nee. She showed me," another one said. He remembered the photos, taken after one of their midday trysts. Nee went out to the balcony and rested her elbows on the railing, taking in the vast city trembling with incessant urgency. From where he lay with his camera, she looked glorious in the harsh afternoon light, which could only break through at the very edge of her shadow, as if she had grown large enough to smother the sun.

"Make room, make room," a waitress interrupted, earning his eternal gratitude.

When he saw the food being paraded out the kitchen toward them, he wished he'd brought the camera with him, so that pressing the shutter button could calm his nerves. This wasn't the ornately plated Thai food he was used to in Bangkok's hotels. Fish came at him, silvery and whole, bathed in plum juice and ginger. Grilled prawns the size of men's hands oozed with orange roe, and bowls of curry the color of flames formed a volcanic ring around the table. He kept eating, teary-eyed, until suffering melted into a mode of pleasure.

At that table, he imagined this was what his life would have looked like, had he come back to his birth city after Surrey. It might not have been a bad life; he might have been happier.

He watched Nee, jubilant among her friends, her place so effortless and rightful, and felt annoyed at how easily she could make herself be loved. His mother had fallen for her, and she'd seen to it that he did the same. How could he deny her wishes?

In bed later that night, Nee asked him if he'd had a good time. Her question made him wonder if it was an instinctive extension of her office training. Has your stay been satisfactory? How else can we be of help? But he said only that he'd had a wonderful evening and her friends were some of the most gracious people he'd ever met.

"That's good. Wonderful memories to take with you when you leave."

It took him a few seconds to recognize that she had meant it as a question. All the time they'd seen each other, he hadn't told her about any of his plans for the future, and she hadn't asked.

"I don't think I'm going to leave," he told her.

She had been on her side, facing away from him. The glow of the city shone through the windows and cast her shadow between them, on the sheets. He could smell flowery sweetness wafting from her hair. A hand reached over to caress her shoulder, and he heard someone whisper assurances, and for a moment he thought a phantom had crawled into the bed, but he had only been watching himself.

She did not turn to him when she said, "It's probably nothing, but my period is late a few days."

□　□　□

Sometimes, he would imagine what his life would have been had he stayed married and living in Sweden.

He would have seen Anja continue her studies and, afterward, likely join the ranks of a ministry or charitable enterprise. He would have tried his hardest to find assignments in northern Europe. He still knew people who owed him favors in London, and on visits to the city, he would have dropped in on Helen and Freddie and his family and, every once in a while, dutifully found the time to pull the weeds at his father's grave.

Anja was also an only child, and the villa on Blidö would have been theirs after her elderly parents passed away. He had thought of building a studio shed in the yard there: a simple Nordic structure of wood and glass large enough for a backdrop setup, a few flat files, and a closet-sized darkroom. He would have found himself spending more time at the villa than at their flat in the city. Anja wasn't the type to stay far from civilization for long, and she would probably be in Stockholm during the weekdays, while he stayed behind to focus on his projects.

It was likely that they would have had children. Anja wanted two, to give each child the early company that their parents never had. He was fond of certain Swedish names, like Magnus, Astrid, Signe, and Linnea, and maybe Anja would have agreed to at least one for their children.

They would have had to renovate their flat, turning the study into another child's bedroom, or to move to a larger place elsewhere, perhaps Bromma, where some of their friends lived. He would by then be able to hold extended conversations about football in Swedish with the other fathers taking their kids to the förskola, and when his kids neglected to take off their shoes in an orderly way on coming back home, he would call out their names from the foyer and point to the little sneakers scattered at his feet. When they had other parents over for fika, he would impress them with cookies he'd learned to make from the well-thumbed copy of *Sju Sorters Kakor* inherited from Anja's parents, who used to make sticky buns with a touch of cardamom when he and Anja visited.

He would be more than satisfied, he had wanted to believe, to make this part of his life everlasting.

It turned out that he had felt then only the first wave of psychic tides that would arrive years apart. The high ecstasy of assured comfort that greeted him when he first landed with the love of his life in Stockholm was followed by depths of dread on staring out at the bluest and most serene of bays and its postcard islands of pine and rock, and spotting only the final resting place of his own contentment.

◻   ◻   ◻

He found Nee by the pool. Around her, children hung from the tiled edge and kicked tiny whirlpools. Parents looking up from magazines yelled encouragement in Thai, Swedish, and Mandarin. Other Sundays, he had watched from the balcony with his 300 mm lens, complying with her rule that they not be seen together on the grounds of the building. She didn't want gossip, but he hadn't seen her in almost a week, and she wasn't returning his calls. He regressed to the impatient, spoiled child that he was. Whenever he threw a rock, it unnerved him if he didn't hear it strike something.

When she gave the kids their ten-minute break and got out of the water, he walked up to her with a towel.

"Here you go, my sea lioness."

"What are you doing here?"

"It's a nice day. I wanted to see you."

"See me? Are you sure?"

Her voice fumed with subdued anger. She wouldn't let it grow any louder, not here with the children she loved to teach and the parents she'd tried hard to keep happy.

"I started thinking about you the second you left."

It was true. He had thought about her immediately because he knew what was coming and she didn't.

"Sammy, I know about the tickets."

"Yes, the tickets."

"Special delivery by motorcycle messenger? You wanted me to sign for them."

Yes, he had bought tickets for New York, and he had asked the travel agent for them to be sent and signed for that day, knowing she'd be the only person in the office.

"I was going to tell you. An old client is flying me in for a shoot. I'll be back soon."

He felt free to give any excuse. None would matter. The curtains had been flung down, and it should be clear to her by now that he was full of it.

"What do you mean by soon?"

"Next month. This year. Sometime."

His rock had hit. A kind of pained spasm, like an animal turning under a sheet, undulated across her face.

"Is it because I'm late, Sammy? You aren't leaving because of that, are you?"

"Of course not."

"But you won't be back."

"What would make you think that? Didn't I just say I would?"

"Because you aren't brave enough. It'll be easier for you to go off to wherever else, again."

"That's not true. You can't say that."

"Then tell me. What is it that you want to happen for us?"

He didn't answer, although he tried. Perhaps it had been his mistake to expect Nee to take his prevarications so easily. He thought she was smarter than to have expected more from him than she had from past lovers, but he also wanted to make sure she knew that she'd had him all wrong.

"I have to go," she said, turning to the children in the pool.

"Come see me," he said, and left the pool area. He genuinely wanted her to come upstairs after the class. It was important to him that they not part on bad terms.

He waited that afternoon and evening. She didn't come. He looked for her at the management office the week before he was due to leave, but she was nowhere to be found. When he finally resorted to calling, the office assistant picked up and evaded his questions of Nee's where-abouts and return. That his flight was in less than a day did not soften her guard. He packed and left for the airport.

He wouldn't see Nee again. He instructed the executor to price his mother's condo and the other units that he had inherited for a speedy sale. He would be relieved of the onerous past that was the cradle of his life, finishing what his mother had started years earlier.

The executor said on the phone that a nice young woman in the management office had been of great assistance with the paperwork, performing her duties flawlessly.

FAR

What could happen at a restaurant over two days? Or the next decade? Nok kept to her routine. She rolled up Erawan's steel shutters. She rolled them down. She kept the sidewalk clean.

The Nikkci would fall off its stilts in the early 1990s, but not before financing a second Japanese landing in Thai cities. Customers started coming into Erawan asking for spicy squid salads and reminiscing about elephant rides across mountain jungles near Chiang Mai. They talked of sacred golden temples and shapely female caddies. Nok and Maru bowed, laughing, and then brought up the day's specials.

Maru's cooking improved. A newspaper took a picture of Nok and him cradling their large mortar and pestle for a food feature. They hired Thai students part-time. New tables and chairs replaced ones coming apart at the legs.

They trained some staff to cook and trusted the restaurant to one of the hostesses a few days a month. They boarded trains and vanished into long straight lines and then reappeared at beaches and mountain towns. At the height of festivals, they lingered in crowded lantern-lit streets and nibbled on skewered takoyaki. Nok waded into the women's side of the hot springs and let steam fill her lungs.

At home, she washed clothes with her favorite detergent and let them dry on the balcony. She wore comfortable pants and open-back shoes bought at a nearby Seiyu.

Maru had an affair with a waitress. Nok chased him out of the apartment with a spatula and changed the locks at the restaurant. They didn't speak for a year. He came back, remorseful. She could have left him as he was, a ruin.

They soon had a child together, to her surprise. She was forty years old, and the thought of becoming pregnant had long left her. When Riku was born, she thought he looked perfectly Japanese. He also looked perfectly Thai. She thought the same as he learned to ride a bike at Yamashita Park and when he said he wanted to grow up and become a pilot.

□   □   □

One night, Nok picked up the phone and heard Nee's voice for the first time in a decade.

"It's me," Nee said, but Nok didn't need to hear it. She'd recognized her sister's voice at the first word.

"Hey," Nok said, and then added, "it's been a while."

"Yes, it has."

"What's wrong?"

"Nothing. I just wanted to talk to you."

Nok didn't believe her but left it at that, not wanting to pry any further and risk pushing Nee away.

They now talked nearly every week. Each call, Nee fed Nok's hunger for the most ordinary details about anything happening in Krungthep—updates on the neighborhood stray cats, which fruits were in season at the market, how hard the rain had fallen that week, or whether she'd visit a temple to make alms for their mother. Nok told her about the exquisite gift-wrapping at the department store or how crowded the train had been that morning or how Riku liked to watch nature shows about crocodiles. They had veered farther in their own directions across land and sea, but little embers like these were enough to light up the shape of each other's life.

Nee flew to visit twice over the next year, each time by herself. Nok and Maru took her to Tokyo Disneyland and drove with her to beaches in Chiba, places Nee thought Riku would also enjoy. Riku called her his Thai aunt. They figured out games to play, even though she spoke no Japanese. Nok came home to find Nee hiding underneath the dining table, a finger over her lips.

Evenings, Nok cooked their mother's recipes. She fed her sister as their mother used to, though without four or five dishes on the table, that overpowering show of love.

"You have everything figured out, Nok."

"I get up and cook at the restaurant and sleep. It's nothing much at all."

"It's not nothing," Nee said. Nok thought that Nee wanted her sister to feel proud, but Nok ended up saddened. Nee would soon return to Krungthep and problems she didn't care to discuss. Her job was fine, no cause for concern. She kept mum on the state of her romances. Nok had no idea if her sister was happy or, at least, fine. *It is only so*, Nee would say when Nok asked if something was wrong. She thought there was nothing that Nok could do to help. Nok didn't disagree.

How could she have? Nok hadn't lost Nee to a bullet or the Chao Phraya's currents in 1976, but having chosen this life in Yokohama, she could claim no part in helping her sister in the years after. Given their estrangement of several years, Nok hadn't even been a spectator. Nee had survived the loss of her lover and of many friends as well, but only to endure a city that barely remembered the events that had caused it—an unpublicized ceremony once a year, a small plaque there. Did that make Nee cling to her horrors even harder? That was very much the kind of thing that Nee did: taking on what no one else wanted to do—this remembering.

In her kitchen, Nok kept a framed photo of Nee, one of the few that showed her smiling. It was taken at the condo building where she worked. Nee posed on the balcony of an empty apartment. Below her grew a garden of TV antennas and soot-blackened roofs, and, beyond them, skeletal towers crowned with cranes, and farther still, the river.

□   □   □

Not long after Nee's visit, Gahn came to the restaurant. He had gained weight, his face even fuller than before. He called out to Nok and lifted clasped hands to his forehead.

"I hope you don't mind that I'm here."

"Khun Gahn, it's been a very long time. Please, sit."

Nok asked one of the waiters to bring him olieng.

"Look at all the Japanese here. They can handle the heat now?"

"More than you'd think."

"And Maru, is he well? I expected to see him here."

"It's his day off. He's taking our son to a BayStars game. Do you follow baseball at all?"

"I'm afraid I don't. So many years here and the game still confuses me."

Nok laughed the way she now laughed, mouth covered with a wrist. For a moment, Gahn seemed familiar, but only because he no longer resembled the Gahn she remembered. With his receded hairline and plain long-sleeve dress shirt, he could be any one of their middle-aged Japanese regulars.

"And how's the colonel?"

Gahn sipped his olieng before answering.

"He's the reason I'm here, Khun Nok."

As Nok looked away, Gahn said, "Please. He isn't well, and all he has been asking for is your food."

□ □ □

She could just fill the bento boxes and hand them to Gahn. But no; she helped him carry them out and then got in the car with him. The ride took them south to a nondescript neighborhood in Naka Ward. High gates drew open with a remote to reveal a two-story house taking up a small lot, barely enough for a corner garden on one side. She followed Gahn up a concrete ramp with stainless-steel railings into the house. On an upright bed in the main room, a man lay motionless except for the slow heaving of his chest.

"The second stroke really did it."

"Does he have children?" Nok asked with a lowered voice.

"They're in Krungthep. They came last year for a week, to shop."

"And he's not going back? Haven't others like him returned to their families?"

"He could have, but like some of us, he has chosen not to go back."

Nok nodded, to convey her understanding and also to acknowledge who they both were. She picked up one of the bento boxes that Gahn had set on a table. It could still warm her cupped hands.

"Will you be the one to feed him this food?"

"I'm sorry I didn't mention it to you sooner, but he can't really chew. The nurse usually feeds him some kind of slush."

"What good is all this then?"

"Their smell."

Nok understood. This food mattered less than the ghosts it would channel.

She stepped closer to the bed and clasped her hands to her forehead. Up close, she noticed the paleness of his flesh, which draped like silk over his bones. The air around him hung salty, putrid—a rotting sea. She breathed through her mouth, as little as she could.

The old man's eyes widened.

"Hello, Khun Chahtchai. Remember me?"

He nodded, his mouth emitting an unintelligible rasp.

"Of course, he does," said Gahn, as he wheeled a small table to the side of the bed and began laying out the bento boxes. "He's still sharp. If his hands were better, we'd be playing cards all day like we used to, isn't that right?"

Khun Chahtchai didn't move or say a word.

"Go ahead, Khun Nok. He'd love to hear about the food you made."

A window by the bed let in pale white light. Here he was in full, a monster, a man. If Nok reached out, she could easily crumple his neck the way she wrung her kitchen towels, for Nee.

"I brought sour curry. I remember you liking it. And you asked for chicken-fat rice. The soybean sauce is in this bag."

Nok gave up on holding her breath. She breathed in.

"I brought hor mok," she said. "My mother used to make it with river fish she bought at the market. It steams well in porcelain, but I wish we had banana leaves like ones from the tree in my grandparents' garden. My sister, Nee, was really good at weaving bowls with them."

Nok let the stink fill her lungs. She picked up a bento box and angled it so that he could see inside it. As she opened the lid, vapors curled out.

She hadn't paused when she'd written down Gahn's requests. She went to the kitchen, took what she needed out of the pantry, and put pots on the range. She thought of Nee, who would find out over the phone from her and not anyone else.

Nee and her dead classmates and their families. Nok couldn't hope to measure their grief with what little she knew of her own. She wanted them to somehow understand that this wasn't forgiveness. She had no right to that. Any punishment owed was theirs and would always be theirs.

Who could say what hers would be?

III

DELUGE

The snakes were the first to seek higher ground. The people of Krungthep began finding them in places they weren't often spotted before—curled around roof antennas or slithering up parking garage ramps. Remnants of the unlucky ones lay on busy roads, cut and flattened where tires hadn't veered away. In one suburb, broods colonized tree branches and replaced leaves with their wriggling bodies, prompting gamblers to bow with a clasped stick of incense, for good luck in their football bets. At a high-end shopping mall, the sighting of a cobra in a dressing room evacuated an entire department store. Nobody was hurt, except for the snake. A country-born security guard found it coiled in the corner of the women's wear section, bludgeoned it, and took home the carcass as an ingredient for a spicy salad. When a boa with the girth of a man's thigh wrapped itself around the head of a revered Buddha, photos traveled fast, phone screen to phone screen. The superstitious declared it an omen. Fortune-tellers and astrologists predicted varieties of calamity, from stock market tumbles to plane crashes to the death of movie stars.

Not too many took notice of news that the rivers flowing through Greater Krungthep were rising. It was another wet season, and who should be alarmed by small pools that had begun to form at drainage gutters? Old memories of the flooded city had faded. It was simply raining hard, like it had always rained around this time of the year. Rain came in the midafternoon and once more at night, and the city woke up to wet, darkened sidewalks and damp air, but the sun would soon appear and steam the roads dry, as it had always done.

Except the city wouldn't be rid of the puddles. The puddles soon turned curbs into ankle-deep streams, rushing toward any outlet or low ground. Some spilled across major intersections, where cars and motor scooters rode over one another's widening wakes, and traffic officers took to directing rush hour standing on borrowed chairs.

Along canals, stilt-house dwellers nervously eyed the waterline. Marks from previous years disappeared into the murky, dirt-stained flow beneath their homes. Newly built waterfront promenades closed, after the Chao Phraya began to wash over seawalls. Condo owners, who for years had listed a view of the river as a feature that buoyed their property value and their daily well-being, lost sleep over the likelihood of evacuation and the potential sell-off that could follow.

News trucks arrived with crews of reporters and cameramen wearing hip-high rubber waders. Officials dropped by affected neighborhoods to survey the damage. The people of Krungthep could rest assured that all necessary measures were being taken to alleviate the flooding and help those who'd been displaced. Videos of a teenage boy going about his daily routines—waking up, eating his rice porridge breakfast, folding his laundry—gained hundreds of thousands of viewers within a few hours, for the floodwater sloshing against his living room walls.

Everyone in Krungthep was watching the TV screens that covered the approaching flood day and night. Somewhere upcountry the water was lapping on the steps of thousand-year-old temples and forcing saffron-robed monks to camp on highway ramps. Produce markets turned into shimmering, rectangular pools. Entire industrial complexes seemingly went undersea. Airports closed due to submerged runways. The people saw clips of politicians rescuing nearly drowned grandmothers and celebrity-filled rafts bringing food and supplies to families waiting on roofs for extraction.

When the rain fell, people panicked. When it stopped, they hoped to hear that water levels had lowered. Phone calls between those who claimed to know and those who also claimed to know gave varying reports. The water could arrive to their neighborhood in a week. The water would come tomorrow. Shopkeepers began laying cinder-block barriers in front of their stores. Predictions were grim. The sea rose higher than it had during past floods. Only mere trickles of river water could drain out.

The most popular online search term for the city that month was *"How to fill a sandbag,"* and when nobody could buy sand due to the inevitable shortage and price gouging, popular questions included *"Can I waterproof my house with plastic wrap?"* and *"highest ground in Krungthep."*

Where water had yet to come, still most of the city, shelves at food stores emptied. Frenzied shoppers swept packs of instant noodles into their carts and hauled multipacks of bottled water out to waiting cars. Hotels and resorts within Krungthep shut down due to canceled reservations by foreign tourists, but those beyond its limits saw an up-tick in reservations by city dwellers who could afford to make an invol-untary vacation out of the impending ordeal. Highway overpasses and parking lots in more elevated provinces filled with cars from already flooded or threatened parts of the city.

Those whose lives had not yet been breached watched the news. When they saw an alert about newly flooded areas, they looked up the approximate cross streets on zoomed-in maps and guessed where the water would flow next. When it came to their own homes, they touted reasons for optimism. There were underground sewers that would pump excess water elsewhere. There was a sacred shrine nearby that would safeguard the surrounding populace from harm. The water would overtake another neighborhood before theirs, which would then act as a dam, and they would be able to watch the flood end its ap-proach there, feeling lucky for the close call. The water was far away until it wasn't.

Some found that the flood management system did not equally fa-vor neighborhoods near its waterways, sparing one but letting lakes be made of others. There were whispers of so-and-so influential persons diverting the water to flood otherwise safe homes to save their own. At more than a few floodgates, rioting crowds reopened the sluice and flooded their neighbors to correct unequal fortunes.

There were public apologies and heated debates on nighttime talk shows. Angry swarms favored scathing postings. Who would be held responsible for this catastrophe? After the previous floods, why wasn't the flood management plan more robust?

As more of the water swelled into the city, supposed photos of croco-dile sightings began to appear on network feeds. A crocodile farm out-side the city was said to have been flooded, and escapees were leisurely swimming everywhere. Reports told of creatures darting out of the water to snatch abandoned pets and strays. A man claimed a crocodile leapt out of the water in an attempt to devour him as he stood peeing into the water outside his bedroom window. Children were disappearing midswim in flooded streets, some swore, and the tale spread of a heroic woman who'd managed to wrestle a dropped phone from the jaws of one ferocious beast.

The floods would recede, but not until nearly two months later, with the return of pacific conditions in the Gulf of Siam. The sea relented, slightly.

The few who'd witness the gradual decline in the waterline were the people who refused to abandon the appliances and electronics they'd raised on concrete blocks in their homes. Others who'd evacuated could only keep track through those who'd returned to feed pets or retrieve personal items. They asked after the condition of their own homes, whether anyone had caught a glimpse of how far the water had risen on a given street.

As officials reopened areas deemed safe for return, photos of damaged rooms became fashionable in the capital. Young and old posed in living rooms, up to their knees in mud, or reaching out to point at a tea-colored wall to show where the flood had reached. They squished their noses closed to hint at the moldy, rotting stench. Where the water hadn't fully receded, they threw damaged items into garbage bags, which were then floated to overburdened garbage trucks on drier land. They left books out for the sun to dry, let clothing and furniture bathe in the warmth of rooftops. They recovered family photos now adorned with hypnotic swirls of bled color, torn where the paper had stuck to glass. When the news anchors declared Krungthep crocodile-free, they cheered.

BECOMING

They recognize each other; they both struggle to say how. Then Mai remembers him from the building where she lives with her parents. She has watched him walk across the outdoor rec area with his daughter. She knows the squeaky sound of his flip-flops on the tile. Dr. Wanich thinks she looks familiar but isn't sure why. Maybe she once accompanied another of his patients and sat on the sofa reserved for family and friends. Maybe she's a friend's daughter, one of the many shown off during encounters at the supermarket. *Come meet Khun Doctor. If you study hard, you can be like him.*

He supposes that he could be wrong about having met her. He likes to think that he never forgets a face and finds it disappointing that his memory, usually so reliable, has failed him. Then he remembers: the long-haired young woman by the pool, there not to swim but to read textbooks beneath an umbrella. Here she is now fully clothed in a university outfit—a white short-sleeved blouse, a black knee-length skirt. She's pretty, he admits, in the way of Thai movie stars from his parents' generation, with a youthful beauty more comforting than striking.

She is the one to bring it up.

"I'm sorry if I'm mistaken, Dr. Wanich, but you live in my building, don't you?"

"I was about to ask," he says, relieved. "Hello, neighbor."

His assistant steps in to guide her inside a yellow circle painted on the floor. The room dims. A blue bar of light appears and slowly swivels around her.

"That's it," he says. "If you'll wait just a minute."

His voice could lull a stampeding elephant, just as Pig had described. It had been Pig's referral that let Mai skip the yearlong wait for an appointment. If there were a calendar for the clinic, like the kind given out to customers at banks and supermarkets before New Year's, Pig ought to be on the cover, with her assembly of pleasing curvatures and contours—that smidgen of a nose, those hypnotic feline eyes. Even before the surgeries, Mai thought Pig the least suitable nickname possible for someone who received weekly declarations of love from strangers. Pig blames the name on her now eradicated baby fat. Mai wonders if, had she grown up with a more damning moniker, her own cells would have divided more pleasingly, in defiance.

"Okay, we're ready," he says. "Have a seat over there."

Mai sees her own face hovering in front of her. The face is staring straight ahead, like it's in line at the twenty-four-hour minimart and elsewhere in thought. A cold glow radiates from its skin. She's reminded of sitting last year in her art history elective, watching detached head after detached head of Sukhothai-era Buddhas blip into place. Sitting down, she hears Dr. Wanich tapping on hushed keys. On the screen, the heaviness under her chin disappears.

"Better?" he says.

"Better. I think."

"You already have a very nice bridge. What I would do is lower the nose only a little."

He models potential options for each procedure. As he taps, the eyes on her new face widen into almond-shaped ovals. He draws three versions of her jawline. The droop of her chin flattens out to the sides. Wordless, she nods at the screen.

The shapes come easily to him. His stylus glides as if it could not have traced a different path. He performs hundreds of surgeries year after year. He knows the spaces his patients long to fill. Some have fled surgery costs in their home countries, flying in from the Arab states, from Seoul, from the gray suburbs of America, where he did his fellowship. They recover in hospital suites that offer hot-stone massages and Ayurvedic consultations. They leave.

"I like this combination best, but it's up to you."

After another tap, her current face appears next to her new face. The comparison shot is his most effective persuasion; he saves it for last.

For Mai, the image is no different from pictures of her and Pig posing together side by side. Pig always posts them online, no matter how much Mai objects.

Pig says that she has a huge responsibility to uphold. With the new face, Pig's following has widened even beyond the campus. Thousands clamor for her every photo. Pig holding up a slice of pizza. Pig pouting with a tilted head at broken sunglasses. Pig brushing her teeth. Likes. Favorites. Hearts.

"Honestly, Dr. Wanich, I'm not sure about this. Some friends just thought I should at least come and see."

"Everyone has doubts. Take your time. Talk to a few people. I can give you references, if you need them."

Dr. Wanich pushes a button on his printer. As it whispers out glossy sheets, Mai peers through a partial opening in the blinds. She guesses the view is why he chose this suite in the medical high-rise. The building where they both live is close enough that if her parents were on the balcony, she would be able to make out their silhouettes. It's a clear, beautiful day. The sky looks as if it has been painted on.

"Here, take these. Any questions, call me."

"Or maybe I'll see you at the building."

"Yes, that, too."

□ □ □

Weekday evenings, he leaves the clinic to pick up his daughter at the tutoring center, joining the double-parked cars idling in front of the shopping plaza. Decals of smiling cartoon children wearing caps and tassels decorate the windows. It doesn't take long for his daughter, still in her white-and-red school uniform, to open the back door and rush inside.

Behind him, the door slams. Juhn drops her backpack on the seat. She brings her clasped hands to her forehead to greet him.

"How was the session?"

"We went over sine and cosine and worked on timed exercises."

She's in fifth grade and learning subjects he had no idea existed until he entered secondary school. When she asks him for help with homework, he talks cautiously and vaguely, to avoid showing how much he, the learned surgeon, no longer understands.

"Oh yeah, this kid threw up on his desk."

"Was he sick?"

"He did it so he could call his mom and leave early. She believes anything he says."

He feels sorry for the mother and also frightened by his daughter's indifference to the boy's subterfuge. He thinks about his patient from this afternoon. He wonders if her parents know that she went for a consultation with him. Children, he realizes, keep their own truth and show another.

Juhn still listens to him. If he says something, she nods, because he has said it. Sometimes she asks questions, as if she could trap him in a cage of his answers, but she usually lets go after a bit, distracted by some newer curiosity. He's thankful. He rewards her duly. On Sundays, he gives her respite from Pia's regimen of study aids and takes her to the pool downstairs. She swims twenty laps, her goal, not his. He admires her discipline. She slaps at the water and keeps at it until she's done. He calls to her from the edge of the pool, with encouraging words he hopes she hears.

□ □ □

Visits to see Pig happen more often in the weeks before finals. As with the last three years, they can expect to sit in the same tiered rows at the university auditorium, the acoustics making every noise louder—the crinkle of turning pages, the faint scratching of hundreds of pens—as they stack arguments and supporting examples in blank booklets. What Mai has a knack for is anticipating exam questions, and Pig has begged her for help with studying. The taxis Mai takes from the Skytrain station never get lost going to Pig's house. All she has to say is, "To the windmill house near Soi 71."

Pig's parents went on vacation in the Netherlands and thought it'd be much too trite to bring back a ceramic souvenir. They brought back blueprints instead. The windmill, built by Thai carpenters out in Ayutthaya Province and trucked into the city piece by piece, stands two stories tall on the roof of their carport. With the wide sloping lawn giving the appearance of a low hill, Pig has said that Van Gogh would have wanted to paint it, minus the office towers in the background.

Pig opens the gate herself. "Bubble and Caterpillar are already here," she says with what sounds like impatience but is simply how she talks after too much caffeine.

Mai has known Pig since convent school. Still, they might never have become friends if not for neighboring seats in second grade. On days Mai's mother couldn't pick her up on time, Pig gave her a ride in a chauffeured Lexus. Mai looked forward to the smell of the trip—musky leather mixed with the crisp, vaguely fragrant air-conditioning. She spent a lot of her childhood in Pig's car, the traffic on Petchburi Road abetting, each sipping from the straw poking from their bagged iced tea, one of the few things to which Mai could treat her friend. Once, in fifth grade, Mai told Pig about her savings account, the one her parents opened to teach her about money. When it was large enough from her small allowance and relatives' gifts, she would buy a car to drive her friends around.

"I can't imagine having a bank account," Pig said. "That's so amazing." Money surrounds Pig, and she barely knows it exists.

Mai follows Pig into the house and up the staircase to the room where Pig's father keeps the audio system. On the wall hang framed blues and jazz record sleeves collected from business trips to America. They find Bubble and Caterpillar, two wavy-haired mermaids beached on the sectional sofa, leafing through foreign fashion magazines and looking very much like they do in their online postings. Caterpillar specializes in seconds-long videos featuring lively adventures with her bangs. Bubble's followers can't get enough of her signature pose: one hand at the hip and a big wink. When Mai checks their posts, she feels she might as well be watching a Japanese cartoon.

"So?" asks Pig.

"Pig told us all about it," says Caterpillar. "We should have gone with you."

"I didn't want anyone with me. It's not like I'm going to do it."

"Then show us," says Bubble.

Mai takes the printouts out of her purse and shields them behind upright elbows. Pointing at her cheek, she says, "I'm sure you can imagine them yourself."

With a sudden leap, Pig snatches the printouts from her. Mai tries to grab them back, but it's too late. Pig is already holding them up to the window light.

"Tell me the truth," says Mai.

"You're beautiful," Pig says to the printout. "So, so beautiful."

"Oh, I love it," say Bubble and Caterpillar, almost in sync. "You look like that Korean pop star—I always get her name wrong—or maybe a Thai Katie Holmes."

"They asked if I wanted to schedule a date."

"Sometime this term break," says Pig. "You can do the procedures in one shot."

"*Shoop,*" says Bubble, her hand imitating scissors. "Done."

❑ ❑ ❑

That night, they go to a new hotel bar near Lumpini Park, somewhere Pig wanted to try. They sit around a booth designed in homage to a scallop shell and pass around the cocktail list. Mai mulls over the names on the menu. What makes this one old-fashioned? Who's Tom Collins? She orders whatever Pig orders. Their responsibilities split that way: Mai reads about political economy theories and tells Pig what's important, and Pig takes care of what her policy professors might call carrots. The drinks come to them in ambers and reds and yellows. They clink the glasses, arms raised, the way they've seen people do in movies about young people living in large, civilized cities.

"Do you think we'll have to buy our next round?" Bubble says.

"Which one do you think it's going to be?" asks Caterpillar.

They chose their booth at a corner where eyes are inclined to converge. Feng shui matters, as Pig says.

"That guy over there is throwing us looks."

"Ew," Caterpillar says.

"He could be a pedicab driver, even with the tie on," says Bubble.

"Actually, he's not that terrible," says Pig. "If he'd use some whitening cream, and if you squint, he might look like Jay Chou."

Mai makes herself laugh with them. She knows her role when Caterpillar and Bubble are around. She's the one not pictured. She's the one to step away. The photo snapping will start, as it always does, and she'll volunteer to get up from the table and capture the triptych.

It's fine. She doesn't need to be in another photo. It's maddening enough that her parents put pictures of her everywhere in the apartment and never shy from showing her off in the most embarrassing ways. Last week they had asked her to meet up with them at the wedding of one of her father's friends' daughters, someone she'd only recognized from a family portrait stapled to one of the delivered New Year's gift baskets. Mai arrived to see the bride and groom up on the stage singing abridged Elvis hits, the crowd delirious. Her mother called out from a crowd of people Mai might or might not have met at other receptions. "Mai, Mai! There you are! Come talk to my friend Auntie Rain." Customary introductions followed. Mai's always late like this when she's out with her friends, they say, but we're never worried. She gets good grades and the rich kids line up for her to tutor them. That's right, international affairs, third year. She wants to go to grad school next, probably in America.

When she's honest with herself, she acknowledges that she doesn't mind her parents' boastful appraisals. The few times anyone ever says something nice about her are when they talk about accomplishments that look great on paper.

What puts her ill at ease are the expectations. She wants; that's true. Also true is Mai not knowing how she can reach for anything higher than what they can afford. She's an international affairs major, but she has been out of the country only twice, once to Singapore on a school trip and another time with her cousins on a group tour to Paris. This is their fortune: they've inherited respectable family names and obtained acceptable jobs. Her mother works as an assistant administrator at a public hospital. Her father spends his days summing up numbers for a telecom company. All their lives, they will move sideways.

Her parents have said that should they ever need the money, there's the condo, which they'd bought from the old owner at a quick-sale price.

Mai excuses herself to go to the restroom but instead finds herself at the bar. With everyone at their own booths, it's quieter here. The bow-tied bartender is wiping glasses dry with a white dish towel. Behind him, bottles lit from the bottom glow like glass lanterns.

"Sawasdee, little lady," a man says. He stands with one arm leaning on a wall. He's older but probably believes he hasn't aged in decades.

"Say, what are you drinking?" he asks. "If you introduce me to your pretty friends, I'll buy you another."

He's not so different from the rest—her friends, her relatives, the department directors at school, the HR managers thumbing through CVs with the requisite candidate photo clipped to the top left corner. She remembers Dr. Wanich at his desk, considering her face as he taps on the keys. He barely looked at her. His eyes stayed fixed on the face on the screen.

To be seen and wanted: the opposite has given her the comfort of being left alone, free of expectations, able to come and go without notice.

"I'm having a Cuba Libre."

She will watch them play with him, like cats with a stunned sparrow.

□   □   □

It's Sunday, time for his daughter's weekly swim. Juhn holds his hand as they walk down the covered walkway to the pool. Through slats overhead, the afternoon sun draws golden bands across them. Juhn shields her eyes with her other hand. Dr. Wanich stops to stretch anti-UV goggles over her head. She drops her towel, and he picks it up. It takes them five minutes to get to the far side, where the shade is best at this hour.

Into the water she goes. He loves the sound of her splashing kicks. He sees her small feet just by hearing them. He sinks into a vinyl pool chair and assumes the position of lording father—shoulders slouched against the chair back, hands hanging from armrests, his phone on the table. He doesn't know if his daughter can hear him. He yells anyway.

"You're doing amazing!"

Juhn has grown taller this year. She now comes up to his chest, and it's looking likely that she'll be at his shoulders next year. She has his energy and concentration. He can leave her to a task and trust her to keep at it until he returns. She's fascinated by nature shows and laughs at dubbed Japanese cartoons. She seems happy, more than he was at that age: an academically promising boy whose duty of future success had meant everything to his noodle-selling parents. If it were up to him, he wouldn't have enrolled Juhn at the tutoring center. She doesn't need it, he said. She'll be left behind, Pia said. With his wife, he has negotiated a balance for his daughter: weekdays of exertion and weekends of joy.

"Hi again, Dr. Wanich."

Mai's standing next to him. She has books in her arms and a backpack slung over the arm straps of her one-piece swimsuit. He stands up, so that he can look at her face without seeming like he's staring at anything else.

"Oh, hello there, Khun Mai. I didn't expect to see you here."

"I come to the pool to study every now and then. That's your daughter, right?"

He nods. They turn to admire the girl in the pool. She's chopping the water in front of her. Mai guesses that the girl had taken lessons at a younger age—a girl whose father is a surgeon always takes lessons.

"Do you mind if I give her some tips? Just something with her stroke."

"Of course not. Do you swim?"

"Yes, since I was your daughter's age. A swim teacher taught me right here in this pool."

"I didn't know they offered swim classes."

"Not anymore, not these past few years."

"You should teach them. Maybe I'll even enroll my daughter."

"Ha, no. I don't swim as much as I used to."

He points a thumb at the books she's carrying. "Well, it seems like other things are keeping you busy." He reads a title out loud, "*Concepts in Global Studies*, your preferred poolside read." He wears the smile longer than when he's not trying to joke.

"Father, Father!" Juhn shouts, hanging from the pool's edge. "I'm halfway through!"

He motions Mai to walk over. She puts down her things on a chair and follows him.

"This is Juhn," he says to his daughter. "Juhn, give Sister Mai a wai."

"Sawasdee kah," says Juhn, waiing.

"Sister Mai here is an experienced swimmer. She says she can help you swim even better."

Mai sits down near Juhn's bobbing head and compliments Juhn on her swimming. The girl looks up, her eyes behind foggy goggles.

"Juhn, your arms are strong, which means it's easy to put a lot of power into your strokes, but, actually, you can save energy and swim longer if you do this."

Mai bends sideway at the waist and gets into a midstroke position. Her arm lunges out and stops a distance from her head. Then she reaches out even farther.

"See that? A very good swimmer taught me, right here in this pool. You shift your shoulder out, just that one little extra change, and it makes all the difference."

"Okay!" Juhn shrieks, and swims off.

For a minute, Mai stands with the doctor. She remembers herself, no bigger than Juhn, in the same pool. She swam so much then, even though she had no competitive meets, and her father didn't come down to watch her swim. She liked the lessons and the satisfaction in answering to Teacher Nee sounding out, *stroke, stroke, stroke*. She loved the feeling of moving forward, her fingers anticipating the pool's edge ahead. Even now, she can feel on her skin the ribbons of water rushing around her, cold at first and then warm. Swimming across the pool, her movements sending out one ripple after another, she comes closer to knowing how a spirit could move a body—this watery thing that gives her a shape and a face to meet all the others.

Juhn reaches the other end of the pool and waves to them. They wave back, and Juhn starts another lap.

"Look at her go. Thank you, Khun Mai."

"It's a small adjustment. She's already a wonderful swimmer."

She says this with a kind of maternal pride, he notices. She has a wonderful smile with upwardly curved ends, even when she's not smiling.

"Dr. Wanich, I think I'm going to call your clinic," she says.

"About?"

"Scheduling the procedures, I meant."

"Yes, do that when you're ready. Or not."

"Thank you, Dr. Wanich. I better go study some more." She clasps her hands to the bridge of her nose and does a slight bow. She picks up her books and finds a seat on the other side. She opens a textbook and doesn't look up.

When Juhn climbs out of the pool, he wraps her in a towel. She stands, shivering, dripping a little wet shadow on to the tiles. She looks at the young woman reading across the water.

"How do you know Sister Mai?"

"She lives here. She's a patient."

"A patient? What's wrong with her?"

In his daughter's mind he's the fixer of broken faces. Juhn knows

about his heroic surgeries. He rebuilt a nose for the noodle shop owner whose face melted in burning oil. He gave back a jaw to the sergeant whose patrol Humvee flipped down a border town hillside. Her father's hands, those that hold hers, restore shape to mangled lives.

He looks over at Mai on the other side of the pool. How many faces like hers have changed under his hands? It's their choice, their design, he has told himself.

"Don't be so nosy, Juhn," he says, pushing her by the shoulders toward the walkway.

◻ ◻ ◻

In the early evening, when the mosquitoes intensify their hunt, Mai heads back up the twenty-five floors. Her parents are watching a dubbed Brad Pitt movie on the sofa. It's one she has seen, though she doesn't remember how it ends. Usually, she sits down in the side chair and joins them, one eye on the movie, the other on her class notes. Today, she teeters on the arm of the sofa and waits. Her father chuckles at a line she has heard before in the English version; her mother grins. They shouldn't ever have to leave their earned comforts to pay for her studies.

"Have you eaten?" asks her mother. "There's grilled chicken and sticky rice on the counter."

"I had a slice of pizza from the minimart."

On the end table next to her, framed pictures surround arrangements of knickknacks brought back from their few overseas vacations. A photo of her, age one, at her grandmother's old teak house. Her grandmother presents her to the camera, cradled, as if showing off a basket of mangoes. She was a beautiful child, her parents like to say.

Strangers stopped her parents at the mall, to congratulate them and nudge her cheeks with pinkies.

She takes out the printout from her shoulder bag and puts it on the coffee table. Her new face looks up at her parents.

"Koreans and Saudis fly in to get worked on by Dr. Wanich," says her current face. "I can try to get a slot during the term break."

Her mother feels her shirt pocket for reading glasses. Her father picks up the printout for a closer look. They look at her new face, up and down, as if it were an electric bill. This is the first they've heard of her visit to Dr. Wanich. She wants to tell them that it's not their fault.

"This is from hanging out with those rich kids, isn't it?"

"No, listen. Next year, I may have to look for a job. They often ask for a photo from the female applicants."

Her mother looks over to her father.

"Is it true, Mehta?"

"Yes, Mohd, they do that at companies," says her father.

"And scholarship applications," says Mai. "Want me to show you last year's recipients?"

□ □ □

Wednesday evenings, they have a pattern: start at the produce aisle and end at personal hygiene. He pushes the cart, and they fill it. It's their weekly ritual. He and Pia pick up Juhn at the tutoring center and stop at the supermarket in the same plaza. He doesn't schedule patients then, and Pia knows not to book piano lessons. She teaches two or three students most afternoons, to keep busy. Most are daughters and sons of residents in the building. Every few months, they host a recital in the living room. Proud parents sip wine and gather around the Schimmel.

Every child's a prodigy, every song worthy of breathlessness. Juhn doesn't study with Pia. Again, this is the result of his negotiations. He knows their personalities and wants peace in his home.

Juhn drops a pack of yogurt cartons into the cart. Pia picks it up to make sure they're not poisonous.

"Whoa, this is full of sugar."

"It's fine, Pia. She's young. She'll burn it off."

"Some doctor you are."

He doesn't resent her remark; he appreciates her watchfulness as a mother, her intentions. At his clinic he meets many mothers who sit next to their daughters and quibble over the angle of new noses.

Pia braves a circle of shoppers for shrink-wrapped cantaloupes heaped between aisles. The crowd, although better dressed, reminds him of those in the market where, as a boy, he bought fruits with his mother—those yellowing mangoes and eyeball-sized longans and hairy piles of rambutan. She showed him how to divine their ripeness with a thumb poke and a sniff. He doesn't remember when cantaloupes started appearing in every New Year's fruit basket in Krungthep.

"How about this one?" he asks, holding up a cantaloupe he has found satisfactory after a squeeze.

Pia looks at it. "That one won't be ready for a week."

"Are you sure? It feels like it's ready."

"I can tell by the color. And not only that, it's bruised."

He turns the fruit around to find a dark dented spot at the bottom. He inspects dozens of faces each week. He shouldn't have missed this.

"Okay, you're right. I'll let you choose."

He leaves Pia to catch up with Juhn, who has been walking in front of them, her legs outstretched, a slight hop with each step. It's her walk of leisure. These aisles are their park trails. He imagines her at fifteen, thirty, fifty, still with that girlish stride.

She stops to wait for him in front of a blue mountain of mouthwash bottles and, behind it, an aisle of creams and moisturizers.

"Don't we need more sunscreen?" he asks, remembering the bottle whistling with each squeeze on Sunday.

"We do," she says. "But, you know, I may need to swim indoors."

"Indoors?"

"My friends tell me that it'll be better for my skin. Less sun."

"There's sun everywhere. We're in Krungthep."

"Please, please can we look into it? Please?"

She tugs at his sleeves. She has inherited his stubbornness and Pia's regal charms. She pleads, but commands.

"Okay, I will," he says.

□ □ □

To get to the hospital, they cut across the city on the tolled highway. Her father drives, humming a country song, while her mother switches radio stations for traffic reports. Mai's in the backseat, her hair still damp from the shower. They are silent for most of the ride, no different than when going to visit cousins in the provinces or attend a hotel wedding. They try their best to make this afternoon feel like a past afternoon.

"May the sacred look over you," her mother says in the hospital atrium. That morning, at the shrine in their building's courtyard, they had made offerings to spirits and angels, for good luck.

"See you guys soon," she tells her parents, as attendants seat her in a wheelchair. She's pushed through double doors that swing out to receive her. In a dimly lit room, she undresses and puts on a beige-colored gown. From a wall mirror, a face looks at her, bewildered, its body submerged in shadow.

"Bye-bye," she says with a smile.

Outside, she is asked to lie on a bed. She's pushed down a corridor, stopping once next to an older woman with ash-colored skin, nearly see-through, and then into a prep room.

"Hello, Khun Mai."

"Hello, Dr. Wanich."

She clasps her hands at her chin, although she can't see him. Her eyes want to shut under the bright lamps.

"How are you?" his voice sounds out.

"I'm all right, I guess."

"Good. All right's very good."

"How's Juhn's swimming?"

"She's a little fish, thanks to you. She'll be taking lessons at an indoor pool, starting next month."

"She's very beautiful, your daughter."

"Thank you. She is, isn't she?"

He steps away when the anesthesiologist interrupts them to check Mai's blood pressure. Dr. Wanich looks at her charts again. He is almost twice her weight, although she is taller, as most well-nourished kids are these days. She's no longer a child, but she hasn't lost her youthfulness. She has bone structure that would have kept her looking young all her life. He pictures her as a teenager, as a young girl, then as she was at a few months old. The medical textbooks say that babies look the same that early, and then they grow into their fated faces. She's already beautiful. She's perfect.

His colleague gives him a thumbs-up. He nods.

"Ready?" he asks her.

"I am."

When she got together with her friends earlier in the week, Pig was set to depart for a term-break vacation in Australia. They ordered in pizza, and Mai provided tertiary opinions while Pig tapped back and forth on the screen with Bubble and Caterpillar to plan which outfits to pack for scenic jaunts through the Outback. At the end of the night, Pig turned to her, bottom lip bitten. It's a face that Pig likes to deploy in posted photos to exaggerate her grievances. Mai isn't used to seeing it outside of a screen.

"I'm so happy for you. You'll have everything now."

"Silly Pig, how's that even possible?"

"No, I'm not. It's almost unfair."

"Stop being ridiculous. Nothing's different. Nothing's going to change."

So here she is. He puts the mask over her mouth and nose. She turns her eyes back to the operating lamp, the off-white ceiling, the cloudless sky. He watches her eyelids flutter, an instinctual fight, and then she's gone. With a green felt-tip pen he draws an incision path a few millimeters below her lash line. He makes trails along the side of her face and behind the flare of her nose.

He does hundreds of these procedures every year, he reminds himself. He has chosen this specialty, in part, because it lets him avoid matters of life and death. Or does it?

"Scalpel," he says to a nurse.

Her skin and tissue will peel easily into flaps to be held open with tape. She will bleed small streams down her cheek before an assistant wipes her face dry.

She will wake up, unsure if the procedures had been successful. She'll be told by a nurse to keep taking pain medication until she's comfortable. Within a week, the swelling will go away. She will remove the bandage patches and inspect herself in front of a mirror. Her new face will seem like a stranger's mimicking her own head turns.

He will see her, too, the first time at the post-op checkup, where he will shine a penlight on her face and see that her reddened seams have faded. She will likely have done something different, maybe cut her hair to her shoulders, but to him, unlike everyone else, she will not look like another woman.

He will hope these things will always be true: that his daughter loves him, that she never suffers for his fault. Tomorrow, as today, he'll go on giving shape to his patients' wishes. He will believe that all he touches is surface, the least important part of all.

He lines the blade where she wants it. He carves into her with the same force he'd use to cut into a fruit.

SONS

I t's ten in the morning, and Sammy sees Betty's pickup truck roll into
the lot from the direction of town. Wayne's driving. Betty opens the
passenger door and hops down, and Wayne waves palm-up with his
gimpy arm, fingers straight and frozen, like he's feeling for rain.
Sammy is glad to be standing about a hundred yards out in the field
and not near enough to require the usual niceties—excitable commen-
tary about last night's Red Sox game that he didn't watch or a general
inquiry of what he was doing with the camera—until Wayne feels that
sufficient banter had been exchanged. After Wayne drives off, Sammy
sees that Betty has arrived empty-handed. Yesterday, she promised to
make a run to Kreissler's. They're running low on everything—paper
towels, detergent, floor soap. This summer season has been far busier

than the last. Since Memorial Day guests have booked every bungalow and nearly all the rooms in the lodge.

Betty waves with one hand to catch his attention. After he smiles and does a half wave back, she begins to flag him toward her with both arms. She won't yell for fear of waking the guests. He supposes that she wants him to come back up.

It is clear to him that Betty doesn't fully apprehend her intrusion into his zoological investigations. He has been up since five o'clock to capture, through his zoom lenses, the foxes living underneath the shed. He tried enticing them with leftover bits from last night's roast, but his cooking has so far failed to draw them out to daylight. Some townspeople have warned him about feeding the foxes—cunning nighttime raiders of garbage bins and antagonizers of small pets, they say—but what can anyone do to stop him? This is America, and this is his land. He owns that decrepit shed and all that lives under it, the field where he's crouched, the main lodge and the ten bungalows, the driveway Betty and Wayne had just driven up, the wooded trail that hugs gently sloping hills all the way down to the boathouse, and the crescent-shaped beach along the lake where Vermont gentry and assorted New Englanders have vacationed for generations. Some walk up to the reception desk to ask for Mr. Portsmith, not realizing that Sammy is now the owner. The brass plaque on the wall bears his meandering Thai name. They struggle to pronounce it. He tells them to call him by his Anglicized moniker.

"Sammy!" Betty shouts finally.

"*What?*" he mouths, making it clear that he won't resort to her kind of ruckus. She turns and disappears into the kitchen's side door.

Just to show her who's who, he will stay out here for another five or ten minutes, before packing his camera and crossing the field and its scattered dandelion patches and slender, prickly grass to find her in the kitchen, where she has likely sat down at the dinette to wait with folded arms. He points his lenses at the gap between the shed's rotted boards where he might see an animal's pointy orange snout poke through, and he waits.

In this place, it's easy for him to become a patient man, and not just in matters involving Betty. Time passes here in a way that makes him feel like he can never run out of it. If he has to, say, fix a broken latch on a window shutter or rake the beach sand flat after a day of trampling and digging by guests' children, he can lavish exorbitant attention on each task. And there's certainly more than enough to do. Five years ago, when he sat with the Portsmiths at the lodge's patio to sign papers for the sale, they warned him, the good people that they are. "It's so much work, for someone our age, and it'll probably be no less for you," said Mr. Portsmith. Unlike their son, who didn't want to take his parents' place at the lodge, Sammy was undeterred. He had spent the greater part of that year searching for some kind of new footing, and when he saw the sales posting for the lodge online, he flew across the country and made the six-hour drive from New York City the very week. Within the next month, the lodge was his.

He likes to think that Betty came with the place. Without her, he'd never have made it past the first year. For years she had worked for the Portsmiths, cleaning the rooms and bungalows, laundering all the sheets and towels, and amassing know-how essential to the lodge's operation, like which switches to jiggle on the circuit breaker and how to prevent bears from getting into the dumpster. Sometimes, it feels to him like the place is more hers than his. She grew up a town away and later came back to the area, having dropped out of college after a few semesters of youthful excess. As contrition, he guesses, she attends nearly every meeting of the town library's book club and has been making her way through a respectable magazine's list of purported top one hundred books. Read this, she'll tell him, despite the likelihood that he won't. In her late thirties, she's more than twenty years his junior and doesn't tire easily, he likes to joke to his faraway friends.

He finds her in the game room, sweeping Ping-Pong balls from under the sofa. She looks up, then takes a pen out of her pocket and tosses it to him. After catching it, he finds that it's not a pen at all but some kind of plastic gizmo that ends in a blue dot.

"I'm pregnant," she tells him, and then leans on the broom, her signal that she's done speaking. He tries to gauge, by the angle of her pinched brows, the implications.

"Ha ha," is all he could say right off.

"I'm not kidding. I tested with two kits from two different pharmacies, one yesterday and another this morning."

"When did it happen? How far along?"

"Maybe six weeks."

In emergencies, he likes to trace back his steps. He does it when he loses things and when he doesn't know where he is, as if by figuring out the course of what has happened, he'll have readied himself for what's due.

"Suite five."

"The laundry room."

He returns to quieted grunts and flesh clumsily grappled in the dark. Two bodies heaving on a hill of unwashed sheets. He remembers again how he had thrust with the "1812 Overture" in his head. The imagination of his little men reaching her verdant spaces thrilled him more than the act itself.

"You sure it's not Wayne's?"

"Better chance it's Zeus's." She has been reading the classics.

Cammy can't deny the awfulness of this situation for Wayne, but he can honestly say that he hasn't schemed to undo what Wayne has with Betty. He certainly wasn't there when Wayne and Betty first met and dated in high school. He had no part in how they settled on each other again after her return to the township. Wayne had taken some nebulous heroic part in the liberation of Kuwait, and she decided she could do worse than someone the townspeople called "Sarge" who received a check from the US government every month in recompense for mysterious bodily symptoms: that barely controllable right arm, nausea, headaches, sudden night tremors, and, as the coup de grâce, terminally sluggish sperm motility.

And yet, Sammy knows, he certainly isn't blameless. If she had been any less pretty, he would have hired someone else for cheaper.

"Praise this modern divine miracle."

"You know what? You're an asshole."

"I'm sorry."

"Well, what do you want to do?" Betty asks.

He won't make a smart-ass joke now. He knows that look: the result of profound exasperation preparing to leap to contempt, but then the anger that spurred her question extinguishes, as if it has run out of something to burn.

He remembers another pair of eyes demanding an answer from him like that. He sees a face he hasn't seen in years. Unexpected things bring her back.

It might be the exacting way the cashier always answers the phone while he's standing in line at the general store. Or it could be the sight of a guest wading into the waters of the lake—some woman with similar shoulder-length dark hair and sharp, clifflike shoulders—that would make him think of Nee in the pool, goading children to finish another lap. Those sudden reminders jar him from whatever he has been doing—buying eggs or drying canoes—so that he needs to take a moment to regain his present facts and bearings, as if he's been away from them for a very long time.

He reminds himself that Betty's waiting for him to answer. He wonders if she even knows what she wants to do. Maybe she's asking him so that she'll have something to feed her own reaction, or it might be that she doesn't want to be the first to make her position known. It's a standoff not at all unfamiliar. Their arguments—over menial things like how the guest beds should be made or whether she should wash the better plates by hand—have never ended quickly. He believes it was one of their acts of reconciliation that led them to the current predicament.

"Don't worry. I already know what I'm going to do."

"Then why are you asking me?"

"I'm curious to see what you want."

In the silence, he gauges how much time he has to respond. He has rolled around in his head the question of children, but only until he's reminded of the his age and the unlikelihood of having any. He thinks of his father and his phantom ancestors before him, all plotted along a line in which he's the pointed tip racing toward oblivion.

"If you want to end it, I trust you to make that decision, but I would be fine if you've decided to do whatever else."

"Goddammit, just say it. Do you want me to have the kid or not?"

Too often, he's been quick to second-guess the choices he's made. He wishes he had taken another county road to get to I-91. He can't say how often he's reversed his steps, after having locked his front door and gotten his car keys out, to change his pants.

"I wouldn't mind it. You having the kid, I mean."

"Good. This one's the surprise I'm keeping. The doctors didn't think I'd ever have one, but here we are."

He nods, relieved, as if he's lucked on the right answer. He remembers to smile, ostensibly at the prospect of his genetic perpetuation but largely to ensure some momentary calm.

Of course, her pregnancy will change everything between them. What scant authority he's held as her employer will crumble against the fact of this future child.

And what is this thing that they have, anyway? Their affair is not the result of unquenchable passion but of a joint impulsiveness that has swept them up and again and again deposited them behind the same closed doors, to satisfy a mutual need for distraction. Is there more to them than that, enough to share the responsibilities of a child? He feels familiar tremors of dread, like when he suddenly realizes that he has swum too far out on the lake.

He walks over to her, and for a long minute, they hug. If they were a real couple who had tried for a baby, he might be feeling overwhelming joy—a prompt for a kiss, perhaps. All they manage to do is lean against each other in this room, among stacks of disintegrating board games and piled tennis rackets—the beginning and end of someone else's youth.

He halfway hopes that a guest will walk in on them and ask for more brewed coffee or for directions to the boathouse. None do. He hears Betty draw long, deep breaths, as if she is getting ready for a sprint.

"Now what?" he asks.

"When I get home this evening," she says, "I'm going to have to tell Wayne."

□ □ □

A younger Sammy would have wished to avoid the evening, the next few hours, the arriving minutes. He would try to hold on to each moment, as if he could slow down time. This Sammy knows that it will always slip from him.

If he's to surrender to the currents and let himself gaze at what's due, he'll see the vague shape of Betty in the near distance, the paper towels and gallon jug of lemon-scented disinfectant that he must buy for the lodge, and a little farther from that, the lake and its shore, gray and hazy, as if he's looking at the view through rain. Beyond that, he can't see much at all. Nothing of him persists, he's afraid, except perhaps, possibly, this child.

He is still, and only time moves. He can feel it dash against him, scraping off grains of his substance; soon nothing will be left.

The future used to be his haven. He escaped to its large open country when he felt his present life constrict around him. It was where he could live out the stories that seemed to happen only to other people.

In England, when he was young, he looked ahead to school breaks, when there would be freedom from the masters and the other boys, and there would be, he was positive, girls. In the futures he dreamed then, his camera and made-up press credentials would broker his way into one-room clubs in Soho where everyone wanted to be photographed. At some point, a woman would pull him into some secret nook and let him touch her in places he'd only seen in the magazines passed, boy to boy, between schoolbooks. And when he did become a professional photographer, the future he saw for himself brimmed with wide admiration for his eye. There would be exhibits and openings, retrospectives and treasured monographs. In interviews, he would regale the public with tales of near misses in war zones and the welcome intrusion of grace and beauty amid unimaginable despair.

When he was no longer able to furnish a future for himself in this way, he found women who did so for him. He could be accused of falling in love just so that new futures would appear, and he would counterclaim to have loved them all: Anja, Matilde, Isma, Nee, and the rest, even as the historical record of his decisions and actions would discredit his assertion.

What is his future now? It appears less and less expansive: no more than a strip narrowing into a corner bordered by the endless dark.

It's the past that now pulls at his imagination. He used to try to flee from it, but still it managed to follow him. It trails him, heavy with decided consequences, wider than the lay of whatever's ahead. It calls out to him and demands that he look back. He feels this monster that has been his life reach out and grab him, and he can do nothing but give in to its strengthening, formidable gravity.

He keeps his old photographs in the shed, having converted the part of it that isn't used to store tools into a small winterized room where, shielded from the elements by plastic sleeves, the photos lie flat in file cabinets he bought at a yard sale, arranged sometimes by year, some by place. He calls this his archives, as a joke to himself. Only he has any use for the photos.

Some inevitable time, not so far off, a stranger will perhaps riffle through them. He has tried to imagine himself as someone else who has shown up to survey what's left of a man. Will they even wonder who these people in the photos are? Where they were? Most likely, this stranger will only try to discern which might fetch a price and which should be discarded. To abet a liquidation sale, they might sort the photos by subject: landscapes, city streets, a few series that look like photojournalism, assorted consumer products.

Some of the photos are of women: a fine-boned blonde shopping for flowers in what looks like a Scandinavian street; and probably in Rome, judging from shop signs, a cat-eyed brunette who looks up from a watercolor landscape she's been painting in a sketchbook; another blonde is captured in a perpetual, cross-legged wait for the train at a graffitied New York subway station; and a small-shouldered Asian woman grins to the camera high on a tall building's balcony.

A few of the photos have been labeled on the backs. If this unknown person were inquisitive enough, they might look up the names online. They'd find nothing at all on Isma and Matilde. Anja's obituary would briefly announce the passing of a beloved wife and respected colleague at the Kulturdepartementet. Nee's face looks out from the website of a condo's management office.

From a manila envelope, the unknown person pulls out photos of an old house. The first few are wide-angle exterior shots. They show a pale, two-story house circumscribed by a roofed terrace and made airy by tall fanlighted windows with low balustrades. The palm trees on either side of the main entrance and the stark light visibly hot on the skin makes it clear that this photo isn't of Vermont. A dull-colored canal flows past a wooden dock. A small school of arm-sized fish gasps for pellets in a garden pond. Inside the house, a wrought-iron staircase curves down one wall of the foyer to land on a floor of inlaid diamond-shaped marble. Ornate tiles adorn the ceiling with blooming flowers. Gray cloth drapes over the shape of an upright piano. Inside the wooden frame of what looks to be a large rectangular mirror, an unsmiling young man with a boxy camera aims from his waist.

□ □ □

It's almost evening, and he's driving back from Kreissler's with re-plenished supplies in the back of the van. He knows the way as if he's driven those roads his whole life. His hands turn the wheel seemingly without his intervention, pointing the car down nameless country roads.

He contemplates stopping for a bite. He hasn't had much to eat all day and probably should have wolfed down a biscuit before he left the lodge. He keeps driving, because he thinks it's more habit than actual hunger that's troubling his stomach, and he should at least get himself somewhere where Betty can find him.

He thinks of Betty in the rec room telling him, "*I can't pretend to Wayne this hasn't happened, not for a minute.*" That makes him picture Wayne in his living room, where she'll likely have found him. He sees him wearing a gray T-shirt with the faded name of a made-up sports club printed across the chest. Wayne has the bulky frame of someone once athletic, but now he sits wrecked on a couch cushion, with an overheating laptop balanced on his knees. If Betty's to be believed, this is how he spends his days. Sarge, people say to Wayne out of respect, but it can sound like taunting.

Five miles past the town's meager Main Street, Sammy turns down a two-lane road to the land that's his.

He sees Wayne smoking in the parking lot. He's not alone. Betty's sitting in the truck, and he recognizes Little Head and Billy Dave leaning against a guest's Subaru. From what Betty tells him, they've been friends with Wayne since high school. He knows they do contracting work on out-of-towners' vacation homes. They're lean and sinewy and lizardlike and remind him of his sun-darkened countrymen whose skinny frames belie their feats—hauling cement buckets up twenty floors at construction sites or, in a ring, swinging knees at one another for the entertainment of thousands.

He squeezes into the spot across from them. When Betty sees him, she gets out of the truck. He looks her over and asks, "Are you all right?" She nods. He sees from her reddened eyes that she's been crying.

"Sammy!"

His name rises out of Wayne like a flushed bird. "Hey, what's going on here?" he deigns to ask.

With the gimp hand, Wayne whips out a plastic wand that ends with a radiant blue dot and points it at him.

He should feel more fear at the sight of these hostile young men.

He's outlived that simple breed of terror, he guesses. He thinks little of pain that would only counterbalance the excessive sum of his life-long leisures. He doesn't tremble anymore at the thought of some terrible thing that could happen to him. He can stand back and watch, as if regarding someone else's life. He used to require a camera for this; his own eyes are all he needs now to step a world away.

Wayne stands there for what must be half a minute, without saying another word. Then he flings the test stick on the ground.

"What?" Wayne yells with the fat jug that's his head. "What the fuck is this?"

Sammy can only let out a sigh as Wayne turns toward Betty, unfurling a finger in his direction.

"Really? Him?" Wayne squints at Sammy as if this were the hardest question he's ever asked of anyone. "Him? Are you fucking kidding me?"

"So messed up," says Billy Dave. Little Head shakes his eponymous knob.

"Wayne, stop," Betty says. "You guys need to all leave right now. This is ridiculous."

Wayne borrows the expression of someone who's seeing, at the same time, the summed horrors of human violence and the sublime beauty of a mountain storm.

"But we just got here, Betty. I brought us all to see the great fucking choice you've made, choosing to betray me with this old piece of dog shit," he says with a smirk.

Sammy stays quiet as Wayne looks him up and down. He feels Wayne's eyes undress him, no doubt comparing his old man's body and its parts with his own and basking in the deepening shame that Betty has chosen to occupy herself with any of it.

"It just happened, Wayne. I didn't choose anything. I'm sorry, I told you already," Betty says.

"This shriveled Chinese fuckhead bum!" Wayne yells. "I can't fucking believe it."

Sammy doesn't feel compelled to correct Wayne's ethnic and social assignation.

Little Head straightens his shoulders. Billy Dave follows. His neck tilts like the bough of an old oak.

"Listen, guys," says Sammy. "I know this stinks, but we can all act like civilized men here."

"You thought you can be an asshole and do whatever you want and not pay for it," says Little Head.

"Yes, but I can pay for it. I swear."

Sammy knows he's too out of shape to bother running. Betty screams for Wayne and his friends to stop and stay where they are.

It's now that Sammy looks up to see a guest peering out a window—Mrs. Moore, the retired schoolteacher from Boston—and, for an instant, he worries that she will rate his lodge poorly on the travel sites.

He feels Little Head and Billy Dave grab each of his arms, and suddenly he's jerked toward Wayne, who's standing with clenched fists. He keeps an eye on Wayne's gimp hand and expects it to swerve at him: a pellet blast of loose knuckles against his face. Fine, have his battered body.

Except what he feels next is Little Head and Billy Dave loosening their grip.

They've done so because Wayne has dropped to his knees, arms slung to his sides. He's sobbing, like a boy who has had everything he's known and cherished stolen from him. Little Head and Billy Dave can do nothing but look in awe.

Sammy figures he should bolt to the car and back it out the road, away from any hurled slurs or objects. He doesn't. He's held back by the sight of Wayne breaking apart.

It hits him in the gut: there's no natural scheme being played out, just his own foul part, all along. He bedded this man's girlfriend and impregnated her with his dusty sperm.

Wayne's crying harder. Sammy feels the broken man's wails batter some part loose inside of him, and all of a sudden, he's bent over holding his knees. In one ear, he hears Betty screaming his name, because he's opened his mouth and endowed his gastric contents to this glorious land where his child will crawl and run.

Betty asks again if he's okay, and, uncertain, he says yes. He wipes his lips with a wrist and straightens up. Wayne hasn't moved from where he sits crumpled. Little Head and Billy Dave are hunched over him, offering words of courage that they must have picked up from game day sidelines.

Sammy still can't guess how this all will end: with his devastation or their retreat. Any second now, they could all still pounce on him.

He looks for Mrs. Moore. She's no longer by the window, and no other guests have come to theirs. He lets himself take in the lodge, its weathered clapboards and carved gables and steep roof. Almost a hundred fifty years ago, tradesmen laid fieldstone on a rectangle of carved earth and hewed and joined milled timbers from the surrounding hills to fashion what would be a rough farmhouse, and then the beginnings of a country inn.

Out in the sloping field, white pitted boulders sleep half buried where long extinct glaciers have rolled them to place. An orange shape scampers across the expanse of meadow fescue and clover, its tail straightened like a rudder. Sammy knows it won't stop until it's home.

POSSESSION

Were the pear trees on the hill again verdant and full? Had his father and Andrew taken the rowboat out on Archer's Pond? Phineas thought of the Smiths and the Pendletons and questioned whether anyone in the valley had asked about him.

Here, bored urchins lit remnant firecrackers at irregular hours. Soon, the Siamese would celebrate their new year, flocking to temples in the morning and gambling dens thereafter.

Whatever jubilation these festivities might bring, however, would be tempered by rampant disease in the capital. The line at the veranda grew longer each day. His patients came after their native medicine had failed, showing him the strange concoctions prescribed to them: pulverized hog jaw and gall of snakes, placed on a clay idol's hand and then boiled.

Miss Lisle and Miss Crawford assisted him. Fewer children now came to the school. He was glad that he had vaccinated many of the children months before, after learning methods from Dr. Bradley on a rare visit to the other side of the river. Most of the children lived in deplorable conditions, nothing more than huts floating above muddied waters in which they both bathed and secreted their wastes. He was unsure whether the inoculants would guard against whatever it was that was ailing the capital, but he remained hopeful that any effect they had would be beneficial.

In the past months, he had seen a greater part of the city. He had been rowed along brimming canals to the homes of noblemen and merchants, had drunk tea served to him in imported silver pots that cost ten times their European prices. He had also tended to the sick in the nether reaches of opium dens and open-air markets, where vendors laid their fevered children next to mounds of fruits for sale. The city radiated from the river outward, and so did her madness.

It was true that each time he left the house he kept an eye out for Bunsahk and his son. He thought of them often, perhaps more than he should. Not knowing the man's fate proved worse than knowing himself a cause of his doom.

"What if you find out that he is no more? What then?" Winston asked, after promising to aid in his search.

"Then I'd know that I have fallen short, but my estimations were correct, and everything I know about medicine still holds true."

"And if you find out that the man lives?"

"I'd still have failed him, but I'd also have an honest test of the substance of my tenets."

He would not have the chance to verify whether Winston would make good on his promise of help in the matter. Not a day after their conversation, the reverend found Winston sprawled on one of the pews, without trousers. Less than an hour passed between the reverend's discovery and his shaking Winston's hand at the gate with words of farewell. Even Miss Crawford was surprised that the reverend had finally acted.

"I am almost saddened," she said, her eyes wet.

Winston told Phineas not to worry. "I've got a few notions whirling about," he said, tapping on his temple. "Have faith in me. In yourself, too."

And so as he ventured out into the forsaken city, he looked out for Winston, as well.

He floated like a black phantom along roads that seemed to darken with his steps, past street dogs backing into alleyways and barebreasted mothers tugging their children into doorways. He had been warned of the dangers after dark. Foreigners were often found bled from opened throats, pierced by crude bamboo spikes, left to liquefy and ferment in their woolen trousers. His fears, however, seemed to lessen in the empty nighttime streets. The dark cleansed his way forward, leaving only flickering lantern lights from windows, the smells of cooked meals wafting from homes propped on stilts, the sudden light of fireflies and shrill screams of bats. The capital was more comprehensible to him when it was subsumed by night, appearing as if it were but one small village after another. Following a native to where his patients lay, he sometimes came across familiar figures passing in the dark—the robed monks silent and barefoot, the night watchmen with stick and cymbal who nodded knowingly to him, as if he were one of their own.

Times turned dreadful not only for the city but also for the mission. Miss Lisle fell ill. Phineas made her take spoonfuls of laudanum diluted in rice spirits, and peppermint tincture dropped into hot water. She had been blessed with beauty, and it made him tremble to see her skin shrivel and her eyes sink into darkened pits. She lay there, pained, as fluids flushed out of her and thirst consumed her. In the steamy weather, she complained of freezing winds. Cholera was cruel but also quick. She breathed her last before the sun rose on a third day of illness and was interred in the Protestant cemetery by sundown. Miss Crawford, who had attended to her day and night, shipped Miss Lisle's few possessions to her family in Missouri. Phineas prayed that they might find solace in a brush still entangled with strands of her fair hair; her stained, roach-eaten dresses; and a hymnal blotted with the blood of swatted mosquitoes.

He believed himself heartbroken, but he could not mourn.

The Siamese capital was dying. Wailing sounded in the streets as families carried their dead to the body carts. A new mandate had put an end to the custom of tying corpses to stones and heaving them into the river. Now the air reeked of burnt flesh.

Many blamed the disease on demon spirits. Phineas had learned that Buddhist belief hinged on a system of ledgered merits and demerits, and now he saw how, in hopes of gaining the favor of their account in this life, the Siamese sought to manufacture an increase of merits. Market fish escaped the fishmonger's block and were returned to the river. Butchers and slaughterhouses were emptied, and once-doomed animals went free, while eating halls went without meat. Hens and pigs roamed the roads, nobody daring to disturb them for fear of karmic repercussions. Noontime and midnight, fireworks and the clanging of pots broke the quiet as families tried to scare evil away from the homes of the diseased.

The living came to him, pleading for more life. He was entreated to come into homes encircled by monk-blessed cords to save men, women, infants soon to die or already dead. As he crossed the city, some bowed down before his path. Others trembled at his presence, thinking him a demon wearing the pale skin of a man. Street children who had once ridiculed him now hid behind trees when he neared. He did not dispel the aura of magic. He felt compelled to embrace it in the performance of his duty. If they believed, and he believed, together they might find salvation yet.

His brother sent him letters, one including a sketch of ships in New York Harbor. He had forgotten all about them. In return, he sketched from memory a picture of the music room in Gransden Hall, more for his benefit than for his brother's. He feared that he might lose the completeness with which he saw that room—his mother's lacework draped over the piano, the blue sycamore leaves imprinted on the wallpaper. In the letter he attached to the sketch, he did not mention the deplorable state of the city but warned his brother that because of growing demands for his medical duties, he might have little time to spare. He vowed he would write again after circumstances improved.

They did not. The next week, the sickness breached him. The hospital closed, but the afflicted still remained, sleeping on straw mats as they leaked into the earth. He walked among them, hiding his condition, and then returned to his quarter. He lay in his bed, feeling his deterioration advance at every hour. Every now and then, he heard through his window the arrival of a cart, the gates of the compound creaking open.

He warned Miss Crawford to let him be, lest his foul humors take hold of her as well. She refused. He was both disappointed and relieved.

Soon, there was no one else left at the mission but Miss Crawford. The reverend fell ill and did not last a day. With no room left in the cemetery, the cart pushers were forced to deliver him to fire.

Immobilized by grief, Miss Crawford stayed at the mission, but Phineas found the strength to accompany the reverend's body to the designated grounds north of the city, so that he could offer rites of committal at the pyre. Two able-bodied devotees carried the body on bamboo rods borne on their shoulders.

At the cremation grounds, the reverend lay with natives on stacked logs topped with dried palm fronds. The cremator bound the body with rope, so that the reverend would not sit up aflame, and doused it with plant oils from a clay pot. Another cremator brought a branch ignited from a neighboring pyre.

Phineas stood before the reverend, releasing words to wake him to Glory. The lit branch shook in his unsteady hand.

Then he saw, among the company of bodies waiting their turn for the pyre, the remains of the witch doctor. The man was lain out in white cloth, his hair slicked and combed, his skin touched with ceremonial powder. Phineas would not have recognized him had he not seen the driftwood stick curled in the corpse's hands. The man had been loved and mourned, as were all who lay there.

He once desired nothing more than to strike this man down. Encountering his former adversary now, Phineas was surprised to feel neither anger nor hate. He considered that he might have become too accustomed to the tragedies around him. He had, at many prior instances, felt thankful that his profession condoned his taking refuge in his role. He could step back from his immediate situation, as if into a different room concurrent with his own life, and watch another man who was he perform procedures in his place. Yet, here at the cremating grounds, he had no patient who would have let him dissolve into his duty, and he could not conjure the revulsion and fury the witch doctor ought to have inspired. He had not arrived at a state of apatheia, as the ancients had countenanced, but its opposite—a multitude of his passions demanded to be heard.

First, panic cried above the din. His memory no longer preserved the man's face.

Then sorrow sang. Where were the secret chambers and nooks and gardens in which his most tender and truest sentiments dwelled, which he had thought everlasting?

BIRDS

*A*ny day now, the people of Krungthep will celebrate the river leaving the city.

This morning, like many mornings these past few years, Pig tunes out when the news anchors start to discuss the flooding situation. They can say anything they want with their cheery voices—*Experts predict . . . powerful pumps . . . relief efforts . . . the government is committed to . . .*

But she's come to know that none of their words matter more than the squawking of gulls and other seabirds that now regularly make a mess of the balcony.

She bends forward in front of the bathroom mirror to dab on foundation, followed by concealer. In front of her, she sees her own face and also the face of someone she doesn't want to recognize. She will have to lay on another dusting of powder. A face can tell too much, especially to Mai.

Thinking to dress well for their lunch, she has picked out one of her reliables—a gray silk blouse and navy blue pants—but now she realizes that it makes her look matronly.

Better-constructed dams . . . zones affected . . . the prime minister gave encouragement . . .

There isn't enough time to change. She should have gotten up earlier, but with her worries she's often unable to sleep until first light begins to erase night from her windows. After a few hours of restless dozing, she usually wakes to recoil from a thought that tires her again: Woon.

She smoothes out creases on her pants, gives herself a reassuring nod in the mirror, and then walks to her son's room.

□ □ □

She has decided to set a number. She will stop after three knocks, and then pick up her purse from the sofa to leave for the day. As she has for six months, she hopes this will be the time the door opens.

"Woon, my dearest, won't you come out for lunch with me and Auntie Mai?" she asks the door. "The last time she was here, you and her really got along, remember?"

She judges from the pale slit underneath the door that Woon's curtains are drawn back. Barely any morning light reaches the hallway, where she stands in near dark, as is the usual case on Tuesdays and Wednesdays when the power in her zone often vanishes without warning. The bulbs overhead flicker out, every appliance humming dead. By now she has learned how to thump across the unlit apartment—

L-shaped, with two bedrooms on opposite ends and a high view of the city. Well suited for her and Woon, as Mai has said.

"We're going to a place you like, the one that makes the tasty dark broth," she tells the door. "You can order extra meatballs, anything you want."

A week or two before her son started to lock himself in his room, she had brought him noodles from that very shop. She had prepared the table for the two of them to eat together, their ritual of sorts after the move to the apartment. But that evening, he took his bowl into his room, to eat by himself, his door closed. He was occupied with homework, she told herself then. Classes had become ever so competitive.

When he refused to leave the room even for school, she screamed and banged on the door. When she used an old five-baht coin to unlock it, and he threw himself against the door as she tried to push through, she could no longer avoid the truth: his door would not open for her, that day or after. After a month of absences, the school stopped calling to ask where he was.

"Fine, you don't have to come with me if you don't want to, but let's not forget your meals." The bowl of porridge she left outside his door earlier that morning has cooled, untouched.

This is the pattern that saddens her: he only emerged when she wasn't around. The last time she saw him was two weeks ago, a swift shadow flitting to the bathroom one night, then shuffling back inside his room. She had fallen asleep on the sofa, and if not for the rousing noise her son made patting the wall to feel his way, she wouldn't have wakened for even that sighting. She stifled the impulse to call out to him. She had promised herself that she would avoid doing anything that might upset him.

"Woon," she says to the door. "What do you want me to tell Auntie Mai? She asked about you. Please answer, so I can tell her how you are."

She knocks again and again, first with knuckles and then with the bony edge of a fist, how many times she doesn't care to count anymore. She rests her forehead on the door and listens. Somewhere outside, a growling plane engine churns the sky.

"Do you want to have him committed?" the bespectacled man had asked. This was at the start of Woon's lock-in, when she made the rounds of psychiatrists. She had brought this one to the apartment to question a door that would refuse to answer.

"It's an option we can take, with your consent," the doctor had told her, out in the hallway.

Pig foresaw the scene of struggle. How could they guarantee that Woon wouldn't get hurt in the process? And even if they were able to restrain him, there'd be no hiding his being carried through the hallway and down the elevator and out the lobby. How could she be certain that neighbors wouldn't talk and that no word would reach Woon's teachers? She didn't want to diminish his chances of going to a reputable university in a few years.

"Let me think it over, Doctor," she said, but she had already decided. If she were patient and supportive, he would come around. He had always been a good son. There would still be a happy life for them both.

"Woon, Woon," she says to the door, banging with both hands. "Come out just this once. Can you hear me? Please don't make me come in there to get you."

By now she should have known not to expect a response, but she can't help putting her ear against the door. She lays her palm on it as she would her son's back.

A piece of paper slides through the gap under the door, a page torn from a math textbook. Scrawled on it in pencil: *Leave me alone.* And a second line: *Or this will happen.* Then a stick figure under a trail of dots, having plummeted from a square window.

"Okay, Woon, you win. I'm leaving."

She lets the apartment door close behind her. She thinks of calling Mai to cancel lunch, but what would she do instead? Stand out in the hall for another six or seven hours?

Besides, this isn't the first time he's done this, and the other times, nothing happened. She shouldn't reward his antics by showing him that they have any effect on her.

No, Woon wouldn't hurt himself. Growing up, he'd always stop on his own at crosswalks, as he'd been told. At the clinic, he'd turn away, eyes closed, when the nurse pricked his arm with a needle. Teenagers like to sound off more than they mean, a normal part of their horrible phases.

The hallway lights flicker on but then go dark again. She doesn't bother to check if the elevators are working but instead heads straight to the stairwell.

A saying has come into fashion in Krungthep in recent years: *No lights, no problem.* At first, it seemed to voice a prideful kind of resilience, but lately, whenever a neighbor says it in the dimmed building lobby, she hears only resignation. It doesn't take much more than ankle-deep water to overwhelm the city's hydro pump stations. Out goes the usual public alert to affected zones: *Due to today's rising flood levels, electrical shutoffs have been authorized to avoid equipment damage and electrocution. Apologies for any inconvenience.*

◻   ◻   ◻

There are hardly any tables open, but they find one near the cooking stand, where they can watch bowls of noodles being assembled under a blur of hands.

After a few spoonfuls, Pig and Mai conclude that the broth isn't as fragrant as they remember it. What makes the shop worthwhile is how much of the old one the owners managed to salvage from the floodwater: the same rickety sheet-metal stools and tables, the wrought-iron light fixtures, the wooden ceiling fans from who knows when. Even the view outside looks the same: the parade of buses and motorcycles passing behind sidewalk vendors and brightly colored tarps stretched overhead, replacing the sun and sky.

Rain dimples black pools in the road. Storeowners drag out sandbags, still soggy from the last downpour, to pile across entryways. This afternoon, unlike others, Pig doesn't mind the prospect of a storm and a power outage.

"Don't worry. There will be a drier day with working elevators, and we can meet at the apartment like you wanted," she says, twirling slippery noodles into a ball with her fork. "Believe me, you'll enjoy not having to walk up twenty-something stories."

Pig reads in Mai's half nod and flattened grin her disappointed agreement. How comforting that so many years won't change someone's facial cues.

"Phee would complain the whole way, as much as she wants to see where her grandparents lived," says Mai.

Mai now lives with her daughter in New York, and after her parents passed away, she let the apartment to Pig, pegging the annual rent at the cost of a dozen limes. By then, Pig was no longer in a position to decline Mai's generosity. It took some time to get used to living in a less spacious place than the house where she had lived with Woon when he was small. She still misses looking out to her long sloping lawn, a reassuring sight in the shadow of packed high-rises.

"I'd be curious about my grandparents, too, especially if I were her. Did I tell you I make offerings to them every year?"

"I didn't know that. Thanks, Pig."

"It's the least I can do. They really were such good people."

"I'm sure they're eating way better now than when they were alive."

The mention of grandparents makes Pig remember her own. As a child, Pig had listened to her grandmother talk about Allied air raids over the city and how sirens sent everyone to pull shut the blackout curtains. Now, nearly a hundred years later, everyone goes to the window to see who else still has light.

"So how are you liking where they've put you up this time?"

"It's another one of those corporate flats that feels too much like a hotel room. I don't know why I expect it to be any different. There's at least a pool, but I haven't been able to take a dip, with my schedule."

"You used to swim so much. I remember that you took lessons at the building."

"That's right. Every weekend. I had a good teacher."

"Yeah, I remember you told me. Well, maybe you should wake up a little earlier and go for morning swims."

"I totally do need the exercise."

"Well, if the power goes out, you're definitely going to get some, trudging up and down the stairs."

"The only remarkable thing about the zone where I'm staying is that the elevators always work. I don't know how I'd make it through the day if they didn't."

"Oh, you get used to elevators being out of commission. Haven't you noticed my amazing calves?"

Pig extends her leg and turns her foot, flexing. Her legs have retained some youth, she thinks, unlike the rest of her. Mai, though, looks as if she has hardly aged anywhere, her crinkles faint, her frame unrounded—and so casually spirited in an ivory linen suit wrinkled at the right places. Pig wonders if the young civil servants and office clerks at the neighboring tables might mistake the two of them for a mother eating with her adult daughter.

"Pig, come to my project site. I want to show you the work I'm doing."

"Are you sure? Do you really have the time? I don't want to bother you."

If she were a good mother, she would have already said no, using the usual excuses: work deadlines to meet, errands to tick off, everything amazing and busy.

"It's no bother. I can always move around meetings," says Mai. "Just nod when I tell people you're a visiting government honcho."

"Okay, well, I'll try my best to look important."

She tells herself again that Woon wll be fine, and she has to believe it.

Before her parents died, Mai had returned only at the New Year holiday, staying for a week at most before some company's crisis—a conglomerate's assembly lines coming to a halt or some telecom giant verging on bankruptcy—demanded her immediate presence elsewhere.

Pig would drive her to the airport, along the way consoling her for having to leave earlier than expected. That was almost two decades ago, when Mai was only an overworked, sleepless fledgling at the consulting firm. The Mai of later years called a car and left early, before light, on her own. This Mai sent one-sentence replies, apologized for the brevity, and then disappeared for months. Five years have passed since Mai last visited. When Pig received the message that she was coming to manage a project in Krungthep, Pig replied that she couldn't wait for all the time they'd spend together, not quite believing Mai would find much. But she has, and she's been quite insistent, making it harder to say no.

"When I last met him, Woon was all into robots and monsters. Call him and see if he can join us."

"There's no way he's going to skip his music rehearsals. I told him not to take on too many extracurriculars, but he couldn't help himself."

"That's too bad, I think he would've enjoyed meeting the birds."

□ □ □

Pig first heard of the birds months ago, from a blurb that interrupted the telenovela playing on her book. *"Sleep well! Safety and happiness for all Thais, no worries!"* floated in bubbles from bug-eyed cartoon citizens, like those from comics she had read as a kid. *"Say hello to the birds! They're working hard to protect happy days ahead."* Cartoon birds fluttered into the message before disbanding out of view.

In waiting halls at the ferry port, Pig has noticed "SLEEP WELL!" banners hung between pillars. The figure of a young boy, curled in his bed like a newborn puppy, floats above a caption proclaiming, *"Knowing he's safe today, he dreams of his future as an environmental engineer."*

Now Mai is about to give her a private demonstration. They have arrived at a fluorescent-lit lab space where a concrete pillar as tall and formidable as a temple gate giant rises from a platform. Next to it, a row of fist-sized metallic orbs—the birds—rest on tripod stands.

After Mai pushes the button that put the rotors in motion, Pig steps back to let a bird take flight. This bird doesn't resemble the usual ones she has seen presiding over car-choked intersections during rush hour. Those look like the hatchlings of helicopters, their blades spinning on jutted spidery arms. This bird, with a belt of petal-shaped wings whirling around the middle of its round body, reminds Pig of a pudgy child doing pirouettes in her tutu. With barely a sound, it lifts from the stand to hover eye level in front of them. Mai hands her glasses with darkened lenses.

"I love this next part," she says, beaming girlishly.

Eyelets that dot the entire bird glow blue on the side facing the pillar. The radiant hue, as if sapphires have emptied their color into the air, sends Pig's hand over her mouth to cover a sudden gasp.

"It's like the ball spinning from the ceiling at one of those clubs, remember?" she asks, without specific memory of one. Two decades have dissolved everything so familiar in her university days to vague, fleeting notions.

"Of course. That one with parties where everybody wore 1990s vintage outfits."

"Le Discotheque. What a terrible place."

"We were such stupid kids," says Mai with exaggerated conviction.

Pig nods at the unintended truth of Mai's joke. Pig, back then, had assumed her own family would take care of whatever was to come after she graduated. How naive of that girl to believe her future lay in stone before her.

"Right behind each of the lenses are thousands of little mirrors taking in more information than we could look at in ten lifetimes," says Mai, motioning toward the bird with an open hand, a gesture Pig thinks more apt for an audience much larger than a lone childhood friend. It's how Mai speaks now, she realizes, always with those gently gliding hands in perpetual tai-chi movements.

"What happens to the information?" she asks Mai.

"Scans tell us about the behavior of subparticles as they're transmitted through a pillar. We quantum-process waveforms they generate in our data to predict what's underneath. I'm just parroting the engineers, but one of them said the analytics are pretty much listening to and imagining what our world's like, outside in."

Mai's voice lilts, which always happens when she tried to make complex subjects appear so happily simple.

"And then you'd go out and stabilize the buildings?"

"My firm's just orchestrating first-step evaluation. Then the government officials who hired us will send teams to actually poke at unstable structures and add supporting elements where they can."

"Well, whatever they say they're doing, I hope they'll actually do it."

Last year, Pig counted three lean-outs in Krungthep proper. With the floods worsening and levees breached daily, concrete foundations and support pillars began to fracture, the ground beneath them more like sponge than stone. For those more fortunate, their buildings at most swayed like tired dancers on windy days. A few hundred less fortunate found that their buildings tipped a few degrees to one side within months. Pig watched live broadcasts of panicked families pointing to their slanted homes, and when it became clear that no tower would collapse suddenly, she went to a temple to make alms for everyone's well-being, especially Woon's.

The bird lingering near them lets out a beep and then drifts to its perch.

"Ready to take a peek?" Mai asks with a wink, before pointing to a swarm of pixels on a screen. A three-dimensional rendering of a pillar appears, same as on the platform. With a swiping motion in the air, Mai peels away its stony outer skin to reveal the grid of steel rods underneath. When she swipes to the next layer, she exposes a snaking vein spanning the height of the pillar.

"That long line right there," says Pig.

Mai pinches her fingers and picks out the entirety of the crack from the surrounding mass of concrete and steel. Rotating on the screen, the shape looks like a bolt of lightning reaching for ground.

"And we would have thought this support pillar was fine. Imagine how many like it are in the city."

Pig thinks of all the buildings that have gone up over the past few decades. Clusters of towers used to rise only from the main commercial districts, but now the entire skyline brushes against low-hanging clouds.

"Well, honestly, this has been both incredible and scary."

"You're not upset, are you?"

"No, I don't think so. Do the VIPs freak out when they see this?"

"It's usually a very persuasive demo. Seeing means everything."

"Thanks for giving it to me. Really, I'm not being sarcastic at all. I'm a nobody, and I'm getting this tour."

"You're my friend," says Mai. "Much more important than any visiting dignitary."

"You've gotten to be such a jokester."

"I'm serious. And let's see each other soon. I'll make sure Phee comes."

"Can't wait. She was just a little girl the last time you brought her along."

"And please bring Woon, if he's not too busy."

"We can always hope," says Pig, and she leaves it at that.

□ □ □

To get back to the apartment, Pig rushes to a ferry that takes her across the flooded area that once was the Klong Toey neighborhood. The boat, a fiberglass long-tail with two huge outboard motors, glides through the canal that used to be Rama IV road, its traffic jam days long over. She passes alongside the second stories of old storefronts. Sometimes, a sliver of signage surfaces just above the boat's wake, and she can make out the names of former dental offices, tutoring centers, barbershops. Few people now call these buildings home, but Pig glimpses a bare-chested old man squatting on what had been a window ledge to shave, guided by his reflection in shaded water.

There were happy years after, weren't there? Whenever she feels sadness return, she would think of the good things: those car rides with Mai, her childhood parakeets, New Year's dinners at the ancient cook-shop restaurant in Silom, Woon as a baby looking up from her cradling arms—those scrunched brows and beady eyes that moved her to tears and promises. They would all come back, as if she were reliving them again. She thinks of how her father, withered nearly to weightlessness, had said the same thing of cherished vacations and favorite pets returning, as he lay dying in his hospital bed.

Her father didn't say whether the not-so-good things also returned. She doesn't want to live again the childhood discovery of her dead puppy, a glass-eyed and fly-swarmed victim of a snake bite in the garden, or the times a certain lecherous professor insisted that she bed him. Most certainly, she didn't want to find herself again speechless on the phone in her old living room after finding out that Sawahng—a most winsome husband candidate, the fortune-tellers had said—had convinced the family to bet a reckless bulk of their investments on the wrong crop derivatives, not anticipating the first floods and the rice shortages that followed. Before that, she had believed that misfortune only visited people without much luck in the first place. How naive that woman was.

At the southern flood wall, she gets off, walking up a ramp kept afloat by truck tires covered in duckweed. She shields her ears as she goes past the row of discharge pipes, a perpetual waterfall even more deafening than real ones in the mountains. The pumps are working this afternoon, expelling the river that has seeped from underneath them onto the river that threatens to wash over the city.

As far as she knows from elevation maps, the building where they live was built on land at least level with current seas. The parts of the city that used to be marshes and rice fields are sinking the fastest. With clear weather, she can see the unnerving tilt of distant towers, perceptibly angled toward and away from each other like wild shoots of bamboo. People still live there. If she looked through Woon's old binoculars, she would be able to make out bedsheets and towels drying on balcony clotheslines and, at night, the flickering white of screens. It's all perfectly safe, a minor lifestyle adjustment, the officials declared.

"Two orders, to go," she says to the fish maw lady at the market. Woon's favorites.

She carries the soup in hot bulging cellophane bags that dangle from her fingers all the way to the building, a half-hour walk from the port. She crosses through torrents of people lurching home in the early evening and others stopping at sidewalk stalls to inspect end-of-day bargains. The streets smell of sweet fruits, engine fumes, and fish guts.

The building has seen far better days. Nobody has bothered to paint over or wash off the sooty grime that has streaked down the sides of multiple floors.

Worse, the once resplendent old house at the base is falling apart. The roofed terrace around it is slowly being turned to digested crumbs by insects, and large parts of it has been blocked off from use. The wonderful flowery tiles at the ceiling are peeling off one by one and only hot-glued back on by the unexacting hands of the understaffed maintenance crew. On rainy days like this one, parts of the ceiling drip water that has seeped through, and she can count on stomping across muddy puddles in the lobby. She often remembers from her youth viral photos of an abandoned Bang Lamphu department store, where gold-and-orange-scaled fish had flourished in the waters of the flooded ground floor, and how back then she'd found the sight wonderful and out of the ordinary. No matter, she couldn't help but feel overjoyed on seeing that the elevators were again working.

"Woon," she announces to a silent apartment. "I bought fish maw soup, the one by the lady with the funny squeaky voice. I'll leave it out here, with a bowl and a spoon."

This is the place she feels most alone and terrified, and yet each day she stands in front of her son's room and tells the door about her day at work, proofing autotranslations for the Ministry of Foreign Affairs, the crazy prices at the butcher, or what funny things their neighbors on the floor were doing. Mrs. Tadpole was walking her pet guinea pig in the hallway, or Mr. Galvin, the retired Scotsman, was flirting with the food delivery boys, wearing nothing but a loosely tied robe. Still, the door stays shut.

"And don't you forget we're going to celebrate your birthday soon. Can you let me know what you want?"

She thinks she hears a noise. Is that the whisper of a song leaking from headphones or the patter of her son's bare feet? She thinks she hears something crumple. Whatever the sound is, it hints of life stirring and persisting and will spare her from hours of hushed panic in bed that night.

□ □ □

She and Mai meet again two weeks later at a floating hotel's restaurant. Whole-floor windows bathe them with views of the widened river. This time, Mai has brought along Phee—short for Phillipa—who sits across the table with her bowl of basil-strewn noodles.

Pig can't tell if Phee enjoys listening to her elders struggle to tell apart things that now are from what had once been. Over there almost at the horizon, near the triangular steeple looming over submerged buildings, was where Pig and her mother followed a trail of trampled grass to get to the campus library. The spot where the tips of rotted trees fiddle the air might have been the university pier where they gathered during Loy Krathong to celebrate the last full moon of the lunar year. There, they made a wish and pushed out candlelit flower baskets to join thousands of others floating in the river.

"My candle always went out in, like, two seconds," says Mai. "Everyone else's would still be lit, and so I thought mine would be the only wish that wouldn't come true. I really thought my bad karma would wash back to me, and I'd cry myself to sleep that night."

It was something the old Mai had mentioned, an admission that would have made their other friends back then roll their eyes. The new Mai is retelling it in an attempt to entertain a daughter visiting from boarding school, but the remark doesn't seem to register with Phee, who gazes chin-down at her mother, saying nothing.

Pig turns to Phee and asks, "Do you know about Loy Krathong?"

"Of course I do, Auntie Pig. I've watched the videos."

"She knows about the famous song," says Mai.

Pig takes Mai's remark as a prompt to begin singing in the high-pitched voice of yesteryear's singers:

> *Full moon night of the twelfth lunar month,*
> *the banks brimming with water*

They all giggle, looking around to see who else nearby noticed. It pleases Pig to see Phee, who seems more at ease each minute, unable to contain herself. Woon used to laugh so much at her age. How long ago was that? Five or six years? Another life?

"Do they still do Loy Krathong in the city?" Phee asks her.

"Yes, but not as much. Fresh flowers are harder to come by, and the discharge water along the shore grosses out a lot of people."

At the next table, waiters arrives to seat a South American family, likely tourists who have come to take in the Venice of Asia, as the waterlogged city now bills itself. Aside from the wide views of the river, diners here can enjoy blue langoustine curry and larb rillettes with mint-lime foams. The restaurant reminds Pig of the places where she used to treat Mai as reward for a productive study session or detailed class notes. Friends joked that Mai was a sort of hired friend. "Where's your lady-in-waiting?" they'd ask whenever Pig arrived without Mai.

Those days, she sometimes felt like she could do without Mai's constant deferral to her. It was Mai, the awkward, unassured girl, who had always depended on Pig's guidance through treacherous years of secondary school and university. Yet Pig found pleasure in being the one who knew which house doors opened to secret parties or how to put on makeup like a Korean starlet. When Mai no longer needed someone to pay for everything, Pig had feared their friendship would fall apart, but she and Mai remained close while other friendships faded.

She wonders how Mai sees her now, after so long. Has she simply become Mai's trusty friend from childhood, the one at the ready on each return to welcome and entertain and sweetly evoke years past?

"Where's your son?" Phee asks. "Mom said he was going to be here."

"You know, he was excited to come," says Pig. "But then he told me he has exams coming up. Advanced calculus of some sort."

"Phee's curious about young people here," says Mai. "She doesn't know many other Thai kids."

"I've told him all about you, Phee. He's way sorry he couldn't make it. Mai, you remember how it was with exams, right?"

"So let's take him some study treats. I loved getting them back then. Phee also wants to see her grandparents' old place. Isn't that right?"

Phee nods and shrugs at the same time. Pig can't help but surmise, with a tinge of anger, that Mai has tactically pushed her words in front of her daughter's. It's a move she herself would've made back when she could expect to get her way.

"When Woon's less busy, we'll have you both over. I promise to ask him. No guarantees though."

She takes a long sip of coconut water, hoping the pause would send the conversation elsewhere.

"C'mon, just half an hour," said Mai. "He won't fail out of school because of that, will he?"

Pig realizes she shouldn't have expected Mai to drop it. This Mai has gotten too used to talking to some secretary or underling she knew she could bulldoze over. A feeling surfaces, refusing to be held under. Pig doesn't immediately recognize it, because she can't remember at any time feeling that way toward Mai, but there it is: hate. Hate for the mannered, spokesperson-like way that Mai speaks, even among old friends, and that cheery voice, chiming out from a world without worry. Hate for the barely aged face and that satisfied, unforced smile on it.

"Listen, Mai, I've already told you no," she says with what even she finds unexpected sternness. Her stomach sinks when she sees Phee recline to the seatback.

"I didn't meant to snap like that," she adds.

"Okay, Pig, we don't have to see the apartment today. It was just a thought."

"I'm sorry, Auntie Pig. I didn't mean to intrude."

"It was my fault, Phee. I don't know what came over me."

"It's fine. Let's not talk anymore about it," says Mai. "I'm going to ask for the dessert menu. That sounds good?"

"Actually, I have to go. I just remembered that I have to pick up basketball gear for Woon at the sports center before it closes." She retrieves her purse from the empty seat where he would have sat and reaches inside for her wallet.

"No, Pig, my treat."

"Mai, I can pay, too."

"Pig, really, you don't have to."

"But I can."

She picks out two ten-thousand-baht bills, nearly half her weekly wage, and lays them on the table. She would have spent much of it at the market for the usual staples, and whatever remains would have gone into the fund she promised herself she'd have ready, in case she and Woon ever have to leave the building.

□ □ □

It rains the entire week that follows, and through the downpour outside the apartment window Pig sees birds in the wild for the first time. At first, they seem nothing more than tiny shadows between her building and the one across, but she can tell they're not the usual sparrows by the perfection of their dart-shaped formation, seven deep. When the flock changes directions and turns toward her building, she scampers to the window to twist the blinds closed.

"Go away," she mutters, and returns to the kitchen, where she has just broken eggs into sugar. She hasn't baked in many years. She took classes before she married, imagining days ahead with a gingham-bordered apron tied neatly across her waist and children reaching across the counter to dip a finger in the batter, like in homemakers' magazines. After she did marry—to a man who couldn't stand the smell of butter—the plug-in oven stayed boxed in the closet.

Where is he now? Hong Kong? Singapore? Woon has heard his aunts and uncles curse his father to be reborn a water lizard, a damned monster of hell. She has assured her son many times that he's nothing like his father.

Her fingers encrusted with dried batter, she lowers the cake pan into the oven and sets the timer for an hour. She searches the cupboards for the nicer gold-bordered plates from when she lived in the old house. She thumbs open the blinds to check if the birds are still there.

Earlier in the week, a coworker shared conspiratorial chatter circulating about the birds. Messages asked why they looked so different from the traffic and weather birds. *What is that blue light? Why have they hired a foreign firm? Structural damage, sure, but what are they really looking for?* She nodded at the suppositions, never mentioning Mai. They haven't met since that last meal.

"Woon, did you forget what day it is?" she asks the closed door. "I baked you an entire cake. I'll cut you a slice and you come and blow out the candles, okay?"

She pictures him bony and pale skinned. She doesn't know if he's bothered to shave. She knocks on his door, just to make sure he knows she is there.

"Woon, I said come blow out the candles," she barks. "Don't make me sing out here by myself."

When Woon was a young boy, they celebrated his birthdays at the zoo. Woon, ever so excitable, would scrunch his face and pout and make noises to imitate the animals he saw, at times using his hands and arms to stand in for beaks and horns. From his face she divined the exuberant, spirited heart in her boy. She had feared she would lose him, in time, to the world, to grand ambitions that would take him far away, to young women eager to lay claim on him. But not to a room.

Just above a whisper, she launches into the familiar birthday song.

She has picked out a long, outsize candle to give Woon ample time to open the door. The flame descends, one lingering second to the next, and then disappears into smoke.

"Well, I guess there's a chance he could get better on his own. How long are you willing to wait?" a psychiatrist had asked in the early months. He looked at her with palpable impatience.

"I'm not sure, Doctor, but I'm his mother. I'll know."

The sight of the cake and spent candle together gives her a sudden shudder. Earlier in the year, out on the balcony, she lit incense sticks and put out boiled chicken and rice for Mai's parents, as offerings. She clasped her hands and whispered for the dead to come feast.

□ □ □

Hey, Pig taps on the projected keyboard she's brought up on the wall.

She knows she can't expect Mai to respond that night. It is already late, and Mai must have suspected that Pig has been brushing her off. Earlier in the week, Mai had sent a note asking Pig if she wanted to grab a bite, and Pig wrote back that the Ministry had been keeping her very busy, best to check back again later. She wasn't in a very social mood, and she certainly didn't feel like going to another one of Mai's fancy restaurants. Mai would have insisted on paying this time, and Pig owes her much more than she could ever pay back. It had felt much less burdensome to feel like she would always be the one to so generously give.

She taps on the wall to refresh her message list. Nothing. She types Hey again and then regrets sending it.

Why should she even expect Mai to reply at all? Maybe every friendship needn't last forever. The one between her and Mai wouldn't be the first to fade, at no one's fault. The inseparable sling out of each other's orbits. Strangers become friends, then become occasionally recollected names. Out the window, the blue shadow of gulls line the railing. They will soon launch from their perch out on their own separate flights.

Her heart leaps when a message bubble appears on the window-pane: Hi, Pig. Is everything all right?

□ □ □

The hall outside is quiet. Through the doors, they can hear the neighbors—mothers yelling at children over the clatter of forks and spoons, the evening's entertainments through muffled speakers. The two of them lean against the railing and look on the echoing space above the courtyard pool.

"He was doing well, and then he wasn't. I kept thinking he just needed time. I'm to blame."

"Pig, believe me, you've been nothing but the best mother."

Pig wipes her eyes with the backs of her hands as Mai rummages through a briefcase for tissues. The evening swelters thickly. Pig dabs her forehead, mixing tears with sweat. A misty light—from windows, headlights, billboard screens—has washed over the sky. On nights like this, the air beading on her skin, the city seems already drowned.

"I'm sorry I've kept all this from you."

"It's fine, Pig, but please don't be afraid to talk to me anymore. I'll help."

"Yes, I know. I've never doubted that."

She takes a napkin from Mai and blows her nose, unselfconscious now that the most painful facts have already been said.

"Where's Phee? Did you leave her by herself?"

"I told her I had to run to an emergency meeting. She doesn't care. All she wants to do is stay up and face-talk to her friends, their daytime."

"Woon used to do that, too. Now I don't know if he talks to anyone at all."

She grabs another napkin, just to have it in her hand. She feels rude for not having invited Mai inside the apartment, but she can't so easily shed the habit of letting friends enter only tidied rooms.

"Mai, do you think Woon's going to make it through this?"

"Yes, I think he will."

"Tell me he's going to be fine."

"Woon's going to be fine."

"Thank you. For some reason, it's comforting to hear you say it."

"I can say it as many times as you'd like, Pig."

It has been decades since she last cried in front of Mai. They were university students who'd come upon a little publicized campus exhibition of photographs from student massacres in the 1970s. She hadn't known about these Octobers. So much had been lost or erased from the books, but taking in the faces of young strangers alive and dead long before her, she felt so keenly their suffering that she hurried to a corner of the exhibit and wept. It was Mai who found and consoled her. "It is only so. It will not be so," Mai said then, her hand on Pig's shoulder. Many times, many years after, Pig would chant those words when she needed to believe them.

"I'm glad you're here, Mai. You've been more generous to me and Woon than you've needed to be, and I've always depended on you, more than I've been willing to say. I've been such a miserable, ungrateful friend."

"Pig, you're the opposite of that," says Mai, stepping over to put an arm around Pig's shoulder. For Pig, Mai's brushing off what was said only confirms its reality, but this isn't the time to think of her own failings.

"Mai, how are you doing with the birds?"

"Are you sure you want to talk about my work project?"

"Yes, I've been wondering about it."

"We've covered over half the city already, from what's left of Chinatown to the old racetrack."

"Will all of Krungthep really be scanned?"

"More or less. Right now, we're focusing on places we think we're in most danger of losing."

"To what?"

"To whatever happens."

Pig can see it. There will be a vast body of water and the shards of a city. There will be falling ruins the waves will turn to sand. Yet on sunscorched days there will still be children vaulting into their own shadows in that new sea.

She will return Woon to this world, but first she needs to see him. She has only let herself think of the child preserved in the framed photos: the one who chased sea crabs at a Bang Saen beach and the one who played chess for hours at his grandfather's bedside. She realizes now that, knowing people their whole lives, she can mistake them for a phantom—the mirage of who they once were.

"Mai, I have to ask you something. Have you ever scanned people?"

"Why are you asking that?"

"Tell me, Mai."

"The birds see everything."

□ □ □

It doesn't take more than a thump for Pig's hand to find the flashlight by the door. She switches it on and shows Mai into the apartment. Standing in the foyer, they nod at each other. Mai's eyes follow the beam around the living room.

"Do you want to see the other rooms?" Pig whispers.

"Maybe some other time. Another week or year, however long you and Woon need."

Pig can hear her son snoring in his room. The snores won't last long; Woon has never been a restful sleeper and will soon flip over and quiet down.

While she was outside with Mai, he came out for the slice of cake she had left for him. She picks up the empty plate off the floor and carries it to the kitchen sink, where she would normally catch up on the news as she washed dishes. Tonight, she and Mai will be accompanied only by the squeak of her fingers on the wet plate and their bare feet on the kitchen tiles.

"Are you sure you don't want me to cross-run a physiological diagnostics module?"

Pig shakes her head. If anything remains of the son she loves, his face will tell her, and this time she promises to let herself see.

"When will they get here?"

"Just listen for the wings."

A half hour later, Pig opens the sliding door and steps out to the balcony. Beyond, in the open windows across from them, multitudes of solar lamps eke out light with their remaining charge, and, farther out, the dim glow of inclined towers, lucky for the night to have power, give shape to the skyline. The air is hot and buzzing with mosquitoes. Louder is the whirring of three small rotors. Pig looks to Woon's windows and wonders if her son is awake.

The birds power on their scanners, dotting Woon's windows and the outside of his room with blue light.

"Avoid looking at reflected beams," Mai says next to her, and Pig shuts her eyes.

The city seems to have quieted, as if all the air has suddenly left it.

The night crackles. Pig feels her body electrify, every particle seemingly humming. Pinpricks of blue and white pierce through, and quivering constellations bloom inside her lowered eyelids.

It all seems familiar, but she isn't sure why. Then a sight returns: a younger Mai, hemmed in by the celebratory crowd, squatting on the last steps of the university pier where it met the river. Mai looked up and handed her a basket made of banana leaves and bright amaranth flowers, purple and orange. "C'mon, make your wish," Mai said.

Pig turns to watch thousands of candles bob away in the ebbing tide, each carrying pleas into the dark. She feels Mai's hand clasp around hers.

NETHERWORLD

The three of us set our alarms to wake us while the stars still cast shadows. We tiptoe outside, careful not to let the screen door slap or to say more than we could with hand signals. It isn't because we're mindful of anyone's sleep. It's just that it's more gainful to let the others stay lost in their dreams. The elders talk wistfully of the olden days when the ocean was so bountiful that all they had to do was reach into a wave to hook a catch by its gills, but we only know of times where there are so many perches to claim and not enough in the sea. Out we dive with splashes no louder than minnows breaching the surface. The fastest and earliest of us break for plum spots where the bottom divots and freshwater flows right over the salty currents. We scramble up the rusty poles, our spears and nets on our backs, until we reach the curved end where the old ones say the lights used to shine, and there we hang a few arm's lengths over the water, depending on the tides. We wait, our grip loose and ready on the bamboo handle, elbows raised in position, eyes searching.

The fish are smarter than a land person believes. We know the fish know we're here. They tease us, darting across our shadows, so close we can see the red inside their gills. We miss, cursing. We never hear them laugh, but we know they do. If we get impatient, the morning totally worthless, we leap in after them. We pair up and unwrap our nets across channels in the underwater dunes. We can hold our breaths for five, six, seven minutes. We kick, propelling forward in bursts, hoping at every second that we will have caught more than baitfish, and when our lungs feel like they've turned to coral, we make for air.

This morning our C-Os buzz against our forearm. Forget the fish, our mothers say, we have a visitor.

We return, the sun-paled wood on the deck darkening where we drip. Our mothers are waiting for us in the lanai with a middle-aged woman, fair-skinned, compared to ours, and already in a wetsuit that looks like her own and not one of our rentals. We clasp our hands and give the woman a wai, before looking again at our mothers.

"Big Sister Juhn here is a seasonal volunteer from the medical corps," they say. "She's making a house call in one of the fishery districts. You'll ready a long-tail boat and take her where she needs to go."

We nod and grab Big Sister's rucksack. *This way to the dock*, we show with our open hands. As we check the fuel cells and make sure to wipe the seats clean of squid bits, the woman waits, gazing at a faded Skytrain map still enclosed in plastic. It dates back to when this dock used to be the first landing for Mo Chit Station, the name on the one sign that hasn't been ripped out for scrap.

It's unusual that anyone ever comes here during monsoon season.

Currents, sped by wash-offs from the mountains, gain eno...
to carry fallen houses far out into the gulf, where the wre...
join other debris tumbling toward the seafloor. Mosquitoes fir...
puddles of rainwater and lay eggs, spawning black clouds low in...
mangroves. The tourist zones with the museums and snorkel-throug...
ruins are closed. The market stalls hawking salvaged knickknacks and
seashell-encrusted furniture—the more water warped and stained, the
more sought after—have shuttered. No diving shows or feats of underwater endurance scheduled, just silt and rust everywhere, staining everything they touch the red of stingray blood.

It's our favorite time, this late in the season. School's still out, and
we can do whatever we like. Best thing, we don't have to pretend not to
have C-Os, or to go around in silly clothing the land people think we
still wear, because of some movie or soap opera made about us. It
should be like this year-round.

When the engine revs to life and sends out high, arcing sprays from
the driveshaft, we tell Big Sister we're ready. We cast off and steer from
the dock with the lever stick, until we've pivoted east toward where she
wants us to take her.

Off we throttle into the brightening day. We dart forward, shifting
speed and direction where swirls at the surface warn us of structures
beneath, or where the tint in the water changes from brown to green
and back, telling of snaggy weeds or shallow runoffs. Mostly, it's the
names that guide us across these waters. Everywhere worth knowing
has a name like Uncle Victory, Auntie Rainbow, the Glass Elephant—
hundreds of them, each embedded inside our heads by our mothers'
songs, by pointing fingers since when we were babies and could barely
say any word at all.

"We'll be turning right in a few minutes," Big Sister says over
the roar of the engine. She's in the middle of the boat, sitting on an

ller we usually use to keep shrimp alive. We look to see if
g her C-O, but it doesn't seem so. She's been here or was from
e guess. We sometimes get these visitors, too: the returnees.
What are your names?" she asks.

"I'm A, that's B, and that's C," our oldest says, pointing first to
herself.

"Easy enough to remember."

We nod. We don't like to say much to the visitors. Our mothers say
that we have to make them happy, because it's part of our livelihood.
Smile, be helpful. Pose for their cameras. We're sick of it, honestly. We
already have our water and our fish and our farmed greens. It's time us
Krung Nak people shrug off the outsiders. We resolve not to smile
at her.

We turn where Big Sister orders us. It's deeper here, nearly all the
two- and three-story shophouses have gone under, their roofs visible as
rectangular tracts of mud through the murky water. Only above four
or five stories do buildings remain above water, for who knows how
long. Anything has a way of disappearing. Every once in a while, we
wake to trembling floorboards accompanied by a horrific sound, like
hundreds of food cans being crushed, and in the morning someone
will report that Uncle W or Uncle Hilton had toppled over, a few kilometers away.

The waterway widens into a lagoon where the old ones say people
once raced horses. Imagine that, the sound of gallops, the cheers, and
not the squawking of thousands of migrant birds.

We speed up across the open water, the wind batting our faces, before we cross under a raised highway. Traffic gets busier near the Asoke
settlements. Larger fishing vessels motor out toward the gulf, their
nets still empty, the menfolk not yet drunk. The glass-bottom boats
find out-of-season use transporting schoolchildren. The air smells of

seafood rice soup simmering in large pots and of fresh laundry drying on clotheslines overhead. It's a fine morning. Big Sister appears to be enjoying the scenery.

Of course, we take her on a slight detour. We round a corner and glide slowly past the white facades of a former shopping center, now bedecked with last night's catch. Ocean fish hang from hooks, their guts ripped out. Everybody has on rubber shoes, for all the blood and slime slick on the ground. The sun bears down. The stench becomes inescapable. We struggle to contain our laughter as we watch Big Sister bring her hand to her nose.

It's fun to mess with people from the new cities. They want to see how things really are. So we show them.

"That was unnecessary," says Big Sister. "You could have gone straight but you didn't. Why?"

"It's a shortcut," says A. "Better the stink than getting stuck in front of the market." We all hope Big Sister Juhn has no idea that the market is half a kilometer north.

"This is not the first time I've come around here; you should probably have guessed."

"We thank Big Sister for taking care of us sea people."

"You don't mean that, but it's okay."

Big Sister doesn't say anything further. We don't either.

We taxi down a small canal. The house she's visiting is at the far end. It's one of the newer houses built from the kits towed in on barges. They no longer look like the shipping containers they once were. They're stacked on stilts and connected, to open on the inside into a courtyard. They have glass walls, jutting balconies, and gardens on the roof watched over by object-identifying quad-propeller hawks, to scare the all-too-common gulls. The owners paint these kit homes in bright colors. This one is green and yellow. Someday all the Krung Nak houses will probably be like this, instead of the ones built from things we find—the different-colored shingles, the glass blocks, the ancient timber that we managed to nail or weld together. And some of the people will say that it's for the better. And the rest will agree.

The woman is lying on a cot in the courtyard. She's maybe a decade older than us. Big Sister and the woman's family convene in a corner while we wait on the sofa. There's lingering odor coming from the woman that no breeze can clear. It's worse than anything we smelled at the fish station. Big Sister approaches the woman and removes some medical equipment from the backpack. The woman's husband and the older pair who are probably her parents look on with sad faces.

"How many times a day did you say she goes?" Big Sister asks.

"We don't know. She was constantly in the bathroom. We asked her if she was sick, and she said no. She went to work at the visitors center but had to come back home midday. Now this."

Big Sister puts on gloves, and we see her pinching the woman's skin at an elbow.

"I'm sorry if I'm causing any discomfort, but I'm going to turn you over," she says to the woman. The woman groans as she turns on her side, and it's then, with her dress partially open, that we see the woman is pregnant. Big Sister takes out some kind of clear stick and wipes it on the woman's exposed buttocks, which have been stained turmeric yellow from her recent shitting.

"This PCR probe will help me figure out what has infected you."

Big Sister inserts the stick into a metal tube that she's holding up to the light. It's nearly noon. The sun hangs above us, glowing white behind a veil of clouds.

There's not much for us to do. We take out our C-Os. We tap on our friends and tell that we got screwed having to ferry some visitor around. Did anyone hear what happened to Winky? That duck-faced bitch dumped her. What's the word on Frog? Did you see what she was wearing? Who going to the lake for the temple fair?

We keep one eye on Big Sister. We watch her take out packets from her bag and ask for warm water from the husband, who looks so pale and bedraggled we thought at first he was going to be her patient.

"Mix in one of these," says Big Sister. "The rest you'll have her drink for the next several days. I'm also going to stick an antibiotic patch on her back. That should do the trick, but if she doesn't get any better, take her to the closest mediplex right away."

"We're in your debt, Dr. Juhn," says the husband. "I also must ask, how is our baby girl? Should we be worried?"

"There's some risk, because your wife's experiencing hypovolemia, but I wouldn't be too concerned. Here, let me connect in and show you."

Big Sister flips the woman on her back and glides her specialty C-O over the woman's protruding stomach.

The glass wall overlooking the canal turns black. The silvery water disappears, replaced by an image of the woman's massive belly, which then becomes a green domelike shape, which then peels away to reveal the unborn child inside. The child glows green, as if her body has been carved out of emerald. Blue webs run like rivers along her body and limbs. At the center, behind the hook of two little hands, a blue blob diminishes and expands, diminishes and expands.

We let our C-Os drop to our laps. B almost falls off the sofa, leaning forward from the armrest she has been straddling.

"She's not lacking for oxygen," says Big Sister. "She's fine."

Afterward, the family sees us off at the dock, insisting that Big Sister take homemade sheets of dried squid back with her. We swivel the boat back in the direction from which we came. C straightens up to wave smiley good-byes, as if she had something to do with the family's relief.

"What was wrong with the woman?" asks A.

"An old disease called cholera. Every once in a while it comes back—luckily for us, this time not much changed from what we know of it."

When we reach open water, we slow down, almost to a stop.

"Anywhere else, Big Sister?" asks A.

"No, that was the only case they assigned for me today. But as long as I'm here, I'd like to take a different route back."

When we hear where she wants to go, we ask if she's sure.

"I used to live there with my parents. They're not in any shape to come here. It would be nice to bring back a photo, before I head back to New Krungthep in a few days."

We're familiar with the area: a dense valley of buildings in different stages of decrepitude. Some are leaning, some have crumbled. Wriggly vines often cover them, erasing telltale floors, so that from a distance they look like ancient cliffs risen out of the sea. The light shines strangely there, passing through gouged floors and the remnants of glass facades. Not the most hospitable part of Krung Nak, if you ask us. The only ones who go there are the swifts' nest harvesters, who are secretive about their sites and not very friendly. They sometimes shoot before warning.

We tell Big Sister all this. We wait to see if we've said enough. Some of it is true.

She's hard to read, this Big Sister. She's like the part of the estuary mouth where the waves look like they wouldn't wash over a three-year-old, but you know that underneath furious clouds of sand are being kicked out by the tow.

"All right, let's head back your way then."

Many thanks to the deities. She doesn't know it, but we're doing her a favor. We see them all the time, like we've said. The returnees come back here believing they'll see their old homes, not so different from what they had been. The waterless years weren't long ago, they like to think. Something must remain. They imagine stepping back to find the marble still shiny, old lightbulbs flickering on for their arrival. Then they find out it's only the bits in their heads that have endured, and everyone's sad.

But what do we know? We're too young to even know about most of the things they mention. We only nod and smile when they talk and talk. We sell them tissue paper so they can wipe their tears. In truth, we're sick of them blotting their eyes. Boo hoo, so what. Enough with the crying. Quiet, already.

Big Sister Juhn's not going to cry. We're going to take her another way, past some of our favorite spots. The tide will soon be washing out. The waterline will slowly lower. The golden tips of submerged pagodas will again greet the sun. We'll pass by tidal flats that will soon be crawling with mudskippers, thousands of spherical eyes poking from puddles on what the old ones say was the roof of a supermarket. Then we will show Big Sister the hollowed-out building where bats have taken over, their screeching noisy even well before the darkening hours, when they'll pour into the sky like smoke. We'll visit the windmill with its turret barely above water and its sails now turned by currents. We should pass by a sundries raft, and we'll tell them to make us iced coffee, to go. The ice will be cold, and we will hardly take a break between sips.

We will ask Big Sister if she has enjoyed her afternoon. We expect a good tip.

CROSSINGS

The building where he works floats ten kilometers west of his neighborhood, anchored to a network of piers in the newly formed sea. Part of its outer structure came from the salvaged national library, and the high-pitched roof over its side entrance is from the archives building on what was Samsen Road. This is the entrance that lets him take a shortcut through the brick-paved courtyard where, among mothballed specimens of Old Krungthep's subway cars, he often stops at the ancient swing that once towered over the traffic of tuk-tuks and minibuses taking tourists to the golden landmarks of Rattanakosin. For good luck, he likes to knock on its wood, pocked by barnacles and bleached pink by caustic tides.

His work area is in an inner building, one with only slitty

black-filmed windows because of the fragility of its contents. He receives the day's arrivals in the docking bay and guides the padded carrier bots ferrying artifacts through the hall. Most of the objects are sealed in hermetic carbon-fiber crates, but some are too big to be contained, so that sometimes it appears as if he's walking alongside a three-meter golden Buddha or a stone lion. Others, mostly ephemera collected from drowned libraries, are so delicate he handles them individually. From time to time he stops to read through the glass sleeves: ledgers from defunct trading houses, diaries of hired Scandinavian generals and Italian engineers, Buddhist texts and prayer scrolls in old Sanskrit, letters from the dead to the long forgotten.

By the scanning chamber, he drums a stylus against his palm as he waits for every atom in the objects to be blipped by eyes in the wall, as precaution against still more calamity.

His real preservation work then begins. He dons a breathing mask and steps into the chamber. Prompted by his voice, the robotic arms swing into action. They spray paper artifacts with alkalizing solutions before lifting them to the wire racks to dry. They reverse age, removing layers of encrusted dust from sculptures and pottery with a brush or a cloth-covered vacuum head, sometimes resorting to a wooden scalpel for more resilient grime. The tougher ones with significant degradation or evidence of old repair he tells the arms to set aside on a shelf, for further consultation with specialists. He works slowly, careful to go through procedural checklists and to give each object its proper deliberation.

He has done this for more than a decade. So why did he find himself earlier this day staring at the scattered shards of an antique sangkhalok urn?

He would learn that it had likely come out of a kiln in Sukhothai Province sometime in the fifteenth century. On its gray pitted surface swirled blue patterns of lotus flowers and swimming ducks. The urn should probably have been put in a less precarious place, someone would say. It had sat near the edge of the cataloging table, surrounded by many other artifacts, so that its presence was unlikely to be noticed. Had it even been blipped?

"Khun Woon, we have people who are very handy with broken things. I mean, hell, this can't be more complicated than patching up an early-modern rice bowl," said Khun Cocoa, the first to walk over.

He'd heard the fast thudding of his own shoes on the concrete floor as he tried to regain his balance. He remembered his arms flailing at his sides, as if he thought he could swim upward in the thick New Krungthep air. Was it possible that someone nearby could have caught him? Did everyone think he could have recovered on his own? He at one point played intercollegiate basketball at university, and even now he tends to stand with his legs slightly apart, as if waiting to receive a pass. He had superb body control and ran pick-and-rolls that silenced gyms full of the opposing university's fans.

The shattering quieted the conversations in the vicinity. He got down on his knees to gather up what remained of the urn. Two coworkers kneeled down to help, but he waved them off. He was focused on the task of sweeping the shards into a pile with the edge of his palms.

"I'm so sorry," he said, when the department director arrived at his table. "I'll make sure to find every piece of it and alert the specialists."

He wanted to tell her that in the many years that he had worked here, he had never damaged an item in his care.

"Don't worry too much, Woon. This happens all the time," said the director. "You should really just get up, and order the vacumatics to take care of it."

"Director, it won't take more than five minutes for a thorough sweep."

"Your time would be better spent on other items. We've hundreds of these, and this one has already been blipped. See?"

She showed him her device. The urn, intact as it had been, rotated on the screen.

"Okay," he said. "For a moment there, I thought . . ."

He got up from the floor, the shards sharp and noisy in his hands. He emptied them into a sealable bag, to be cataloged and carted off to a storage warehouse that might as well be oblivion. He moved on to the next batch of artifacts.

Yet the bowl—its many shattered pieces on the floor, its intact counterpart on the screen—has stayed in his mind. As he blips and tags, and inspects and catalogues, his thoughts wander to the people in his life. What are they but flesh, bone, and water?

If his mind should move past his worries, the displays themselves remind him, with their animated touting. He can't help but look.

Surveys show high ratings by satisfied customers. They love having a choice in their fate. They cherish not having to say final good-byes.

"I'm not feeling very well," he says to Khun Cocoa. "Tell the director I'm off to the doctor this afternoon."

He exits through the side gate and boards an interdistrict vaporetto. He takes out his C-O and reads the brochure he had requested:

Choose from financing plans tailored for your future.

Enjoy peace of mind with cold storage backed up by generators.

Feel safe with systems protected by advanced defense intelligence.

Look forward to your better forever.

□ □ □

His children, his wife, his mother—they're why Woon has left work midday to come to a low-rise, limestone-encased building built on top of a hill. Upcoming Songkran festivities means that it has taken more than an hour for a slot to open at this portal. He passes through steel gates painted in tasteful whites and signs in at the guard booth.

To get inside the building, he crosses a walkway that zigzags over a blue-tiled pool where schools of golden carp bob between lily pads and kiss duckweed. As he walks, he notices that the fish appear to be following his reflection in the water, and at the end of the walkway, about a hundred paces across, he signals his good-bye to them with the wag of a finger. A glass door slides open, and he's inside an atrium brightened by daylight. One of the receptionists at a long wooden table confirms his requested time slot by waving at his C-O. He's told that he's about to be blocked from all outside networks, for everybody's safety, and before he can say that he knows the protocol, his C-O goes red. A young woman walks over to show him through a long corridor to the reconnection rooms. She offers him what's politely called tea. He accepts the cup with both hands and sips, knowing he needs to bear with the ferrous taste in his mouth so that he can raise the electrical conductivity in his body. In the sci-fi books and movies of his youth, the imagination of this technology always showed effortless use: lie down on a bed and put on the goggles or tap a glowing button on a headset, no harder than tucking into a dream. He does lie down on a leather reclining chair, and the woman does lower cushioned ellipses over his eyes, but there is also the seemingly endless ten-minute wait for the nano-material solution to circulate throughout his body, his limbs bound to the chair by leathery straps all the while so that he can't flail around and hurt himself before dissociation, never mind the tiny, tingling zaps that he thinks he feels as scanners map his nerves.

"Almost there," the woman says to assure him, and he tries his best to believe her. He feels the cold metal of hundreds of probes descending to kiss his skin. Static fills his ears. With his eyes closed, his field of vision shifts through a gradient of blues that always makes him feel chilly.

The woman's voice fades. He's alone in the room, which is now no longer a room but a spot he remembers from his youth. They're in the building where he used to live with his mother.

"How's this?" says a different woman sitting across from him at a small wooden table. "We can shift somewhere else if you want."

At some point, the condo managers decided to lease out this space to a café. It's all here: the hard, cushionless chairs, the Japanese porcelain cat beckoning by the entrance, the receptionist/barista, head down, staring at a screen in her hand. He even recognizes this particular table for its wobbliness if the wadded napkin got kicked from under a leg. He nudges it. Perfectly still and even.

"This will do, Auntie Mai. I liked coming here when we lived in the building. Sometimes I'd even slow down going past it, so I could smell the espresso being made. It's all probably driftwood now."

"Yeah, I remember when the management office first announced a café was opening here. By the tenants' reaction, you'd have thought they were putting in an opium den or massage parlor."

"I know. People hated it if a wastebasket was moved a step over."

"Do you still drink a lot of coffee? I remember your mother being worried at one point."

"Yes, I still do, but probably less than what you remember. Maybe two cups a day. Now people like to take their coffee vaporized in a sound field. Have you heard? Enhances the notes, quickens the effect, they say."

"Even though my family sends me update credits, I admit that I don't keep up with trends. Especially with consumables and things of that sort."

"Why would you if you don't have to?"

"I don't know. Curiosity, maybe nostalgia, or that old person's fondness for being horrified by the present. Speaking of old people, how's your mother?"

"She's well. Healthy for now, but the doctors are closely monitoring her cell count. When did you last see her?"

"It's been a few years, your timeline. She's still not keen on coming to the gateways much, I take it. Such an ordeal, she always tells me first thing."

"Mother does that to remind everyone to pay attention to her."

"I think she's also afraid something might go wrong."

"Silly Pig. She should to be used to how things are by now. It's been a decade since Oslo."

He remembers that day too well. He had recently finished his master's program and was apprenticing at an archive in Shanghai. A woman, hands over mouth, stood up from her desk. For a few seconds, she remained fixed on the news on the screen, and then her eyes met his. The headline tickers scrolled: *Hundreds of thousands feared lost . . . Assailants disabled life systems.* He still sometimes pays attention to the ceremonies in white that mark the day, which evoke a lingering sadness and disbelief. He's thankful not to have known personally anyone who met their final end that day.

"It's a pity, these security restrictions," says Auntie Mai. "I think I feel safe, but I know I'm supposed to feel safer, what with the things they say they've done to prevent something terrible from happening again. Am I wrong to keep worrying?"

"I don't know, Auntie Mai. I'm not a technician of that sort."

"Of course, what can any of us know? I should stick to thinking about things that make me happy, like the people dear to me, like your mother. I hope she'll come again soon. Won't you give her a nudge?"

"I will. She probably figures you'll always be around. You know how she procrastinates."

"Maybe. My question is, will she be around?"

His mother doesn't like him talking about her illnesses. A few years ago there was that stroke, luckily recognized before any great harm could be done. But there's also the mysterious come-and-go pain in her back, hard to address even with regeneration therapy, and now a burgeoning lymphatic syndrome that announced itself only this year, when one afternoon his mother asked why her grandchildren looked so blurry. "The cause is likely idiopathic," her doctor said. "Things happen. We'll do what we can."

"They've kept the inflammations in check, but her numbers aren't getting any better," says Woon. "Still, she's against any suggestion of a transfiguration procedure. I tell her how well you're doing, but she only shrugs."

"It does take some getting used to, certainly not as easy as they advertise it."

"Beats the alternative."

"It's the absence of a bodily component that deters prospects. They don't think it's real. I understand that, trust me. I had so many questions before I went through with it."

But there is a body, or what's left of it: the plugged-in brain and the stringy nerves, kept from further degeneration. In documentaries, the host inevitably walks past row after row of enclosed preservation racks.

"Oh, believe me, Auntie Mai. I've told her that pretty much all her questions about transfiguration have already been settled by researchers, but she doesn't want to hear any of it."

"With age comes either extreme faith or extreme doubt. Usually both."

Sometime, every visit, he clenches his fist to check the fidelity. This is flesh. It's definitely his, or feels like it.

"Even with the slight unknowns, the positives make the procedure worth it, don't they? For one, you look like you're about twenty."

"I do? I don't always keep track of my settings. I should probably try to look more recognizable to you."

"You can appear however you want."

"Are you sure?"

A giant hamster sits across from him. It flashes him a smile under its pink nose and twitchy whiskers.

"No, not that? How about this? You probably saw me most often when I was in my forties."

The hamster blinks into an older woman wearing a white linen suit. This is the Auntie Mai who dropped by when she was in the country to visit his mother. Here's the woman who radiated infectious self-assurance, so that he couldn't help but envy how even his mother would immediately brighten up for her.

"Yes, right about then," says Woon, "perhaps under less than ideal circumstances."

"Doesn't matter. You're here now, and not behind a door."

"Not one of my finer moments."

"But one of your mother's. I was with her, Woon. She did everything she could to get you out."

"I still can't believe I fell for the cakes. What a gullible little glutton I was. You know, I probably have trust issues with food now. I see an ordinary pastry, and I'm wondering if it will make me topple over, passed out."

"If not for that, who knows what might have become of you."

"Still there in that room. My beard from here to the floor."

"It's easy to laugh now, I suppose."

"I've only begun to admit that I ever went through that period."

"Have we previously discussed this? Do you feel comfortable talking about it?"

"About that phase? That's what Mother calls it, if she even brings it up. It was more than that. I really had the conviction that I could live that way forever. Air-locked in that room, like an astronaut hurtling through space on a hundred-year mission. Funny thing, it's even more vivid to me now. I look at Puk and Mint and I tremble. I'm afraid they'll take after their father in his worst ways."

"When you have children, your own childhood comes back in full relief against theirs."

"They're such stubborn children. I recognize it like my own face. Look where that stubbornness got me, Auntie Mai."

"I don't think you went through with that because you were stubborn."

"It certainly didn't help. I hated everything. I didn't want to deal with anyone. I just wanted to put on my headphones and listen to music. Locking myself in was my method of protesting, and I really had the crazy notion that the world might yield to my boycott of it."

"The whole world's one formidable adversary, your mother aside."

"You know, she was in a bad shape before then. Did she ever tell you, Auntie Mai?"

"You well know she's not one to speak ill of herself."

"Well, you didn't hear it from me, but she had been drinking well before that phase of mine, and it wasn't like she had just a glass of wine or two. I have no idea how she was able to function at all. Well, oftentimes, she didn't. She'd yell at me for hours, about my father or me, and then she'd try to play nice, asking what I thought of this or that program on TV, all facedown from the couch. She never remembered those episodes. She'd just wake up and ask me what I wanted for break-fast, as if everyone had had a good night of sleep."

"I wish she had reached out to me sooner. Or perhaps I should have."

"It's not your fault, Auntie Mai. It's not any of our faults. That was just how she was. I don't blame her now, although she might have actu-ally worsened my situation. The times I stepped out of the room when she wasn't there, I noticed that there were no more empty bottles left out for the recycler units. With me to worry about, I had a feeling she was paying less mind to whatever was eating her up. That gave me an-other reason to stay where I was. My being crazy was saving my mother from herself."

"So now you're again trying to save her."

"I only want her to think about her future. Maybe get her to visit a facility and take a look around."

"Is that why you're here? To get me to help you do this?"

"You've known her the longest of anyone. Why is my mother being so difficult? Why won't she even let me get a word in about it?"

"Asks the man who locked himself in his room for months."

□ □ □

That room. Has he ever left it entirely? Woon's standing on a second-level deck among hundreds of passengers, his hands gripped on the bar overhead, his body swaying to the ferry's unsteady propulsion upriver. All he has to do is close his eyes for a second or two, and he's again re-turned to an indeterminate daybreak years ago, with dawn's grayness, as fine as ash, sifting through gaps in the curtains to touch the con-tents of that room—the mounds of spiral-bound textbooks, the pajamas dangling from a chairback, and, leaning on a desk leg, a schoolbag un-touched for more than half a year.

The songs return to him, one by one, in snippets, as if he were hearing them on the ferry's PA speakers. How many times did he play each one? Lying on his bed, his headphones engulfing his ears, he devoured entire albums and then feasted on them again. He played the usual greats, Ellington and Miles and Coltrane, but he was held captive more by musicians few had heard of, like Arturo Watanabe and Emilia Z, whose names were evoked with reverence on online music boards, for deserving reasons. Or the older forgottens—say, Alfie Watkins or Morris Clemens and gang—whose sessions he downloaded from bootleg archives, back when downloading was a thing.

"Stop it, you morons," a teenage girl in school uniform, unchanged since his own schoolboy days, yells at her two friends for no apparent reason. They giggle and shove each other, paying him no mind.

These schoolkids, coming home from their hyperlearning sessions or whatever, probably have no idea anything exists beyond Nairobi quarto or rup-pup. They've probably never known what a piano can do under deft hands, the way a capriccio once swept him up to a state as close as he's ever gotten to levitation, or how a drum solo can enliven the beat of a troubled heart, for better or worse.

He remembers the moment before he resolved to stay in that apartment and lock out the world outside it. He was listening to a newly discovered bootleg recording with Clemens, Jenkins, and Thompson all going at it one long-ago night, something he'd played at least a dozen times before, when a song suddenly coiled around his entire being, note by note, with the unexpected aggression of a pet boa long thought tame. As songs shuffled to the next album on his list and then another, he grew certain that some musical matter had condensed from the air to become palpable essence filling every crevice of the room. Beyond, the city boiled in immeasurable suffering. Inside his cocoon of sound, there was only undisturbed, perfect communion with miracle after miracle. The dead were alive to sing into his ears. Time flowed in every direction, until there was no such thing as time. He let himself sink, like a prehistoric insect into sap. He couldn't bear to leave. What was it his father had said about that collection of LPs inherited from his grandfather? A shelf full of songs outweighs all the gold in the world. Probably some quote the man also stole, well before he'd disappeared on Woon and his mother.

The high-speed ferry takes him to the Kanchanaburi suburbs, part of the second resettlement area after the floods. He disembarks at a port built into the first floors of a shopping complex. He walks past brightly lit, white-walled shops in compliance with neatness and signage codes, located along the one corridor so that anyone who has to get to the mainland or other barge colonies won't be able to avoid them. The sun has dipped under the billowy silhouette of the Tenasserim Mountains, and a lingering stripe of orange sky is fighting for its life. At this hour, the evening rush has thinned. He can actually see the wide, smooth pavement in front of him.

From the transparent trash bins, human street cleaners on work furlough from a detention facility are carting away a day's worth of drink cartons and lunch kits. He avoids looking at their faces. What were their crimes? Not making a night's curfew? Shouting too loudly at the market? Each week brings in new orders and codes. He can't keep up. Perhaps one day he will be stopped and fined, or worse, for wearing brown in the wrong month or parting his hair in the wrong direction.

There was so much desperation for normalcy at the start of the migrations that almost everyone was willing to nod for whatever rules were proposed. Onward. Let the catastrophes of those years sink with the old city. Few liked to talk anymore about the many who didn't make it—often those who had held off from leaving because they couldn't afford to—or how much had been lost beyond the buildings and property.

He was certainly complicit; he'd let his own children learn of the troubles in whatever way least disturbed their happier future.

He never told them about the time he'd volunteered at a refugee camp. The official order had been to use the word *evacuee* not *refugee*, because the former gave some dim hope of return, but few complied in private. They knew by then what they were. He counted himself a refugee, albeit one not as unfortunate as most others. A relative owned an empty condo on higher land, and he and his mother were able to stay there, dry and at least with clean food at prices less flesh-gouging than in the areas closer to sinking Krungthep.

At the nearby camp, he started out as an assistant in the makeshift commissary warehouse, checking inventory mostly and taking note of when they were running low on certain supplies. It was the kind of job a specialized bot would have done faster and more thoroughly, but most of those had long been left behind in the city to rust underwater at their charging stations. A human like him would have to do.

He tried as best he could. Inventory levels proved unpredictable. Some nightshifts, he could climb on top of a pallet of bottled water and leap across a warehouse full of them as he scanned. Other times, there was so little water available, the refugees had to line up with their issued canteen—or more likely, a cup or bucket—to claim their share of a bottle. He stood at the commissary window, measuring out water, until his ankles ached.

One night, while taking a break outside, he heard a cry from one of the nearby tents. He couldn't make out what the voice was saying. He looked around to see if anyone would respond, but after a minute passed and nobody did, he decided to unzip the tent and climb inside. The shit and urine stink immediately struck his nose, followed by damp rot. He held a hand over his face and turned on a headlamp to find an old woman lying on a pad stained green and brown.

"Is anybody there?" she pleaded. "Hello? Anyone?"

He took her hand and felt a cold web of creased skin slide against his palm.

"Yes, there's someone," he said.

The woman didn't seem to acknowledge him. "Anyone there? Hello?" she went on.

"Yes, someone's here," he said. She looked to him to be in her late seventies. She wore a blouse that used to be white, and gold-rimmed glasses. She might once have been a teacher or accountant, he thought.

"Hold on, okay?" he asked her. "Let me radio for someone."

He let go of her hand, and although she still hadn't acknowledged him, the pitch of her voice rose as he left. "Is someone there?"

He did as he'd promised. He scanned and sent her tent number. Then he got busy with an onslaught of supply problems. He never saw the old woman again.

Things are different now, they say—siwilai, to use the old-time term. Order brings greater peace and a prosperous future for all, the public service signs declare. For anything else, he'll have to wait for a better forever.

Home is one of the units in a block of ten-story, multiwinged buildings with a narrow food garden separating each wing from its neighbors. Woon thinks of stopping at the garden to check on the year-old kaffir lime plants he recently replanted into larger racks. The plants haven't borne any fruit, but he likes to rub their leaves, which make his fingers greenly fragrant.

He appreciates the garden and the pastime it gives him on days off, but he also knows that it's not wholly for the benefit of the families here. These food gardens are good PR for the officials talking about how the garden harvests are part of the initiative to maximize yield when so much arable land is now underwater. Everyone, though, knows

that almost all their food is being imported from a consortium of cor-
porations, with the city's debt rising every day, but nobody likes to say
it in public. Nobody wants to end up sweeping the streets.

Let the rackbot feed the lime plants. When he gets to the elevators,
he decides to head up to his flat instead and arrives just in time for
dinner.

Dao's making a pan of pad Thai, a favorite with the children and
certainly good enough for his mother, whatever her recollection of the
street stall version sold in Old Krungthep. The twins clear and set the
table. Puk brings out the glasses, and Mint fills up a pitcher with water.
Everyone piles on noodles from the steaming pan in the middle. It took
Dao years to find a proper pan like that—flat and round and blackened
by years of burnt fats, unlike the composite glass in everyone's kitchen
now. They were on their honeymoon in Lisbon, of all places, and there
it was, on the wall of an antiques store, hung between an old Dutch
beer sign and a sun-faded one-sheet for one of the early-century super-
hero movies.

His mother is spearing the noodles with her fork, turning them over
to judge the color and the doneness of the strands.

"I went to visit Auntie Mai today. Do you remember Auntie Mai,
Mother?"

"Who's she? An old woman forgets. Don't be smart. Of course I do."

"I think I've met Auntie Mai before," his wife says. "At our wedding.
A very pretty woman for her age."

"She had some work done," says his mother.

"So did you, Mother, if I remember correctly."

"Back in the day when people went to the clinic and still left as
humans."

"I agree with Mother," Dao says, winking at him. "The word *human*
is going to soon become meaningless. What's stopping me from taking

Mumu to the clinic and turning her into a puffy-tailed girl? Didn't you always want a cat-daughter, Woon?"

"Yes! Yes! We want a cat-sister," say the twins, nearly in unison.

"She might as well be, the way your mother treats her," he says. "I presume she's enjoying the nice piece of mackerel in her bowl?"

"Only the freshest for Mumu," says Dao proudly.

They laugh while his mother picks at her plate. She must be enjoying the noodles, at the least, given that she has yet to make a complaint. He's surprised she hasn't brought this up: that a well-balanced Thai dinner should bring together a curry soup, a vegetable dish, something meaty, and, of course, properly cooked jasmine rice. There's no one more cooly viperous than an Old Krungthep matron thinking a meal not up to her standards.

It doesn't help that she isn't very enthusiastic about most things that he suggests. *Let's go picnic in the mountains. How about checking out the Loy Krathong festival at the river?* His mother says no outright, as the default response to every suggestion. *You all go and have fun,* she says, waving them away with her words. Sometimes they win her over, sometimes not. It's a minor feat that they've convinced her to go to the waterfalls with them tomorrow.

For his mother, the telenovelas suffice, especially the older ones she calls up from the archives service. Great-Grandmother liked them, she says to the twins, who often watch them with her as the drama unfurls in lavish living rooms likely lost in the sunken city.

He's thankful for the twins, for many reasons, one of which is that they regularly get his mother out of the house. Every weekday afternoon, while he and his wife are at the office, his mother picks them up at school, taking the three o'clock ferry and returning on the five o'clock, stopping at the market so the kids can help haul back groceries in their backpacks. He has offered to hire someone else to do this. She rebukes him for even thinking of it. He's worried something will happen, with her being over seventy and not in the best of health.

"How's homework?" he asks the twins, who've finished their papaya slices. "No playtime in the envo until you're all finished."

"We've done everything except maths."

"Dao, do you want to help them finish that part?"

"Father thinks logarithms give him migraines."

"Tell you what. You all can go finish that homework. I'll take care of the dishes. Mother, will you help me?"

Dao and the children disappear into the living room. He looks at his mother.

"Ready?"

Of course, he does nearly all the work, picking up the stacks of bowls and plates with open palms. His arms bent out as if weighing the dirty dishes, he keeps his balance as he strides like a minor Hindu god into the undersized kitchen.

"I told you I can carry some," his mother says.

"Don't worry. It's nothing. All you have to do is load them into the autoclaver after I do the rinsing."

He lets her do what she does best: putting things in their assigned place. She has a good eye for what fits where, a real knack for spatial geometry that lets her double the load he normally manages.

"By the way, I've got a message from Auntie Mai. Let me play it for you."

He reaches to tap the wall next to them. She grabs his hand.

"No, you don't have to. I'll visit her soon."

"She said that she hasn't seen you in quite some time."

"She's right. It's been far too long."

"I'll take you anytime you want."

"No, I can go by myself. I much prefer it if there's no hidden agenda."

"Agenda?"

"Look, I know what you're trying to do, and as your mother, I appreciate the efforts."

"Then you understand my concern."

"There are all kinds of reasons that I can say, some I have already, but you won't listen. You want things your way. You always have. You're my son."

"Mother, if not for me, then think of your grandchildren. Don't you want to see them grow?"

"Of course I do. It's thoughtless of you to even suggest that I don't."

"Then why?"

"Why what?"

"Why won't you even come to an informational tour with me? Auntie Mai can shift in. It won't be such a horrific experience, whatever you imagine."

"We can't afford it."

"We'll find some way."

"They'll say anything to have your money, and your children and then their children will get stuck paying for the upgrades. Much cheaper to burn paper money or give alms at the temple, I say."

"Mother, there are financing options. You have some savings."

"It's late, and the dishes aren't even halfway loaded. Are we done here?"

By the way she enunciates the word *done*, it's clear this is as far as she's going to discuss the matter tonight. Her stances have a way of hardening to stone. He hopes a trickle of dew can break immovable boulders, as they often say in old martial arts movies. He'll find some other occasion to bring up the topic again. He'll keep at it; he has to.

"Yes, Mother. We're done."

□ □ □

It's early morning. The whole family boards the special weekend boat crowded with sightseers and migrant workers returning to mountainside towns. They had wanted to avoid the later crush of people, but it seems that everyone else had the same thought. The overburdened boat, a small converted cargo runner, pushes through the water like a hurrying giant turtle. Waves wash out at its sides in long, unbroken ridges to lap at the shore.

At first, they're surrounded by small craft—fiberglass canoes heavy with entire families under sun-shielding umbrellas, repainted barges that drift together to form a floating bazaar—but not far outside Kanchanaburi settlement proper they find themselves the only boat on the water for long stretches, passing unawakened riverside villages along fingers of the river, until a cargo convoy or another passenger ferry roars past them in the opposite direction. Every once in a while, they spy leaf-darkened orchards behind electric-fencing, the fruits dotting trees like faint stars.

□ □ □

An hour later, having arrived at the national park's piers and taken a trolley up the mountainside, they come across a gaggle of other sightseers in line to buy tickets or waiting to use the public bathrooms.

The last time Pig was here, she was a university student. The waterfalls were just as crowded then, with tour buses and two-rowed passenger trucks lining the roads to jockey for legal parking. Who did she come with? Mai, most likely, maybe Wiangsuk, whom she had a crush on. Must have been some kind of departmental trip, part collegial bonding, part excuse to haze the first-years. She remembers the same park insignia she now sees on a trail sign: the three-headed elephant Erawan drawn in a way that makes it seem as if it's standing tiptoed on an unseen dot of land. Welcome, reads the sign, before warning about littering fines. A garbage can nearby shares its ample harvest with a flock of pigeons and sparrows.

Even with decades of flood, most Thais aren't shying from water. It feels good having it all around, misting faces even while hiking up the trails. Water means home.

"Listen, keep your eyes on us and stay together," her son says to the twins. "I don't want one of you carried off in a tiger's mouth."

"We know you're just saying that," the twins say back.

"Here, help your grandmother. Walk alongside her to make sure she doesn't fall," says Dao.

Pig hates how they sometimes act as if she's helpless, showing outsized concern for her health and comfort even as they entrust her with the weekday delivery and pickup of the children, which she's managed for years without as much as a cane in hand. Filial piety serves both young and old. That's how it works.

How dare Woon tried to take that responsibility from her. She wakes up early and looks forward to seeing Puk and Mint eat breakfast, half in their pajamas and half in their uniforms. On the way to school, she holds them, one in each hand, and lets their little energetic legs pull her forward, up sidewalks and steps. They can very well break free of her and walk at their own true pace, but they don't—this young, not yet teenagers, and already so considerate, if only to their grandmother. What wonderful adults they'll become. Her greatest worry: With her weakening body, how much more of them will she get to see?

She's tempted to stay, of course. Some semblance of her could have the pleasure. It's not as if she hasn't thought about it.

"The funicular's out of service," says Woon, with that dour expression of his. "Mother, can you walk for a bit?"

"I'll be all right. There wasn't even one the last time I came."

She recognizes the visitor center and its multiple flagpoles and the grimy leaf-covered roof, not much changed at all, except for the glass-walled gift shop added at one side. Even here, by the bottommost falls, the continuous rush of water pouring over limestone shelves begs her to speak louder. Strangers' children call one another's names across milky turquoise pools. They laugh, gawking at wriggly fish nibbling their feet. Her own grandchildren squat on the rocks, clandestinely dropping crumbs from their snack biscuits onto a mob of gasping mouths.

"Puk, Mint, if we get fined, it comes out of your allowance," Woon says, and strong-arms them back to the trailhead. Up the wood-planked paths they go, slowly for her sake, she knows. They walk past young children running down the steps in soaked clothes, bathing-suit-clad farangs with translation modules over their ears. Bamboo growths as tall as streetlamps curve overhead, breaking sunlight with thin, feathery leaves. She acquiesces to posing for a 4-D capture in front of an animated sign warning of thieving monkeys.

At each level, the falls grow taller and more powerful. Silky white curtains veil sloping rocks hollowed under the waterline. Their roar deafens. The twins shout at each other, pointing at foamy swirls in the water.

"I see cows. I see horses."

"Keep up, kids. We still have several levels to go," calls Woon, up on the next landing.

It's good that he's having fun, Pig thinks. When he was young, Woon was always running around, making silly. It's been too long since she's seen that boy.

"Your father wants to show that his legs still have it," says Dao, who's helping her up the stairs. "Look, you're impressing nobody! Come down and look after Mother, you hear?"

" I'm fine on my own," says Pig. "You can go make sure Puk and Mint don't run off a ledge."

"Okay, I'll be right back," Dao says. Pig watches her daughter-in-law, arms spread, keeping balanced over moss-nibbled rocks, her pointed, crescent feet slipping yet somehow finding the next step. Not the most graceful woman, but in what Pig once regarded as uncouth she now tries to find some endearing virtue.

Truth is, for some time, Pig didn't think her son's marriage would last. She had suspected eventual self-sabotage on Woon's part, that he would end up doing something stupid one day, just as he'd done as a young man, unable to escape the fantastical impulsiveness she'd once found charming in his father. Yet, there's something in Dao—her practical head, her calm command when the mood turns tense for others, ever the schoolteacher—that has provided ballast for her son, the woman's sharp tongue aside. No, she isn't someone Pig had imagined her son would marry—someone with at least a halfway respectable family name—but what do the elders ever really know? Her own father had been ecstatic when he'd heard that she and Sawahng were going to marry. Sawahng had come from a finance family with a trusted surname in their circles. A most beneficial alliance, was how her father put it. What had all that led to? A case of exorbitant malfeasance and then flight, she and Woon left to bear the shame.

"Grandmother, Grandmother, look at the pretty clothes," Puk says, leaping up the stairs. "What is this, a fashion show?"

Beside the trail, bright dresses have been left under a large tree— offerings for some wish answered by the mountain spirits. Collarless blouses in magenta and green, edged with golden threads. Knee-length wraparound skirts, like the kind worn by her grandparents' grandparents. Where on earth did they even find these?

"Be respectful, Puk," she says. "Watch what you say, or they might come visit you tonight."

"No, no! Don't scare us, Grandmother!" Mint says, plugging her ears.

"Serves you right," Dao says.

"Hey down there," a voice calls out.

"Father! We see you."

Woon's leaning on a bamboo railing at a ledge far above them. If his wife wasn't here, if he were two decades younger, Pig would have yelled for him to be more careful. One never knows how rusted the nails are or what has devoured the insides of a bamboo rod.

"Woon, don't put your whole weight on that," Dao yells up.

This is also true: Pig has realized that, at one point, she not only expected her son's marriage to fail, she wished for its doom. She had felt guilty for his early troubles, with a wastrel of a father and then fatherless, and with a mother who couldn't keep up the life he had enjoyed as a young boy. That useless, foolish woman who expected that her life would comply with her sweetest imagination of it. She had thought she'd have a chance to be a better mother and make it up to him. Instead, it's Woon who has been more than good to her. Not very many in his generation bother to treat their elders with so much reverence or warmth. Yes, she's been lucky, but does she deserve the luck?

"Grandmother, come, come. We're going to catch up to Father."

"Don't worry about me. I've been to these falls so many times. Look, there's a bench under that tree."

"Mother, you know we can't leave you here."

"I'm okay. You all go ahead; just don't forget to fetch me on your way down."

"Dao, what's going on?" Woon's voice reaches them from the ledge above.

"Mother wants to stay at this bench," Dao says.

Pig sits down on the concrete bench and drops her bag on her lap. Her knees thank her. She hadn't realized how much they ached until she took her weight off them.

"Grandmother, come, hurry. We only have a few more levels to go."

"You two blink some images of the higher falls for me. It'll be like I've seen them with my own eyes."

She says it, but she knows it's not true. It is absolutely not true.

They're interrupted by a man with spotless white shoes and the telltale optical modification. He first bows a wai toward Dao, and then remembers also to bow to his elders.

"Excuse me, do you mind if we leave my mother with yours? We don't want her to get overtired."

"I don't know. Would you expect my mother-in-law to chase her if she wanders away?" asks Dao.

"Don't worry, she'll sit here and won't move one step. It's what she does all day, with us."

"I wouldn't mind the company," Pig says before Dao can answer.

A woman wearing an untucked blouse pitter-patters to the bench and gingerly lowers her bottom onto it. The woman, maybe a decade older than her, has a pretty, congenial face that reminds Pig of Caterpillar's, back when they were all at the university. Whatever happened with Caterpillar? That's right, gone, like they're all beginning to go, one by one, each into her own black-and-white photo set on an easel at memorial rituals.

"Are you sure, Mother? Will you be all right?"

"Dao, pretend that I'm not here and take the children up to Woon. I'll be happy here."

"Okay. Don't be shy to tap us if you need us to come down. Come on, children. Let your grandmother rest here with her friend."

She watches Dao and her grandchildren trudge up the steps and disappear behind a cliff. They reemerge at the ledge above, where Woon stands, puzzled. She sees Dao talking to him, and Woon looking down to the bench where she's sitting. She waves up at him, and he waves back, along with the twins. They disappear up the next level of steps.

"Isn't it beautiful? All that water. These trees and rocks," the woman next to her says, pointing to the falls. "What's your name? I'm Lucky."

"My name is Pig, and yes, it is. I've always loved these falls."

She gazes up into the canopy, away from the crowd gathered at the rocky shallows. Misty slivers of light shoot through wavering treetops. Long wispy branches trace dark shapes against the bright colorless day. A cool breeze sweeps through, sending dried leaves into lofty, airborne rolls, except those dried leaves are golden-winged butterflies thickly clinging to the edges of branches. They return to perch after a few short spirals, settling and resettling on different parts of the trees, as if visiting old friends and lovers.

She loves it so: to be a woman breathing on this earth.

A tap on a shoulder interrupts her. Her new friend is smiling and pointing to herself.

"What's your name? I'm Lucky."

Pig nods. "Yes, I know. . . . My name is . . . "

Lucky points up at the waterfalls. "Do you hear that? I think it's raining outside."

PARTINGS

The wind, always the wind. It carries drier sand from the dunes in prickly waves. It rattles Mai's sunglasses, and by instinct she squints, without any real need. She walks back toward the ocean and the wet sand. Not far away, a kite—white and dovelike, with a long streaming tail—floats and dives over the family holding its line. Everyone's looking up at it, including her. She's afraid the line will snap, all the while knowing that it won't. The kite, this family of four with their striped shirts and partially wet shorts: they've retained their quality of memory, beginnings and ends encapsulated, witnessed as if all at once. A man wearing red track pants is about to jog from the dunes with his golden retriever. Soon, a flock of seabirds will land near the tidal pool ahead. The bluffs above appear golden yellow now, but in the evening, near twilight, they will appear chalkboard gray. A crew of surfers are paddling out on their boards, and she knows that one of them is about to wipe out under a spectacular blue curl, his friends cheering.

"Am I interrupting your swim?" Pig asks her.

"No, I was just walking, drying up."

"Where are we?"

"Near Cornwall in southwest England."

"Have you visited here before?"

"No, not before I afterbodied. None of this is mine."

Every atom on this beach had been scanned at some point by the seeing machines, every subparticle guessed by processing units. Then there are the other details—the gritty sand between toes, the children hunting for seashells along the shore—each a memory someone has deposited in the public map room. Only when a visitor from the other world shifts in does Mai feel it's anything other than normal.

"How was the water?" asks Pig.

"It's still too cold for a long swim, although I probably could have tweaked that."

"Well, why didn't you?"

"I tend to prefer things the way they were."

They walk along the curve of the beach to the next outcropping of rocks without saying a word. The wind picks up again. Their clothes flap like sails. The tips of dune grass lean with each gust and then ease back.

"You haven't told Woon about my visits here, have you?" asks Pig.

"No. It's been years since I last saw him, the last time probably with you, before he got married."

"I have a feeling he might seek you out, to convince me."

"If he does, what do you want me to tell him?"

"Nothing. I don't want to encourage him."

"Your son means well, for what that's worth."

"A lot of headaches. Good intentions mostly come to that."

"We've grown so cynical."

"Just a pair of miserable old women grumbling by the ocean."

"Speak for yourself," says Mai, conjuring her twenty-year-young self for a second before returning to her usual manifestation. The joke never gets old for her.

"On the topic of young people, how's Phee?" asks Pig, ignoring the joke.

"She's on what's supposed to be her sabbatical year, but mostly busy with her ten-year-old. She doesn't come to the portal as much as she said she would, but I understand that she has her life."

"Raising kids is so much more complicated and expensive now. I don't know how my children do it, even with my help."

"I'm sure they appreciate you being there."

"I do wonder. I worry. For them, for everyone. I meditate, I pray to my ancestors and whoever else might be listening, and I go back to being anxious. That's why they shouldn't waste anything they have on me. I've had more than enough."

"You don't have to worry. I'm not here to try to change your mind. It has to be you who wants this."

"I know."

"I talk to other friends here, and we all seem to agree on that. It has to be an individual, personal decision."

"I'm happy you're not lonely here."

"I've told you about Bubbles."

"Yes, I think so."

"It amazes me how much closer we've gotten. I remember hating her stuck-up guts so much. Now she shifts in almost every week, your time-line, or I go to her vineyard near Lyon and have a nice picnic on a hill."

"You did tell me this. She spent tons on the amenities upgrades. A Versailles for anyone who can afford it."

"It's tastefully done, especially her gardens."

"That's right. She's now a woman of the land, her fingernails stained by earth, if you can even call it that."

"You're being unfair again."

"Sorry. Didn't mean to make fun of you and your new best friend."

"Stop it."

"Okay, okay. Just trying to be funny. Am glad that everything's great with you all."

"For the most part."

"I hope so, for you."

The beach ends ahead at a bluff, so they follow a trail flanked at first by grassy dunes and then thickets with mustard-colored flowers. On a hill up the beach, Mai spots a large sign warning beachgoers of undertows and rip currents. To sink. To struggle without air. She's surprised that she fears drowning, even when it no longer threatens her.

"If it pleases you to know," she says to Pig, "I've often thought about the facts of my afterbody and the time right before I went ahead with the procedure. It seemed like a decision of life or death then. Now it doesn't. I only paid for more time. That's all. A freak solar phenomenon could happen tomorrow, or another Oslo, and I wouldn't even know it. I'm relaxing by a clear, blue lake in South America, and then what, that bright light they always say would appear? Will everything then go dark, like it would have before?"

"Not unlike what befalls those of us out here, I guess. Breathing. Breathing. Poof."

"Aren't you the least bit afraid? Of not being here in some way?"

"I like to think not. Besides, haven't you already kind of partway left?"

"I'm still me, and I'm still here, Pig."

"Are you?"

"Come, I want to show you something. It might help you ease worries you haven't admitted to, or it might not. In any case, you'll probably find it fascinating."

"You're always wanting to show me something. Why do you always have some surprise up your sleeves?"

"C'mon, shift with me."

"All right."

The next step they take isn't on sand but on sun-heated concrete. Flip-flops appear on their feet, courtesy of Mai. They're standing on the front steps of a building she trusts Pig will recognize right away. High above the ornate old house is the condo tower with its many curved balconies.

She sees on Pig's face the startling recognition and, soon after, the disbelief. She has felt the same way. The totality of the capture shouldn't impress her more than any other place in this world, but it does. How remarkable: the extent and detail of what is now here, so much that she can forget there's still a there, in whatever condition time and nature has willed. Here is everything that's been cataloged of there, within reach like books lined up on a shelf, so that she can step wherever she wants into the old city, busy and smelly and incessant, and feel like she's never left it. She likes best arriving not directly to the building but to a Skytrain stop a quarter kilometer away and retracing the sidewalk route she used to take coming back near dusk from the university. How wonderful, to move along shadows of people unknown and the familiar strangers she didn't know by their actual names, but whose storefront or daily commute had installed them in her daily life then, distinct from the faces inserted there by someone else's recollections or filled in by the processing units. To be back here again and look up fondly at the endless silhouette of telephone and electrical wires entangled above, and the brief, particular shades of gray and pink the dying afternoon has colored the surrounding shophouses. And, with every floating stride, to see the building closer and closer, each of its lit windows shining out a welcoming beacon for her.

"I haven't thought about this place for a very long time," says Pig. "Do you shift here a lot?"

"I sometimes keep this experience open, even as I've shifted to other places."

"We haven't met here."

"You never asked. I thought you might not want to kick up old history."

She doesn't tell Pig that she has never gone beyond the lobby. Never rode the elevator up to the condo, not wanting the possibility— permission's more like it—of unlocking archive settings to bring back the specters of her parents, reappearing as they were, raised to seeming life from the museum of her mind. Safer to bring them up as still photos that can only draw up brief, vague notions of a person before flowing away like a stream through an open hand. Photos will never bicker with each other or ask about her day or insist that she eat the freshly cut pineapple, bought at the market some afternoon long before it was possible for anyone to avoid the rude interruption of mortality.

"It's funny, Krungthep in the 2010s and 2020s doesn't seem that long ago," says Pig.

"A handful of decades can feel like a few seconds. Do you miss it, that old city?"

"Every day, painfully. What is it that you want me to see?"

Mai already knows where they are on the timeline, but she looks at the watch on her wrist, out of habit.

"Should be soon. I can quicken the minutes, but I think it's better just to wait a little. Come, follow me. I want to be close, when it happens."

She grabs Pig's hand, and they walk down the steps to the garden beside the old house. The guard on duty at the entrance booth, whom she doesn't recognize, squats on the ground, reading a newspaper folded in one hand. He's definitely sourced from someone's public memories. Does he even notice her and Pig in front of him? There's a vast difference between him, this ornamental figure inserted into the scenery, and her, a conscious, feeling entity, isn't there? What's alive and what's not: there has to be an inviolate line between them, somewhere.

"Mai, let me ask you something," says Pig, tugging her hand.

"What?"

"Will you miss me?"

"Pig, don't be stupid, talking like that."

"Because I'm sure I'll miss you, whatever I'll be then."

"Some angelic being, I'm sure, reborn on the tenth level of the heavenly realm."

"More like a wandering ghost. Nobody thinking to make alms or offerings for me. I'll go hungry."

"You're always thinking about eating."

"Can you blame me? It's hard enough as it is, having to bear with my daughter-in-law's cooking."

"You'll think this unfair, but I can bring up almost any one of my past meals. Guess what I'm tasting right now."

"Don't say Den Pochana."

"Den Pochana when we were at university, not the replacement. That broth."

"Now that's a reason for me to change my mind."

"I would love it if you did."

Mai wishes to unsay the words. She'd promised herself: *you must let Pig make up her own mind.* Still, more words leap from her lips.

"Pig, I don't want you to think that I'll be okay when you're gone. I really won't. If it's only money, let me help. I don't care how much."

She spent decades donning a suit of professional coolness for her job. Her self-control and discretion ranked highly among her peers in performance reviews. It was much easier then, wasn't it? Bosses losing their tempers, the lawyers barking across the table, clients saying something awful. She held in her thoughts behind a smile that was also a fortified wall.

"Mai," says Pig. "For once, I'll find out something before you. Is that why you're upset?"

"Stop kidding around. I'm not."

"I've had a good, fortunate life, even with the parts that weren't so great, and it's hard to think it won't last for much longer, but—I can't explain it—I'm not afraid. Nothing comes after, or everything does. I feel all right not knowing. I'm actually more used to that, by now."

"I'm sorry. Forget I said anything."

"I won't. I know you mean well. I appreciate it."

Mai draws Pig into a tight one-arm hug. For a long while they stand there, not another word between them.

Then comes the roar, loud and horrible, as if the building has come crashing down on them. But it's not the kind of a sound that an ear might hear, as she's found out and as Pig, with eyes widened, is now discovering, too.

When she sees the ground darken, she whispers to Pig, "Look over there."

Pig turns toward the driveway in front of the building's garage. Mai guesses from the squinting that, at first, Pig must not have noticed the particular spot. She waits for her friend to look in the right spot. A dept at wonder that announces itself by

ange grayish area?" asks Pig. "Is it a shadow.

They walk closer to the spot. On the gray concrete is a shape s getting larger and darker. Here's an arm, then another, then legs.

"It looks like a person," says Pig. "A small person."

"A shadow of a child perhaps. I've often thought so."

"What happened here?"

"I wish I knew. Much of the old newspaper records went with the floods."

"Is this not from someone's memory?"

"That's the thing: there's no source for this. I've checked. The shadow is here at this spot, part of the scan at the time, yet also not here."

"Wait, where did it go?"

"Here and then gone."

"This is kind of frightening. If you weren't here with me, I would run."

"There's nothing to be afraid of. It was only a child's shadow."

"A child lying here, not moving. Whatever happened couldn't have been good."

"I suspect that, too. Even so, I can't help but come back here to watch this shadow appear and disappear."

"Like a ghost."

"In your world maybe, but there are no ghosts here."

"What do you think it is?"

"I suppose that it's an error or artifact that the system never detected. I also think that it might be memory, just not human memory. I admit, I find it strangely comforting. That's why I wanted to show you, because I know what you're going to decide."

"Wait, wait. Who's doing the remembering?"

"Here. This building, this ground."

. do that?"

ı had a better explanation, but I think that maybe yes, they
. when we don't. Places remember us."

◻ ◻ ◻

Make a fist, spin and spin. Mai can't help but mouth the song when it
sounds again, unprompted, tinny on the conical speakers hung high on
metal poles. She spreads her arms and then touches her shoulders, as
the song tells her to do. She's there at the morning assembly with Pig
and the other children, all in their uniform of white blouses and blue
pleated skirts and those drab Velcro shoes. Her arms and hands, like
the others, circulate about her, the instructions by now unnecessary.
She thinks of their history exam later, having spent the night memoriz-
ing the names of old kings and queens, generals and noblemen, the
Greek consul and Japanese mercenaries and French priests. When she
finally went to bed she slept soundly, while in her dreams head-
wrapped Burmese marched quietly across the porous mountains and
fang-infested forests, and soon she was watching the doing of those
men: the smoke-eaten old capital in Ayutthaya, its glowing pagodas
dripping melted gold into steaming puddles, flashes of swords where
steel had yet stained, and through a terrified sparrow's eyes, surging
above its intended flight to escape the heat, she saw the spread of the
land, the tall wicks of orange where thatched roofs spewed starry embers and the ashen villages and blackened stubs of men, women, and
children curled still on the charred earth. When Pig, in the middle of
the calisthenics routine, nudges her at the elbow and asks what questions she thinks the teacher will ask, her arms continue with their
movement, stretching out, fanning air, and then her palms extend flat,
pushing water. She's young, her leaf-sized feet slapping water behind

Khun Nee's encouraging shouts. She's older, her long legs like oars. She smells the chlorine, familiar in the sun-warmed water she's spitting out, her head turned for a quick breath before sinking again to face the deepening blue of the pool, where she feels she could swim forever, across the length of seas, over wavy kelp and side-walking crabs, over reefs and schools of comical fish, the creatures larger the darker and farther out she swims, so that she's soaring across leviathans and mile-long serpents and the yellow-green phosphorescence bursting from their fins, and then there are larger creatures, so endlessly massive that it would take the span of her whole life to swim a width of their hair, and as the purple hues blacken above the city, her ears again detecting its enormity waking to night, the car horns and street babble outside the walls, the lawn lights buzzing on, the choir of cicadas under grassy shrubs and security guards by the car park leaping to kick around a takraw ball between shifts, she surfaces to walk up the sloping wet sand, stepping through the cold foamy surf on this beach, where an older Pig has shown up. "Am I interrupting your swim?" Pig asks. So good to see an old friend, yet always so sad, too. A different view opens. The silhouette of the Empire State Building looms in the far distance, in First New York. Glass towers surround her, reflecting the afternoon's incandescent blue. She bends down, and it's to pick up her grandchild, who has scampered across the balcony to collapse against her knees.

"Don't hurt your grandmother," Phee says to her son from behind the potted rosebushes, kneeling on a blue tarp where she has laid out crumbling mounds of black dirt.

"Neil's grown so much since last I saw him. A month or two ago, was it?"

"Well, you're busy, I'm busy."

"I want to come by more, if that's okay with you."

"Whenever you want, Mother."

"It will be good to spend as much time as possible with him before I afterbody. And with you, of course. I imagine things will be very different next year."

"You can always delay it later."

"No, I'd like to just go through with it. Who knows what will happen if I wait longer?"

"Who knows."

Phee's worried. The technology's too new. There are no long-term studies. Why is her mother rushing to jettison the world she has?

"What are you doing to those poor roses?" Mai asks.

"I'm mixing this new fertilizer into the soil. Mrs. Hernandez said that I should try it. You should see her Eau de Nil varieties."

"Hope it works well for them. I've come to learn in a roundabout fashion that every flower blooms in its own odd way."

It's summer. The balcony tiles singe the balls of her feet. She picks up her grandson, who lets out a protesting whimper, and carries him over to Phee. His fine black hair, almost umber in this light, brushes the tip of her nose. She smells the shampoo from the morning bath in his little tub and the dried talc on his neck. She hasn't let herself lock up this memory. If she could, she would tell Pig, in the wherever, that this alone is worth every doubt. Those doubts would disappear, for her, and so would the term *afterlife*. There is only life, and there is meaningfulness inside it that can never be destroyed or again created. Any physical thing can be recorded—the micro-details of appearance, the sound something makes, its motions and conditions, in whatever encoded distillation of its original—but no one else is going to feel the way she does for this boy at this moment. They say that not long from now, whenever that is, it will be possible for ten thousand years to pass here and only minutes out there. No matter, the machines must someday crumble into rusty mounds and water will leave the earth. This joy within her will always be true.

"You'll bring him to see me often."

"Yes, yes, I promise. We'll go see you every week."

With her free hand, Mai reaches out to grab a small bud dangling at the end of a stem. It looks like an unripened fig, with fine bristles on its green cover, a sliver of blue peeking from within.

"These are going to be so beautiful. I know it."

RETURN

My Dearest Andrew,

If you should ever find yourself stricken with disease in
the tropics, dispense with any shame for wailing as would
a babe left in the woods.

I'm fortunate not to have been so abandoned. My worst
night, Miss Crawford stayed by my side to repeatedly apply
mustard poultices for the immense pain in my abdomen,
and when I could, I swallowed copious amounts of saline
solution and castor oil, so that its purgative effects might
help to eject the morbid matter that had invaded my
bowels. Cloudy fluids smelling of bile and salt poured from

me into earthen bowls, which Miss Crawford emptied after
each administration. I had earlier requested that she
sheathe me with a wool blanket recovered from the
reverend's trunk. It had been wrung, by my instructions, in
a hot bath and was then wrapped around my body so that
it enshrouded me from head to tremoring limb, with the
hope that it would draw blood to the capillaries and
improve my circulation. On my sleeping mat, I simmered,
drenched in sweat. At times, I found myself laboring to
breathe, every draw of air a kick of sawdust in my chest,
in contradiction to the wetness everywhere else. The
pain in my abdomen always found haste in its return,
and my insides felt as if they had been stuffed with
sharp gravel. Poor Miss Lisle, poor Reverend, I fully
understood the horror of their suffering. I waited for
the moment that would be my last, when I would surely
join them.

Nevertheless, even as my body failed me, my most
instinctive faculties refused the same fate. Like a deer that
had found itself cornered by wolves, I fought to persist. I
spotted a crooked nail on the ceiling and clung to it with
my eyes. I made myself believe that I would immediately
perish if I looked away for a mere second. I did not look
away. I kept my eyes open. I took in the surface of that
rusty nail, which to a man of infinitesimal size must have
seemed an endless red desert, pocked by vast craters where
moisture had nibbled away the iron.

I know this because, as I fixed my sight on the nail, I
became that man in miniature. Although my body had
been lain supine underneath that nail, I was also making

my passage across its pitiless landscape, tormented by the unceasing stillness of that world. It was quiet, with the exception of faint noises emanating from somewhere in the distance. It was song, I recognized, and I moved toward it. I couldn't gauge how far I had to go. I simply followed this most peculiar sound.

When night arrived and I could no longer see the nail, my journey did not pause. I continued in darkness. Instead of rusty dunes, I was now crossing through black space sometimes interrupted by gossamerlike ribbons of light that, farther upon my trek, I came to recognize as streets lined by faint contours of edifices and doorways, and at times, moving forms that resembled, if only for a second, human shapes. Gradually, I realized that this devil's scenery was alarmingly familiar because I had walked it before, during my stay in New York, before leaving for the Orient.

Do you recall my telling of those visits to the Bowery? Can you conjure the scenes I then described or drew for you—the desperate leisure-making of debauched souls in damp saloons and the wriggling of bodies in the perfumed parlors of bordellos? Do you remember my pride at having resisted their invitations to degenerate leisures? The truth is that I did more than pass through that temptatious scenery. I drowned in Babylonia's drink and pleasured in flesh many times, yet I saw myself separate from the men who fell. I feel compelled now to tell you this, with apologies for having made you believe otherwise. I almost missed my opportunity to reveal my truer face and for you to see me as He does.

Have no fear for me, brother, if you still believe me worthy of your love and trust. My disease has since lifted. I can again sit upright at my desk. I can eat and drink by my own strength and even make brief visits to patients. The best of it, the cooks accommodate my requests without rancor.

I am told that the carts no longer have need to come around. The streets of Bangkok are returned to the living and slaughterhouses are enlivened again with the bleats of doomed creatures.

A letter from the Society arrived yesterday. With the loss of the reverend, and considering the progress of past efforts, the board thought it best to dissolve the mission. I have been offered my choice of postings in China.

I shall decline it. You will find me here in Siam.

After my recent ordeal, you must think my decision folly. Would it not be easier and far more prudent to return to Troy to join Father's practice, or to seek another fellowship at the medical college? Yes, it would be. And I realize that what remains of Father's and Mother's years will diminish each day, and that among our friends, my name will be mentioned with shaken heads. I suspect I will soon become but a shadow occasionally recalled, perhaps a memory discarded altogether.

And yet I know my decision to be the right one. I've been thinking of when I knew it so. I could say it was after that harrowing night passed, when I opened my eyes not to a red desert but to a bluing dawn, and the familiar shrieking of parrots in the trees made me aware of where I'd returned, but it was not then. And it was not when I saw

Miss Crawford enter my room, and I could guess from the radiant joy on her face, and the tears in those kind eyes, that I had regained some visible vitality. I did not have any extraordinary vision. I was not visited by angels. Yet the godly I did see, as I lay in my room.

In my most dire state, I came upon a grand house atop a hill in the rusty desert. I knew, by some intuition, that the song I'd been hearing had come from here. I thought it to be Gransden Hall, yet I could not be certain. Every aspect of the house was at the same time familiar and strange. There were wooden chairs on the porch that I didn't recognize, yet it seemed natural that they should be there. A glimpse through the window revealed dark wood furniture in the style of our parlor, I was sure. The scene felt welcoming, and I did not want to question why I had failed to identify our home with confidence. Does it make sense that I could feel utterly lost and, in the same heartbeat, delighted by my return somewhere?

I entered through a side door near the kitchen hearth and wandered, room to room. It appeared that I had arrived on the occasion of a banquet. There was commotion in the house—the sound of hurried footsteps upstairs and the bumping of jars in the pantry—and then my ears registered laughter from the parlor. Someone was telling a story, and I imagined it was either Father or Uncle Merton regaling the room with the usual tales from their time in the western territories. I heard a child playing in the hall, and I was seized by joy, from not having seen our little sister for a very long time. It was unapparent to me then that it had been decades, and I did not question that she had lived. Yet, as I roamed through the house, I was met by no one. There was only the house, as pristine and glorious as ever, with the furnishings and floors unmarred by any dust, as if they had been cleaned and tidied that very morning. I was upstairs in the midst of my search, frustrated by the belief that everyone, even Mother, was playing some cruel trick on me, when I heard the rising notes of a piano through the floor slats, and I immediately rushed down to see if Annabeth was practicing from her songbooks or if the devil himself was fingering the keys.

An unexpected face floated before me. It was Winston's.

How odd, I thought, that he should come into the music room.

"You look terrible, Dr. Stevens," he said.

He told me he had come back to the mission house after hearing of the reverend's passing. He took hold of me and sat me up against the wall.

Then, I saw a man and a child step into the room, with clay pots in their hands. The man's face, dented and flattened at an acute angle on one side, I recognized at once. The boy I could never forget. I believed I had been summoned to the Netherworld.

Bunsahk brought a bowl filled with dark liquid to my lips. His son dipped a rag into it and wrung trickles into my mouth. I swallowed, not knowing what I drank, medicine or poison. I only knew that I was thirsty. With every drop, I drew in the spirit of oxen and snakes. Great jungle beasts ran inside me, growling. I tasted dirt and rubies and thousands of years of rain.

Believe me, brother, I still harbor great skepticism in the Siamese's treatment methods, so thoroughly devoid of scientific rigor. I do believe, however, that what I actually drank contained more than what was material in that medicine. I'm certain that, by way of it, I was touched by His Spirit, and Mercy and Grace did I receive.

I drifted away from the house that might have been Gransden Hall and back to where a crooked nail had caught me, and there, clinging to it, afraid to let go, I witnessed Winston and the boy scrubbing away the filth encrusted on my skin, and Bunsahk washing me with saline. They held little fear, in spite of the perils present, and it may well be that in their courage and generosity, I have also renewed my own.

I beg that you understand my intended course even if you believe my wits lost. Please do not burden your heart with any concern; my well-being belongs to our Lord. This I know when I hear the last rasping breaths of the dying sing out their wants and fears, when Miss Crawford's voice settles coolly on the assembly hall as she leads her young charges in prayer, or at twilight when the river shimmers with rippling fire as I'm being rowed out to attend to a patient, for whom I shall feign practical confidence, even as I wander, bewildered in the great mystery of this earthly place, because each poor soul I encounter, I've come to know, is also my own. The lifelong accumulation of their hours; their betrayals, blindness, and failings; their genius and heart: mine, too. I shall come to God through their eyes.

We will soon have to leave the mission compound; my funds are insufficient, alone, to continue the reverend's work. The Siamese landowners have expressed their wish to raze the current edifice so as to build more structures on the property. I will see to it that we keep the wood and whatever other material we can salvage, for construction elsewhere.

Where will I find the necessary means to continue on here, you ask? I have discussed with Winston the formation of a partnership for the export of teak and silks to the West, and the import of European and American goods to Siam. The plan is for me to help manage the trading company at the capital and take the reins when Winston travels to trade in the Siamese countryside or the British Malayan settlements. Whatever time remains to me, though I fear there will be little, I will continue tending to the sick and injured among the populace. I've asked Miss Crawford if she will join me, and I anxiously await her answer.

I look with awe and gratitude at the immensity of the work to be done. The sum of it may prove to become my true, lasting mark on this world, more than medicine or faith alone could hope to effect. There are illnesses to remedy, libraries to fill, roads and homes to bring to modernity with the most healthful and uplifting of civilized comforts. In time, I hope that we will have helped the Siamese and her neighbors in this Asiatic region to construct an enduring society that wholly nourishes all its citizenry in body and spirit, and that the means of this well-being will have arrived by the provision of the highest-quality wares within reach of the most common man, which will in turn foster further humane advancements, ad infinitum. I foresee happiness and peace ahead, Our Father's heaven on this earth if I may be so bold to proclaim, and I am committed to playing my newfound part to the fullest.

A curious happenstance occurred just today, by the way. The customs men at the port, perhaps by the work of mysterious hands or their own repentance, located the trunk lost at my arrival in Siam. On opening it, I found my old shirts. They were barely recognizable to me. Some had been perforated by the nibbling of worms and moths, rendering them unsuitable for public appearances, and some had been yellowed by moisture and rusted iron parts, while others remained intact, as whole as I remember them. These appear to me the strangest of all, like bodily shadows I shed in a past life, if I'm to adopt the Siamese beliefs. They did remind me, fondly, of the trips we made to the city, when Father would take us to old man Barrie's. You could never stay still while he measured you with his yarn. Do you remember that? Such a troublesome imp you were, and Father so young then, with his gait erect and shoulders wide, like the mainmast of a galleon. What I would do to see him as he was. What I would give to see us then.

UPSTREAM

Yeah, it was probably a nightmare again. Sometimes he feels like he's woken up to a mind that's collapsed on him, and he's still buried in the rubble of a terrible dream. He can count on his bladder to alert him to who and where he is.

"As long as I'm up, might as well go," Clyde says in his accented Thai, still rusty after all these years. It's late, and the lights in the room are off. He searches for the shape of the woman in the dark.

She only comes up to his shoulders, but he trusts her broad, solid build. He hooks an arm into hers, and she guides his pitter-patter to the bathroom. She helps pull down his drawstring pants and steps behind him to give him privacy, all the while keeping a loose grip under his arm.

"My butt's freezing in this place," he says. Like many Thai folks, the young woman doesn't like to give the AC a rest, even if the weather cools down. It's so cold he thinks he can feel each staple holding his chest closed.

"All right, Ms. Ducky. I'm done."

"Hey, Khun Clyde. It's Lucky, same as you forgetting how lucky you are to be alive."

◻ ◻ ◻

He doesn't agree with Lucky's choice of words on his current state, although technically speaking, she's right. A few weeks ago, he was on his way to join everyone who's already gone ahead.

In the middle of a set, his chest tightened as if an invisible assailant was bear-hugging him from behind. He breathed, but it hardly felt like he breathed. A man drowning on nothing. He knelt on his knees, and his bandmates rushed to hold him steady. His vision dimmed outside in, and from the flashes whitening the periphery of his eyes, it seemed like somewhere above him an unannounced fireworks show had started. They'd ended the war, someone said on the radio. He smelled charcoal fire and cooked meat. Top of the fifth, Yankees down two, someone says on the radio.

He woke to a beige ceiling and spent a minute staring at his arms and the tubes and wires they'd stuck on him. On the glass door of a dark, empty room opposite his bed, he spotted his own reflection: a face webbed at the eyes and draped thinly where his skin sagged, but a boyish part of the man has stubbornly hung on so that a younger man might still be seen if he squinted. Every few minutes another patient somewhere behind the curtain moaned, a man, he thought, but he couldn't be sure. He'd heard cries like that the years he worked the afternoon cleanup shift at a movie house near Times Square—always careful to thoroughly scrub his hands and arms before heading off to his gigs.

The nurse stopped by, a clipboard under her arm.

"Mr. Alston, I'm looking at your forms here. Any next of kin we can contact for you?"

"Nope, not really, not here."

"You're not going to be able to do much of anything for a while."

The surgeons had to open him up to repair his ruptured right ventricular valve. It would take one or two months for him to recover.

"This ain't nothing. I'll manage," he said, gazing at the long strip of bandage down the middle of his chest. He wouldn't fault them for not knowing the history of Clyde Alston, who'd bounced back from his share of broken ribs and bruised lips and all kinds of other wreckage to play his next show. Still, after discovering himself too weak to hold the TV remote, he asked the nurse to call Bobby Blue Eyes.

It was Bobby who arranged for Lucky, having used the same home health aide placement company after his mother got sick. "I pay," Bobby said on the phone, and Clyde relented. It was good of the man, who'd made much more on other clients these past few years. Clyde, hoping to make it to 1998 without emptying his savings, had lately even agreed to play at a piano showroom, tinkling out tunes mallgoers might recognize from the movies or the supermarket aisle. He thanked the Buddha and all the heavenly deities that nobody from his night gigs saw him there, but he was sorry when the showroom had shuttered this past month after something or another happened in the unearthly realm of global finance. The Thai baht took a dive, and there were far fewer parents furnishing their kids' future with an imported baby grand.

"Economy like tom yum goong," Bobby explained in his accented

English. "Soup is hot and spicy. So delicious. People eat too much. Everyone now pay."

"I guess that makes sense to someone. Thank you, Bobby."

The next morning, the young woman arrived at the hospital to ride with him in the transport van back to his flat.

□ □ □

Whenever she speaks to him, she smiles. She smiles when she helps him into his layabout clothes and when she gives him his pills and when she asks him to turn on the AC. By the end of their first day, he understood her smile to mean that she's on duty.

She looks young to him, no more than thirty. Instead of wearing a secondary school or university uniform, she wears dark pants and a knit shirt with the name of the placement company stitched over the chest pocket. He notices that she has at least five sets of the outfit in her rolling suitcase. She washes them in a tin basin that he doesn't remember owning and then sun dries the wet clothes on his balcony.

They keep to a routine. He wakes early in the morning, and she takes off her headphones and gets up from the foldout cot to help him. He still can't stand up for long, so she sponge-bathes him in his bed and then takes his blood pressure, jotting the numbers in a small red notebook. Breakfast is rice porridge with maybe pork foo or boiled garlicky fish. She spoon-feeds him, and he feels like a child eating by someone else's hand, but he doesn't mind. At least someone's here while his chest creaks like wood in a decrepit house, each gulp emptier than it should be. A dull pain jabs at him when he least expects.

When he's done, she clears away the plates and hands him the remote control. They watch a bit of a Thai channel's midday news—the usual politicians' interviews outside of parliament, the same kinds of bad accidents and flooding in the far provinces, but these few weeks, the anchors dedicate half the show to the economy. Grim-faced experts fear the baht soon won't be worth a grain of sand. It's a relief when the telenovelas come on.

"Remind me what happened last time?"

"So okay, like, the little wife has hired an assassin to go after the major wife, but the major wife has found out and has now hired a witch doctor to attack the little wife with ghost children."

A delivery person brings them Styrofoam boxes of noodles for lunch. He eats slowly. Even chewing tires him. After the meal, he takes a nap and lets an hour or two dissolve away. He sometimes peeks out to see Lucky reclined on the sofa, wearing headphones attached to the CD player at her hip and nodding to music he can't hear.

She doesn't say much about herself. He pieces her together from the details she drops. He knows that she was born in Lampoon Province and came to Bangkok to study and never left. She doesn't have her own place. Where she works is also where she stays, with a day off here and there. He gathers that her previous charge was a paralyzed lawyer who enjoyed having ghost stories read to him, and sometime before that there was a former TV personality and actress who spent much of the day singing karaoke in the living room. Of course, she's had to put up with dirty old men and incredibly stingy people, but she doesn't go into the details.

"You don't have to worry about that with me, except for maybe the stingy bit," he says.

"Oh, I know," she says, and lifts a spoonful of rice porridge to his lips.

"Still hot."

"It's warm. You can't handle it, Khun Clyde?"

"Know what I say to musicians when they're afraid to get into a song? I tell them to dive into the gator's mouth. Hit me again."

She does. He slurps from the spoon and asks for another.

"Good?" she asks.

"Can use more fish sauce and chilies, if you don't mind me saying."

◻ ◻ ◻

He recovers faster than the doctors expected. By their third week, he's able to walk without much discomfort, Lucky holding him by the elbow and leading him downstairs near evening, after the weather has cooled. They inch their way to the sundries store down the soi and back, for his exercise. He eyes the olieng stand every time but only buys a bottle of Singha soda for himself and a Yakult for her. Back at his flat, they pick up the bag the bento service has hung at the door. She takes his blood pressure again and then plates their meal. They eat. She washes the dishes and afterward takes him to his practice keyboard. To appease the neighbors, he keeps the volume low. She sits next to him as he plays. He asks, "What do you want to hear, young lady?" and she tells him to play whatever he likes.

One night he surprises her with a famous Poompuang loog toong song. She claps and giggles and mumbles the lyrics the whole way through. Good thing she doesn't want to be a singer.

They sleep at eleven, on the dot. If he doesn't fall asleep right away, he listens to the music hissing from her headphones. He can't tell what it is. Just waves after wave of drums and machinelike noises, sometimes human voices, crashing against his ears.

He knocks on the floor to get her attention. She takes off her headphones and props herself up on an elbow.

"I can't help but overhear a bit of you what you're listening to," he says.

"This? I'm so sorry, Khun Clyde. It helps me sleep, what with the construction noise outside, you know. I can turn it down."

"It's quite all right. I'm only curious about what it is."

"Oh, it's just music. Probably nothing you'd like."

"Is this what young folks are listening to? I don't think I've heard anything like it."

"Well, it's not Thongchai or anything popular. My friends make copies or get songs from the internet and then burn them for me."

"You're going to have to help me out here."

"Did you know you can plug a phone line into the computer and dial up the modem and look for anything?"

"You did what to the phone?"

"I don't really know how it works. It just happens when you push the right keys, I guess," she says, and reclines back on the cot.

He doesn't press further and returns to puddling on the bed. Lucky seems to fall asleep, and he's left alone with his raspy breathing and the far-off shouts of nightshift construction workers outside. Saws scream their whirling songs to him. He hears hammers, one closer and a few higher and fainter, take turns forcing some steely thing into its final shape. Sometimes a motorcycle roars by, going faster than it ought in a small tributary soi. The dark city hisses at him from every direction, and he folds into himself.

□ □ □

He can't tell where he is. He could be at Minton's, or the Lenox, or Nick's basement spot. He thinks he sees the 134th Street crowd in a booth. Max and Eagleface and the gang. Ada and Jeanine.

Also in the room: so many headcutters in one spot. Many in the crowd probably don't know what's coming. They're probably expecting a pleasant jaunt uptown, letting themselves loose clapping and whooping when they see the colored folks do it, so they can tell their friends, and then a speedy cab ride back to well-heeled Bohemia. The evenings always start out tame, never seen cats so well behaved. Light applause and thank-yous all around.

Then someone like Ellis has to go and bring it. Starts double-timing on a number and staring down Mitch Jenkins the whole time, and everyone knows that Mitchy isn't going to let the young ones think they could lop off one of their elders' heads. After Mitchy goes, he finds out that he's only riled up Jimmy George, who can't stand show-offs and so has to show everyone better himself, and by then, the audience's confused as all hell about what happened to their night. They probably feel like a knife fight's going to break out, and they're not wrong.

When he looks down, he sees that he's in his signature blue suit. He's slapping shoulders and shaking hands like he's running for mayor of New York City, peace-making between sets and showing everyone what a congenial big man he is. Good thing he doesn't know what some of them are already whispering. He avoids being pulled into a duel with Batty Eddie, who's machine-gunning the keys, hands stretched across elevenths with gigantic chords. Of course, he fails.

"You showed Eddie up good. Everyone heard it," a man says, and then kisses him in a shadowy alley. They're on their walk home. It's wintry and cold as the moon. Every shopfront has closed for the night, except for the Chinese restaurant. He looks through the security bars to see the cooks gathered at a table for their own meal, a beer bottle to each. They look up at him, and he sees that they don't have faces, only pale, featureless swaths looking less like flesh than smudged paint. He looks at the man he's been walking with. He, too, has become a smear of a figure.

"Morris, what in hell's going on? What's happened to you?"

"Hey, Khun Clyde. Are you okay?" asks a young woman, her hand tight on his arm.

He recognizes Lucky. He's on a bed in a room, his back sweaty even with the chilly air. Outside, metallic clangs welcome him back. Unseen parts of the building tell him that they've hit the ground through thuds he can feel up through the floor.

"Probably just a nightmare," she says.

"Yeah, it probably was," he says, trying to push himself up so that she'll help him. "As long as I'm up, might as well go."

□ □ □

Every two weeks, Lucky takes a Saturday off and stays with a cousin in Nonthaburi. In her place, the agency sends a dour-faced woman who doesn't have much patience for him, and he submits to being tugged and pulled through the day. With her, he doesn't practice on his keyboard, choosing instead to turn on the radio and tune in to the VOA jazz show—not the same since Conover left, but better than sitting in silence with the woman.

He sits in his circular rattan chair, too low to make it easy to get up from but worth the comfort he feels sunken in that old and stained yellow cushion, the radio music sealing him in from above. The aide reads celebrity magazines on the sofa next to him, but soon he forgets she's even there, she's no different from the furniture.

A curtain of black falls over him. He lays himself on the thinnest skim of perception—no light, no darkness, only solid immateriality. He lets go of the radio music to attend to the hum coming from where his songs have always called to him. It's occurred to him, after decades of playing, that it's only the buzzing of a much grander ruckus, muffled, like sound coming from behind a thick wall. Here he is again, as he has been all his life, trying to listen in. He's spent many years trying to piece together a likeness of that grand but faint noise, feeling its shape note by note, and failing. He thinks he hears it, and then he knows he hasn't. It's only the tired dance of his own heart.

□ □ □

When the piano showroom closed down, the manager handed him an envelope, commending him on his friendliness with the customers and wishing him the best. The amount was maybe enough to pay a water bill. He thanked the manager and folded the check into his pocket.

Good thing Bobby found a gig for him: Fridays at an off-Sukhumvit piano bar popular with the jumble of farang expats on ever-extending visas. There, he was all at once in Bangkok and Chicago and Manchester and Frankfurt and Smolensk. He played songs he knew the crowd would like, and they often got up and sang along, raising and swinging their steins of watery beer—Oi and Donut and some stranger farang getting up to do a clumsy cha-cha in front of the stage—and he loved each and every one of them for as long as the songs lasted and he was the center of their leisurely night. Between sets, he and his young Thai bandmates sat around the bar, where they munched on the free cocktail nuts and cheese ball, and where he also fed them stories from his own youth, when everything was so wild and delicious. They lapped up the names he'd played with and the sweaty all-night sessions and the fist-swinging personal antics and the joy of being unafraid. He made sure to frame the stories so that they'd know that those days could never happen now, that they were privileged even to hear about it from someone who'd been there to see it all.

His drummer, Mickey Plengjai, asked him if he was ever going back to the States, and he told them yes, when he was sick and tired of them asking dumb questions. "You water lizards, I'm going to buy my goddamn ticket tomorrow," he said, to everyone's laughter. He didn't tell them that when he called anyone in New York, the talk started boisterous and ended fast. Cats would say they'd got to help others, like the old days, and then never call back. He imagined them sitting at their card games, pulling the same stories from under the rug over and over, as he was doing. Someone asks what happened to that Clyde. They all grin and shake their heads as an answer.

"I got a big bonus last week. The next round's on me," he declared. Joey Wonderboy brought them a whole bottle of SangSom, and Clyde went around the table to give everyone a good splash. It was in the middle of the next set that his chest tightened.

□ □ □

"You hear that?" he asks the substitute aide.

"What? The radio?"

"Nope, listen. Really listen."

"What are you talking about, Mr. Clyde?"

"Listen. It's completely quiet out there. They stopped," he says. With his own strength, he pushes himself up from his chair and walks over to the window. Outside, the construction site has gone dark. He sees no workers on the ground or up on the building's naked, unfinished floors. The shadow of the crane high above is still.

He motions for the aide to come look out the window. She does, shielding her eyes to look up into the darkness.

"I see nothing," she says.

"That's not nothing. That's tom yum goong."

❑ ❑ ❑

When Lucky's back, Clyde returns to the keyboard.

"What do you want to hear, young lady?"

"Anything you want to play, Khun Clyde."

He stretches out his arms and starts to play. This one's a train he hops on, like he did when he'd first listened to the song on his grandma's record player while she wasn't around to limit him to songs of worship. Except now he's the one telling it where to go.

He notices Lucky nodding along with him. He nudges her and flicks his head in the direction of his left hand.

"Here, Ms. Lucky, play with me. Press the keys like this and then this and badeedumdeebumdeebum."

"Are you sure? I've never played before, Khun Clyde."

"There's nothing to it. Don't be afraid. C'mon."

She presses the keys in the sequence that he's showed her.

"Yeah, that's what we call a bass line. Don't stop now."

She's nowhere close to playing it right, but he's not going to tell her. He hasn't spent this much time holed up alone with anyone in years, but he knows it doesn't take much for two loons under the same roof to start to want to claw at each other.

❑ ❑ ❑

It also doesn't take much for things to go the other way. One summer, he and Morris stayed at a beach, just the two of them. This was at a seaside town close to the city, no more than a two hours' drive out on the Long Island Expressway. Lizzie, back before all the mess between them, had made friends with a black couple who owned the beach house, and they needed someone to stay there for the three weeks the couple went to visit family in Maryland. He took her up on it. Said that he was going to stay there with a few friends. Didn't bring up Morris.

Unlike at the other beaches, nobody here would bother them for being there with reasons other than to clean up after white folks. They walked the pebbly beach and chased scurrying crabs at low tide, went for a swim when the sea returned, and lay down on the dock after the bay had chilled them down. No fear of being wrestled away by the crowd or spat on, like what them brave kids had to deal with at the lunch counters, none of that. Still, they kept to themselves, told anyone who asked that they were brothers.

The couple had an upright at the house, and Morris would wake him up to try something different than what they'd tried out earlier. Morris's face comes back to him as a smudge of eyebrows and lips and not much else, but it's all right, because he can still hear Morris's voice. He won't forget the way the man plays.

"Let the notes float a little longer," he tells Lucky at the piano.

"Like this?"

"Even softer at the end, like you're patting a baby's head."

Lucky starts playing again, fingers lighter, and so does Morris. The song floats off into the blue surrender of the day's light. One day it'll hit back down like a rainstorm.

"Yeah, there you go," Clyde says to them. "Don't you stop now."

It was September, and the weather had begun to turn. Looked like there wasn't going to be a hurricane or some other awful weather that season, so said one of the neighbors, and relief had spread into joy humming all around. Underneath their song, he could hear joy in the sputter of lawn sprinklers outside, the radio drifting from someone's window, left open without care. He thought he could hear roots spidering underneath the trees, the scratching of worms tunneling through the soil, and they, too, were happy.

He promised Morris this was going to be how it always would be. Easy as that.

"Hell, that was fantastic," he tells them. "Every last bit."

"Khun Clyde, you're going to turn me into a nightclub piano player by the time I leave you."

That day won't arrive for another two weeks. She has the day marked on a pocket calendar in her purse. The agency has already assigned her a new placement in Bang Khen, and after that there'll be another placement and then another.

If they have the awareness, it's pretty normal for her charges to become saddened by her departure. They ask her not to go, looking at her with pleading eyes, and she smiles and tells them that everything will be all right and keeps on smiling.

"But who will I play with, Ms. Lucky?"

"You'll be back playing your shows, Khun Clyde. Wouldn't that be nice?"

"I suppose. I don't know."

"Everything will be all right, Khun Clyde."

He motions her to help him to the bed, and she does, even though she knows he doesn't need her to get up anymore. They walk arm in arm across the room, and she lifts up the bedcover before he sits on the mattress.

"They've stopped construction," she says, looking up into the dark skeleton of a building outside.

"Indeed, they have. I kind of miss that noise."

"Yeah, so weird, Khun Clyde. Me, too."

She helps him recline, and he straightens himself. She unfolds a silk Chinese blanket and lets it billow down to shroud him. She feels a tug on her elbow.

"Ms. Lucky, you mentioned something about that look-up computer machine. Can you remind me what you can do with it?"

◻ ◻ ◻

It's another Saturday, and Lucky's headed not to Muang Nontha but to Fangthon. She's told everyone at the agency about the cousin in Nonthaburi, so that the extra distance to get there would warrant her having the whole day off. It still takes a good two hours for her to get across the river. She has to take a bus from Khun Clyde's building in Klong Toey, ride crosstown to get off near Thammasat University, and walk to the pier for a long-tail boat. If traffic's bad and the bus gets stuck, she hops off to look for a corner with waiting motorcycle cabs and then weave through gauntlets of side mirrors. She wears a medical mask over her nose and mouth. Still, the exhaust fumes get through, and after the ride, when she can pull out a sheet from her pack of tissue, she'll see a dark gray stain where she's blown her nose.

She finds a seat toward the front of the boat, so that she doesn't feel sick. On weekends, the boat doesn't fill up with students, and she's glad to have room to put down her rolling bag next to her, instead of having to hug it in her lap. She's still wearing the health aide company's shirt. She doesn't change into her regular clothes in front of Khun Clyde or anyone else. Better to keep consistent, she was instructed at orientation, and best to avoid the substitute ratting her out to the manager. She's heard of people getting demerits in their postassignment reviews for less.

The trip across the river never lasts more than ten minutes, dock to dock, but it's the part of the commute that she looks forward to the most. When the ride's gentle, the river calms her. The boat cuts across

the brown and milky water, pushing farther from the shores of Krungthep, with its garbage-lined banks and the music-blaring waterside restaurants perched on stilts and the green islands of entangled hyacinths
and, up farther along the banks, tall white buildings looming over their
half-built siblings, ghostly and lifeless now, with construction halted,
but sooner or later they, too, will be born into Krungthep, the city of
angels and yet higher angels and even higher ones.

□ □ □

After she arrives at the flat, she collapses on the bed—how she needs to
black out her mind for an hour or two after all that—and wakes when
she hears Den's jangling to unlock the door. Her body jiggles with the
mattress when he sits down next to her.

"Hey, you're all sweaty," she says. "Don't lie down. It's disgusting."

"Sorry," he says. "I'll hop in the shower."

She can tell he was out playing takraw with his waiter friends. How
many hours was he leaping and kicking out there? He's going to destroy
his ankles one of these days, and she reserves the right to laugh in his
face. She's not going to remind him that he's supposed to be looking for
an electrician job. He'll only blame the economy, and then they'll fight
again, and nothing different will come of it. When his rent is close to
being due, he'll still come up with some excuse or another and ask her
to help cover him—until things get better, he'll say.

"Den, before you go into the bathroom, can you unlock your computer for me?"

"I thought I told you the password."

"I don't know it anymore."

"It's BangkokStud2515."

"How could I have forgotten?"

"Don't be nosy."

"Trust me, I won't go looking for the porn files you downloaded."

"You sure? That reminds me. I ripped a new CD for you. If you're nice to me, I'll let you have it."

"Is it the same one you made for your other women?"

"There's only you, my love."

He shuts the bathroom door, which doesn't keep his singing to himself. She recognizes the song: a loog-toong number about having to be willing to wait so long when you're in love with a truck driver. Above the sound of water splashing from a hand bowl, his voice cracks at every start of the chorus.

At the computer, she sighs and types in the password. The screen turns on and she stares into the square of light that has brightened the room. With a few clicks, the computer modem screams a birthing agony before a window tells her that she's connected. She remembers which one of the squares to click. A web browser opens up, and she searches for a name she wrote in her notebook: Morris Clemens.

There's not much, she'll have to tell Khun Clyde. She's found a lot of names spelled the same way, but only a few results look promising, according to her passable reading of English. The most likely of them is a brief obituary for a Morris who passed away in New York eight years ago. He had been a music teacher at a high school. Former students remembered him for his passion and devotion. There's no photo.

Another result takes her to a music forum. She spots the name again in a thread about obscure jazz albums. She ignores much of the discussion and homes in on where it mentions Morris's name. At a stoop sale, a user had bought three self-released albums from the 1970s and 1980s and wanted to see what people thought of this guy. She clinks on a link, and a new window pops up to show a WAV file download.

This will take forever, so she gets up to pour herself a soda. It's warm, having sat out on the table. Den's fridge is way too small, and he's already loaded it up with little bottles of energy drinks that slide all over the place. She's told him that stuff will probably burn through his brain, but that makes him buy even more of them, as he has apparently done.

□ □ □

Static suddenly bursts from the computer speakers when the download auto-plays. As a trumpet begins to blare from the computer speakers, she takes another sip of soda and sits down on a stool by the window. Clouds hang low and dark outside. Sidewalk vendors are bringing out umbrellas and sheets of plastic to cover their goods. The music closes her eyes.

It's no longer cloudy where she's arrived. She sees a spiky cluster of metal and glass, thinner in the middle where a long strip of green clears out the buildings. It's Central Park, if she remembers correctly. She's seen the view before in farang movies, and now it's playing for her again, as she floats over a tilework of gray roofs and air-conditioning units and the dark lines of traffic yellow and black far below to hover over a brick apartment building. An old man as dark as Khun Clyde stands in the shade of a water tower. He's wearing a collared, long-sleeve shirt and wide-legged olive pants, and on his head is a beaten Panama hat with a blue band salted by sweat. The man's lips are puckered around a trumpet's mouthpiece. He keeps his elbows high as he fires off note after note, fingers fast on the valves. Below him, people and cars in the street barely look like people or cars, more like the aquatic creatures she's seen writhing across the ocean sand in the sea-life documentaries that Den likes to watch. She floats closer to him. He doesn't see her. He's blowing into his trumpet, but she can hear him speak.

The man Morris is saying that he's always had a peculiar ear. When the man was a child, his school organized a trip to an American Civil War battleground, now only a hilly field. He can still hear his teacher telling her students what had gone down where they stood: cavalries charging against cannon, rows of men tumbling into pieces, picked off by clouds of bullets. Like the other schoolkids, he stood there as his teacher waved across the field with an open hand, pointing to strategic hills and the long-past carnage all around, but he swore he could hear the screams and the booming explosions, so loud that it amazed him no other kid said a word. He didn't know then that he'd be spending his whole life hearing things. *Toot-de-toot-de-tat.* He'd pluck sounds out of the air that he was sure had taken centuries to reach him, and he'd string them up together. *Toot-de-toot-de-tut.* Does she like it?

Does it hurt to look back to what you and Khun Clyde had? she thinks to ask him. *But this song's not about that,* he replies with his trumpet. *I want to know,* she thinks back. *Why does it matter?* he asks. *Just tell me,* she thinks. *Fine, here you go,* he plays. *Wait for it. There.* His trumpet comes to a quick halt, and the drums accompanying him rush through to explode inside her head.

She feels herself shatter over one unreal city, sitting by a window in another. A glass of soda fizzles in her hand, as she opens her eyes to see the rain tap darkly on the gray dustiness of the ledge.

□ □ □

"What's this you're playing for me?" says Den, leaning from the bathroom door with his wet hair drenching the floor.

"Just music, nothing you'd probably like."

"I like everything, my love."

He walks out with a towel wrapped around his head. The rest of him is naked and dripping. He tries to wrap himself around her, and she pushes him away with a foot to the stomach.

"Go put your clothes on," she says.

"Ow, that wasn't a soft kick."

"You of all people should know better."

He walks over to a pile of clothes and picks out whatever's on top. She's afraid that she's overdone it with the kick, so she gets up to hug him as he wrangles into his T-shirt and shorts.

"What do you want to do today?" she asks.

"There's a free concert later on. We'd have to hop on a bus and head a few kilometers out. It's in a condo building the developers abandoned half finished this year. Heard it from Yohn, who probably just wants me to come fawn over some spiky leather jacket he got some dude to buy for him in Germany."

"We can go if you feel like it."

"Should be fun but we don't have to, if you're feeling lazy."

The computer's playing the next song on the album. She hears Morris's trumpet but she no longer sees him. The screen's gone dark again. She's forgotten to turn on the lights, and she and Den are holding each other in a grayed-out dream.

"Look, it's raining so hard outside," she says.

HOME

All day, she's been looking forward to a swim.

Nee doesn't know how long building staffers will treat her with some reverence, but she's so far been able to continue teaching swim classes here on weekends. Sometimes she even takes the two bus routes from where she lives to come for a swim on her own. She has more time, now that Roong is away at university and there's really nobody to take care of but herself. It's been good to see some familiar faces here, be it the security guards or the receptionists, although she also doesn't mind the times she can slip in and out without being noticed.

In front of her locker, she undresses, puts on the swimsuit she's tucked into her ample old-woman's purse, and then exits barefoot out to the walkway. She rinses herself off at the outdoor shower, respectful of sanitary rules that everyone else ignores, and then steps into the shallows. The incline drops as she wades. Soon, she's chest-deep, the ripples from her own arms washing over her shoulders.

Middays like this, there's usually nobody else around, but today at one of the poolside tables, she recognizes a girl who had been one of her swimming students. The name of the girl doesn't come to her. It's been a long time, and she taught so many children in this pool. When they get older, they no longer come to the pool. No time for that anymore, a few have told her. Sometimes they don't even remember their old instructor. This one does. The girl puts her book down to do a wai from her seat and then walks over.

"Teacher, are you getting ready for a class?"

When talking to students, even ones from years ago, Nee can't help but raise her voice a pitch higher.

"No, it's only me today, swimming on my own."

"That's so great," says the girl. "I need to come here to swim more. Haven't done it in a while. Anyways, I'm heading back up, but I just wanted to warn you about the snake."

"What snake? What are you talking about?"

"Look up."

The girl points up, and Nee cranes to look. A green snake has wrapped itself around a tree branch giving shade to a couple of lounge chairs. It's not a big one, not much longer than the length of two arms and as thin as a broom branch. The way it's coiled, she can't see its tail. When she stayed with Nok in the provinces, her grandmother had warned: all green is good, stay away from the black-tailed.

"What is it doing there, do you know?" asks the girl.

"Probably just hunting for sparrows. I wouldn't worry too much. It's probably more scared of us than we are of it."

"Well, be careful, Teacher," the girls says before giving another wai and then walking back inside.

After the girl has left, Nee lunges out and sweeps herself forward in the water. The deep calls out to her, as it always has. Her legs begin to kick. Her muscles tighten and stretch. Joints creak between bones. Her arms and legs move like a weight has been cut from a rope pulley, and they're now put in motion by the turn of wheels and gears releasing forces held back for who knows how long. If she's sunburned from her walk, the hurt on her skin dissolves away, as if it had only been lathered on.

The pool, though, can only do so much. There are other parts of her that she can't wash away.

After awful things happen, she's found that a woman has to make herself appear inviolate, so that she can live the good life expected of her and be a productive, contributing member of the society. If she gives it her amicable face, maybe she'll also find herself loved, unconditionally if she's lucky, as her husband has loved her, as her son does, and still there'll be a lingering ache underneath, made more palpable as her years begin to wear thin. The more terrible memories manifest as more than an ache. She feels them alive and aflame within her, and she can't just abandon them to oblivion. She must tend to them. She feeds them with her heart.

It's been so long, almost fifty years now, yet she can still see the day play out like a terrible movie. She can still hear Siripohng mumble to her, the bullets having torn through him, the blood gurgling from his mouth, urging her to get up and run.

Siripohng. Siripohng. Sometimes she wants to believe that if she says a name so many times, anyone can be brought back to life. Siripohng, Siripohng, she's muttered into clasped hands after giving alms at the temple. By the canal, she poured fish rescued from the monger's block at the market and followed their fanning dark tails until they disappeared into the murky, brown water. She hoped that they would take to Siripohng whatever merits she'd sent him from this world.

Few remember names like his anymore. Faces have been made ashen. Those October dates swallowed everyone who'd been there into history's giant unlit belly, and that history into silence. The forgotten return again and again, as new names and faces, and again this city makes new ghosts. Can the dead ever forgive? What do they still remember of their old lives? It's only a hunch, but she's come to suspect that nothing true ever dies. Doesn't matter that the bullet holes have been filled and the walls painted over. Truth lingers, unseen like phantoms but there to rattle and scream wherever people try hardest to forget.

She thinks of ghosts all the time: Siripohng and her poor late husband up in some heavenly dimension or born again as another good man or woman, and her parents, and others she's known in this noisy life. She misses Khun Crab saving the best gossip for the visits to her mother's sundries shop, and the cat that slept on Khun Mahm's lap as she sold lottery tickets, Uncle Fah stirring a giant pot of broth in his open-air kitchen, and the older monks who used to shuffle barefoot past her house on their morning routes. They're all here, haunting her mind while she still has a mind, and also drifting in seas where their bones are scattered, and hanging on to the dust of Krungthep and dancing and carousing in lungs, and looking out from old newsprint buried in libraries and landfills and from altars and walls and shelves to watch over the messy business of the living and breathing. Even in this pool, she's swimming among them.

When she reaches the end of the pool, she flips over to do the backstroke. Glancing up to the tree, she sees that the snake has disappeared from the branch.

Still, she keeps her eyes on the gray-blue sky. Propelled by the hopeful certainty natural to the most stubborn and the most desperate, she pushes on blindly, the pool's edges invisible to her. She can only hope to swim on and touch the other end of the pool, or maybe her fingertips will stop her at a rock she's never known to be there—a large, grayish protrusion rising from the water like an emerging moon. When that happens, she'll recognize that she's reached the shores of a Krungthep other than the one she's known.

Her father used to like to scare her, back when she was little, with folklore from his native province. He said villagers went into the mountains to make extra money by foraging for honey and trapping creatures they could sell to buyers in Krungthep, and that the elders often warned them to walk away as fast as they could, and quietly, if they should come across anything that shouldn't be there, like a village in the forest that would look like any of the other villages they'd visited in the mountains—the usual red clay road flanked by wooden homes high on stilts and the chicken pecking unmilled rice outside their coop and the vegetable gardens in rectangular clearings—except that the air would pass into their lungs more thinly and the sky would have a menacing shade, like rain was about to arrive any minute, and they would meet only people who would not look them in the eye or utter a word back to their greetings. Do not eat their food, the elders said. Do not stop to linger in this in-between place, because a day there would turn out to be decades in ours, if it wasn't already too late to make an escape and avoid the fate of others.

She wonders what might happen if she doesn't heed the advice of her father and the elders. She imagines her outstretched hand feeling the heft of that gray rock.

She's pulling herself up from the water and lying down on her back. She's listening to the waves, as they arrive one after another at the rock, and will go on arriving long after her. When she's here, she doesn't feel lost.

Acknowledgments

I am grateful for the kindness and generosity of so many.

Great gratitude goes to Rebecca Saletan, who saw something in this novel beyond its earlier, cruder shape and helped me find its truer expression, and all the astounding people at Riverhead Books—Jynne Dilling Martin, Glory Anne Plata, Michelle Koufopoulos, among many others, as well as Emma Herdman and the team at Sceptre.

I'm very thankful for the reliable brilliance and wisdom of Nicole Aragi. Thank you, as well, to Grace Dietshe and everyone at Aragi, Inc.

This book would not have been possible without thoughtful advice and support from friends in my writing circles, including Jenny Blackman, Julia Fierro, Cheryl Fish, Nathan Ihara, Jessica Francis Kane, Paul Lucas, Mark Prins, Rajesh Parameswaran, David Rogers, Susan Chi Rogers, Jeffrey Rotter, Sujata Shekar, Casey Walker, and Karen Thompson Walker. I am particularly grateful for Alexander Chee and Ted Thompson, who not only helped me find footing in my early attempts at the novel chapters, but also showed how I might be able to proceed with grace as an author.

I'm indebted to these organizations and the people there who do good work: the New York Foundation for the Arts, for awarding me a fellowship that allowed me the time I needed to finish the first draft of my novel; the MacDowell Colony, for providing the concentrated attention I needed to complete the last major edits and re-energize from the process in such inspiring company; and the literary journal *StoryQuarterly*, for publishing an early version of one of the chapters.

Books and other historical sources that stirred my imagination in writing this novel include: *Historical Sketch of the Missions in Siam*, revised by the Rev. A. Millaro Coopci; *Missionary Sketches: A Concise History of the American Baptist Missionary Union* by S.F. Smith; *Siam and Laos as Seen by Our American Missionaries* by the Trustees of the Presbyterian Board of Publication; *Lao Rueng Bahng Gog* [Telling Stories of Bangkok] by S. Plainoy; *Siam and the League of Nations* by Stefan Hall; *Addresses* by Teddy Spha Palasthira; *The World Without Us* by Alan Weisman; and the many *Tuay Toon Phiset* magazines read in my childhood.

I owe my informal literary education to the great independent bookstores of New York City, whose talks and readings I hungrily attended, and, since my earliest days as a young reader, public libraries everywhere that should always be well supported in their work to cultivate and nourish minds.

Other friends have been very supportive throughout various stages of writing this book. My thanks go to: the Blanchard family, the Nagella family, the Shadows, the crew at *The Morning News,* and various work colleagues who recognized the time and attention I needed for fiction writing.

An infinity of thanks goes to my parents, whose brave striving made so much possible for me, and who, in the course of my childhood, never hesitated to drop me off at a library or bookstore. Many thanks to all of my family, for their stories and love.